The Prince

The Prince

Vito Bruschini

Translated by Anne Milano Appel

ATRIA BOOKS

NEW YORK   LONDON   TORONTO   SYDNEY   NEW DELHI

ATRIA BOOKS

A Division of Simon & Schuster, Inc.
1230 Avenue of the Americas
New York, NY 10020

Copyright © 2009 by Newton Compton Editori, s.r.l.,
Roma, Casella postale 6214, Italia

English language translation copyright © 2014 by Anne Milano Appel

Originally published in Italy in 2009 as *The Father: Il padrino dei padrini*
by Newton Compton Editori

First Atria Books hardcover edition March 2015

ATRIA BOOKS and colophon are trademarks of Simon & Schuster, Inc.

For information about special discounts for bulk purchases,
please contact Simon & Schuster Special Sales at
1-866-506-1949 or business@simonandschuster.com.

The Simon & Schuster Speakers Bureau can bring authors
to your live event. For more information or to book an event,
contact the Simon & Schuster Speakers Bureau at
1-866-248-3049 or visit our website at www.simonspeakers.com.

Manufactured in the United States of America

10   9   8   7   6   5   4   3   2   1

Library of Congress Cataloging-in-Publication Data
Bruschini, Vito.
    [Father. English]
    The prince / by Vito Bruschini.—First Atria books hardcover edition.
      pages   cm
    "English language translation . . . by Anne Milano Appel"
    Originally published in Italy in 2009 as The father : il padrino dei padrini by
Newton Compton Editori.
    1. Mafia—Fiction.   I. Appel, Anne Milano, translator.   II. Title.
    PQ4902.R76F3813   2014
    853'.92—dc23
                                                        2013035380
ISBN 978-1-4516-8719-4
ISBN 978-1-4516-8721-7 (ebook)

For Giuliana and Giuliana

Part One

Chapter I

"The night of the damned" was how the inhabitants of the Salemi valley would recall that night in late July when the massacre at Borgo Guarine took place.

There was no moon to illuminate the vast fields of the large Sicilian landed estate, but the pitch-black sky was studded with billions of points of light. At its zenith flowed the river of the Milky Way, seemingly close enough to touch with an outstretched hand. In its brightness, the dark outlines of the surrounding mountains were just visible. The earlier heat had given way to a light breeze blowing in from the sea, and the magic of that landscape, so harsh and brutal during the day, was sweetened with the scent of wildflowers and lemon groves.

That fatal night, Gaetano Vassallo came down from the foothills of the Montagna Grande with two of his most trusted men: Corrado and Mariano. He hadn't seen his children since he'd gone into hiding over four months earlier.

His two bodyguards showed up at Borgo Guarine first, while Vassallo remained behind a clump of prickly pear to steer clear of a possible ambush.

The night's silence was ruptured by barking dogs alerted by the hoofbeats of the bandits' horses. Corrado and Mariano approached the settlement's small cluster of houses cautiously. Fearful eyes peered at them from behind the slats of the shutters, which were then quickly bolted. The two men spurred their mounts, splitting off to check both sides of the village. But there were no interlopers around. That was when Corrado gave a faint, prolonged whistle.

With a jerk of the reins, Gaetano Vassallo emerged from his hiding place and galloped toward the two men. Once they had regrouped, the three continued along the path leading out of the village and came to a halt about a quarter mile later in front of the farm of Gaetano's brother, Geremia.

In a trench that had been dug into a gully by soldiers from the Royal Guard, a young soldier named Gaspare had heard the dogs barking, then a prolonged whistle, and finally the patter of horses' hooves. Lifting the sod covering that the guardsmen had placed over their hideout as camouflage, Gaspare trained his binoculars on the farm.

Darkness and distance did not allow him to make out the details of Geremia Vassallo's small farmhouse, but when the door opened a crack and a flickering ray of light spilled out, he glimpsed a shadow stealthily enter the house.

Gaspare's heart gave a start, and he recalled Captain Lorenzo Costa's orders: "If you have even a trace of a doubt, report it immediately." This nighttime visit was definitely unusual. Gaspare crawled out of the ditch and started running as fast as he could to cover the mile or so separating him from an outpost manned by fellow guardsmen. After several minutes of frantic sprinting, he reached them and from there alerted headquarters by means of a field telephone.

An hour later, under the command of Captain Lorenzo Costa, forty Royal Guardsmen inched forward quietly in groups of three to surround Geremia Vassallo's farm. The Royal Guard, a special branch of the military police numbering in the tens of thousands nationwide, had been alerted that Gaetano Vassallo, the most dangerous bandit in the territory of Salemi, was inside his brother's house. Their orders were to prevent him from escaping and, if possible, to capture him alive. As for the other two outlaws, they could decide on the spot: dead or alive, there were no specific instructions.

———

Mariano, the first of Vassallo's bodyguards, was covering the rear of the farmhouse, while the other, Corrado, kept an eye on the entrance.

Their long stay in the woods had heightened the bandits' sensitivity to any sounds and movements that were not part of nature. When Mariano suddenly heard a suspicious, stealthy crawling nearby, he lifted his rifle and spun around, staring into the shadows in an attempt to penetrate the darkness. A young guardsman jumped out from behind a bush and leapt on him, clamping his mouth shut and then slashing his throat from ear to ear. The guardsman was swiftly joined by the other two soldiers from his group. But the outlaw Mariano had already breathed his last.

Corrado, the other bandit, heard a slight scuffle coming from behind the house and quietly called out to his friend.

One of the guardsmen let out a whistle in response. Corrado, suspicious, headed with his rifle around the side of the house, his finger on the trigger. The signal hadn't convinced him, but his moment of hesitation was enough to allow the two foremost units of guardsmen to leap toward him. Corrado sprang like a cobra. As soon as he saw the first soldier's figure outlined against the sky, he fired and hit the man right in the chest. An instant later he was overwhelmed by a superhuman force that slammed him to the ground. Then two, three, four, five Royal Guardsmen were upon him, finishing him off with their daggers and bayonets. A dozen other soldiers stormed the front door while still others, following the captain's orders, guarded the windows of the farmhouse to block any means of escape.

As soon as they broke down the door, the first two guardsmen shouted for the occupants to surrender. But they found Geremia standing in front of them, holding the double-barreled shotgun he used for hunting. He shot the first man point-blank in the doorway, and in rapid succession fired at the second. The two young soldiers slumped to the ground with bloodcurdling screams. Inside the house, a woman was shrieking, and children were crying hysterically.

As Geremia hastened to reload the shotgun, ten other guardsmen acting in unison charged into the house.

Just inside was a kitchen with a fireplace; a large table stood in the center, with two cots placed against the walls. Brave little Jano, frightened but not crying, had rolled out from under the blankets to hide beneath his cot.

In his aunt's room, directly adjacent to the kitchen, he heard his brother Giovanni bawling with all the force his young lungs could muster. Jano stuffed part of a blanket in his own mouth so a moan wouldn't slip out. From under the bed, he saw a flurry of people break into the room and rush at his uncle Geremia, wresting the gun from his hands. Then the slaughter began. In horror Jano saw a severed hand fall beside the bed where he was hiding. Then he heard gunshots and immediately after that, pieces of bloodied legs and arms rolled to the floor. Drunk with terror, little Jano closed his eyes, covered his ears, and shrank back into the farthest corner of his makeshift shelter.

He could hear his aunt Rosalia's strangely altered voice but was unable to see the woman fall desperately upon his uncle, gathering missing body parts off the floor in an irrational attempt to reassemble them. The next ten minutes were an orgy of screams, gunshots, objects torn to pieces and dashed to the ground. Luckily for him, the child did not see what his poor aunt had to endure, though her screams would remain fixed in his ears for many years to come.

Someone wrenched the woman away from her husband. Covered only by her blood-soaked nightgown, she was taken brutally, every part of her body violated. In the tumult, the woman, crazed with grief, managed to grab a gun from the floor and shoot herself. Fragments of her brain splattered the face of the man on top of her, who collapsed when the bullet ricocheted and reduced his eye to a pulp. It was a signal for yet another bloody frenzy. The Royal Guardsmen, not yet sated, went on to defile her corpse.

The mayhem ended with the arrival of Captain Lorenzo Costa, who had to fire several shots in the air to make himself heard by those men who had turned into savage beasts. Finally, exhausted, blood smeared, having had their fill of violence, the soldiers quieted down.

Captain Costa surveyed the wreckage in the rooms, taking care not to tread on any organic remains with his boots. In the bedroom, he found a child five or six years old lying on the floor with his head crushed. In a large cradle a few feet away he discovered two seemingly dead babies. But then he realized that only one of the twins had been strangled. The other, a girl just a few months old, seemed to be still alive; maybe she had been knocked unconscious by a blow to her face, which was now swollen. No one noticed Jano, huddled under the cot in the kitchen, hidden by a tangle of blankets.

"Where's Gaetano Vassallo?" the captain shouted in a tone that made the men around him shudder. "You let him get away!"

"Captain, sir, no one got out of here," one of the guardsmen spoke up. "We kept watch at every window. No one left the farmhouse."

Suddenly something caught Costa's attention. He noticed that under the cradle the floorboards were loose. He had them move the crib and saw a trap door leading to the cellar of the house; from there a natural tunnel led out to the slope of a nearby hill.

Evidently Vassallo had escaped by that route as soon as he heard the shot fired by his bodyguard.

The discovery infuriated the captain. He realized that the responsibility for all that havoc rested solely on him. He had subjected the young men to intolerable pressure for too long, anticipating their confrontation with the bandit. So inured had they become to death that life itself was now of little importance to them: he had turned them into a pack of wild animals. After this unprecedented bloodbath, they were sure to undergo a trial from which none of them would emerge unscathed. It would be a total scandal. Unless he quickly found some way out, his career and his entire life would be ruined. If only they had captured Vassallo, everything would have been more acceptable. They could say they'd been attacked by the bandit and his men and had defended themselves. But how could they justify the slaughter of two children, one still an infant, along with a woman and her husband? At dawn, the whole town would know. He had to find a solution fast. The blame would have to be pinned on a scapegoat, and the culprit had to be someone who stood to gain from wiping out the Vassallo family.

His decision made, he ordered his men to give him a pistol and one of the bloody daggers. Wrapping them in an undershirt he found in the bedroom, the captain charged one of his most trusted men, Michele Fardella, to go and stash the bundle on Rosario Losurdo's farm. Next, he directed that the bandits' three horses be led away into the woods, instructing his men to get rid of their saddles and harnesses.

Lastly he addressed his forty thugs and made a dire pact with them.

Chapter 2

Seventeen years later, the echo of those events had become no more than a hazy legend among Salemi's younger farmers, though for the old-timers, the episode continued to represent the darkest chapter of their desolate past.

The town had undergone some transformation, not in terms of its way of life but in its social and political fabric. Many villagers had been forced to immigrate to more hospitable nations, while fascism had raised some dubious individuals to positions of honor.

The days passed by, no different from the next, as in every provincial Italian town. One clear autumn afternoon, however, the village's peace and quiet was disrupted by the rhythmic drum roll of Nini Trovato, the town crier. The townspeople interpreted it as a cheerful summons for some kind of proclamation.

Over the years, Salemi's residents had grown used to those booming declarations by the mayor's factotum. Everyone, even children, generally knew the content of the announcement that Nini would soon bellow out to the village.

But that afternoon, the decree had not already been read by the usual "well-informed" individuals, so when they saw Nini passing by outside their windows, people wondered what it could possibly mean. Several women leaned out their windows and shouted to him, asking what all the racket was about. But Nini, his manner very professional, nose in the air, didn't deign to look at them; continuing along the path that climbed toward the town's main piazza, he went on pounding the instrument's cracked skin.

Mimmo Ferro's tavern, which overlooked Salemi's central piazza, was on the side opposite the church. *Chiesa Madre*, facing the imposing walls of the Norman castle where Giuseppe Garibaldi had proclaimed himself dictator of Sicily in 1860. The tavern, along with the house of God, was the only area of town where one could gather after a hard day's work. The church was favored by women and the elderly; the tavern, by men and the young.

That late October afternoon, Mimmo Ferro served a second carafe of red wine at the table where the game of *Tocco* was being played. The table was crowded with townspeople. There were workers from the stone quarries and sulfur mines, along with managers and private guards from the landed estates. Rarely did farmers or shepherds join the game—not just because you had to have a little money to participate but also because you had to have a certain degree of oratorical skill, which peasants and flock tenders were known to lack.

Around the table were Nicola Cosentino, one of Rosario Losurdo's guards, and Curzio Turrisi, one of the Marquis Pietro Bellarato's. Seated near them were Domenico the barber, Turi Toscano the salt miner, Pericle Terrasini the charcoal burner, Alfio the quarryman, Fabio from the sulphur mine, and an indeterminate number of villagers who clamored behind them, some standing, some sitting on small stools, rooting first for one group then the other.

The object of the game was to allow one's cronies to drink the most glasses of wine and at the same time humiliate one's rivals by getting one of them drunk and leaving the others thirsty. The "boss," who was responsible for doling out the carafe of wine, was chosen by drawing lots. But the one who actually determined the outcome, by deciding each time who would drink and who would lose—that is, go thirsty—was his helper, the real boss of the game, which lasted the time it took to consume three carafes of wine. No one would move from Mimmo Ferro's tavern until the last drop of nectar had been poured into the glasses, even if it meant returning home late.

Ninì Trovato's drum roll attracted the attention of the tavern's customers. Those who weren't playing headed for the door, going outside to hear what the old town crier had to proclaim.

At that moment, Prince Ferdinando Licata and Monsignor Antonio Albamonte were strolling up Via Garibaldi, a narrow winding street that terminated at Piazza del Castello.

Licata loved talking with the cultured monsignor. They often met toward the end of the day while both were awaiting the dinner hour. Their frequent discussions led them to endless ruminations, since their concepts of the world and of life were drastically different. Nevertheless, they respected each other: the monsignor had given up on converting the prince to his mystical notions, and Ferdinando Licata had abandoned his attempts to modify the priest's views on Voltaire.

Together they were an odd couple. Licata, tall and slender, towered almost comically over Don Antonio, who was short and stout with a plump, round face and big eyes that twinkled with cunning and wit. Physically, aside from the prince's wavy black hair, there was nothing typically Sicilian about him. In addition to being over six feet tall, he had eyes as blue as the May sky, a trait inherited from his father, a nobleman of Welsh origin. Nor did his extremely formal manner correspond to the Sicilian temperament. However, he did betray his ancient island origins, on his great-grandmother's side, in his behavior: his actions were always measured, and he was reluctant to reveal his emotions. Licata's humor and "stiff upper lip" suggested the Anglo-Saxon strains of his great-grandfather, a member of the venerable English aristocracy to whom he owed his title.

Nini Trovato had shaken the town's peaceful atmosphere. Several children ran gleefully around the crier trying to touch that fascinating instrument, likely an ancient relic from the Napoleonic campaigns. A number of people went to their windows, among them Peppino Ragusa, the district physician. He was even more impoverished than his fellow townsmen, who were rarely able to pay him for his miraculous interventions.

Interrupting his examination of a little boy afflicted with lice, he moved to the window to hear the words of the proclamation. The boy's mother, curious, went over as well, though she respectfully remained a step behind him.

The two looked on as Nini approached the center of the piazza and in a loud voice began his incredible announcement.

The words bellowed by the town crier made Dr. Ragusa shudder. Nini pounded his drum again and repeated the odious edict: "Hear ye! Hear ye! Hear ye! . . . The mayor decrees that all Jews must be reported to the authorities and recorded in the civil status registry. And he demands that all residents of the town belonging to the Jewish race appear at the registry office."

On October 6, 1938, the Fascist Grand Council had issued the infamous "racial laws," a series of decrees intended to exalt the Italian race as pure Aryan. This was the apparent justification, subscribed to, moreover, by ten scientists of dubious principles. But the entire world realized that it was a concession that Premier Benito Mussolini had made to his friend Adolf Hitler of Nazi Germany, who just a few months earlier had come to Rome on an official visit. The aim was to crush the Jewish people. Their Italian citizenship was taken away, mixed marriages were nullified, and the race was declared unfit for military posts and public employment, as well as for several professions, such as teacher, lawyer, journalist, and magistrate.

For a segment of Italians, including Dr. Ragusa, the future promised to be more wretched than the already bleak present.

"Those poor Jews still haven't finished atoning for their deicide," observed Don Antonio Albamonte, stopping in front of Mimmo Ferro's tavern.

Not even on this score did he and his friend the prince find themselves in agreement. Licata, in fact, shook his head. "Don Antonio, don't you understand that the Jews are just a scapegoat? It's been that way for centuries, and it will always be so."

"Still, they're a greedy people," the priest concluded as, trailed by the prince, he entered the tavern. The monsignor purchased his Tuscan cigars only from Mimmo Ferro. The entrance of the two interrupted the excited voices of the men playing *Tocco.* Everyone turned toward them. Those who were seated rose as a sign of respect, and those wearing caps took them off. Don Antonio asked Mimmo for his Tuscan cigars and glanced at the little crowd of players.

"You see, Prince, the entire philosophy of our people is summed up in this game. Never mind Aristotle and your Voltaire." Mimmo handed the priest five cigars wrapped in wax paper. Don Antonio took one out, lit it, and inhaled a few puffs with pleasure.

"This is one of my many vices." He smiled with false modesty.

"The cigar is a perfect symbol of pleasure," remarked the prince. "Exquisite, yet it leaves us unsatisfied." He smiled ironically and headed toward the door, followed by the monsignor. "But what did you mean to tell me about that game?" Licata prodded him.

The priest waved his hand in a sweeping gesture, as if to embrace the houses, the palazzi, and the people passing by. "You see all this? Here in Sicily, this is by no means reality. It is only a facade. The real world— who controls things and who makes the important decisions—remains underground. Invisible. Like in *Tocco.* The one who decides things is the boss's helper, who only *seems* to be under the boss but is the real one calling the shots."

Chapter 3

Back in 1920, the Italian population was experiencing a period of intense crisis, with discontent among all social classes contributing to levels of extreme intolerance. The harvest that year produced the most disastrous yield farmers could remember, forcing the government to buy two-thirds of the country's required wheat abroad, at a price much higher than what the average Italian could afford to pay. In many cities, clashes between protesters and police became commonplace, with numerous strikes by the working classes, professional groups, and even government employees and teachers.

The situation was not as dramatic in Sicily as in the rest of Italy, because the farmers' discontent lacked the crucial backing of the masses of workers in large industries; but even there, the common people managed to make their voices heard violently, supported by socialist and popular fronts.

For these reasons, the great feudal landowners of western Sicily chose to meet in a secret assembly to chart the course of Sicily's economy in such a way that they would not lose control of power.

The meeting took place in the heart of Palermo on October 14, 1920, in the rooms of Palazzo Cesarò, whose proprietors were the Count and Countess Colonna, descendents of a branch of a famous Roman family that had arrived in Sicily in the thirteenth century. Invitations were distributed secretly to thirty-eight large-estate owners, as well as representatives of the clergy, politicians, and members of the press. Thirty-four turned up at the meeting; all of them men. Wives and lovers were excluded from the assembly, with the exception of the Countess Paola Colonna—in fact, the originator of the conspiracy—who acted as hostess. Ferdinando Licata, who had recently turned forty, was among the last guests to arrive. He kissed the countess's hand before addressing her.

"Donna Paola, it is an honor for me to meet you. I must admit that what they say about your charm is inadequate to convey what is felt in person."

The noblewoman, advanced in years, was flattered by the prince's words and impressed by his elegant appearance. "Prince Licata, when a woman is young, she is said to be 'beautiful,' but when she is on in years, the best thing that can be said of her is that she is 'charming.' I would like to be remembered for my brain."

Licata smiled. "Men are frightened of a woman who is beautiful and also endowed with intelligence. Your husband has indeed been fortunate."

The countess gave him a smile of complicity, and, with that, let him know that he could consider himself free to move on.

Ferdinando Licata knew most of those present, and the few whom he had not yet had the pleasure of meeting were introduced to him by the host, Don Calogero Colonna himself.

Almost all of the attendees were noblemen who had inherited feudal estates that they held by the grace of God and the king. Among the political figures invited were the liberal Antonio Grassa, the republican parliamentarians Vito Bonanno and Ninì Rizzo. There was even a delegation of journalists with Raffaele Grassini, the official spokesman of the Agrarian Party, and in addition, there was a representative of the Church, Don Antonio Albamonte, who was also a member of the island's nobility.

At that time a simple parish priest of the Cathedral of Salemi, Don Antonio was the youngest of three brothers. Due to family arrangements, he had been forced by his father to embrace an ecclesiastical career. But in character and unscrupulousness, he did not differ significantly from the others present.

When introduced, Licata and Don Antonio took an instinctive and immediate liking to each other.

Ferdinando Licata approached the group that seemed most passionate. At its center, a baron waved his arms like a rabble-rouser. "It's all the fault of that idiot of a prime minister Salandra! To urge those few lazy good-for-nothings to fight during the war, he went and promised them that when they returned home, they would have 'a piece of land all their own.'"

"Salandra should have his tongue cut out," echoed the honorable Ninì Rizzo.

"No one can stop them now. And it's not only the socialists," ventured Marquis Pietro Bellarato, a short, stocky man who lacked the aristocratic bearing of a Licata.

"That plaster saint Don Sturzo and his Popular Party have also gotten into it," a quarryman concurred. "Now they too want to divide up our estates to distribute them to the people. What kind of a revolution is this? I for one am against it."

Paolo Moncada, the elderly prince of Valsavoia, joined in. "Devalua-
tion is at historic lows and shows no sign of stopping. In one year, gold
has risen from 5.85 liras per gram to well over 14.05 liras. That's 240 percent. A staggering figure!"

"The real plague to eradicate is the socialist scum," Marquis Bellarato
interjected firmly.

"The problem is that they possess a majority of seats in the Chamber of Deputies: one hundred fifty-six," said Moncada, stroking his long
white beard.

"But let's not forget," the republican Vito Bonanno concluded with
satisfaction, "that the socialists didn't even get one seat from Sicily."

"True," agreed Moncada. "And the fascists were also left empty-
handed. In a couple of years, they too will disappear. The ones that worry
me, on the other hand, are the hundred seats held by the Popular Party,
by that damned priest—forgive me, Don Antonio—that Don Sturzo,
who wears a black cassock, though it might as well be red."

Raffaele Grassini, the journalist, joined the discussion. "Let's not over-
look the fact, gentlemen, that these were the first genuinely free elections
since the unification of Italy. We have to recognize that the socialists are
the true representatives of the people."

"This is the consequence of the right to vote, which our political signori chose to extend to all male citizens!" exclaimed Bellarato, the most
hotheaded of the group. "Still, you have to consider that hardly more
than fifty percent of the electorate voted."

"That's because no one has ever had faith in parliament," the quarryman offered. "Especially since the deputies were ignored by the king
when it came time to decide on entering the Great War. Remember?
The majority of deputies were in favor of not intervening, but the king
decided all the same that we had to fight."

"Today, however, it is parliament itself that sets the political price of
bread. We can't support these prices anymore!" Marquis Pietro Bellarato
shouted, attracting the attention of all present. "We're selling wheat at a
quarter of its real price. Why should we have to take it out of our own
pockets? These reds are ruining us!" The assembly nodded, concerned.

"They want to sow terror among the peasantry; their goal is to create
panic. They provoke us in order to fuel the people's resentment and in-
cite them to take up arms to revolutionize the system, and gain possession of everything we own!" His final words silenced the entire gathering.

Taking advantage of the lull, Count Calogero Colonna moved to the center of the room and, clapping his hands, requested his guests' attention. "Dear friends, thank you for coming and participating," he began, clearing his throat. From his jacket pocket he withdrew a sheet with a list of names. "I must inform you that four of us are absent. In the interest of protecting our holdings, you should know who they are: Baron Vincenzo Aprile, Count Gabriele Amari, Marquis Enrico Ferro, and Baron Giovanni Moleti. It is important to understand who are our friends and who are our enemies. And now I turn the floor over to our spokesman, the eminent Raffaele Grassini."

That said, the count sat back down. The journalist stepped forward to the center of the room and, wasting no time, began speaking, turning to the countess, who was sitting in the middle of the semicircle:

"First of all, our thanks to our gracious hostess, Countess Paola Colonna, who has been kind enough to welcome us into her beautiful home." He waited for the applause to die down before continuing. "On the agenda, and the reason why we are meeting this evening, is the need to decide what stance we should take regarding the provocations that all of us have had to put up with in recent weeks. Tenant farmers occupying our lands, who no longer want to pay rent; thieves who steal our livestock and then sell it to estate managers in distant areas. The situation is grave.

"The central government is far away and at the point of economic collapse itself," Grassini continued. "The budget's expenditures exceed revenues three times over. The farmers who fought in the war, where they were able to eat at least one meal a day, have returned to a miserable, poverty-stricken life. Now these same farmers look with envy on those who stayed home to make their fortune. The lands are abandoned, partly for lack of workers, but in greater part because it's to our advantage to let them lie fallow. Under these conditions, it doesn't take much for the fuse of rebellion to be ignited, and, I assure you, there are certain ringleaders who are capable of fomenting revolutions even when there is much less rancor in people's hearts. The question is, What should we do to stop this madness? The debate is open. To avoid confusion, try to speak one at a time and raise your hand first. Thank you all." He moved to the side of the room and remained standing.

"There is only one answer." First to take the floor was Marquis Pietro Bellarato. "An answer that comes from the depths of centuries past, from our ancestors; an answer that has never failed: the force of arms! I, like all of you, have in my service an army of killers that cost me a fortune.

Let's give the people a good example, and everything will go back to the way it was before, you'll see."

He sat down again. A hand went up beside him, and Baron Adragna spoke up: "The peasant farmers are like children to me. And children need to be spanked to make them obey. That's all they listen to. I agree with the marquis."

The assents from the assembly seemed to indicate a general consensus. Prince Ferdinando Licata, who had remained silent and for the most part unobserved until then, raised his hand to speak.

"I don't think that's a wise idea," he began in a resolute voice, quieting the assembly. Marquis Bellarato, in particular, stiffened in his chair. Licata continued in a decisive tone. "Times are changing, and we must change with the times. Enough violence. We've had far too many deaths and losses. Our farmers want to form cooperatives? Let's allow them to do so. They want to occupy the lands and petition the courts to recognize their rights? Let them make their demands. Let's not oppose them; on the contrary, let's support their petitions, help them prepare the papers.

"I will go even further and say let's make a little effort and participate in these cooperatives ourselves along with our most trusted friends. Let's help them request funds from the Cassa Rurale, the agricultural bank, for the collective tenancies."

He paused, surveying his audience, and then continued in a more insinuating tone: "Who manages the Cassa? Is it not we? And won't we be the ones who postpone the loans indefinitely?" He smiled slyly, and those present breathed a sigh of relief, though not everyone had fully understood the prince's subtle humor and had to ask his neighbor to explain.

"If I understand correctly," Marquis Bellarato replied sarcastically, "we should assist them in their designs. Is that right?"

"Exactly," Licata confirmed. "We can control their movements, indefinitely put off the applications for expropriation, and later shelve them permanently, if it suits us. Let them think they will obtain loans for the leaseholds; we can deny them the funds with the excuse of some bureaucratic oversight or simply because the applications were lost in a fire and new documents will have to be filed. Or when it is to our advantage, we can give in and grant them those blessed pieces of paper."

"One gunshot, and everything will return to normal more quickly," the marquis maintained defiantly.

"Marquis, would you have our superb lands invaded by police and *carabinieri* from all over the continent?" the prince countered calmly. "Besides, violence leads to violence, death begets death."

"Prince Licata is right! We can't have our lands invaded by the military police!"

Everyone's eyes turned to the source of the statement.

It was Salemi's parish priest, Don Antonio Albamonte, one of the most authoritative presences at the meeting despite his mere thirty-five years of age.

"We are a civilized people," Don Antonio began. "Violence must be avoided. Our farmers are like a flock of sheep that need a dog and a shepherd to guide them. Perhaps we can allow them to choose their own path, but we must see to it that we are always the ones leading them. While we can recognize the desire for reform on the part of those we protect, we also have a duty to ensure that ultimately nothing changes."

"But Don Antonio," retorted the marquis, "if we do that, we'll be like capons, who think they're roosters even though they don't have the balls!" The marquis's laughter was echoed by most of the assembly. "Forgive me, Countess," he apologized to the only woman in the room for his indelicate remark, before continuing. "They'll eat us alive! It's completely wrong! The shotgun is the only music these people understand, and the shotgun's tune is what we must play for them!" He looked around at his neighbors, seeking approval. But the room had fallen silent.

The moderator took the floor again. "Well, then. If I may interpret the thinking of this assembly," said the journalist Raffaele Grassini, "we must choose between two streams of thought. That of Marquis Bellarato, who advocates the use of force, versus that of Prince Licata, who by contrast urges us to support the peasants' ambitious pipe dreams while maintaining control over their initiatives. At the entrance, you were handed invitation cards. Indicate on the back which of the two proposals you wish to support."

The result of that vote would turn out to be a milestone for the Mafia in Sicily.

Chapter 4

– 1938 –

The morning following Nini Trovato's pronouncement, Ragusa, more distraught than ever, went to the town hall to try to find out what the absurd ordinance meant from a practical standpoint. He couldn't understand what being recorded as a member of the Jewish race in a civil status registry might lead to. Was it a good thing, or could it have ominous consequences? Someone would have to explain it to him.

He put on his best suit, knotted his tie, and, accompanied by his son, Saro, hastened toward the town clerk's office. He felt certain that fate did not have anything good in store. His thoughts went to his children. He had hoped for a better future for them than his own, even if it were far away from that grudging land. Stellina, his youngest daughter, had married a quiet boy from Marsala, a city on the west coast of the island, and was perhaps better off than all of them. But Ester, the eldest, his first wife's daughter, had just turned twenty-eight, and, despite her teaching diploma, she could not manage to find a job, much less a good husband. And then there was Saro, the little orphan they had adopted when he was still an infant and raised as their own son.

Saro was shy, too sober for someone his age. A very intelligent boy, a ray of sunshine, with a thatch of light brown hair that he tried in vain to keep out of his eyes. At school he had always been the brightest in the class, but he'd had to settle for working for Domenico the barber, and for this, Ragusa could not forgive himself.

When they arrived at town hall, Ragusa asked to see the town clerk. At that time, the appointed mayor of Salemi was Lorenzo Costa, a Ligurian who had landed in Sicily in 1918 as commander of a troop of Royal Guardsmen. Costa had managed to adapt to the changing times and, after his experience with the Royal Guard, had gone on to the new police corps, eventually founding a section of the Italian League of Combatants in Salemi. His political climb ultimately had led him to the town's highest office. As mayor, he had appointed his most trusted man as town clerk: Michele Fardella, the only one who knew about all

his misdeeds. He had assigned command of the local *Fasci*, the action
squad or combat league, to Jano Vassallo, the son of Gaetano Vassallo.
The elder Vassallo had been the leader of one of the most violent outlaw
bands in the Salemi region prior to fascism and hadn't been heard of for
many years now.

The action squad was made up of a group of dissolute young troublemakers, always ready to use their fists, emboldened by the authority con-
ferred on them by Rome and by the personal protection of the mayor. In
addition to Jano, the gang of tough guys included five of Salemi's most
desperate young men. The youngest was Ginetto, a real coward, though
in a group, he punched harder than anyone else. Then there was Nunzio,
the eldest son of Manfredi, one of the many emigrants from the early
days. Prospero Abbate, Cosimo, and Quinto were the other three for
whom the word *bastards* could be considered a compliment. Jano, their
worthy leader, was a strapping young man with brawny shoulders and
legs, whose presence aroused dread among the area's inhabitants.

Lorenzo Costa, who now had to think mainly about maintaining
public order in the territory under his jurisdiction, tolerated him and
tried to contain his rages.

Jano had survived a rebellious childhood. He had been the despair
of every teacher who, one after the other, had tried to tame him. The
slaughter of his family, which he had witnessed as a child, had scarred his
psyche for life. He hated the world and had turned violent. Luckily for
him, with the dawn of fascism, he had been placed in an unprincipled
organization that readily welcomed him. In some ways, the action squad
represented his salvation, though paranoia had by that time enclosed
him in a dark labyrinth.

Jano wanted payback, in blood. He hated Dr. Ragusa because the
physician had failed to save his mother when she gave birth to twins.
He hated Rosario Losurdo, Prince Ferdinando Licata's estate manager,
because he had gotten away with only five years of prison for the massacre of Jano's family. He hated his own father, the outlaw Gaetano Vassallo, because at the time of the murders, he had thought only of saving
himself, abandoning his family to the mercy of the killers. He hated his
mother too because she had chosen that vile man as a husband. In short,
he had a grudge against the entire world.

Jano and his militiamen had turned a room of the municipal building
into their base of operations. Seeing Dr. Ragusa there in the town hall
was a welcome surprise for them, an excellent chance to have some fun.

"Well, well, Doctor, you've come to pay us a visit?" Ginetto said loudly as he leaned against the doorway, smoking.

Ragusa strode past him without slowing down, followed by Saro. "Ginetto, why aren't you in school at this hour?" the doctor scolded him, asserting his authority.

The boy broke away from the door as if caught in the act and said uncertainly, "But I don't go anymore. I'm big."

"Big? Don't make me laugh." But by now Dr. Ragusa and his son were already climbing the staircase leading to the main floor, where the offices of the mayor and the town clerk were located. At that moment, Jano intervened.

"Hey, Doc, where do you think you're going?" Jano yelled after him.

"I was summoned by the town clerk," Ragusa lied, not slowing his steps. Moments later, he entered the office of Michele Fardella and stood before him at his desk.

Fardella did not use the desk for working, since he couldn't actually read, much less write. It was merely a pretense to justify his salary. The real work was done by the clerks on the ground floor, crammed into a large room spilling over with papers and file folders.

"Signor Fardella, I won't waste your time," the doctor began as he took a seat. "Yesterday I heard Nini say that we had to come down to the town hall. Do you mind telling me what the hell is going on?"

"What are you talking about, Doctor?"

"What do you mean, what am I talking about? Who sent Nini around to tell the Jews that they had to report to the public records office? Was it a joke?" The doctor was beginning to lose patience. Saro gestured to his father to calm down.

"One moment," Michele Fardella, who didn't like being caught off guard, stood up and went to the door. "De Simone!" he shouted at the top of his lungs. Then he sat down with Ragusa again, smiling, and held out a pack of Popolari, which the doctor refused. Ignoring Saro, the clerk stuck a cigarette in his mouth and lit it, leaning back in his chair. "A little patience, and we'll clear up the mystery."

Seconds later, in came De Simone, an elderly clerk who performed the work of ten people at the town hall. He was out of breath after running up the stairs. He didn't even have the strength to introduce himself.

"What is all this about the Jews?" Fardella asked.

The old man caught his breath and finally said in a hoarse voice, "It's a notice that arrived a week ago from the Ministry of the Interior. Racial laws have been enacted. Jews are no longer citizens like us Christians," the clerk summed up.

The doctor's blood froze, while Saro didn't really understand what they were talking about. Even Michele Fardella had a hard time understanding what that decision meant in actual practice.

"It's all written there," said De Simone, going toward a stack of documents arranged on a corner of the desk. He rapidly scanned the folders and spines, deftly slipped out a *Gazzetta Ufficiale*, the official journal of record, and handed it to the town clerk with the writing deliberately upside down, to make fun of him. Michele Fardella pretended to read it quickly, and then gave it back to De Simone.

"What is it about? Tell us in so many words," he ordered in a tone that brooked no argument.

"Well, what I said: the Jews must be entered in a register that we must then send to the ministry. They can no longer practice their professions." He leafed through several pages of the royal decree. Then he began reading in a singsong tone: "Measures for the Defense of the Italian Race. Vittorio Emanuele III, King of Italy and Emperor of Ethiopia by the grace of God and by the will of the Nation, considering the urgent and absolute necessity to take measures, given article three—"

"Enough. That's enough, De Simone. You may go."

Dr. Ragusa had a whirlwind raging in his head and didn't notice the understanding look his old friend De Simone gave him as he bowed slightly, turned, and left the room.

Saro had been silent until then. In deference to his father, he had not intervened in the discussion. But now, seeing his father's struggle, he sought Michele Fardella's attention.

"Are the regulations already in force?" he asked with a certain naiveté.

"What do you think? Don't worry about it. Doctor, Doctor, take it easy. Don't get so excited. You know how things work here in Italy. Many laws are made, but how many are enforced? This is just one of many. The government does it on purpose. What do they say? 'Too many laws, no law.'"

From the floor below, desperate screams could be heard; then individuals yelling, a woman shouting, and frantic footfalls, as if people were running away.

Michele Fardella leaped to his feet. A character more suited to action, he quickly grabbed a Beretta from the drawer and ran to the door. Saro followed him, while his father remained bent over the desk, envisioning a future of despair.

From the landing, Fardella and Saro looked down and saw that a man had taken De Simone hostage in the middle of the entrance hall below, holding the old clerk with his left arm, while his right hand gripped a pistol pointed one moment at the poor clerk's temple and the next at the crowd huddled against a wall.

"Nobody move! I'll kill him, I swear to God!" the man yelled. Some of the people had their hands up; others cowered on the floor. The man was unaware of Michelle Fardella's presence just above him.

"Calm down, don't do anything stupid, nothing's happened yet!" Everyone's attention turned to Fardella, who, hiding the gun behind his back, had started slowly down the stairs, followed by Saro.

"Stop! Stop, I said! I'll shoot him if you don't stop!" The man shoved the gun against De Simone's throat.

"Okay, I'll stop. See? I'll stop." But Fardella kept heading down the stairs, though as slowly as possible. "Tell me, what is it I can do for you?"

"You can't do anything. There's nothing anyone can do now!" the desperate man cried.

Near him stood a chubby matron who was clasping a younger woman to her. It was Mena, Rosario Losurdo's daughter, and her governess, Nennella. Saro had seen Mena around town on other occasions and had been struck by her radiant beauty and her vivid green eyes. Now there she was, her life in danger, the madman's gun barrel just a few feet away. Saro was afraid the man might make some reckless move.

Jano Vassallo, stationed near the hallway door, had his hands up, as did his squad members, awaiting the right moment to act. As long as the gunman had his pistol leveled, he was careful not to move.

Michele Fardella spoke again: "What do you want? Who do you have a complaint with?"

At that instant, someone in the crowd inadvertently made a motion. The frantic gunman must have spotted it, for he turned around and fired a shot toward the ceiling as a warning. Immediately all hell broke loose, with people screaming and trying to rush out the door, knocking some to the ground. Mena and her governess also tried to escape, but the crowd shoved them, and they were separated. The girl fell, a step away from the mob. Jano and his men raced to their command center to grab their guns. Michele Fardella ducked behind the staircase's marble balustrade, keeping his pistol aimed at the man. All he could do was yell, "Easy now! Don't shoot! Don't shoot!"

Saro immediately sprang to the spot where Mena had fallen and, shielding her, rolled over with her on the floor to avoid the path of the crowd.

The armed man, dragging De Simone, positioned himself in a corner of the hall. He was completely beside himself, no longer rational. He kept on shouting: "I'll kill you all! All of you! Bastards! Goddamn bastards!"

Mena raised her frightened gaze to the young man who was protecting her with his body. Their eyes met, their noses nearly touching. "Don't be afraid," Saro whispered to her. Mena closed her eyes and clung to him, terrified.

Michele Fardella tried to draw the man's attention: "Take it easy . . . Talk to me. Tell me who you are . . ."

In the depths of despair, the man uttered a cry that shattered the hearts of everyone present. "God forgive me! Forgive these people!" He shoved De Simone aside as forcefully as he could. The elderly clerk, who was expecting the final blow, fell facedown on the floor. Then the poor wretch turned the barrel of the pistol up under his chin and pulled the trigger.

The roar made those in the hall recoil. The bullet came out of the center of his head, shattering his cranium and causing the brain to explode into a thousand pieces that ended up splattered against the wall. The man slid silently to the ground and sat there like a puppet whose strings had been cut. Some people screamed, while others stood stock-still, paralyzed.

Michele Fardella, joined by Jano and the other militiamen, went over to the gunman.

Saro helped Mena to her feet. "These are terrible times," he murmured to her, genuinely frightened as well.

The girl, though still upset, was bold enough to look into his eyes. Then she lowered her gaze as soon as Nennella appeared to resume care of her charge.

"May God bless you, Saro," said Nennella, who evidently knew him. Then she led Mena out of the building, heading for their carriage.

Saro followed the young girl until she disappeared through the door. Next, he turned to the knot of people that had formed around the man who had taken his life.

Prospero, one of Jano's men, crouched beside the corpse and lifted the man's head, or what was left of it.

"Do you know him?" Jano asked.

Saro shook his head no. "He must be someone from around here, though," he replied.

An elderly farmer made his way through the townspeople. "It's Davide Zevi," he said loudly, in a disapproving tone.

"A Jew?" Jano asked him.

The farmer's only reply was a nod.

"Good. He saved us a bullet," Jano remarked cynically, pushing through the crowd.

Some made the sign of the cross, others went to notify the carabinieri, while someone else went off to summon the undertaker. Saro suddenly realized that in the commotion he had stepped on a document. He picked it up and saw it was Mena's identification card. The young woman must have come to town hall to obtain it upon turning eighteen. As he looked at the photo, seeing again those magnificent eyes framed by jet-black hair, he confirmed that she was the most beautiful girl he had ever encountered.

He slipped the card in his pocket and looked up. At the top of the staircase stood his father. Ragusa had witnessed the suicide in silence, literally shaken. It wasn't like him to stand back at such a scene. Any other time, he would have rushed to the man to avert a foolish act, to make the man talk, to reason with him somehow. For Ragusa was strong and confident in his skills, both dialectical and humane. But now something seemed to have broken in him. The stability and assurance that had made him one of the most influential figures among his fellow townsmen had suddenly abandoned him.

Saro rushed up to his father and, taking him by the arm, led him slowly out of that hell.

Chapter 5

– 1938 –

Annachiara Ragusa lingered by the fireplace in the kitchen after supper, to finish basting a dress she was making for the elementary school teacher's wife. The flickering light of the oil lamp fell on nimble fingers that moved as swiftly as those of a magician.

Reaching the hemline of the dress, she stopped and stretched, her torso stiff from sitting so long in a contracted position. Her eyes were tired, her shoulders ached. Suddenly she felt a familiar weariness that she recently found herself having to endure almost every day. She put the needle and thread back in the shoe box and went into the bedroom, where her husband was still tugging at the blankets, tossing and turning in bed.

"Peppino, can't you sleep?" she asked, unbuttoning her sweater.

The doctor grumbled and turned over for the hundredth time, pulling the heavy army blankets over him.

Annachiara sat down on the edge of the bed. "Peppino, don't torture yourself. You know how things work here. In a month, no one will think about it anymore. Besides, who's going to bother us down here in Sicily?" She shook him, to get him to agree.

Ragusa sat up. "This time won't be like the others. You'll see, they'll hound us, the Duce will try to please the Führer. Did you hear what they said to each other in Rome?"

"You've worked all your life, you were in the trenches during the Great War, the Austrians even wounded you—who do you think could be out to get you? When you act like this, I don't understand you." Annachiara rose from the bed and, slipping off first her sweater and then her wool dress, was left wearing a black cotton slip.

She was not yet forty, but life's hardships, the three children to raise, the struggle of having to find something to put on the table each day for lunch and dinner, the work as a seamstress that she did at night, stealing hours from sleep, had aged her prematurely.

Ragusa looked at his wife, feeling a sense of guilt. "We must leave the country."

His tone made her freeze. "You can't be serious. Our life is here," she replied patiently, putting on her heavy nightgown.

Ragusa turned over again in the bed. "It will be difficult for us Jews to live in a nation where they'll take away all our rights, even the right to work."

His wife tousled his hair, trying to play down her husband's paranoia. "Peppino, we live in the most remote corner of Italy," she said with that charming Venetian cadence that had made her Sicilian husband fall so deeply in love. "Don't worry, no one will come looking for you here."

Ragusa pushed away his wife's hand. "You should have seen that man's despair."

"Oh, come on, don't think about it anymore. Put out the lamp instead; we'll run out of oil."

The following Sunday was the feast of Saint Faustina, patroness of the fields. From early dawn, the streets of Salemi would be overrun with stalls and street vendors from all over the province. Later in the day, the celebration would include a Mass, followed by a solemn procession led by the bishop. Toward evening, a band from nearby Calatafimi would entertain the residents with opera passages and regional songs. Then it would be time for *tombola*, a kind of bingo, in the piazza, with prizes offered by several of the province's wholesalers: bottles of wine, olive oil, ricotta, and salami. Finally, with the first shadows of evening would come the most awaited event: the fireworks, a thrilling show that children dreamed of throughout the year and that even adults wouldn't miss. The arrival of stalls crammed with all sorts of wonderful things provided a chance for the local women to be able to find dresses, shawls, soaps, stockings, and other items that were hard to come by in town. That morning, Mena, accompanied by the ever-present Nunella, strolled through the market, which occupied the entire Piazza del Castello.

Although the day was gray and somewhat windy, it didn't look like it was going to rain. The townsfolk wore their Sunday best, the women abandoning their everyday black and wearing their most elegant, colorful dresses.

Mena wandered from one booth to another with the joy and curiosity of a child let loose in toyland. It was hard for chubby Nunella to keep up with her, and she sometimes let Mena get ahead of her a little, content to merely keep an eye on the girl from afar while she took a rest, leaning against a doorway.

That morning, even the barbershop had closed for the holiday, and Saro was enjoying the day off. Like all the young men in Salemi, he knew that the market drew girls like honey, and he strolled through the stalls glancing here and there, in the hope of meeting Rosario Losurdo's daughter again.

Since the day of Davide Zevi's suicide at town hall, Saro had done nothing but think of her, her thick black hair, her eyes shining like emeralds. So it was no coincidence that the two eventually found themselves side by side, rummaging through the antique objects of a secondhand dealer. Their hands brushed as they went to pick up the same Art Nouveau figurine of a veiled vestal.

Mena politely withdrew hers first. "Oh, sorry—"

"Mena."

The girl looked at Saro's face, and her eyes lit up with pleasure. "Oh, Saro."

They shook hands for an unreasonably long time. "Hi, I'm glad to see you again," the boy said with a smile.

"I never thanked you for what you did," Mena said in a ringing voice.

Saro felt his heart leap into his throat. "Don't mention it; it was nothing."

"That poor man could have killed us all." Then she burst out laughing, covering her mouth with her delicate hand. "There I was on the floor with a man on top of me. I saw Nennella's eyes—she was about to have a stroke."

"I did the first thing that occurred to me," Saro said in excuse.

But Mena was still smiling. "Yes, but you didn't jump on Nennella to save her, and she was right next to me. Clever, hmm?" Mena touched him affectionately on the shoulder.

The contact once again thrilled him, and Mena was aware of it. "Go on, I'm joking, silly. Saro Ragusa, don't tell me you're touchy?"

Actually, he was very embarrassed. "Of course not," he lied, feeling exposed.

"But wait." From the pocket of his cheap wool jacket, he pulled out the ID. "This is yours; you lost it in the confusion." Mena's eyes widened, and possibly she overdid her show of happy surprise. "My ID card! I thought I would have to get another one! You really are my guardian angel!" She clapped her hands delightedly and then took the document from Saro. She saw that with it was a slip of paper, folded in two.

"Oh! Oh! What's this?" She took it and opened it up, discovering that it was one of the *tombola* tickets. She was ready to hand it back, not realizing that Saro had intended it as a gift. However, Saro was no longer in front of her. She searched for him among the crowd, but he had disappeared. Instead, she saw Nennella coming toward her.

"Was the young man you were talking to Saro?" she asked in the tone of an inquisitor.

"He brought back my ID card. He found it."

"Good thing. That way we won't have to get another one," the governess replied distractedly.

Mena hid the bingo ticket in her hand and continued strolling among the stalls.

At precisely noon, the saint's heavy baldachin was carried out of the doors of the church, not without some difficulty. It was borne on the shoulders of sixteen of Salemi's most robust men. Around her neck, Saint Faustina wore a necklace of dried figs along with many five- and ten-lira bills. In front of her, the florid figure of Monsignor Antonio Albamonte could be seen along with the young parish priest, Don Mario, who held up a tall metal crucifix. On either side of them, a swarm of altar boys scurried along to keep up with the procession, and behind them came the women of the cathedral's congregation. Don Mario chanted litanies that were repeated first by the pious women and then by everyone else, with the same cadence and intonation.

As the saint passed by, farmers came out of their doors and tossed handfuls of wheat grain, saved from the last sowing, at her effigy, to promote the coming harvest and bring good luck to the family.

In the crush of the procession, Mena and Saro seemingly by chance found themselves side by side again. Saro had made quite an effort to reach her.

"Where are you going to watch the fireworks?" he asked.

"In the piazza," she replied, speaking loudly to be heard over the boisterous din of the crowd.

"I know a fantastic place where we won't miss a single burst," he said, fearful that she might reject him.

"Saro, see Nennella?" She pointed to the heavyset woman in front of them, she too dragged along by the flow of people. "She's always with me."

"So we'll bring Nennella along with us," he said with a smile, glad of the complicity that had been established between them. He wanted to add that he was happy to see her again, but the crowd separated them: Saro was pushed in the opposite direction from Mena, and as they were drawn apart, the two smiled at each other, surprised by the feelings well-ing up inside.

————

The stentorian voice of Ninì Trovato read the number that a child had pulled out of the *tombola* drum: "Forty-three!" he shouted, showing the ball to the villagers crowding Piazza del Castello, to prove the actual drawing of the number.

"*Quaterna*! Four in a row!" A girl's voice rose in the piazza, and an arm waved the ticket with the number that had been drawn. The voice was Mena's, and the lucky ticket was the one that Saro had given her. "I won! I won!" she cried excitedly.

Nennella, standing beside her, smiled happily at the win as well.

Ninì Trovato invited the lucky girl to come up to the platform, while a young man from the planning committee hung the chosen number on the large bingo board.

Mena made her way through the crowd and headed for the spot where the prizes were on display.

When she reached Ninì, a barrage of jubilant whistles and warm ap-plause showered her. She laughed good-naturedly and waved the ticket at the crowd. Then she approached the loudspeaker and repeated the four numbers that had won her the *quaterna*. "Three, seventeen, twenty-nine, and forty-three!"

"Are you Mena Losurdo?" Ninì asked her, though he already knew the answer.

"Yes, I'm Mena." Ninì brought his mouth to the microphone. "The young woman, ladies and gentlemen, has won four bottles of red wine, four salamis, four *caciocavallo* cheeses, and a dozen feet of sausage," the crier announced.

Everyone clapped, and the prizes were placed in a gunnysack that was then given to the lucky girl.

"Can you carry it?"

"You fill the bag, Ninì, I'll do the rest," the winner replied with a con-tagious smile.

Coming down the steps of the podium, Mena looked around for Saro as everyone congratulated her.

But there were too many people in the piazza, and finding him was impossible. When she reached Nennella again, the woman threw her arms around Mena and took the bag from her to peek inside.

When a half hour later the *tombola* was awarded to the person getting all the numbers on the card, and the swaying crowd erupted into applause for the lucky victor, Mena felt someone take her hand. She turned and saw Saro, who had once again materialized beside her. She didn't have time to tell him that she'd won with his ticket because Saro immediately pulled her aside, elbowing the people closest to them.

Nennella, still holding Mena's sackful of winnings, was shrieking joyfully. Turning to where she thought Mena was, and not seeing her, she wasn't too concerned, entirely taken up with cheering the lucky winner.

Mena, meanwhile, pulled along by Saro, did not resist, but she had stopped laughing and was beginning to worry. "Where are we going?"

"You'll see, trust me."

"But I don't even know you."

"Trust me," he said firmly.

He entered the door of a house facing the fortress and started walking down the stone steps leading to the cellar. But Mena yanked him back, forcing him to stop.

"Hey, come on! What do you take me for? I'm not going into the cellar with you."

"Mena, I'm asking you to trust me. I want to surprise you!" He made the request so eagerly that Mena couldn't help but give in.

"All right . . . let's go," she agreed after a moment's hesitation.

The two reached the bottom of the steps and then entered a tunnel that opened alongside a cask.

They walked down the long passageway that seemed to descend underground, and then finally came to an open space, barely illuminated by light coming from above. From there a set of wooden steps led up. Saro went first. Mena followed him nimbly, never once betraying the anxiety that gripped her. When they reached the first landing, she grabbed the boy by his jacket, jerking him forcefully around. "Saro Ragusa, I hope for your sake that the surprise is really a surprise; otherwise I'll see to it that you end up badly. Remember that I have two big brothers, not to mention my father."

The threat was serious, and Saro replied in kind: "You won't be disappointed." With that, he moved to a wrought-iron spiral staircase. "And now we have a long climb ahead of us. Do you think you can make it?"

"Worry about your own legs," the girl replied, pushing him aside and tackling the stairs first. Saro followed her. He tried looking up. He caught a peek of slender ankles and firm young legs under her skirt, but Mena's sharp voice stopped him: "Keep your eyes down! Either you do, or I'll kick you and knock your teeth out!"

The climb took several very long minutes. The steps seemed never ending. Finally, the last, even steeper flight was signaled by a thick rope hanging from the cone-shaped ceiling, since there was no longer a railing to hold on to. Mena grabbed the rope, as did Saro. She climbed the last steps with some difficulty and reached a small, round ledge inside a kind of sentry box, with a low wooden door.

"Here we are. But now close your eyes." Saro went to the door and opened it. Mena, somewhat impatient but more curious than she had ever been, closed her beautiful green eyes. Then Saro led her through the low door, gently making her duck her head to avoid the lintel. At last, they came out into the open.

On her face, Mena felt the cool air of evening that was lowering its dark mantle over the entire valley. Opening her eyes, she saw a panorama that made her shiver with emotion.

They were on the highest rampart of the fortress, whose vista took in the entire plain of Salemi. The shadows of night had not yet shrouded the mountains, forests, and farms in the valleys. The mistral had risen and was sweeping away the clouds that shortly before had threatened rain.

Toward the horizon, the luminous points of light from oil lamps in the windows of houses clinging to the mountains, gave the impression of an antique Nativity scene.

Mena looked at Saro and with eyes full of gratitude thanked him for the breathtaking sight. Saro smiled tenderly at her. He was about to take her in his arms, but all of a sudden he heard a whistling sound. From the bottom of the gorge, just in front of them, a flare rose to the sky. Mena turned to look and squealed with wonder. With a bang, the rocket burst into a thousand tiny stars. From that moment on, there was a succession of launches, explosions, radiant cascades, multicolored clusters of firecrackers, red, yellow, and white pinwheels, and showers of golden light that were projected and went off overhead, giving the two young people an endless thrill. Mena clung to Saro, as if seeking protection from the volley of blasts and booms. Saro put his arm around her waist, drawing her close. Then came the final detonation announcing the end of the show.

When the roar had faded among the valley's ravines, Mena raised her face to the boy. Not moving, the two continued to cling to each other, trembling with desire—but then they broke free of the embrace.

"We have to go back. Nennella must be looking for me," Mena said shyly, holding out her hand.

"Come on," Saro said sadly. He took her hand and led her into the sentry box to begin their descent. Neither of the two dared speak a word, preferring to savor the memory of those moments holding each other close at the top of the Castello.

Chapter 6

The suicide of Davide Zevi in the town hall had deeply shaken Dr. Peppino Ragusa's spirit. He'd lost his appetite and didn't want to see anyone; as soon as he could, he would close the medical office and take refuge at home. He had even decided to terminate the evenings he devoted to tutoring the town's illiterates.

Annachiara was desperate and furious over the depression her husband had sunk into and tried to rouse him by whatever means she could.

"You can't abandon them like that. It means forsaking your ideas, your ideals," she chided, waving her index finger under his nose.

Ragusa didn't answer, not wanting to quarrel with his wife.

"Have you thought about them? Or are you content to feel sorry for yourself? Play the victim?" But Ragusa just shook his head, inconsolable.

Annachiara then tried using compassion. "Peppino, please, you mustn't give up. Don't let those idiots win."

There was a timid knock at the door. Worried, Annachiara wondered, "Who can that be?" Ragusa raised his head, seized by panic.

His wife opened the door and, seeing who it was, broke into a smile. "Turi! Pericle! What a surprise! Come in, come in."

Ragusa stood up and went to greet his elderly pupils, moved by their gesture of solidarity. He embraced the four men, and they held him warmly in silence, choking back tears.

When they broke apart, Turi Toscano handed him a black-covered notebook.

"Here, Doctor, I managed to do my homework." Turi's fingertips were corroded by salt, and he had a hard time holding the pen steady.

Ragusa opened the notebook and read aloud Turi's sentences, written in a hesitant script. "All men are born with equal dignity . . . Only decent work sets us free . . ." He wasn't able to go on, and once again he embraced the old salt miner, touched.

"Turi, thank you. Our evenings were not wasted."

"Doctor, why do you want to abandon us?" Turi Toscano finally asked.

"Dear friends . . ." The doctor looked at them as if counting them. "And Gerolamo? And Vincenzo Valli?" He waited for an answer from them, but the four men withdrew into an uncomfortable silence and lowered their eyes to avoid meeting his gaze. "There, you see? That's the reason. Didn't you hear Nini's proclamation? What I feared would happen has started. From now on, life will be difficult for us Jews. For that reason, I don't want to drag other people into my troubles."

"We won't let them harm you." Toscano was the first to break the silence. "Besides, who do you think cares about us, way down here? Rome is halfway around the world."

"Turi is right," spoke up Ottavio Gravina, the youngest and toughest of them all. "We're not afraid of anybody."

"This battle can't be won with force, however," the doctor went on. "They will always be stronger."

There was another knock at the door. Everyone turned around.

A smile lit up Annachiara's lovely face. "It must be your other friends. You see? They've come too." She went to the door and opened it, ready to welcome the latecomers.

But in front of her, in the darkness of night, stood a leering Jano surrounded by three of his most loyal comrades: Ginetto, Nunzio, and Prospero.

"Good evening, Annachiara, aren't you going to invite us in?" Leaning against the doorframe, Jano took a quick look inside.

At that same moment, at the farmstead of Prince Ferdinando Licata's *gabellotto* or overseer, Rosario Losurdo, a small party was being held. One of Losurdo's armed guards, his *campiere* Manfredi, had just returned from Africa, from Addis Ababa, where he gone a year and a half earlier to try his luck as an immigrant, prompted by the regime's illusory promises. He had traveled to Ethiopia in the hope of becoming the owner of a piece of land—a large estate—where he could live out the rest of his life, but those eighteen months had proved a bitter disappointment.

The farmhouse was lit in celebration. Everyone had questions for Manfredi, but he responded impatiently in monosyllables.

Rosario Losurdo was very attached to Manfredi. When Losurdo had been imprisoned on charges, later dropped, that he had been behind the massacre at Borgo Guarine, Manfredi had held the reins of the estate for five years, without anyone bemoaning the gabellotto's absence.

Manfredi had devoted himself to protecting Losurdo's family as if it were his own. He had not let them lack for anything and had continued carrying on the affairs of the estate, collecting the taxes as if the gabellotto had never been away. This honesty and dedication had won over Losurdo, who, once he was released from prison and assumed control of Prince Licata's property again, began treating him as an equal, like a brother.

Among the young men most interested in Manfredi's venture was Saro, who asked him what the land was like, if it was true that it was easy to get permission to plant there, how much farms cost, if seeds had to be brought from Italy, what were the most productive crops, why he had come back after only eighteen months, whether the people there were very hostile toward whites—and if it was true that the girls were beautiful and that they were all willing.

At that question, the other young men burst out laughing, making risqué remarks under their breath and whispering double entendres.

Manfredi dampened their enthusiasm. "It's all a fraud. Everything they tell us to convince us to go to Ethiopia is false."

"But what about the empire, the place in the sun, the promised land?" Saro asked dejectedly.

"All lies. The only ones really getting rich are the 'sharks': the upper echelons, military men, diplomats, big contractors—in short, friends of friends of the government. They live in houses that have been expropriated from the old Ethiopian bourgeoisie, and their wives drive around the city in official cars that should be off-limits to them, but their use is tolerated."

"I've always said it: it's America that's the promised land," Saro told his friends.

"It's true. Those who have come back say that in New York anyone can become a millionaire," claimed Michele, one of Losurdo's sons.

"Then what are we waiting for? Let's get out of this thankless land." Setting out for other worlds had been Saro's dream since childhood.

Rosario Losurdo approached the group of young men who were besieging Manfredi.

"Give this poor soul a chance to breathe." His voice had the presence to silence them all as they turned toward him. "And you, Saro, where do you want to go? To America? Do you want your father and mother to die of a broken heart?"

Glasses began being passed around. Everyone toasted Manfredi's return and drank good wine from Rosario Losurdo's vineyards.

"So, you want to go away?" The feminine voice made Saro spin around, nearly spilling his wine on Mena's dress. "You want to go to

America? Haven't you thought about me?" Those words only increased Saro's embarrassment.

"Actually—"

The girl burst out laughing. "Come on, I'm kidding, I'm teasing you, silly."

"It's just an idea. I'd like to, but I don't know if I'll ever have the courage." He stared into her eyes. She couldn't hold his gaze. "But why did you say I don't think of you?" Saro asked.

This time it was Mena who felt embarrassed. "Is that what I said?"

"Don't pretend you don't remember."

"I meant just what I said." Her voice cracked a little, and Saro noticed it.

For a few moments, the two young people stared intensely into each other's eyes.

"You know what I say? You can go wherever you like, Saro Ragusa."

With that, Mena turned around and walked off, mingling with the other guests.

Jano, trailed by his three bloodhounds, entered the doctor's home without waiting for an invitation from the hostess, not giving a damn about the rules of hospitality. "Well, well. I see that you continue to hold subversive meetings, Dr. Ragusa, even though you've already received a warning from the mayor. Am I right?"

Annachiara, with her innate cordiality, invited Jano to come have a seat. "Jano, Nunzio, can I offer you some of our wine? Sit down, our house is your house." So saying, she went to the cupboard to get some glasses and a bottle.

But Jano's voice made her freeze. "Don't bother, Annachiara. We're not here to have a drink. Or at least we won't be the ones drinking." His jeering smile was imitated by the other three militiamen, who threw him looks of complicity. "I repeat. Don't you know that it's forbidden to hold seditious meetings? What are you cooking up?" he asked, turning to the four villagers sitting at the end of the table.

Mimmo Ferro, the one who least feared Jano's authority given the many times he had seen him drunk, replied sarcastically, "Anyone who has a clear conscience either has a bad memory or has never used his conscience. My dear Jano, we are guilty like every man who breathes on this earth."

"You're being a smart-ass, right, Mimmo?"

Turi Toscano came to the aid of his companion. "Jano, you know very well why we come here to the doctor. Certainly not for a revolution."

"At first I didn't even know how to do arithmetic," Pericle, the charcoal burner, added.

Annachiara had brought four glasses and was filling them with wine.

"But I know that the doctor doesn't only teach you to count and read, isn't that so, Dr. Ragusa?"

He bowed his head, refusing to defend himself. He had nothing to say to the thug.

Jano pounded his fist violently on the table, making Annachiara cringe. "Answer me when I ask you a question!" One of the glasses toppled, and wine spilled onto the table. Jano reared back and stood up so he wouldn't get wet. He was furious. "In any case, your time has come, dear doctor. I know all about what you do during your meetings. The multiplication table is just an excuse. What interests you is putting socialist ideas in the heads of these dunces. You, Doctor, are plotting against the regime. For that alone, I could throw you in jail."

"I am at your disposal, Jano," Ragusa finally spoke up. "Go ahead and throw me in jail. You don't have a shred of evidence to prove what you say. You'll look like a fool in front of everyone, as usual."

Jano rushed at him and struck him on the face with the club he always carried with him. Annachiara threw herself at Jano, screaming, but Ginetto stopped her, pulling her away. Mimmo Ferro tried to interfere, but Nunzio shouldered him, knocking him to the floor. A stream of blood ran down Ragusa's face. Turi, Pericle, and Ottavio Gravina tried to reach the door, but Prospero blocked their way out.

"The party isn't over, and you want to leave already?" Jano barked at the three men. "I need witnesses. Someone will have to report what happens to those who oppose us."

Ragusa wiped his wound with his shirtsleeve.

At a sign from Jano, Nunzio and Prospero pinned the doctor's arms. He tried to free himself, but they were stronger, and after a while he stopped struggling. Annachiara kept screaming at them to leave him alone.

Jano appeared with a bottle in his hands. Annachiara saw him and let out a piercing shriek. Ginetto shook her forcefully to silence her, and when that didn't work, punched her in the face, knocking her out. Ragusa, seeing his wife on the floor, began thrashing about furiously again, yelling "Killers! Killers!" Nunzio and Prospero were having a hard time restraining him, so they threw him to the ground and held him down.

Jano went over, grabbed him by the hair, and lifted his head. Then he shoved a bottle of salt water into his mouth and began forcing him to gulp it down.

The salt water had the same effects as castor oil, but in addition caused a feeling of nausea that lasted several days.

Ragusa, in part due to his position, in part because of the deluge of water he was forced to swallow, began coughing to expel the liquid from his nose and other parts of his body. But Jano's job was finished only once the bottle was empty. Finally, Nunzio and Prospero let go of him. Ragusa, in a pool of filth, wheezed and went on vomiting, while Annachiara remained unconscious. The four friends were stunned and crushed by such callous cruelty.

Jano pulled an embroidered cloth off the table and wiped his hands with it. "Remember what you saw. And tell everyone that this is what's in store for the Duce's enemies." With that, he threw down the cloth and walked out, followed by his comrades.

At that moment at the farm, Rosita—Signora Losurdo, recognized as one of the best cooks in town—entered the party room carrying a huge fig and honey tart, borne with the care generally bestowed on newborns. Mena accompanied her mother with a bunch of teaspoons, while her brother Donato carried a stack of dessert plates.

Rosario Losurdo, like most of the *gabelloti* in Sicily, had become a powerful figure in the town, and the Limoges porcelain service with gold trim had been one of his wife's first acquisitions once they became rich. The crostata was cut, and plates flew from hand to hand.

Mena cut the last slice and personally took it to Saro. "Enjoy it, Saro, because in America there are no women who know how to make desserts this good," she told him wryly, handing him the plate.

"Your mother is a great baker," Saro said, licking his fingers, sticky with honey.

"Actually, I made the tart. My mother helped me, but I was the one who made it!"

The boy's eyes widened. "You're a phenomenon! I've never eaten any-thing so delicious."

Mena smiled, and Saro impulsively gave her a peck on the cheek, but his fig-and-honey-smeared lips left a mark that he clumsily tried to wipe off using the edge of his shirt.

The young woman drew back, amused. "Saro, stop that. You're hopeless." Then she took a handkerchief and wiped the traces of the tart off her cheek.

"Sorry, Mena," he said sheepishly, embarassed and blushing.

"What's going on here?" Rosario Losurdo had witnessed the scene from across the room. Mena was still his little girl, and he didn't care for that behavior at all. His stern tone made Saro spin around hastily; when he saw the girl's father, he gave a start that was almost comical.

"Don Rosario—what's going on?" All he could do was repeat the question the host had asked.

Mena shook her head, smiling. "Papa, what do you think is going on? Saro is about to leave, and we were saying good-bye." She pushed her father toward their guests. "Go back to your friends."

Rosario Losurdo had a soft spot for his little Mena. Only she would dare to be impertinent toward him.

Saro held out his hand to say good-bye to Losurdo. "*Baciamo le mani*—my respects—Don Rosario."

The man shook his hand, giving him a look that spoke volumes. When he released Saro's hand, he realized it was sticky with honey. He casually wiped it on his pants and walked away, proud of the "Don" that until then no one had ever afforded him.

Mena, who had noticed the little mishap, burst out laughing. "You're really impossible." She took Saro by the hand and dragged him across the room, toward the door. "I'm sorry, but you really must go now. Otherwise if my father realizes I fooled him, I'm finished!"

"Sorry," Saro stammered.

"If it was up to him, he'd keep me inside one of those glass bell jars we put patron saints in."

"He's not all wrong. Who knows how many guys make eyes at you."

"Oh, loads of them, I'd say."

They both smiled. Upon reaching the door, they faced each other, and suddenly their expressions turned serious. Mena made an imperceptible movement, her face moving closer to his. A few very long seconds went by. Then Saro took her hands, deliberately ending that magical moment.

"I really should go." So saying, he rested his lips gently on Mena's palms and let them linger there a second or two. Then, without turning around, he moved off into the evening shadows.

On the way back, Saro shivered with pleasure at the thought of having touched Mena's delicate skin. The girl was the daughter of Losurdo, the richest gabellotto in Salemi. And he was merely the son of a dirt-poor Jewish doctor.

Surely Losurdo had very different ambitions for his daughter; he'd better get her out of his mind. With these thoughts swirling in his head, Saro reached his house and saw a knot of people in front of the half-open door. He immediately realized that something serious had happened. As soon as people noticed him, the group parted to let him through.

Saro saw his mother lying on the bed. Mimmo Ferro and Turi Toscano were sitting at the foot of the bed, while his father was bent over his mother, giving her an injection. As soon as his sister Ester saw him come in, she ran crying to him and threw her arms around him.

"What's going on?" he asked. But Ester was sobbing and couldn't get out a word. Saro broke out of her embrace and demanded to know what had happened to his mother. Then he noticed how disheveled his father was, his shirt wet and soiled with blood and vomit, his hair dirty. Moaning, Annachiara turned her head to one side, opened her eyes, and saw Saro. She moved a hand weakly to touch him, and her son rushed to her and held her close.

"Mama . . ." He managed to choke back the lump that had formed in his throat. The woman seemed to feel better at the sight of her husband, who had remained beside her. Her gaze also took in Mimmo and Turi at the foot of the bed, and Ester, crying distraughtly. She closed her eyes again, and the sedative's action made her sink into a dreamless sleep.

Saro got up. The room was in complete disarray, a pool of water on the floor, a bottle upended. He turned to his father. "Who did this to you?" Ragusa didn't answer.

"It was Jano. Him and his Black Shirts," said Mimmo.

"I'll kill him!" cried Saro.

But his father took him by the shoulders and gripped him firmly.

"Calm down. You're not killing anyone. We have to pretend that nothing happened. We have to disappear. They're the stronger ones now. Not even the carabinieri can do anything against the fascist combat league."

Chapter 7

Prince Ferdinando Licata was pessimistic about the island's future. Not a day passed when he didn't hear about some injustice, some abuse, suffered by the poor at the hands of those who held political and administrative power in the town. Fascism had put men lacking any moral value in positions of control, crushing admirable men of profound ethics and demoting them to marginal roles.

In its own small way, Salemi itself was a perfect example of how corrupt the regime was. The town's mayor, Lorenzo Costa, was said to have ruthlessly wiped out entire families, and had appointed a pitiable misfit, Jano Vassallo, perpetrator of ill-advised, reckless actions, as head of the town militia. Now, though, that psychopath had begun to exceed all limits, and some residents of Salemi felt the need to redraw the boundaries of common civic decency.

With these thoughts in mind, Prince Ferdinando Licata decided to confront Jano and his notorious associates. Not just because Dr. Peppino Ragusa was a dear friend but also for his own mysterious reasons that were buried in the depths of his heart. Otherwise he never would have stooped to come to terms with such a mediocre individual as Jano.

The libertarian spirit and profound sense of justice that flowed in the prince's veins came from his great-grandfather, a Londoner named Frederick Leicester, who at the end of the eighteenth century, following in the footsteps of those who made the grand tour of Europe, had traveled far and wide throughout Italy. Finding in Sicily not only the colors and landscapes he had been seeking but love as well, the young Leicester decided to remain there for the rest of his life. When the birth of his son, Ferdinando's grandfather, was recorded, his surname was misspelled, thanks to an error by the registry clerk, though some said it was to deny his past: from Leicester it became Licata, and so from that day forward, Sicily acquired a new pedigree of princes.

When Ferdinando Licata was still a child, his family was struck by a tragedy. While traveling to Palermo, both parents were killed by a gang of bandits during a robbery. From then on, his grandfather and his sister, Lavinia, served as father and mother to him.

Thanks to his abilities and educational preparation, Ferdinando had been able to skillfully manage the few lands inherited from his grandfather. For many years, he was considered an excellent match by blue-blooded, Sicilian young ladies. But Licata was very reserved, not believing in marriage and, though he'd had numerous lovers, he'd always managed to escape being shackled by a wife.

He was also a great diplomat and had always avoided disputes with his neighbors and the various "dons" of the surrounding area. He had never wanted to get mixed up with them, men whom he considered extremely coarse and uncultured.

One Sunday morning at a little past six, Prince Ferdinando Licata stationed himself near the drinking trough two blocks away from where Carmela Petrulli lived. He knew—the whole town knew—that every Saturday night Jano sneaked into Carmela's house and left early the next morning at dawn. Carmela was not the town prostitute, but one of several war widows, another victim of the emigration that had depopulated many of the towns in Sicily in the 1920s.

At the customary time that Sunday morning, Carmela's door opened, and Jano slipped out furtively. He drew a black cloak over his shirt, also black, which he now wore like a second skin.

Ferdinando Licata's dark horse was drinking at the trough when Jano came around the corner. Though he was startled to see the prince, he concealed it. Licata, on the other hand, pretended to be surprised at running into him at that hour.

"Jano, it's too late to go hunting and too early if you're not going hunting. What are you doing here at this hour on a Sunday?" he asked, tugging the horse.

"Hey, Prince, I already shot my load, with all due respect." He quickened his pace without stopping, but the prince was swift and came up beside him, leading his horse by the bit.

"Do you know what's tragic about aging? It's not so much actually being old, as one might think, but being still young in your mind and all your senses." The prince touched his arm and stopped the horse, forcing Jano to stop as well.

"You young people see us old and graying now, but our desires, our will to act, is exactly as it was when we were twenty. How old are you, Jano?"

Taken aback by the question, Jano answered almost automatically, "Twenty-four."

"Congratulations." He started walking again, and this time it was Jano who followed him. He wanted to see what the prince was driving at with that gibberish. "Very few young men get to where you are at your age, Jano. You're clearly destined for a rewarding future. You deserve it, evidently."

"But?" Jano beat him to it, showing an uncommon intelligence.

"It's true, there is a *but*," the prince agreed, realizing that he was not dealing with an ignorant thug, as he had always thought. "You see, in life, we may care little about people, but we will always need a friend. It is essential to have someone you can trust."

"Prince, why are you giving me this sermon?"

"Jano, I can see that you are also a fine young man, and I want to offer you my friendship."

"That's very flattering, Prince Licata. And what do you want in return?"

"Well, it doesn't exactly work that way." Ferdinando Licata was beginning to lose patience with the young man and his blunt, insolent ways. "Let's say that if we were to become friends, my friends would automatically become your friends, and, conversely, your friends would become part of my world. Do you understand what I'm offering you, Jano?"

"I'll become a prince?" Jano was beginning to act disrespectfully, but Ferdinando pretended not to notice.

"There's a friend of mine, Dr. Peppino Ragusa, whom I believe has been denounced as a subversive. There is nothing more unfortunate than an accusation like that. The doctor is a fine man, as demonstrated by the fact that all these years he's worked unstintingly for the good of us all, never asking anything in return. If the doctor were to decide to leave Salemi"—the prince kept pressing—"it would be a great misfortune for the entire community. For our town physician has also taken the trouble to teach reading and arithmetic to our peasants who've never gone to school."

"Yes, but he also puts revolutionary ideas in their heads. He preaches socialism, the sharing of land, he's against the Duce. How can an individual like that be your friend?" Jano wasn't aware that he had raised his voice.

"But what harm could he do? I myself don't see eye to eye with him, but he's absolutely harmless, Jano, promise me you'll leave him in peace."

"He's a dirty Jew besides," was Jano's only reply. "The Jewish race is the cause of all evil. After the Great War, it led to the Russian Revolution, it advanced communism."

"You imbecile, don't you understand that those are just stereotypes?" Ferdinando Licata realized that he wouldn't make any headway with Jano. The young man, not at all intimidated, replied just as aggressively, "Prince, don't you understand that you aristocrats have had your day? For you and everyone like you, it's over! The fascist revolution has brought you to your knees. We're the ones who now impose order and command respect in the cities. No other power can exist within the fascist state!" An icy contempt came over Ferdinando Licata's face. Making no reply, he placed his foot in the stirrup and mounted his horse.

"Jano, do you like *porchetta?*" he asked scornfully.

"What a question! Of course I like roast pork. Why?"

"I'll send you some. We're slaughtering a pig." The prince spurred his mount and the horse cantered off toward the fields.

In other times, no one would even have dreamed of talking to the prince that way. Jano looked around to see if anyone had witnessed their exchange. There wasn't a living soul in the streets, but Jano was certain that behind the shutters a thousand eyes had observed how high his power now reached.

Encouraged by his victory over the powerful Prince Licata, Jano decided to take action and initiate the bureaucratic process to remove Peppino Ragusa from his official post as district physician. He knew it wouldn't be an easy matter, but you have to start somewhere. Thus he wrote a letter to the mayor, his friend Lorenzo Costa, requesting that Dr. Ragusa be removed from his post "in order to safeguard public order, and because of his Jewish origins, in accordance with the recently enacted racial laws."

Costa recorded the request and sent it on to the provincial governor. The official took note of it and turned it over to the prefect of the province, who in turn—without looking into the matter—forwarded the demand to the provincial health center director, who—without even reading it—passed it on to the administrator of the medical center of the town of Salemi.

All the latter had to do was choose a replacement for Dr. Ragusa. The administrator's decision was easy, because a certain Dr. Attilio Bizzarri had been working in the medical center for some time, badgering him with his perfectionism, finding flaws with everything. Though Bizzarri was highly respected by his colleagues, the bureaucrats in the health care world couldn't bear his fastidious character. He had a generous spirit, made no distinction between aristocrats and peasants, and was greatly esteemed by all his patients. Bizzarri also had a knack for diagnosis and an extraordinary intuition for deciding on the proper method of treatment. However, the administrator had a desk covered with letters of complaints the doctor had sent him. Bizzarri had even written to the Duce himself, griping about some sanitary deficiencies. It was a good opportunity to get rid of him.

So Dr. Attilio Bizzarri received a letter ordering him to take over the post of town physician of Salemi within one month of the date stamped on the envelope.

At the same time, the medical administrator wrote Dr. Ragusa a letter with the opposite orders to leave his assigned post within one month from the date on the envelope. Unfortunately, a postal service glitch prevented the letter from being delivered to Dr. Ragusa.

———————

On a cold morning in 1939, Dr. Attilio Bizzarri boarded the bus that would take him to his new post. Bizzarri was just past fifty, but the profession's hard work—along with an altruistic nature that left him always ready to sacrifice for others—had worn him out so that he looked older.

When the doctor arrived at Peppino Ragusa's medical office and rang the bell, a dark-haired girl open the door. It was Ester, Ragusa's older daughter, who assisted her father as a nurse. Bizzarri introduced himself and asked to speak with Dr. Ragusa.

"Good morning, Doctor, I'm Dr. Bizzarri," he introduced himself moments later, extending his hand with a smile. Ragusa didn't for a moment suspect the reason for that visit. Bizzarri realized his discomfort and came to his aid.

"Didn't you receive the letter from the provincial administrator?"

"In fact, I didn't receive any letter," Ragusa replied, beginning to understand yet still unwilling to accept the evidence.

"I know it was sent to you a month ago."

Ragusa glanced at his daughter, but she shook her head to confirm that no letter had come from the administration.

Dr. Bizzarri was crestfallen. "The usual bureaucratic slipup. You didn't receive any letter. Wonderful, what a sense of timing."

"Have you come to replace me?" Ragusa finally asked.

"Exactly. Only they were supposed to inform you ahead of time and give you a chance to make plans." He pulled a folded sheet of paper out of his breast pocket and handed it to his colleague. "Here is my letter of appointment. Note when it was sent to me: on that same date, they should have sent you a letter about your new destination. They are truly bungling incompetents."

Bizzarri went to a chair and sat down, setting his bag on the floor. Ragusa, meanwhile, quickly read the letter that assigned his medical post to Bizzarri. When he had finished, he passed it on to Ester, who hurriedly scanned the words in silence.

"After twenty years . . ."

"Unfortunately, it's the law. You're a Jew, aren't you?"

But Ragusa couldn't hear him, because he was clinging tightly to his daughter Ester in a despairing embrace. Finally, the girl said, "Come on, Papa. Let's go home. You'll see, we'll be all right."

They left the medical office arm in arm and headed home to break the sad news to Annachiara.

Chapter 8

— 1939 —

That year too, as was the custom, Ciccio Vinciguerra had been invited by Prince Ferdinando Licata to the ceremony of the *Cento Santi*: the One Hundred Saints. It was like a reminder each November 1 that his impoverished condition had not changed. The destitute farm worker had no family. No one knew his origins, no one knew where he had come from, but one day he had appeared in Salemi begging for a few days' work as a field hand. Thanks to Prince Licata, he began working and became well liked by the town's residents. Ciccio Vinciguerra spoke very little and, when questioned, responded in monosyllables. That's why everyone in town had nicknamed him *U pisci*, because he was mute as a fish. Later on, however, his submissive character, his untiring strength, his discretion, and his skill with weapons won him the trust of Rosario Losurdo, who, with the blessing of Prince Licata himself, had enlisted him among his *campieri*, his army of private guards.

As in previous years, Ciccio Vinciguerra arrived at the service door of the Licata palace and walked down the long corridor leading to the large downstairs bathroom. There he met the other "hundred saints" who, like him, had been summoned to the celebration of Saint Christopher, the patron saint of the prince's ancestral family.

After all one hundred of the town's poor had washed their feet in preparation, they were led, barefoot, to the Hall of Globes, which was on the main floor of the palazzo. Ciccio Vinciguerra, herded along with the other peasants, walked through the sumptuous corridors with his face upturned, admiring the designs and colors of the ceiling frescoes commemorating the triumph of Jupiter, driving a chariot.

They entered the hall and took their places along the walls, preparing to wait patiently for the arrival of their host and his sister.

———

At that moment, Ferdinando Licata was speaking with Manfredi, Rosario Losurdo's most trusted campiere, who had recently returned from Ethiopia.

Now close to sixty, Manfredi had served the Licata family as an armed guard from time immemorial. Before him, there had been his father, and even before that, his grandfather. For him, land was a religion, and ever since he was a child—seeing his parents devote themselves to it until they were worn out—he had dreamed of owning a piece of it. That morning, Manfredi had made a big decision, prompted primarily by the insistence of his wife, Adele, and his son Nicola. He had taken advantage of the feast of the *Cento Santi* to go ask a favor of the prince. It was an ancient tradition in Sicily, on certain feast days, to present pleas to those in power.

"*Parri*," he began, using the customary term of reverence for the prince, after bowing and kissing his hand. "I have a request to ask of you. You've known me since I was a child, and you've seen my little ones born. All my life I've served you and protected the lands that you gave me to look after. You've never had to complain about me or my family."

"Manfredi, you are one of the most loyal men I know," the prince indulged him, to hasten along the pleasantries, "but please, go on. Between us, two words are already too many. What is it you have to ask me?" The prince conveyed an innate sense of authority, and therefore inspired fear.

"*Parri*," the campiere went on with considerable emotion, "I would never dare ask you, but I've reached the age when a wife and children prod you. . . . In short, Father, over the years, my family has made many sacrifices. There are three of us who work on your lands."

"Two," the prince corrected, "it seems to me Nunzio has been busy with other matters for quite some time now."

"Prince, it's not easy to raise children these days. Someone puts certain ideas in their head and all our teachings go to hell—with all due respect."

"Honesty is praised by all, but dies of neglect," the prince made a long story short.

"Father," the campiere continued in a supplicating tone, twisting his cap in his hands, "during the months I spent in Africa, I put aside some money; just a little, actually. There's a piece of land down in the valley of the Madonnuzza. I'm talking about just a small plot; a *salmo*. It's barren, abandoned for a hundred years or more now. There's no water nearby. But *vossia* would fulfill an old dream of mine if you would offer it to me for that little bit of money."

The prince was surprised by the request. "My dear Manfredi, I wouldn't want to rob you," he said at last, moving toward the door.

"Why on earth should you take for your own that piece of land abandoned by God and by man? Do you know the effort it would cost you to
make it yield a few potatoes?"

"Consider it an obsession of mine. I beg you." Manfredi grabbed the
prince's hand to keep him from leaving the room.

The prince freed himself from his grip. "We don't divide up the land;
you know that. It's a rule. But how much do you have to offer me, Manfredi?"

"Everything we've saved up till now: six thousand liras." Ferdinando
Licata wasn't easily moved, yet the man's moral strength touched him.
He also knew that the money wasn't the result of years of scrimping,
otherwise he would have said "everything *I've* saved." It was the result of
the cheating and stealing his son Nunzio carried out along with Lorenzo
Costa and Jano Vassallo at the expense of the poor farmers in the area.

But he pretended to be unaware of the origin of that small fortune.
For one thing, he didn't want to completely alienate the friendship of the
family that for three generations had served the Licatas so devotedly. So
he answered with a winning smile: "With five thousand liras, I can buy
half a Balilla sedan. It would be a good deal . . .

"All right, Manfredi: give me five thousand liras and consider the
other thousand my personal gift to you to dig a well. You get a plot of
land down in the Madonnuzza, in Sòllima, okay? Let's shake on it."

Manfredi needed a few moments to realize that the prince had accepted his proposal, and for only five thousand liras! He responded with
a big smile and devotedly shook the hand that Ferdinando Licata offered
him, indicating a signed contract.

Adjacent to the Hall of Globes was a vestibule furnished with two massive cherry-wood armoires reaching to the ceiling, similar to those found
in cathedral sacristies. The prince headed there after his meeting with
Manfredi and removed his velvet jacket while his older sister, Lavinia,
assisted by the maid, took several white lace-trimmed garments from
one of the wardrobes. The ceremony that was about to begin was one
that Ferdinando Licata himself had insisted on in recent years to make
his presence felt by his most needy fellow townsmen. In actuality, it was
an expedient that he had contrived to silence his sense of guilt or at least
appease it for a few hours.

The doors of the Hall of Globes were thrown open, and an eerie si-

lence immediately descended within those ancient walls. All one hundred peasants looked toward the door, and soon, as in a miraculous
apparition, the unmistakable figure of Prince Ferdinando Licata loomed
before them, an image of extraordinary nobility, touching in its humanity. Instinctively all the peasants bowed their heads and upper bodies
in reverence. The prince acknowledged this with an imperceptible nod
of his head. Then, like a pope, he walked to the center of the hall, followed by two maids carrying several white cloth towels folded over their
arms and by other servants bearing enameled basins and large pitchers of
water. Bringing up the rear of the procession was the stern figure of Lavinia, who with precise signals directed the servants as they silently and
efficiently prepared the staging for the rite of ablution.

Among the group of farmers, the tension was palpable. They all stood
in awe of the prince, and they weren't able to fully understand this ceremony in which Ferdinando Licata washed their feet, much as Christ had
washed the feet of his disciples at the Last Supper.

At a sign from Lavinia, one of the maids took the arm of one of the
peasants and led him to the chair, making him sit down. Meanwhile,
the prince approached a basin, rolling up the sleeves of his linen gown.
He bent down, dipped the farmer's foot in the water and performed the
ritual cleansing.

When the ablution was completed, the farmer stood up, leaving the
chair to another poor peasant. The ceremony was repeated, amid the
commotion of the servants and the embarrassment of the peasants, until
the last participant had his turn.

Then everyone moved to the nearby dining room, where several tables had been laid with the finest dinnerware and where, with the help
of his servants, the prince himself served his friends, until the final toast
was made.

The other noblemen in the area considered Ferdinando Licata eccen-
tric to say the least for these practices of his. Moreover, they didn't understand why he refused the title of "Don" from his fellow townsmen, given
that he had a double right to it: both because he was of aristocratic ancestry and because there in Salemi he was the head of a great community,
including blood relations and farmers. But Ferdinando preferred to have
those under his protection call him *u patri*, because to them he was like a
real father. And the people in the territory of Salemi reciprocated with respect for his authority and with a reverence that verged on the fanatical.
Licata subjected himself to that mortifying ritual for a number of rea-

sons, all well concealed and buried in the deep recesses of his conscience. From time to time, one of them presumptuously cropped up to claim his attention. The most frequent one was associated with the memory of an English girl named Carole.

The young woman had traveled throughout Europe before landing in Sicily, where mutual friends had spoken to her of Prince Licata. The meeting between the two was a classic case of love at first sight. For weeks and months, they were lost in each other. The days spent with her were joyful, full of vibrant scents and colors. In her company, the world seemed like paradise. Licata had never experienced that intimate emotion called love, though he'd had many women before Carole. And she too was in love with his thick, wavy hair, his sky-blue eyes, his authoritative ways, and his physicality. But then something happened that shattered the beautiful dream. Although the coming of a child is generally a blessing from heaven for two people who are in love, that was not the case for Ferdinando Licata. At the age of thirty-nine, he did not feel he could take on the responsibility of a wife, let alone a child, and so he made a mistake that he regretted for the rest of his life.

The celebration of the One Hundred Saints, as well as a number of munificent donations he made to a convent of orphans and to a monastery of Franciscan friars, had led him to become one of Monsignor Albamonte's beloved favorites. From as far back as anyone could remember, the monsignor had counted the prince among his most trusted friends, initiating several lucrative deals with him. And for some years now, Monsignor Albamonte was in the habit of taking part in the One Hundred Saints day. It cost him nothing, and what's more, since the townsfolk associated it with the prince's philanthropic actions, he received many indirect benefits from it.

———

After having seen to serving his guests, *u patri* went to sit beside his friend the monsignor.

"My dear prince," the monsignor said, shifting a chair to make it easier for Ferdinando to sit down, "the day when you no longer burn with love, many here in Salemi will freeze to death." The prelate had a perpetual smile stamped on his face, to express his benevolence.

Ferdinando replied jokingly, "It's really true that you only live as long as you love. And for us, my dear monsignor, not much time is left."

The priest fittingly touched wood. "Prince, what are you saying?" He smiled, touching the tabletop with his pinkie and index finger extended to form the sign of the horns. "Let's not stop Providence's wheel from turning."

Don Antonio, thanks to his acquaintances and the gears he'd been so capable of oiling, had managed to become bishop of Salemi in just a few years, and consequently enjoyed a true economic power within the territory.

The two old friends, whenever they met, never missed an opportunity to talk about the good old days. The monsignor recalled once again the evening of their first meeting at Palazzo Cesarò in 1920. A simple parish priest at the time, he had found the ideas of the young Prince Licata to his liking. And he wasn't the only one they'd made an impression on. Indeed, after that meeting, the Sicilian aristocracy's esteem for Prince Ferdinando Licata skyrocketed. Gabellotti, campieri, estate overseers, the armed guards, sharecroppers—all the way down to the last farmer—the populace saw in him the enlightened spirit of a true leader.

Chapter 9

For the first time since anyone could remember, the "party of noble agrarians" was faced with the new demands of the times. The "agrarians," as the large landowners, or *latifondisti*, were called, felt entitled to intervene wherever lawlessness had gone too far, not relying on the help of a distant, inept government. They even considered seceding from the national state, an idea that the journalist Raffaele Grassini would carry to the extreme several decades later with his proposal of an independent Sicily, or "Trinacria."

Meanwhile, during that period of feverish upheaval, Ferdinando Licata, along with some of his most trusted friends, including Don Antonio Albamonte, was able to seize ownership of many lands. He did this by unscrupulously exploiting the same laws that allowed cooperatives — some formed by returning war veterans, some by socialist "reds," some by the radical priest Don Sturzo's "white" peasant leagues—to acquire uncultivated or neglected lands in perpetual lease. Ferdinando Licata expanded his estates enormously, becoming one of the largest landowners in Sicily. Thanks to his reputation as a wise and generous man, seemingly in favor of ceding lands to the peasants and averse to violence, it was not difficult for him to find people willing to accept his protection. For the farmers, the majority of whom were illiterate, it was a relief to have someone like him manage the cooperative to which their land share was apportioned. He was accustomed to repeating to his most trusted collaborators his basic principles: "I take and give to others, I eat and let others eat." The fact that he got the roast while the other diners got the crumbs mattered little in a society where meals were often skipped entirely.

Naturally, this approach caused him violent pangs of guilt toward his fellow townsmen. Prince Licata had a strong sense of innate justice, and knowing that he too helped make the lives of those poor unfortunates more miserable had caused him a number of physical problems, the most obvious of which was an ulcer that for years tormented him day and night.

His first masterstroke of politico-speculative diplomacy was achieved

a couple of months after the meeting at Palazzo Cesarò. It was Don Antonio Albamonte himself who gave him the opportunity to participate
in one of the first Sicilian peasant cooperatives.

The reverend father, to avoid having his "sheep" be lured by the
"reds," had set out to help his parishioners become owners of small plots
of land, in accordance with the guidelines of Don Sturzo's Popular Party.
He gathered a good number of farmers around him and formed a cooperative called the Veterans, even though many of them had only participated in the war vicariously through the stories of some friend who had
fought in it.

In fact, the enterprising Don Antonio Albamonte immediately went
to work to find an estate that could be shared with his partners. Someone suggested the former Baucina lands, owned by a certain Count Val-
guarnera, of Catalan origins, which extended for more than 2,500 acres
between Castelvetrano and Santa Ninfa.

The total savings of the cooperative's members, combined, did not
cover a fraction of the amount needed to meet the asking price, but the
sum was more than enough for them to obtain a purchase option.

A few days later, however, a second offer appeared on the same estate,
made by a cousin of the Marquis Pietro Bellarato, whom Ferdinando Licata had met during the meeting at Palazzo Cesarò. If the Veterans cooperative was unable to meet its obligation, namely, come up with the sum
required to purchase the land, the marquis's cousin would step in with his
offer, which was decidedly lower than that of Don Antonio's parishioners.

At this point the priest had to scramble to find the remainder of
the stipulated amount; otherwise, when the option expired, the farmers would lose all of their hard-earned savings. Don Antonio therefore
turned to the agricultural bank, the Cassa Rurale, through the good offices of the bishop, who exerted a strong influence over the bank's direc-
tors. At first it seemed that the loan would be granted very quickly, but
days passed and then weeks, with the concession of funds from the Cassa
Rurale postponed time after time. The expiration of the option was in-
exorably approaching.

The Veterans cooperative members were in a state of panic and the
priest didn't know how to hold them off except by acting calm and reminding them that he too had invested his savings. But Don Albamonte
was seriously worried, realizing that someone was scheming against his
cooperative. It was then that the priest got the idea of asking Prince Ferdinando Licata for help.

The prince gladly accepted the priest's request for help and agreed to become a member of the Veterans in the role of guardian-protector of the cooperative. The first thing he did was look into the reason why the loan from the Cassa Rurale hadn't come. Through certain "friends" he learned that it had been Marquis Pietro Bellarato who had prevented the loan, in an effort to further the chances of the cooperative run by his cousin, who was also interested in purchasing the former Baucina estate. There were just ten days left before the option expired, too little time to secure the capital they needed: Don Antonio had made up his mind too late to ask for the prince's help. How to find a swift, effective solution? That was when Ferdinando Licata decided to address the problem directly at its source, that is, by talking to the marquis.

To begin with, he summoned his trusted gabellotto, Rosario Losurdo.

———————

Before becoming the prince's caretaker, Losurdo, a native of Gangi in the province of Palermo, had begun his career as a carter, transporting goods to villages throughout the Madonie Mountains when the only means of conveyance was still the traditional Sicilian cart. Rosario was indefatigable: he allowed himself a little rest between trips, only enough so that the patient horses wouldn't collapse from exhaustion. When he wasn't delivering goods, he helped the farmers hoe the fields, but he was also skillful with a mason's trowel, and more than one house in the Madonie region had been drenched with his sweat. The fact that he traveled around put him in a position to know the affairs of many families in the area. He knew the anxiety of the noblewoman who, year after year, saw her daughter fade away while waiting for a good match to come forward, as well as the ambitions of the wealthy notary who wanted an aristocratic title for his son. He knew where to find animals that could be easily taken from their rightful owners either because they were poorly guarded or because the shepherds could be bribed with a few liras. Sometimes he sent them to the illegal slaughterhouses that supplied sausage factories, other times he offered to act as intermediary between the thieves and owners to recover the livestock, in exchange for a kickback.

He did this and that to wet his beak, or *fari vagnari u pizzu*. In Sicily you "wet someone's beak" with a symbolic glass of wine offered to friends who have not refused a favor or who have performed a job well done. Thanks to these expedients, Rosario Losurdo had managed to set aside a fair pile of money, which, with skill and some not entirely lawful tactics, he had been able to double in the span of a few years. But the circumstance that had changed his life was meeting Rosita, the daughter of a gabellotto from the Gibellina estates.

He'd met her at the feast of Santa Rosalia in Palermo. They'd looked at each other and immediately liked what they saw. Rosario proposed that they run off secretly together, and Rosita, more impetuous than he, agreed. They say there was no premeditation on the part of Rosario Losurdo: that he hadn't had his eye on the enviable position of Rosita's father, though for a long time the gossips swore that he had been snooping into the man's financial affairs. But the girl was very pretty and theirs was beyond doubt a great love. Soon the union was blessed by two fine boys, Michele and Donato, and a girl, Mena, born one year after the second brother.

Rosario Losurdo and Prince Ferdinando Licata first met before the outbreak of the Great War. The encounter would prove truly fortunate for both men.

One of Prince Licata's lands bordered on the Asinomorto estate of Prince Bongiorno of Gibellina, a young scion orphaned at an early age, who in a short time had been deprived of a large portion of his assets thanks to his guardian's greed and the dissolute life he himself had led. Not for the first time, the young Prince Bongiorno found himself in the position of urgently needing cash to pay off certain debts owed to some shady characters. He therefore proposed that Prince Licata buy the Asinomorto estate for 200,000 liras. They agreed on the figure of 180,000 liras and made an appointment with the notary.

On the morning of the established day, however, something unusual happened. Prince Bongiorno's elderly grandfather, while making the rounds of his estates in his horse-drawn carriage, was attacked by masked bandits who knocked him unconscious with a blow to the head and stole everything he had on him: his watch, a few liras, and the family ring. The injured old prince was immediately brought to his palace, where his grandson summoned the local doctor. So as not to break his agreement with Licata, Bongiorno sent a proxy to the notary's office: a man he trusted blindly.

But, as they say, every man has a price, and the proxy signed the purchase contract with an added clause stipulating that, to commemorate the opportune transaction, Ferdinando Licata would present Prince

Bongiorno with seven fig tarts every September for the following nine years.

In point of fact, the proxy never collected the agreed-upon sum, though he swore that he had duly left it at Prince Bongiorno's home, in a desk drawer where he usually hid documents and money, so as not to go around with so much cash. Bongiorno placed his full trust in the proxy and, despite many reservations, ended up believing him, in part because the notary confirmed that the exchange of money and deeds had actually taken place before his very eyes. Although he hadn't received a single lira from the sale, Prince Bongiorno could not prevent Ferdinando Licata from taking possession of the Asinomorto estate, and in the years that followed, Licata never failed to send the prince seven fig tarts when September rolled around, though they invariably ended up in the pig trough accompanied by the bitter curses of the cheated young man.

It goes without saying that the proxy's name was Rosario Losurdo, who some time later—when Bongiorno's grandfather had died and the young prince decided to settle in Rome at the home of certain noble relatives—entered Licata's employ as his chief aide and overseer.

Thanks to that propitious transaction, Losurdo received twenty-five acres of the former estate as a gift from Prince Licata. And over time a strong friendship was established between the two men.

So when Don Antonio Albamonte's Veterans cooperative had trouble purchasing the Baucina lands, Prince Licata summoned Losurdo and explained the problem in broad outline. "I first want to try and persuade the Marquis Bellarato to become my friend. Not to let his cousin stand in the way of my cooperative. But I need a show of force, in case he may have some hesitation. Nothing violent—you know me. Let's say we'll settle for some cattle this first time around. You steal some cows, we'll hide them for a few days, then I'll go talk to him, and, if he agrees to back out of the Baucina deal, we'll give them back."

"And if he refuses?" the gabellotto asked.

"In that case, we'll return the cows, but after slaughtering them."

Not batting an eye, Losurdo asked who he should have do the job.

"Either way, I'd say Gaetano Vassallo is up to both tasks."

———

Don Antonio Albamonte was seriously worried about the farmers in the cooperative. Every morning, when the first mass was about to begin, a handful of the 395 coop members confronted him for information about their investment. For many, the amount advanced for the option was the result of years of sacrifice, and the possibility of losing their money had become an obsession.

That morning, after talking once again with a delegation of farmers, Don Antonio went to Licata's palazzo to seek information directly from the prince.

"Don Antonio, don't worry. I've already told you, it's as if the deal were already a sure thing. If worst comes to worst, all the farmers will get their money back," Licata tried to reassure him. "Someone is already working on your behalf."

"It's just a little more than a week before the deadline," the priest insisted.

"That's more than enough time," the prince lied.

The failure of the venture would be catastrophic, not so much because of the loss of the farmers' savings, but due to the bad image it would give to Don Sturzo's Popular Party.

Chapter 10

Rosario Losurdo had already been riding for four hours, headed for Portella del Pianetto, the area where Vassallo and his gang had their camp.

In the early decades of the century, a large number of armed bands operated undisturbed in Sicily. It was the logical result of the extreme poverty to which shepherds and farmers were doomed from cradle to grave. The more intolerant ones, dissatisfied with their existence, rebelled and decided to live by raiding and looting. Often the switch to lawlessness was triggered by some injustice inflicted by the authorities: unfair taxes, excessive lease terms, the unkept promises of politicians or prominent figures of bourgeois origins who turned out to be more rapacious than the aristocrats.

Gaetano Vassallo's story was no exception to this scenario. When he was a boy, one of his master's hunting dogs, chasing after a hare, reached his family's hut and entered the chicken coop. His mother tried to chase it away with a stick, but the bloodhound sank his teeth into a hen and was about to make off with her. The woman cut him off, and as the dog tried to leap over the fence, she managed to hit him on the snout with a strength born of desperation, causing him to drop his prey. The hound collapsed on the ground, and the hen, though frightened, scampered off to the hen house, saving her feathers.

Shortly thereafter the master, a marquis, arrived and, seeing his dog lying moribund in the pen, lashed out at Gaetano's entire family. Unfortunately, his father was at work in the fields, and only his mother and his brother Geremia were in the shack.

In those days a hunting dog was worth more than a farmer. The marquis, distraught over the loss of his hound, began to take it out on the woman and beat her so violently that it caused her to abort the third little brother. She remained an invalid from that day on and was admitted to an institute run by nuns and emerged a few years later in a coffin.

Two years after that, the marquis was the target of a shotgun blast that wounded him, permanently paralyzing his right hand. The carabinieri arrested Gaetano Vassallo's father, and the judge sentenced him to ten years in prison for attempted murder, though he maintained that he was innocent. Only a few years later, an old villager confessed on his deathbed that it was he who'd shot the loathsome marquis, because of a wrong he'd suffered. And, despite the fact that he was about to surrender his soul to God, the old man declared that his only regret was not having killed him.

The boy therefore got his father back, but by then his hatred toward padroni, or masters, and any institution that represented the state was so ingrained that he had no other goal in life than to take revenge on the world.

Gaetano Vassallo began his life as a bandit by robbing everyone who had the misfortune to cross his path. Then he went on to extortion, far more reliable and profitable than looting. He would send a simple demand letter to the victim—a gabellotto or an attorney or a tax collector—and wait for payment to arrive. If the victim resisted, the reprisals started: sometimes he would slaughter cattle, other times he set fire to sheaves of grain or to storage sheds filled with a newly harvested crop. Only on rare occasions did the victims respond, and that happened only when they hadn't heard of him. In the midst of all these exploits, Vassallo also found time to marry, after meeting his future wife on the farm of some friends.

Located in a remote part of the Ravanusa countryside, the farmstead was an ideal hideout. After one of his extortions, which ended with a carabiniere being wounded, Gaetano Vassallo thought it was a good idea to lay low there awhile. That's where he met his host's daughter, Teresa, a young woman of twenty who lived the life of a virtual recluse on the farm, unable to see people her own age for weeks at a time. The arrival of Vassallo, a man at the peak of maturity, was an exciting event for her, and the story of the bandit's adventurous life, so far outside the rules, also held a seductive attraction. In short, the young woman saw the crude outlaw as the embodiment of an alluring romantic dream.

Gaetano was honest with her. He told her in no uncertain terms that their relationship had no future. They couldn't live together, he was a fugitive, he had to move about constantly. If he were apprehended, he could be sentenced to thirty years in prison.

At the time, Vassallo knew only the girl's sweet, gentle side, not her stubbornness. Teresa not only married him but also had two children with him, within one year of each other: the oldest, Jano, and the second, Giovanni. And now Teresa was pregnant again, but this time she was expecting twins, as Peppino Ragusa, Salemi's appointed physician, had confirmed.

———

Gaetano Vassallo had established his base of operations among the mountains and valleys between Monte Polizzo and Montagna Grande, a region of dense undergrowth, broken by abrupt cliffs and deep ravines, and virtually impossible to negotiate if you weren't born in the region. Vassallo and his band knew every gully, every hideout in that territory, and rode high and low through the area on their swift chargers, making raids in Calatafimi, Vita, Ummari, Mendola. They replenished their food supplies, imposed tributes and other duties, and distributed part of their earnings to the poorest farmers and shepherds, who in exchange kept them informed of the carabinieri's movements and gave them sanctuary when needed.

The meeting between Losurdo and Vassallo took place at the camp in Portella del Pianetto. The refuge was a simple recess in the ridge, which formed a sort of cave and overlooked the mountain pass. Gaetano Vassallo was frightening just to look at. A long, unkempt beard hid his face, and a sheepskin coat protected him from the cold.

"Gaetano, Prince Licata has a favor to ask of you," Rosario Losurdo began, after shaking his hand and sitting down beside the fire.

"You know I've never refused the prince a favor. He is a just man, and it's an honor for me to work for him," Vassallo responded, lighting a *toscano* that he'd taken from the packet Losurdo passed to him; the cigars ended up in the pocket of his sheepskin jacket.

"It has to do with the Marquis of Campo Allegro." The gabellotto wanted to test his reaction first.

"Who? The Marquis Bellarato, that bastard?" the bandit retorted, blowing a cloud of smoke.

"That's right."

"So the marquis's hour has finally come?"

"No, no, you don't have to kill him," Losurdo hastened to explain. "It would it be too charitable. All we want is for you to make off with some of his cattle. You have to keep them hidden for a few days, then I'll tell you if you should return them or slaughter the whole herd."

All the men who were in the camp at the time witnessed the conversation: Vassallo had no secrets from his band. Two of them in particular listened with interest to the requests of Prince Licata's gabellotto: Curzio and his brother, Salvatore Turrisi. The latter was a poor peasant, twenty-five years old, who had joined Vassallo's band because of Marquis Bellarato.

Until some time before, Turrisi had been one of Bellarato's campieri. His duty was to hold off trespassers and poachers on the Balestruccio estate, which the marquis had reserved for hunting. Salvatore Turrisi was an excellent hunter whose aim was infallible, and for this reason the marquis had taken him on as one of his armed guards. Thanks to that job as campiere, Salvatore was able to live with dignity and was grateful to the marquis.

One day it happened that Salvatore Turrisi, roaming through the woods of San Michele in search of pheasants, found the marquis's horse grazing alone in a ravine, saddled up, the reins dangling from the bit. But Bellarato was nowhere around. The young man immediately thought he might have fallen, but the light westerly wind carried the sound of moaning and sobbing. He strained his ears to hear better, and recognized the marquis's voice. He climbed the ridge of the densely wooded hill and at the top came to a grassy clearing surrounded by oaks. At the center of the clearing, Turrisi witnessed a sight he should never have seen.

The marquis, in the throes of a fit, was flogging a young shepherd boy, no more than twelve years old, who was completely naked. The boy was on the ground and could not defend himself. The marquis kept whip-ping the poor body that was already covered with gashes, whip marks, and blood. Turrisi instinctively sprang into a gallop and charged toward the marquis. Leaping from his horse, he grabbed the man's waist from behind, trying to pull him off the young boy.

Bellarato, howling like a wild beast, his mouth smeared with saliva and blood, thrashed about trying to free himself from Turrisi's grip, but the campiere wouldn't let go and yelled at him to calm down. After a final lunge, seeing that he was now at the mercy of a force which he could not oppose, the marquis finally crumpled as though he had fainted. Salvatore's attention was then drawn by the boy's faint cries. A few yards away he spotted his pitiable clothes: a tattered shirt and a pair of trousers, all he wore to shield himself from the harsh cold of the re-gion's high altitudes.

Raising his eyes, he saw a flock of sheep clustered silently in the shade of a crab apple tree, a dreamlike vision. He approached the young shep-herd to try to help him, but realized at once that the boy's condition was hopeless. Turning to get up and fetch some water, he saw the barrel of his hunting rifle appear from behind him. He had no time to get over his surprise. The marquis aimed the gun at the young shepherd's face and fired a shot. The boy's face exploded and a spray of blood spewed onto Turrisi's face and chest. The marquis threw the weapon on the ground, and then mounted Turrisi's bay and galloped away following the path leading down to the valley.

Turrisi stood alone, paralyzed with horror. The first thing that occurred to him was that he would surely lose his wonderful job. With the marquis in jail, the lands would be abandoned, and he would no longer be needed on the estate. Then he thought about the poor boy. He went to the marquis's horse, down in the ravine, hoping there was a blanket tied to the saddle. When he saw that there was, he brought it to the top of the clearing, wrapped the boy up and hoisted him onto the horse. He picked his rifle up off the ground and got ready to return to the farm with that sad burden.

The sun was already sinking below the horizon. In the distance Salvatore saw a whirlwind of dust rising from the trail. He stopped to see who was in such a hurry.

Curzio was coming toward him at a full gallop and a minute later reached him. The two dismounted.

"Salvatore!" Curzio yelled with tears in his eyes. Then he noticed the bundle behind the saddle and went to lift the blanket, uncovering a bloody leg. "So it's true!"

Salvatore Turrisi didn't yet realize the inferno that was about to engulf him. "You've already heard?" he asked.

"I want to hear it from your own lips, before the carabinieri take you away." His brother started yelling again, waving his arms around wildly. "Salvatore, is it true you killed the shepherd boy? Why? Why?"

Now he was beginning to understand. "What are you talking about? It was the marquis! It was him! Who told you such a lie?" He grabbed Curzio by the collar to press for a response.

"The carabinieri are waiting for you at the farm. The marquis said first you flogged the boy and then you shot him point-blank."

Salvatore Turrisi knew he had lost; there was no way out. His word was worth nothing; that of the marquis was gospel. All he could say to his brother was "It wasn't me. I swear on my honor."

"May God bless you! I knew it! I knew you weren't capable of such a thing." Curzio hugged him impulsively, almost knocking him to the ground, and kissed his brother's face. "If you had done what the marquis said, it would have killed our mother."

"I tried to stop him—" Salvatore began.

But his brother was already thinking about the next move. "You have to run away, hide out in the mountains. The carabinieri are too busy to go after a desperate creature like you." He hugged him again. "Leave the boy's body here and go. Join Vassallo, if you don't want to end up shot. Salvatore, my brother, now you too," Curzio said in anguish. A similar injustice had happened to him as well years before, and he had been forced to join Vassallo's band to avoid long, unmerited years of imprisonment. At that time, heaven help anyone who crossed an aristocrat.

"Vassallo is in the foothills of Montagna Grande, in the San Giorgio district. Tell him I sent you and explain to him exactly what happened." Curzio instructed as he helped his brother lay the corpse on the grass. Salvatore Turrisi, his heart pounding, remounted his horse. With a jerk of the reins, he turned the animal around and, after waving good-bye to his brother, headed for the mountains, cursing the Marquis Bellarato and his entire clan.

———

Gaetano Vassallo, always in search of patronage, was all too happy to do Prince Licata a favor. Less than forty-eight hours after the encounter with Losurdo, Vassallo showed up at Baglio di Buturro with fifteen of his men. Every autumn, the campieri would round up some of Marquis Bellarato's cattle so they could spend the winter there. It was a simple task for Vassallo and his band to steal the cows, since no one dared put up a fight.

At that very moment, Ferdinando Licata was climbing the grand staircase of Marquis Bellarato's palazzo in Salemi. The marquis knew about Licata's involvement in the Veterans cooperative and had guessed the reason for his visit.

"My dear Marquis, I am here in the role of ambassador," Ferdinando Licata began after the customary pleasantries, "so don't take my words as a personal affront."

"You know what they say in my village, Prince?" the marquis joked. "A man who butters you up more than usual is either cheating you or has already screwed you."

Ferdinando Licata did not respond to the vulgarity and continued seriously. "Nearly three hundred ninety-five farmers have invested their life savings in the purchase of the former Baucina estate. It would be a shame if they were unable to fulfill their dream of owning a piece of land."

"Prince Licata, since when are you interested in the farmers' welfare?" the marquis asked sarcastically.

"Since they began realizing that they too are human beings," Licata stated. Lowering his voice, he went on in a confidential tone: "And also to live up to the Palazzo Cesarò accord." Then, seeking the marquis's complicity, he concluded, "Mark my words, we relinquish something today so we won't have to give up everything tomorrow."

"I disagree with your theories. We are the *padroni*, the landowners. Nothing else matters. I never accepted what was decided at Palazzo Cesarò."

"Marquis, the people I represent are firmly determined not to lose their money. They told me that they are capable of any action, even going outside the law. In fact, I believe that at this very moment they have taken possession of all the cattle at Baglio di Buturro."

The marquis sprang to his feet. The doorbell then began ringing furiously, and someone knocked at the door. A voice from the street shouted, "Open up!"

"Perfect timing," Prince Licata thought.

The marquis, like an enraged husband who has just discovered his wife in bed with his best friend, stormed out of the room.

Ferdinando Licata went to the window and peered out at the scene in the street. A man was gesturing and explaining to the marquis what had happened a few hours earlier at Baglio di Buturro. The marquis didn't say a word but clenched his fists until his knuckles went white. Then he left the man and reentered the palazzo. Ferdinando Licata watched the messenger get back on his horse and gallop away. He sat back down in his chair, and shortly thereafter the marquis burst into the room.

"Prince Licata, how far will this blackmail go?"

"I told you before. I'm merely an ambassador." Licata displayed a seraphic calm. "I was simply instructed to ask you to withdraw the preemptive offer on the former Baucina estate. That's all. The property will end up complicating the lives of you and your cousin. It's too sprawling and almost entirely abandoned. To undertake any reclamation, you would need a lot of cash—and at this time, neither you, Marquis, nor your cousin has coffers full of gold *tarì*. Listen to me. I respect you, and

I know you can be a practical man. If you will be kind enough to pull out, I will see to it that your cattle are returned safe and sound." After a moment's pause, he concluded, "I advise you to be reasonable."

The marquis was seething with rage. He felt like kicking the prince but managed to restrain himself. "The little bastards, sons of bitches, ignorant assholes, penniless cocksuckers! They want to tell me what I can and cannot do? How dare they give orders to the Marquis Pietro Bellarato? I don't take orders from anyone, least of all from a gang of mafiosi! And you, Prince, how could you lend a hand to this extortion! I'll denounce you all, every last one of you, to the carabinieri!"

Ferdinando Licata smiled. "Let's leave the carabinieri out of our disagreement. They have enough headaches to resolve as it is."

"I will never give up Baucina. Go tell your charges that the estate will be mine." He moved closer to Licata. "You will never succeed in getting the full amount in time. The Cassa Rurale will not be able to grant you the loan within a week."

"How can you be so sure?" the prince asked, this time seriously worried.

Bellarato cheered up, and the shadow of a sneer crossed his face. He responded enigmatically: "I know."

Ferdinando Licata saw that the discussion was not leading to anything positive. He rose from his chair. "I think our conversation must end here. I'm sorry, but not for me; I'm sorry for you." So saying, he turned to leave without bidding his host good-bye.

Bellarato, surprised at how the prince had broken off their talk, became apprehensive. "What are they planning to do to me?"

Ferdinando Licata paused at the door. He turned and said, "You have no idea what a desperate mind can come up with. And when there are three hundred ninety-five of them, they can trigger a real earthquake. I don't know what they're planning to do; they didn't tell me. All I know is that you, Marquis, will be wiped out, economically speaking."

"How much do you want to stop them? Now, right away, that is." The marquis moved to the center of the room.

"Marquis, did I give you the impression I came here to beg for a few gold coins?" Ferdinando Licata, his manner cold, his eyes narrowed into slits, continued. "I'll pretend I didn't hear that, because I understand that you are beside yourself." And with that, he disappeared from the marquis's sight.

Chapter 11

Never had the prince's words been more prophetic. Gaetano Vassallo was ordered to slaughter all the livestock belonging to Pietro Bellarato, marquis of Campo Allegro, and set fire to the farm and its stores.

That night a cloudburst poured down from the heavens, and Vassallo, with a half dozen of his most trusted men, had a hard time setting fire to the storehouses. They had to use five buckets of gasoline. After several attempts, the flames finally engulfed the wooden planks and the straw, prevailing over the pounding rain.

Gaetano Vassallo and his bandits were watching the results of their efforts with satisfaction, when Geremia, Vassallo's older brother, arrived at a gallop to inform his brother that Teresa, his wife, was about to give birth to the twins. The midwife was in Palermo, so they would have to resort to the doctor in Salemi, and there was no time to lose. Gaetano Vassallo jumped on his horse and, leaving his men, sped to Salemi to muster the town physician, Peppino Ragusa.

The house where Teresa lived with her two sons was a few miles from town. The bandit wasn't worried about being seen by the carabinieri, since, for one thing, they rarely went out on patrol at night, preferring the safety of their headquarters. Besides, the rain was coming down in buckets, a downpour that hadn't been seen in months, and this favored his movements.

When he reached the house with the doctor, Teresa was on the verge of collapse, fading fast. She could not manage to birth the two infants. Her two sons, Jano and Giovanni, were hiding under the table, terrified by their mother's screams. Peppino Ragusa immediately understood the gravity of the situation. He would have to perform a Caesarean section, but the sanitary conditions in that hovel made it extremely risky. There wasn't even a horse and cart to transport her to the medical center in Salemi, and in any case, it would be too late. He decided to risk it, hoping for a stroke of luck, though fortune had long since forgotten the address of that shack. He had them boil the surgical instruments and bring him some sheets, and ordered Vassallo to stay nearby. Soon afterward, Geremia arrived back at the cabin; he got Jano and Giovanni out from under the table and led them into the adjacent room. Vassallo was standing near his wife, pleading with her to stay calm, just a little more and it would all be over . . . and at the same time urging the doctor to hurry.

Peppino Ragusa, who at the young age of thirty-four had presided at the births of almost half the town's population, had previously found himself in similar situations—often with disastrous results. He felt that this time things would not go as they should, and, in fact, shortly after he started to make the incision, Teresa surrendered her soul to God with a gasp. Vassallo immediately realized what had happened. His years of experience with death had made him an authority. A roar erupted from his chest. His brother Geremia held Jano and Giovanni tightly and closed his eyes, distraught. The younger boy started crying, while Jano broke out of his uncle's desperate embrace and bravely went to the door to see what was happening. He saw his father clinging to his mother's face. The doctor, with his back turned, hastened his efforts to at least save the two babies. They had just a few seconds of self-sufficiency, and then they too would almost certainly die, by asphyxiation.

Ragusa finished cutting open the poor woman's womb and finally extracted the first infant. He lifted him in the air, holding him upside down by the ankles. With a slap on the back and one on the chest, he helped him breathe, and then cleaned the mucus from his nose and mouth. He wrapped him in a piece of sheet and shouted to Vassallo to take him. The bandit, in a daze, left his wife, whom he had showered with kisses, and took the crying little bundle in his arms. He couldn't make up his mind whether to hate that dumpling of flesh that had killed his wife or worship him like the infant Jesus. The doctor focused his attention on the other infant, a baby girl, who showed no signs of life. He quickly cut the umbilical cord and then repeated the steps he'd just taken with her twin. The infant girl, however, remained lifeless. So he massaged her heart, breathed into her mouth, and the next instant, as if by some miracle, the second baby began to breathe and started wailing.

Dr. Ragusa then noticed Jano, the older brother, hiding behind the leg of the table. He called to him gently so he wouldn't frighten him more than he already was. He motioned to the boy to come hold his newborn baby sister. Jano moved closer, and the doctor placed the poor infant in his small arms.

Now he had to see to the mother. Unfortunately, all he could do was ascertain that she was dead. He sewed up the incision and covered her lovely face with the sheet.

When Gaetano Vassallo saw that definitive act, he raised his infant son to the heavens and with an inhuman howl cursed himself and all of mankind for having allowed such an atrocity.

That ferocious roar would remain in Jano's ears throughout the rest of his miserable life.

Marquis Bellarato, during one of his rides through his lands to hunt for game and obliging shepherds, crossed paths with Ninì Rizzo, one of the republican parliamentarians whom he had first seen at the Colonnas', during the famous meeting at Palazzo Cesarò.

Rizzo was out riding with his campiere, hunting partridges, when he saw the marquis in the distance and rode toward him with a shout of recognition. The campiere remained behind at a distance for the entire length of their talk; whether the encounter was accidental or deliberately sought, no one ever knew.

"Marquis, I heard about what the bandits did to you," he began, leading his horse alongside. "I think you are right to insist on harsh methods."

"I'm glad to hear you say that, *onorevole*," Bellarato replied guardedly. "They destroyed my entire herd and set fire to the storehouse."

"We can no longer tolerate such barbarism," Rizzo said emphatically.

"But those of you up there in Rome, what do you say?" the marquis challenged him directly.

"Rome is far away, my dear Bellarato," Rizzo replied. "However, I want to prove to you that some people up there think about us. I will have a special team sent to investigate the fire and identify those responsible. Will that satisfy you?"

"I hadn't hoped for so much."

"An example is needed. They must understand that there's no place here for anarchists and subversives," the politician continued. He was silent for a few seconds and then added: "Nevertheless, Marquis, you might also be less inflexible with friends."

Bellarato went on the defensive. "What do you mean? Which friends?"

"Well, if I do you a favor today, I expect that you will consider me a friend. I don't know if I've made myself clear."

"I don't follow you," the marquis replied.

"Yet it's simple. We must stand united." At last, he came to the point:

"Why don't you withdraw the preemptive offer on the Baucina estate? It's all rocky land; not even a turnip would grow there, no matter how much effort you put into it. Plus, it makes no sense for anyone to start a quarrel over nothing."

Marquis Bellarato finally understood the reason for the encounter. He dropped all show of diplomacy and asked abruptly, "Did Prince Licata send you?"

Niní Rizzo was stung to the quick. "Why, my dear Bellarato, that's no way for a gentleman to talk. No one sends me anywhere, keep that in mind." So saying, he touched the brim of his hat with two fingers and rode off at a gallop, followed at a distance by his campiere.

By now only two days remained before the Veterans cooperative would see its option to purchase the former Baucina estate expire. That morning, most of the 395 shareholders gathered in front of Salemi's town hall, near the Cassa Rurale. In Sicily at the time, as elsewhere in Italy, no family was spared from unemployment. Field workers and sharecroppers, supported by the socialist leagues and the Popular Party, went on strike, refusing to work. The most enterprising competed for the little bit of land that could be obtained illegally. When the Falcioni decree of April 1920 ruled that even lands illegally occupied prior to that date could be lawfully assigned to the squatters, the landowners as well as the more enlightened overseers declared that abandoning the law that way was an injustice to all those who had remained law abiding. Above all they insisted that it was extremely dangerous to endorse the concept that armed rebellion could sometimes "pay off."

Also present that morning in front of Salemi's town hall, along with the 395 members of the Veterans, were representatives from another cooperative, the Farm, which was supported by the Socialist Party—specifically, by the party's delegate: a certain attorney named Nicola Geraci from Petralia Sottana. They too were demanding ownership of lands to be shared among the members.

The mayor, seeing the piazza packed with people, began having serious concerns. The four carabinieri assigned to the town were out in the field that day, occupied with various duties, and the fifth couldn't leave the station.

Not knowing which way to turn, the mayor got the idea of having *u patri* intervene. The prince, among all the aristocrats in the region, was the one closest to the people. Maybe he might be able to control the crowd. Ferdinando Licata didn't wait to be asked twice and shortly thereafter arrived at the town hall astride his black horse. Someone whistled in protest, but the others silenced him.

The mayor explained the situation, and Licata, with his usual composure, reassured him.

A few minutes later, he had representatives from each of the two cooperatives brought into the council chamber. The mayor and his entire council had taken their places on the high-backed chairs. Ferdinando Licata, standing, positioned himself at the center of the dais. When everyone finally fell silent, the prince began to speak.

"Well, my friends. The time has come for justice. Many of you went to war, and it is to many of you that we owe the victory. So let's come to an agreement and bring about this blessed socialism."

The peasants couldn't believe what they were hearing. Many nodded, satisfied, and an old man wiped his eyes.

After a short pause to let what he had proposed sink in, he continued. "Now, I'll call you one at a time. You," he said addressing the clerk, "get a new register and start writing." Then he turned to the assembly again. "So then, let's get started right away, given that there are so many of you." He pointed at the farmer nearest to him. "You, come forward." The man, a peasant around the age of forty, scorched by the sun, approached with some hesitation.

"State your name."

"Alvaro Di Paola, son of Giuseppe Di Paola, deceased," he replied, stammering.

The clerk glanced at the mayor, awaiting his assent which was not long in coming, and quickly began writing in the big records book.

At that point Nicola Geraci, the Socialist Party delegate, was granted the floor. He was defiant and self-assured. "Excuse me, but what's the purpose of all this? Is it a new census?"

"Be patient, Mr. Geraci," interjected the mayor, who had figured out what the prince was leading up to. "Let the prince carry on, since all of us here place our confidence in him."

"So then, Alvaro," the prince resumed, "tell us what you own, whether the house is yours, the animals, the vineyard, the olive trees—in short, declare all the things in your possession."

Alvaro Di Paola was puzzled and suspicious, like all peasants when asked what they own. The interrogation smelled like a trap. Nevertheless, he answered diligently.

"Yes, the house is mine. I have three acres of vineyard and twenty olive trees. Then I have two cows, a mare, and a donkey, that's all," he hastened to say.

"Clerk, did you write it all down?" Licata asked the man, who nodded. "Good. Next, please, step forward." The peasants, in orderly fashion, went before the prince and declared the things they owned.

This went on for a few minutes before Nicola Geraci interrupted the assembly again. "Now, hold on a minute! I don't care for this business." He moved toward Licata, as if to confront him on an equal footing. "Why are you taking down all this information? Where I come from, we say, 'Where's the catch?'" His laughter was echoed by a few others.

Ferdinando Licata remained impassive. "We have to institute socialism, don't we? First we have to record the possessions of all the members in the register, then we'll add them all up and divide everything equally, according to what's fair. It may turn out that someone who owns two cows will have to give one to someone who doesn't have any, and a person who has ten olive trees will have to relinquish three of them to someone who only owns four, so that each of them will have seven trees. That's socialism."

Everyone in the room was taken aback. "So that's what this socialism is all about?" more than one man asked his neighbor.

From the center of the hall, an elderly peasant called out, "Well, I don't like it! If that's what socialism is, count me out."

The others agreed with him. "It's no good; cross my name out of the book." "Mine too."

There was a headlong stampede from the socialist revolution.

Nicola Geraci was demoralized. All his efforts to persuade the men to stand together had been fruitless. He addressed Prince Licata harshly, his eyes flashing with hatred: "You think you're clever, don't you, Prince?

Well your days are numbered, individuals like you. We no longer have any use for your class of people: in Russia, we hanged them from lamp-posts." He spun around and left the council chamber, followed by the compassionate looks of those in the room who saw him as a doomed man.

Chapter 12

That afternoon, Marquis Pietro Bellarato returned earlier than usual to his palazzo in the oldest district of Salemi. He was irritated and in a bad mood. With increasing frequency in recent months, his brain was assailed by a flurry of images at that hour that drove him to seek ever more intense and extreme forms of excitement. He would begin fidgeting, yawning, though he wasn't sleepy; rather, it was a lack of oxygen—a restlessness—that forced him to get on his horse and go charging through his lands looking for someone who could satisfy his insane cravings.

The shepherd boys had at first considered it an honor to be able to satisfy their master, but since he'd begun hurting them, they now went to hide as soon as they heard the distant gallop of his horse. They abandoned the flock and ran to take cover among the rocks and cliffs, where the horse couldn't get to them. Terrified, they watched him prowling back and forth near the flock like a hungry wolf, looking for them. The marquis called to them, whistling and shouting, his mouth thick with dust and saliva. He cursed them because they were supposed to stay with the sheep.

Then, when he realized that they would not come out of hiding, he galloped off to the next flock, his head about to explode, in the hope of finding another victim on whom to vent his brutal impulses. And if the unfortunate boy was found, he paid the price for himself and for the other ones who had been smarter than him.

His campieri, with no disrespect, but firmly, had informed the marquis that there was risky gossip about him floating around. But Bellarato was too sure of himself and his authority: no one could stop him. That afternoon had been one of those instances when he'd been unable to satisfy his desires. Returning home, he poured some marsala into a glass and then sprawled on the couch, exhausted by the long ride. He sipped his drink, his hand lying loosely on the armrest.

Tosco, the servant who had grown up with him, finished stoking the fire and asked if the marquis had further need of him. But his master did not answer. The devoted servant had learned when to disappear from the marquis's sight. Tosco left the room shaking his head. He was furious over the marquis's decline. It tore him up to see him in that state. But there was nothing he could do about the insanity that seized Bellarato more and more often lately. If the old marquis, his father, had seen him like that, he would have died of a broken heart.

The marquis closed his eyes partway and fell into a deep lethargy; when he opened them again, he wasn't able to immediately collect his thoughts and had to strain his memory to remember that it wasn't morning but late afternoon. He looked straight ahead—and saw a dark figure, completely covered by a cloak, with a hood lowered over his face.

As soon as he saw the stranger, he leaned forward, frightened. It was then that the mysterious individual let the hood drop and revealed himself.

The marquis recognized him and relaxed. "Oh, it's you," he said, sinking back on the couch. "What are you doing here?"

Then it occurred to him that the unexpected guest had appeared in his study without being shown in by the servant. He didn't finish that thought because, all of a sudden, the figure drew a long knife from under his cloak. He was on him immediately, trying to pin down his arms, but the marquis broke free of his grip and ran toward the door. The man was quicker, however, and with a lunge gave him a powerful shove that sent him spinning to the fireplace. Bellarato crawled backward, looking for something he could use to defend himself; he reached for the poker, but the man kicked it away from him. The marquis, desperate, then grabbed a burning log from the fireplace and threw it at the intruder. But the man dodged it, continuing his relentless advance. The marquis tried to get up, but the man jumped on him, forcing him to the floor. He stuffed his mouth with a lace doily from the sofa that was used as a headrest. Holding him down, he stunned him with two powerful blows to the head. The assailant then stood up and with the tip of the knife sliced off all the buttons on the fly of the marquis's trousers.

Bellarato, though dazed, was still terrified of the threat posed by the long knife; spitting out the doily, he shouted: "Why are you doing this to me?"

The man's only response was to force him to lie on the couch and then plant a knee on his chest, to prevent him from moving. Realizing that he was going to die, the marquis fought back, kicking with his last ounce of strength and thrashing about like a man possessed. So his attacker punched him as hard as he could, this time squarely in the face. He felt the nose bone crack and a spurt of blood gushed onto his hand. Despite the pain, the marquis did not lose consciousness. He began to cry. The figure in black opened Bellarato's pants all the way and with one hand grabbed his member, stretching it out as much as he could. The intruder's facial expression held no trace of compassion. He brought the sharp blade of the knife to the flesh— the marquis was rasping in terror—and then one clean stroke hacked off the culprit guilty of so many rapes. The marquis let out a bestial howl as a stream of blood began to pulsate rhythmically from the wound, pooling on the couch. The assailant, who had not yet had his fill of revenge, stuck what was left of the limp organ into the shrieking mouth, crammed it down the marquis's throat with two fingers, then held his jaws closed until he began to gasp and sputter, struggling for air. The last words Pietro Bellarato heard were those spoken by his executioner.

"'Today Salemi will drink a toast to your death, Marquis.'" It was his epitaph; with a last desperate rasp, Bellarato expired, his eyes bulging from their sockets.

A dense cloud of smoke invaded the room. The killer turned and saw the heavy velvet curtains go up in flames as the fire swept quickly to the other wall coverings and antique furniture. The man began coughing. Shielding his mouth with his cloak, he made his way through the blaze, heading for the door. But as soon as he opened it, fresh oxygen burst into the room, reviving the flames that licked at his cloak.

When by dawn the following day the fire was completely put out, very little of the palazzo was left standing. All the antique furnishings, paintings, tapestries, and mirrors had perished. Salemi's carabinieri recovered the unfortunate remains of two people: one was certainly Marquis Pietro Bellarato, according to the testimony of his servant who had left him dozing in the palazzo's drawing room. But he knew nothing about the other person. Nor could the individual's name be ascertained by his identification papers, since they had been completely destroyed.

Chief Brigadier Mattia Montalto arranged for the remains of the two bodies to be transported to the morgue at the nearby hospital. Then he summoned the town physician, Peppino Ragusa, and requested an autopsy. He wanted to know how those two people had died and whether the doctor could identify them.

From a brief preliminary inspection, Ragusa established that it was a man and a woman. But afterward, he had to change his opinion, because upon a more thorough examination of one of the two corpses, he discovered that the one he had mistaken for a woman had in his throat—something that looked like a male member. And it was his own.

They were therefore dealing with an explicit Mafia symbolism, according to which severed genitals, stuffed in a corpse's mouth, were meant to settle an affront committed against the wife of a "friend" or some other offense of a sexual nature.

The murder of Marquis Bellarato caused quite a sensation throughout the territory of Salemi and, as the mysterious killer had glibly predicted, many people drank a toast to his death that day.

But the greatest satisfaction over Marquis Bellarato's demise belonged to the 395 members of the Veterans cooperative. The farmers were unable to contain their elation. Some even wept for joy: with the marquis dead, they no longer had to fear that a competitor might steal the Baucina estate away from them.

The term of the Veterans' option expired the very morning on which the corpse was discovered, and the cooperative had still not obtained a loan from the Cassa Rurale.

As soon as news of the death spread through the town, Don Antonio Albamonte headed immediately for Prince Ferdinando Licata's palazzo to tell him what had happened. The priest found him starting his breakfast of oranges, biscotti, and jam. Sitting down opposite him as the prince spread some jam on a crispy biscotto, the priest asked, "Have you heard about the Marquis Bellarato?"

"What a terrible death, poor fellow," Ferdinando Licata remarked, and went on eating.

"The fire broke out yesterday afternoon, and they managed to extinguish the flames only this morning at dawn," the priest continued, breaking a biscuit as if it were a host. "I spoke with Tosco, the servant. He is the only witness. He says he has no idea who the second corpse might be, because he swears he didn't let anyone in to see his master." After a brief pause, the priest continued. "Prince, don't you think it's quite a strange coincidence that Bellarato died a day before our option was to expire?"

"Of course, Bellarato can no longer acquire the Baucina estate now. We no longer have his option hanging over us like the sword of Damocles. This time destiny played out in our favor," Ferdinando Licata pronounced.

"Could it be that someone guided destiny's hand?" the priest asked boldly.

The prince spilled some orange juice on his shirt. "Don Antonio, do you mean to suggest that the marquis may have been killed over that transaction?" he asked, wiping it off with a linen napkin.

"Many of our farmers were seriously worried about losing their savings. I wouldn't be surprised if someone decided to settle the matter by creating an inferno."

"I understand that Dr. Ragusa found a foreign body in his throat," the prince said glancing at Albamonte.

The poor priest made the sign of the cross. "May the Lord have mercy on him."

"As he had for his poor victims," Licata concluded. "The marquis had many enemies. What he did to his young shepherds was truly unspeakable."

"In any case, peace be with him now. The marquis can no longer trouble us. It's as if the estate were already ours."

"Don Antonio, your farmers can rest easy. I told them they didn't have to worry."

The marquis's sudden death indeed meant salvation for the members of the Veterans cooperative. Ferdinando Licata, through a friend, was finally able to obtain a loan from the Bank of Sicily, which was crucial to the successful conclusion of the purchase. The 395 farmers rejoiced at hearing the news that the former Baucina estate now belonged to their cooperative; they applauded the prince and, naturally, Don Antonio, who had insisted on having him in the cooperative as honorary president. Finally, they would own the lands that they themselves would cultivate: a dream that many couldn't even imagine. They would have kissed the ground the prince walked on, so great was their gratitude for his generosity.

Malicious rumormongers tried to suggest that he was directly involved in the matter of the fire, but they were immediately silenced by those around them who pronounced: "*U patri* would never do anything that dishonored himself and his friends."

From then on, Prince Ferdinando Licata became *u patri*—father—to one and all.

Don Antonio would never forget the favor that Licata had done for him.

After the success of the Veterans cooperative, many farmers wanted to form other cooperatives under the patronage of the church and *u patri*, steering clear of the lure of the red leagues with their socialist and anticlerical talk.

The prince himself derived a significant profit from managing the cooperative. For the next four years, he let the farmers cultivate the land as tenants, while waiting to become its rightful owners. In practice, they paid rent to the cooperative, which went into the pockets of the prince's agents. These payments, rather than being counted as amortization of the loan obtained from the Bank of Sicily, to be deducted therefore at the time the individual contracts for the collective purchase were executed, were considered simply a *"terraggio"* rent—just as if the owner were still the original *latifondista* from whom the peasants were leasing the uncultivated land.

And when the cooperative—namely, the prince and Don Antonio—finally decided that it was time to transfer the estate to the members, it was still the two leaders who established the rules governing the division. They assigned the best lands, the most fertile ones with plenty of water, to a few friends and all the others to the rest of the members. And so it came about that Ferdinando Licata acquired about 250 acres, and assigned another 250 adjacent acres to his older sister, Lavinia Licata, and the same to Don Antonio. Another 500 acres were divided among six or seven friends, while the remaining small plots went to the more than 390 members of the cooperative.

Ragusa, determined to unravel the mystery of the second man who had been burned to a crisp, spent many hours in the medical center's laboratory that night, analyzing the two cadavers.

Ragusa had the stubborn perseverance typical of his fellow citizens. Moreover, during the Great War he had fought on the barren plateau of the Karst, near Trieste, where his protective shell had only grown thicker and more impenetrable. In Bassano del Grappa, where he had been hospitalized for a bayonet wound to his hand, he had met Annachiara; having lost both her parents, she had been an aide there for many years.

Back in his village, Ragusa had left behind a daughter, Ester, in the care of relatives, and the grave of his wife, who had died of malaria. He never would have thought he could fall in love again in his lifetime. Until then life had held in store for him only painful trials and superhuman struggles. But upon seeing that blonde angel, the alchemy of love flooded back, stirring his head and his heart. He was charmed by her gentle, reserved manner. But only toward the end of his convalescence, a few days before being discharged from the hospital in northern Italy, did he get up the courage to reveal his feelings.

So it was that the two promised to marry as soon as the war was over. Almost a year later, Italy signed the peace treaty with Austria at Saint-Germain-en-Laye, France, and the couple was finally joined in matrimony before facing the long journey to Salemi, where Annachiara had promised to raise Ester like her own daughter. Soon the little family was augmented by the arrival of a baby boy, a foundling, abandoned in front of the churchyard by a desperate mother. Don Albamonte convinced the Ragusas to take him in, even though the doctor was of Jewish origin. He had confidence in Annachiara, who was a God-fearing woman of faith. She had proved an incomparable wife. In just a few years, she had managed to fit in perfectly with the townsfolk, and had used her skill as an expert seamstress to help her neighbors cut and stitch clothes that looked like they came from a shop in Rome. And so Saro became part of the town doctor's family, and a year later, a boisterous little girl, Stellina, was born, the cherished darling of her older siblings.

In the evening, Chief Brigadier Montalto went to the doctor's office to hear the autopsy report. "They are two men, I have no doubt," the doctor began.

"The marquis was identified by his gold Breguet watch that we found molten into a solid lump," Montalto told him.

"Before he died of asphyxiation, he was castrated. Then the murderer stuffed the shaft of his penis into his mouth," Dr. Ragusa said.

"Yes, it's a very old practice around here, to avenge a sexual offense," the chief pointed out, adding, "We found a long knife beside the man who must be his murderer."

"The man must have been around five feet three inches tall," the physician continued. "Judging from his skull, I'd say he hadn't yet reached forty. But there's not much else I can tell you. The corpse was in very bad shape."

"We may be able to identify him as well. I found a medal in the remains of his clothing," Montalto informed him.

"Is he known here in town?"

"Of course. He's a member of Vassallo's gang," Chief Brigadier Montalto said confidently. "This murder is going to stir up a heap of trouble. Just between us, Doctor, Bellarato was a real bastard. But he had friends in high places, and they've already sent word from Palermo that they're dispatching a captain in command of a troop of Royal Guardsmen to capture whoever was behind the killing."

"That's all we needed in Salemi, the Royal Guard," the doctor sighed. "Difficult times lie ahead."

"I'm afraid so," the doctor concluded bitterly.

That same week another incident occurred which caused a sensation among the population of the Salemi and Madonie regions: the disappearance of the spokesman for the socialist leagues, Nicola Geraci, who during the meeting at town hall had been disrespectful to Prince Licata.

His wife had reported him missing after Geraci failed to return home to Petralia Sottana for three days. The carabinieri alerted all police stations and command posts in Sicily. In a flash, the news spread throughout the area. But the place where it really caused a stir was Salemi, for the entire town knew about Geraci's altercation with Prince Licata, publicly insulting him. People whispered their doubts but didn't dare expose them to the light of day.

Nevertheless, everyone agreed that you couldn't offend a figure like Prince Licata and expect to go unpunished.

These were the topics that intrigued the elderly peasants who attended Dr. Ragusa's evening gatherings. That evening, they dispensed with the health care lesson and let their imaginations run wild over Nicola Geraci's disappearance. "It has all the earmarks of a *lupara bianca*, a white shotgun," the doctor remarked, referring to a Mafia-style execution in which the victim's body is deliberately concealed.

Pericle Terrasini, a charcoal burner who had never known anything in his life but hard work and sorrow, declared, "Geraci asked for it. You don't offend a man of honor, like he did."

The doctor smiled to himself at that atavistic submission to everything that power represents. Would he ever be able to make his dear townsmen see that we are all born equal? That whoever commits a wrong, be he noble or poor, must pay a debt to society?

It was getting late. In the country, people rose before dawn and those hours of lessons were stolen from the farmers' sleep. The doctor accompanied his "class" to the door and said good night to his willing pupils, confirming their meeting for the following week. The men all bowed respectfully to him and his wife.

Ragusa closed the door, satisfied.

He did all this without pay. While he did not profess his ideas openly, they were genuinely democratic. Some labeled them "socialist" to malign him, but the fact is that the doctor was firmly convinced that only an educated people can truly be said to be free.

Chapter 13

Ever since Dr. Bizzarri arrived in town, Ragusa found himself in serious financial straits. Few of his patients went to see him anymore because they were afraid of Jano. The only work he was allowed to do was butchering; they would call him to the slaughterhouse, and he'd perform the dirty work. Sometimes he got a steak, other times they gave him a few liras. The most dependable economic support came from Annachiara, who had gone back to work as a dressmaker for the ladies of the town.

Unlike the men, the women were less influenced by rules and regulations. No one bothered to check whether Annachiara was the wife of a Jew or a Christian. Her work was good, she was inexpensive, and that was enough for them. Then there were Saro's small contributions from his job at the barbershop. After the racial laws, Ester was unable to find work and helped her father with whatever patients still came to his office.

That Sunday, Jano Vassallo awoke determined to torment his enemies. As usual, the first person who came to mind was Ragusa. But he had forgotten that it was Sunday and that Ragusa, accompanied by his son Saro, had gone to tend to his land, as he did every weekend. To call that piece of rocky ground "land" was a euphemism, since it was just a steep, paltry plot that had been obtained thanks to a law of February 13, 1933, granting veterans the opportunity to own parcels of uncultivated land.

All the same, Jano and his four grim, black-shirted thugs decided to descend into the valley. They went on horseback, riding five worthless nags that they had stolen from some aristocratic families who had fallen on hard times.

As soon as Grappa began to bark, Ragusa realized that strangers were approaching. In the onion field, Saro was the first to straighten his back and peer into the distance. Ragusa went over to him.

"I hear hoofbeats," Saro said. Ragusa sensed a note of anxiety in his son's words. "It sounds like more than one," he added.

Grappa continued barking in the direction of the horizon until the five horsemen finally appeared on the rise. It didn't take long for Ragusa to see that it was Jano and his henchmen, which did not bode well. Jano was brandishing a rifle, something unusual, since he typically favored his club. Now he was holding a M91 Mauser Carcano carbine.

"It's me they're looking for," he said quickly to Saro. "You leave by the pass. I'll hide in the woods." He tied the dog to a tree trunk so the animal wouldn't follow him.

"I'm not leaving you alone. We'll face them together," Saro cried with youthful vehemence, gripping the hoe he was using to weed the ground.

"Saro, don't disobey! Do as I tell you! Go on, go!"

Saro felt a special reverence for his father. When he reached his adolescence, Ragusa and Annachiara had revealed to him that they were not his natural parents and that he had been placed in their care as an infant. Saro worshipped them because they had never let him want for anything and had always showered him with love; after they disclosed that he'd been adopted, he loved them even more for their generosity and nobility of spirit. His father, moreover, by example and through his teachings, had instilled in him a sense of justice and integrity. Saro was proud of his family and would have given his very life if anyone dared harm them. He didn't feel right leaving his father alone. Ragusa knew how stubborn his son was and stepped closer. "Listen to me, Saro. I don't want a confrontation with them. If you're with me I'll have no way of defending myself. You must do as I told you." This time it was an order, and, pointing to the track along the mountain pass, he ordered, "That way!"

Saro hesitated, then turned and began running toward the trail that climbed along the pass of Monte Sant'Angelo. As soon as the doctor saw that Saro was out of harm's way, he ran and hid among the tall corn stalks in the nearby field. If he made it to the thicket of trees, he could consider himself safe. He knew every recess and hiding place in the woods. He raced in that direction, while behind him he heard the shouts of the Black Shirts getting closer and closer.

Ragusa dashed through the entire field and finally reached the San Clemente forest. His chest wheezed with each breath; his heart was pounding wildly. He didn't know how much longer he could continue. He found an oak tree with a large bush at its base and crawled inside to hide. He tried to slow his breathing, so they wouldn't hear him.

Soon enough, Jano arrived with the other four riders. The horses, worn out and foaming with sweat, whinnied as the men stopped in a clearing not far from where the doctor was hiding. Ragusa heard Jano exclaim angrily, "He's nearby, I'm sure of it!"

Jano made his horse trot around in a circle, as his eyes swept the woods. Then he yelled, "Peppino Ragusa! Come out, I have to talk to you!" Lowering his voice so that only his buddies could hear, he added, "I have to play you a serenade—with this." And he waved his rifle mockingly.

From his hiding place Ragusa heard the other militiamen laugh scornfully, and he shivered. "Peppino! Don't be afraid!" Jano yelled again, and, following his lead, Ginetto, the youngest of the group, added under his breath, "We just want to rough you up a little." Ragusa heard another burst of laughter and held his breath. Meanwhile, the five men had begun scouring the underbrush.

All of a sudden, as though in a dream, the notes of a waltz drifted through the woods. Ragusa looked around and recalled that he was not very far from Ferdinando Licata's palazzo. The prince might be his salvation. He saw his pursuers far off in the clearing. From the spot where he was hiding, the vegetation became wilder and more tangled. Centuries of neglect, first by the landowners and later the gabellotti, had caused this part of the woods to become so dense that it could only be entered on foot, whereas at one time gentlemen would ride their horses there to hunt and even drive their carriages through it.

Ragusa crawled backward out of the bush. Then he straightened up, took a deep breath, and plunged headlong through the tangle of brambles, indifferent to the thorns and dry branches that scratched his face, arms, and chest.

The noise of his mad sprint and the snapping of trampled bushes made the five Black Shirts spin around. One of them spotted him and alerted the others, and they immediately rushed in his direction. But Ginetto's horse balked in front of a large bush. The young man flew into the air and landed in the middle of the brambles. The others paid no attention to him and continued their chase. Ginetto emerged from the bush in a sorry state. The thorns had torn his shirt and pants to shreds. Furious as a wounded animal, he vilely took it out on his horse, striking it on the back with his club. Then he remounted and set off after his buddies.

Ragusa, with a good head start, kept running as fast as he could. He had now reached the edge of the woods and not far away, at the top of a hill, he saw his destination.

Meanwhile, Jano had emerged from the dense thicket and was wait-ing for the other four: as a group, they were invincible. When Prospero, Quinto, Nunzio, and Ginetto caught up with him, they resumed the chase, shouting savagely.

Ragusa kept going, struggling along the dirt road leading to the pala-zzo. He was now a few dozen yards from the front door, while behind him his pursuers' cries were coming closer.

The door of palazzo Licata opened and two burly campieri appeared with cartridge belts slung on their shoulders and hunting rifles in their hands. Both wore the classic *coppola*, a flat cap that shaded their pitch-black eyes, and high, shiny leather boots over woolen pants.

As soon as he saw them Ragusa fell at their feet and barely had the strength to say: "Help me . . ."

The younger one gave him a hand getting up and led him inside the house.

Meanwhile, Jano and the others rode up, raising a huge cloud of dust. Once the dust settled, Jano barked at the older campiere, "Don't get mixed up in this! Hand him over to me." Meanwhile, the younger camp-iere reappeared at the door.

The older guard didn't turn a hair and, moving only his lips, was even more unyielding: "My friend, here you are on the lands of Prince Ferdi-nando Licata."

Jano dismounted, faced the man, spread his legs wide, and said, "I just want that miserable piece of trash, and I'll be on my way."

The campiere spoke softly, his words measured: "Here there's only one person who can say 'I want.'" As he spoke those words, the younger man slowly and deliberately moved to the side, so his companion would not be in his line of fire.

From the gruff guard's resolute tone, the conversation appeared to be over. The four minions turned their eyes to Jano, curious to see how he would settle things. Not one of them thought of getting off his horse to lend their leader some support. Jano was thinking quickly about how to respond when the door opened again and this time the imposing figure of Ferdinando Licata appeared. "Bettino!" he said peremptorily, "can't we even have some peace and quiet on the feast of our patron saint?" Though he reprimanded the campiere, it was clear that his words were meant for the intruders. Then he pretended he'd just noticed the new arrivals. "Have you offered our guests a glass of wine? Can't you see how hot they are?"

"We didn't mean to disturb *voscenza*," Jano interjected to get the prince's attention. But Licata didn't deign to look at him. Instead his eyes were on Ginetto, the youngest of the band.

"Ginetto, why aren't you with your father?" he reproached the young man gently. "He's inside."

The boy didn't know what to say other than an offhand "I had things to do."

The prince frowned, irritated. "I see that regretfully there is no longer any proper respect; the respect that at one time we young people showed our elders. You should know, however, that everything that is modern will sooner or later be superseded."

"Our ideas will live on for a thousand years!" Jano Vassallo had the gall to say.

The prince threw him a blistering look and took his leave: "I have guests waiting for me. You may go in peace." So saying, he went back into the palazzo, leaving the five foaming with rage.

As soon as the door closed behind him, Licata went to Peppino Ragusa, who was sitting on a chair in the entrance hall, utterly drained, still terrified and panting. From the prince's tone when he spoke to him, there seemed to be a long-standing complicity between the two. "Peppino, why are they after you?"

Ragusa rose from his chair and was about to kiss his ring, but the prince drew back his hand.

"*Patri*, they've been hunting me for days. They've accused me of being a subversive."

Ferdinando Licata did not conceal a slight smile. "Well, is that all? It's what everyone says, isn't it?"

But Ragusa couldn't manage to smile. "*Patri*, you know it's not true. I give a few private lessons to our townsmen who can't read or write. But they say I mix these lessons with antifascist talk."

"And isn't it so?" The prince was having some fun with the earnest Ragusa.

"I try to open their eyes. Make them use their heads and think."

"Calm down now." Licata squeezed his shoulders, as if to give him courage. "You may join us if you wish. Today I have the 'one hundred saints' here for lunch."

"Maybe I'll just wait here awhile, before I go."

The prince was about to leave him. "And how are things at home?"

"We have our health. Saro is a big comfort to me. He's a wonderful boy."

"Well, make yourself at home," the prince said. With that, he returned to his guests and to the monsignor, whom he had left alone for too long.

In the dining room, a brand-new gramophone was playing the notes of a Viennese waltz. Ferdinando Licata returned to his seat beside Monsignor Antonio Albamonte, who was enjoying a vanilla cake along with the four other diners seated at his table.

"Forgive me, Monsignor; some rude intruders." The prelate nodded with his mouth full, while a servant brought the prince his piece of cake. Ferdinando began eating it with gusto, and then, eyeing the medal that adorned the priest's cassock, asked with a tinge of irony, "Monsignor, I didn't know you had been to war."

The bishop scoffed, touching the medal. "This? I won it at the carnival." He laughed, but quickly turned serious. "I'm joking, of course. This is the medal I recently received from the Fascist party secretary, Achille Starace himself: Meritorious of the Battle of Wheat. I was awarded it along with sixty other bishops and more than two thousand priests from all over Italy. We were received by Pope Pius XI. It was an unforgettable day, so I've worn this ever since."

"From what I've read, I don't think the Pope agrees much with our Duce's decisions. Last year's encyclical condemned the Nazi ideology in no uncertain terms. Yet our Duce does nothing but sing the praises of his friend Adolf Hitler, and now he's even looking to him as a model. A few months ago, he introduced the 'Roman step,' to imitate the German army's goose step. Isn't it grotesque?" the prince suggested, leaving his guest to draw his own conclusions.

"Not as grotesque as the Roman salute. I'm truly embarrassed when I have to salute some party official," the prelate explained. "However, to even the score, the Pope criticized communism as well," the monsignor promptly added. "We'll see. Our Duce knows what he's doing. Have you seen the order and stability he's brought about here?"

"What he's done is simply replace the Mafia." The prince repeated: "The fascist state has supplanted the Mafia. However, the roots remain intact. All they changed was the name, but the methods are alike. I'm willing to bet, Monsignor, that when these gentlemen in black shirts are gone, the Mafia will return, stronger than ever."

"We must be patient. Wait for the storm to pass," the bishop replied placidly, stuffing the last bit of cake into his mouth. By now the numerous glasses of good wine had loosened his tongue and his inhibitions. "As far as I'm concerned, nothing has changed." He leaned closer to the prince's ear. "I'm hiding the bandit Giuseppe Spagnolo in the convent of Santa Margherita, near Calatafimi. A lost sheep who wants to return to the fold, but the laws won't allow him to. I can't tell you how many souls Spagnolo has sent to meet their Maker. I'd like to send him to America. There he can rebuild his life . . .

"I know that you are well connected to the Florios."

"True," the prince confirmed. "They don't ask questions when I ask them to take some poor devil on board."

"Good. Giuseppe Spagnolo can be a generous man if we save his hide," Albamonte concluded.

"Let's put it this way, Monsignor. I'll arrange for your bandit to sail, and I don't want anything for myself—"

"If?" The prelate beat him to it.

"If you'll be kind enough to hide a townsman of mine in one of your monasteries for a few months," Prince Licata requested. "I have to make a good man disappear."

"How many did he bump off?" the monsignor asked slyly.

"No, no, he's truly a good man. His only misfortune is to have made enemies of the Black Shirts."

"Is he a subversive? A socialist?" the priest asked suspiciously.

"Monsignor, ideas are sacrosanct, no matter where they come from. The important thing is to avoid bloodshed," the prince replied. "I assure you, he's just a poor devil. His name is Peppino Ragusa."

"So may I count on you?"

"If the trade of favors is satisfactory to you, it's fine with me. As they say, one more won't hurt."

Chapter 14

Since the day of the pursuit, Peppino Ragusa tried to be seen as little as possible around Salemi. He went to the clinic, in the vain hope that a patient might turn up on the doorstep, but then quickly returned home and shut himself in until the following morning. He also suspended the evening lessons during this time, fearing that Jano might reappear and rough up his elderly pupils. Annachiara couldn't understand Jano's persistent rage, and this time it was she who proposed that they go back north, to the Veneto region. But Ragusa was too attached to the colors of his Sicilian homeland, the ancient landscapes, that sun, to be able to give it all up. Leaving everything behind to start over again at their age, in another part of the world, was not an appealing prospect. They had to be patient. Sooner or later Jano would calm down. He'd known Jano since he was young; he'd always been the most reckless hothead of all the kids, but as a boy he'd been less disrespectful.

Actually, Jano had never gotten along with the doctor's son, Saro. True, the two were five years apart. But they had two very different temperaments. The one impulsive and arrogant; the other thoughtful and introverted. Saro spoke little and was always guarded, never revealing his emotions. He preferred to be viewed as antisocial rather than to appear too receptive and thereby open himself up to others' prying. This demeanor made him all the more intriguing in girls' eyes. In addition, his athletic build, his wrestler's shoulders, and his sky-blue eyes were an irresistible magnet for girls, who would turn around to cast furtive glances at him when he passed by.

Saro worked at Domenico's barbershop, the resonating chamber for every incident, large or small, that occurred in the community.

One day while he was soaping the face of Nini Trovato, the elderly town crier and factotum, Donato, one of Rosario Losurdo's sons, came into the shop. Saro stropped his razor, then took a little rubber ball that was kept in a bowl full of water and stuck it in Nini's mouth; with his tongue, the old man positioned it in between his denture and his cheek. This ingenious technique, devised by Domenico for his elderly clients whose wrinkles were pronounced, smoothed out the skin, thereby making shaving easier.

Ninì Trovato was the most well-informed man in town. If you wanted to know whose son a certain kid was, he could list the entire family tree for you. Carlo Vacca, Roberto Naselli, a livestock broker, a certain Armando Caradonna and three other villagers were also in the shop.

That morning, Ninì was holding forth and recounting yet again what had happened in Partanna a few years earlier to an elderly attorney who was president of one of the agricultural cooperatives formed to help war veterans, though their real aim was to reinforce a coalition of gabellotti to oppose the initiatives of the socialist leagues.

A clapping of hands from the door, like faint, mocking applause, made all heads turn. Jano entered the shop, headed for Ninì's chair and said, "All reds should hang swinging from a hook."

Ninì glanced around and saw who had entered. He rose from his chair, taking the rubber ball out of his mouth and wiping the soap off his face. "Jano Vassallo. Take my place. I'm not in any hurry." He dropped the little ball into the bowl of water.

Jano approached Saro and faced him. The two looked at each other. "Shave, Jano?"

"Yeah," the other said, sitting down.

"Aren't you afraid of my razor? After what you did to my father."

"Saro, you wouldn't hurt a fly. Your father is another story. . . ."

"So, with and against the grain." He smiled, and with that smile everyone could breathe again.

Saro began soaping him, using another brush. "Jano, leave my father alone. We're peaceful people."

"Saruzzo, I have nothing against your father. I'm against people who won't fall in line. It's time we got it into our heads that there is only one man in command and it's *him*, the Duce! Have I made myself clear? Your father teaches those poor illiterate fools without asking a lira, but he puts subversive ideas in their heads, and that's not good. The result, in fact, is that even priests are being shot at now. You heard what happened last Sunday, didn't you?"

"You mean Don Mario's sermon?" Carlo Vacca threw in.

"I was there," Armando Caradonna chimed in, "and I can tell you that no one had ever spoken so strongly against the signori."

"I'm talking about the gunshots that were fired at the door of the rectory the following day," Jano explained.

"_Well_, my father would never dream of shooting at the church," Saro said heatedly, still soaping him.

"They're people who think like him, though!"

But Jano was mistaken. The man who had reacted against the harsh tones of the sermon was certainly not a socialist. Because Rosario Losurdo could be called anything, but not a red—and it was he who had shot at the rectory.

———

That morning Ferdinando Licata had dressed in his hunting outfit: pants, brown corduroy jacket, and high leather boots. He mounted Lightning, the handsome colt with the black coat, and headed for the Taféle Farm, where Rosario Losurdo, his family, and the retinue of campieri lived.

Losurdo was ten years younger than Licata, but his hard life in the fields, his family responsibilities, and the charges brought against him years earlier—of which he continued to declare himself innocent— seemed to have aged him prematurely. Although he was still in his for- ties, his hair was nearly all gray, and his beard was completely white. He and the prince looked as though they were the same age. But under that prematurely white hair was a sharp mind capable of calculating the value and productive potential of land in a fraction of a second, to within a few pounds of its eventual yield. Moreover, his physical strength was prodigious, rendering him invincible at arm wrestling, even against the strongest, most strapping young men in the area.

Licata paused at the top of the hill, where he could look out over the entire terrain. He saw farms scattered throughout the valley, surrounded by green fields.

The largest of these was that of Rosario Losurdo.

Losurdo had come up in the world, the prince thought, rising from the carter that he had been. In fact, after prison, his gabellotto had be- come one of the most powerful men in the territory of Salemi. The in- justice he had suffered had eliminated any allegiance he might have had toward the law. He was convinced that justice was an ideal that could not be pursued on this earth; the law, because it was written and interpreted by men, could be twisted, obstructed, and adapted as needed.

Licata saw some commotion in the courtyard of his gabellotto's farm- stead and realized he'd already been spotted by the campieri who worked for Losurdo, but were paid with his money. He gave Lightning a gentle spur and started down the path.

It didn't often happen that the prince went to go talk to a subordinate. In fact, as far as anyone could remember, it had never happened. But this time he had a favor to do for the monsignor: no one should ever again dare to shoot at the rectory.

Rosario Losurdo had already been at the gate for some minutes, awaiting him.

"*Bacio le mani*—my respects—*patri*," the gabellotto said as he approached and helped the prince dismount.

"Every time I see this land, my heart fills with joy, Rosario," Licata said, looking around. "I can see that you tend it with love."

A thrill of pride made Losurdo smile. "Voscenza is always generous with your praise."

"Unfortunately, Rosario, I'm not here just to pay compliments."

The prince's grave tone dampened Rosario's smile. "I know what you want to talk to me about, Prince, but Don Mario spoke too boldly against us men of honor on Sunday. I'll tell you right now that it was an impulse I couldn't resist. You could say that the shotgun almost fired itself. However, it won't happen again."

"Good, Rosario. You know how much I value the monsignor. And his friends must be our friends. Even if they sometimes speak out of line. The matter is closed."

But Losurdo too had an issue to settle with the prince and took advantage of the rare opportunity to mention it. "*Patri*, there has always been the utmost sincerity between us," the gabellotto said. "There's something I'd like to clear up."

"What is it?"

"It's about Manfredi and his son Nunzio," Losurdo continued.

"Nunzio is a bad apple," the prince remarked bitterly.

"He's likely to poison the whole bushel. We need to take a firm stand against that family," the gabellotto insisted.

"Do you know that Manfredi asked me if he could buy a small plot of land in the Madonnuzza?"

"I wanted to talk to you about that too. I remind you that Madonnuzza borders my Giovinazzo property. You can't let him have it. Forgive me for being blunt."

"Are you concerned about Nunzio or the adjacent lands?" the prince asked seriously.

"Manfredi is my best campiere. When I was in jail, he helped my family. For this I will always be grateful to him. And I also know how important it is to him to become the owner of a piece of land. But I can't allow a member of his family to behave that way with us."

"You're putting me in a difficult position, because I've already given my word. I can't go back on my decision. I've never in my life done that."

Prince Licata was truly very sorry.

"I already told Manfredi to keep his son in line," Losurdo went on. "But now that damn kid is out of his control. He blindly obeys that crackpot Jano."

"Jano isn't a crackpot. He's angry at the entire world, and I can't say I blame him," Prince Licata replied, shaking his head.

"For some time, he's been hanging around my house, and I don't like it," Losurdo told him.

"There's a beehive here, my dear Rosario. And flies buzz around wherever there's honey," Licata said, smiling. "Nevertheless, you don't have to worry. It seems to me that Mena is a young girl with a head on her shoulders."

"But she doesn't have an easy disposition. She wants to do things her own way, that's the truth. She'll make her mother die of a heart attack," Losurdo concluded with a sad smile.

Chapter 15

— 1921 —

In spring the valleys of Salemi, thanks to the brilliant colors of the patchwork of fields, shone like a fistful of diamonds. One morning this peaceful landscape was disturbed when a flock of doves suddenly rose in flight from the trees, frightened by the roar of engines. A convoy of gray-green trucks and jeeps appeared around a curve and climbed up the road leading to the town. In the lead jeep, seated beside the driver and protected by dark, antidust goggles, was Lorenzo Costa himself, captain of the Royal Guard.

After the Italian occupation of the Croatian city of Rijeka following World War I and the uprisings that in those years had devastated many Italian cities in the North, Prime Minister Francesco Saverio Nitti had decided to strengthen the nation's police forces by giving them actual military power: and so the Royal Guard were formed.

Lorenzo Costa, a native of Genoa, had been transferred from the Royal Guard headquarters in Rome to Palermo in order to counter the riots that in recent months had flared up in some Sicilian provinces. It was thought that an outsider could handle the command in a more impartial way, without being influenced by precarious local interests.

Captain Lorenzo Costa had been given specific orders from Rome: he was to get to the bottom of the murder of Marquis Bellarato and find out who his killer was, whether there were others behind it, and why the brutal castration. It was essential that a determined resolve to punish the guilty parties, whoever they were, be demonstrated to the population. The captain was also responsible for investigating the disappearance of Nicola Geraci, the attorney for the socialist or "red" leagues of Petralia Sottana. The state had to present a show of force and the Royal Guard were just the solution, since they were composed of ex-soldiers who, discharged and unable to find work after returning from the Great War, had settled for joining a paramilitary body.

The battlefield of the Royal Guard turned out to be the streets and piazzas of the cities, and their enemies, the citizens. Before long their uniform was loathed by any political group that hoped to organize demonstrations or public gatherings. The Royal Guard were particularly determined and vicious in their interventions, so that often their appearance in the piazzas was enough to turn even the most diehard demonstrators into docile lambs.

The convoy entered a deserted Salemi and headed for the piazza of the Convento di San Francesco, a massive red brick building surmounted by a tall crenellated tower. One wing of the convent had been assigned to the forty men who were under the command of Captain Costa.

As soon as Lorenzo Costa stepped out of the jeep, Chief Brigadier Montalto went to meet him as though he were an old friend and gave him a military salute. "Captain, did you have a good trip?"

Costa snapped rigidly to attention and did not reply to the courteous question. "I wish to set up our headquarters immediately."

"But don't you want to rest a little, freshen up? Shall I have them bring you some lemonade?" the chief brigadier continued amiably.

"I don't have time for all that. I'm afraid there's a lot to do before we can return home. So let's get a move on."

Montalto filled him in on the facts concerning the investigation of Marquis Bellarato's death. Lorenzo Costa insisted on making an immediate inspection of the palazzo that had been destroyed by fire. He brought along half of his men, who poked around through the rubble searching for clues. However, they had no idea what to look for, since they weren't investigators but ex-soldiers who had experienced the horrors of trench warfare.

The work done by Montalto and his team had been more than satisfactory. The only clue that might identify the second body, the probable murderer, was a medal that had been spared by the fire, stuck between the remains of the victim's clothing and his skin. The chief brigadier opened a locket and removed the medal from a small envelope.

"Here it is," he said, handing it to Costa, who examined it closely. It was one of those aluminum medals that are given out in school to children who distinguish themselves for the best essay or the best performance in gymnastics. One side portrayed Saint Christopher crossing a river carrying the child Jesus on his shoulders, while the other side displayed the symbol of a winged victory.

"I know for certain who owned this medal. It meant more to him than anything else," Montalto explained. "He had won it in a cross-country race during the feast of Saint Christopher."

"His name?" the captain asked curtly.

"Salvatore Turrisi." Montalto opened a register that listed everyone who had a police record. He leafed through its pages until he found the name. "Here it is: he was born in 1895."

"Barely twenty-six years old," Captain Lorenzo Costa thought.

"Turrisi also had a motive to kill Bellarato," the chief continued. "The marquis had accused him of having sexual relations with a shepherd and then killing the boy. He went into hiding and became an outlaw because of that accusation. He was a member of Gaetano Vassallo's band."

"Vassallo's gang will be wiped out; that's what we're here for. And we won't make any allowances," Lorenzo Costa decreed. "This time they really went too far.

"Was the fire started by them?"

"I think it broke out accidentally," Montalto told him. "Bellarato may have tried to defend himself with a burning log from the fireplace, where, we've established, a fire was lit . . . In short, I believe Turrisi got trapped in the flames."

Afterward, the captain wanted to hear about all the notable events that had occurred in Salemi over the past six months, so the meeting with the chief brigadier went on for another two hours at least. By the end of the lengthy conversation, the captain had formed a very clear idea of the social dynamics that characterized the most recent period in that Sicilian town.

His first order was to have the Turrisi family's house placed under secret watch. He had two of his men stationed in a dwelling that had been abandoned years earlier by a family of emigrants, located opposite the entrance to Salvatore Turrisi's brother Curzio's house. Curzio too was in hiding with the outlaw Vassallo. Costa knew that bandits periodically returned to their families, for one thing, to see their children again and embrace their wives, and also to replenish their supplies.

The trap snapped shut on Curzio one night in late spring. The Royal Guard were kind enough to wait for him to perform his conjugal duties before violently taking action. After the lights in the house went out, they waited one more hour. Then Captain Costa gave a signal, and about a dozen men moved in; the other twenty or so remained outside the house to close off any escape route. The Royal Guard broke down the door and rushed into the house in pairs.

Biagio, Curzio's six-year-old son, woke up with a start and began to cry. One of the guards grabbed him and covered his mouth. Meanwhile, the others climbed to the second floor of the dwelling, where they burst into the bedroom, surprising Curzio without his underwear and Vincenza, his wife, with her long white petticoat pulled up to her belly. Curzio just had time to get off his wife when two guards pinned him down, pressing him into the floor. The woman straightened her clothes with unexpected composure. Thinking immediately of her son, she shouted, "Biagio!" Then she was about to leap out of bed, but she too was immobilized by two other Royal Guard.

Shortly thereafter Captain Costa appeared at the door. With a look, he signaled to the two soldiers holding the woman to let her go. As soon as they released their prey, she raced out of the room and down the stairs to her son, violently yanking away the soldier who was clutching him. She hugged the child, and the boy was able to breathe again as he wept. Captain Costa approached Curzio, though with his head pressed against the floor, the man couldn't see him. "Curzio Turrisi, the day of judgment has arrived for you too. Let's go have a little chat." From that day on, throughout the entire territory of Salemi, the words "Let's go have a little chat" became synonymous with trials and tribulations for the poor devils to whom they were directed.

The captain had set up a kind of interrogation room in one of the cellars of the convent where the Royal Guard was quartered, and in the months to come, the people of Salemi would describe it as "the slaughterhouse," for those walls witnessed atrocities that would shame the human race.

The room was furnished only with a dark wooden chair, its two arms equipped with sturdy leather straps, a plank-bed secured to the wall by two clamps, and, in the center, a zinc tub filled with water. Nothing more.

The Royal Guard had bound Curzio's wrists with the two straps. Little more than thirty, the poor farmer had not been born to lead the life of a bandit. For him, the family was the center of the universe, but he had been forced to go into hiding and increase the ranks of Vassallo's band because of a dispute he'd had with his master, Baron Adragna.

Now imprisoned in the chair, Curzio raised his head and saw Captain Lorenzo Costa, in his impeccable blue uniform, approaching with a blackened medal resting in his palm.

"Do you recognize it?" the captain asked, turning the medal over so that Curzio could see both sides. Since Curzio seemed to be ignoring him, he repeated more vehemently, "Do you recognize it?"

Curzio looked at the medal, and then looked up and nodded.

"Whom did it belong to?" Captain Costa pressed.

"You know who, Captain. My brother, Salvatore," Curzio replied, his eyes growing moist.

"You know what happened to your brother, don't you?"

He shook his head "no" and lied, because word that Salvatore had died in the blaze at Marquis Bellarato's palazzo had spread not only through the valleys of Salemi but also even beyond the Madonie Mountains.

"Your brother first emasculated Marquis Bellarato, then murdered him like a dog," the captain summarized. "Too bad he too was killed by an unforeseen event: the fire that the marquis himself may have started when trying to defend himself. But these are things that everyone knows by now." Costa moved close to Curzio's ear and whispered, "What I want from you is information that few, except those directly involved, know." Those words made Curzio, who was not a lionhearted soul, shiver. "Both of you were members of Gaetano Vassallo's gang. It's clear that someone first ordered Vassallo to make the socialist politician Nicola Geraci disappear, and then, just to confuse the investigators, sent your brother to kill Marquis Bellarato, since Salvatore had a score to settle with him."

"Vassallo has nothing to do with these events," Curzio mumbled, though not very convincingly.

"So tell me: Were you present when Gaetano Vassallo met with Rosario Losurdo?" the captain asked.

"What does that have to do with anything?"

"And by chance, isn't Losurdo Prince Ferdinando Licata's gabellotto?" Costa persisted.

"I'm not saying another word. You're trying to set me up; you want to put words in my mouth that I don't want to say. I don't know anything about this." And he shut his mouth defiantly.

"We'll see about that," was Captain Lorenzo Costa's only response.

Curzio then got a personal introduction to the tub found in the middle of the room. It was one of the most common methods used at the time to force suspects to confess to things they would otherwise never have confessed to.

The prisoner was made to undress completely, and then, summer or winter, he was plunged into icy water. The tub was too small for him to fit in entirely. His arms and legs, which were left dangling, were secured with wire to the sides of the tub, where metal rings had been specially welded. Immersed in salt water, the unfortunate victim would then be flogged with a scourge made from dried, braided ox tendons. The lashes stung more because of the salt water, but in return they did not leave any marks. If the man managed to resist the whipping—since often they had nothing to confess—the torturers would rip out his beard or mustache, one hair at a time, then with pliers move on to his nails, and finally burn the soles of his feet. If he still refused to talk, then it was time for the electric current, applied to his most delicate, intimate parts. During the interims, a funnel was shoved in his mouth and, with his nostrils pinched, he was forced to swallow salt water until his stomach distended grotesquely.

Though this method would have made even the Jesuits of the Inquisition blanch, it managed to contain the spread of criminality and the rise of subversive organizations in Sicily well past the end of fascism.

Curzio Turrisi did not experience all the variations of the *cassetta*, or "box," as the tub was referred to in jargon. He was only able to endure it until they started tearing out his whiskers; then he succumbed and said he was willing to sign any document. Captain Costa then personally dictated a statement accusing Gaetano Vassallo's band of having carried out the two murders on behalf of an anonymous third party. That confession was enough to give Lorenzo Costa license to operate above the law itself.

The strategy used by the captain to find Gaetano Vassallo was the same one he had used to capture Curzio Turrisi. Searching for the bandit in the mountains would have been like trying to find the proverbial needle in a haystack. So instead of hunting him on his own terrain, where the chances of success would be much slimmer, Costa decided to keep the dwellings and farms of Vassallo's relatives under surveillance from a distance. Especially the homestead of Geremia Vassallo, the brother who, with his wife, Rosalia, had taken on the care of the newborn twins and the two other children: Jano, the oldest, seven years of age, and Giovanni, a year younger.

Geremia, a sharecropper on the estate of a nobleman from Palermo, lived on a modest farm in Borgo Guarine, not far from Montagna Grande, the mountains where Vassallo's band gathered when they had to plan some villainous deed.

Captain Lorenzo Costa was able to wait. He knew from experience that it was only a matter of time, weeks or months maybe, but sooner or later the rat would return to its hole, triggering the trap.

Finally, one evening in late July, the trap sprang shut—and by the following morning, Salemi's world would never be the same again.

Chapter 16

– 1939 –

Ferdinando Licata was packing his own suitcase for the trip to Trapani. As he threw his personal effects into the leather bag, he found himself wondering whether he had more friends or enemies. It wasn't the first time such strange thoughts had surfaced. At first he had driven them back into the black hole of the mind, but recently his brain had begun to embellish them, and sometimes despair prevailed, casting him into a deep state of gloom. Even the trips to Trapani to which he periodically treated himself had become the source of poignant reflection. Up until ten years ago, those trips had taken place weekly. Then he had begun to spread the visits out to a couple of times a month, and then once a month. But finally he'd let a good three months go by since he'd last set off. He considered the constant packing and unpacking one of the many failures of his life. Turning his back on a family of his own, a wife, a child, was a decision that at the beginning hadn't cost him much concern. On the contrary, when he saw married men his age continually complaining about their wives, he felt privileged. He had managed to dodge the snares of marriage and boasted about it when other aristocrats held him up as an example. And all thanks to his sister Lavinia, who took care of running the palazzo.

Over the years, he had become a devoted customer at Francesca Gravina's brothel, known as one of the most exclusive in all of Sicily. He'd had sexual relations with young girls experiencing their first encounter as well as with more mature ladies, not to mention noblewomen who in the privacy of Francesca's alcoves sought to commit adultery with one of the island's most renowned men, though few people could claim to truly know him. With some of these women, the encounters had even gone on for several months. But when he began to see that feelings were outweighing passion, Ferdinando Licata always managed to very gently break the hold and continue the life of a perpetual bachelor.

Lately his visits to Francesca's establishment had become increasingly sporadic. His mind was not as blithe and carefree as it was when he was young.

That day, as he packed his suitcase, a hundred questions arose in his mind. He felt an overwhelming need for affection other than the kind he had known so far, a deep attachment that only a son can give. For some time now the many mistakes he'd made in his lifetime had been rising to the surface of his consciousness. The prince had attempted to silence those inner voices, but so far without success. He had hoped that the humiliation of the *lavatio*, the washing of his peasants' feet, could produce the desired result, but it had all been useless.

He decided that after the visit to Trapani he would face Manfredi and tell him that he could no longer sell him the Madonnuzza land. He would go back on his word. And what is a man if he loses his honor and dignity? Rosario Losurdo, his partner in villainy, had asked him for a favor. He could have refused him, he had the power and authority.

For days and days Ferdinando Licata was undecided whether to follow the path of honor or that of expediency. In the end he chose the path of least resistance. Crime is an unyielding partner. You can only break away if you are very strong and determined to free yourself, despite having to suffer the consequences.

So he climbed into the Alfa Romeo, and, saying good-bye to his sister, Lavinia, headed for Trapani. He was still driving along the back road in the direction of Calatafimi, before reaching the state highway, when he saw the Fiat pickup belonging to Jano's gang of Black Shirts emerge from a side road at moderate speed and proceed in his direction. Only the driver was in the cab, sniggering while glancing into the external rear-view mirror to see what was happening behind him. In the truck bed were five rowdy thugs, shouting and waving clubs in the air. Ferdinando Licata followed their gaze to see who they were harassing. Finally, he realized who the object of their excitement was. He recognized the unmistakably thick beard of Ciccio Vinciguerra, the destitute farmworker who had been at the Hundred Saints ceremony. His hands were tied to a long rope attached to the truck's tailgate. The poor man had been running for countless miles, pulled along like an animal, trying to avoid falling to the ground and being dragged. He was exhausted and had no more strength left. His torturers' sadism, however, was well calibrated, because the truck was moving at a slow enough speed so that Vinciguerra would not stumble and fall. Seeing what was happening, Licata made an abrupt U-turn, accelerated, passed the truck, and with a sharp swerve stopped his car crossways on the road. Since the driver was distracted by his comrades' shrieks, Licata thought it wise to run toward the truck and shout for him to stop. When the driver finally noticed the obstacle, he stepped on the brake as hard as he could. The pickup slid a few yards along the dirt road. The five in back, taken by surprise, tumbled over one another on the bottom of the truck bed. Meanwhile, Ciccio Vinciguerra kept running from inertia and collapsed behind the stopped vehicle, worn out, his lungs gasping for breath.

Licata went to him and began undoing the rope's knots. Meanwhile, Jano appeared over the side of the truck bed, enraged by the unexpected occurrence.

"What the hell is going on?" he yelled, his eyes bulging from their sockets. He jumped down with his club in hand, ready to use it. "Who the devil is butting in?" he hollered.

Prince Ferdinando Licata rose to his full height. Jano came up to his chin. The prince was angrier than he was.

"Jano, I'm going to report you to the mayor! This man is one of my farmhands! You are forbidden to lay a hand on any of my laborers, do you understand?" he shouted in a commanding voice.

Meanwhile, Jano had been joined by the other four Black Shirts.

Nunzio, Manfredi's son, appeared to be the most ruthless one. "Jano, let's give him a little taste of our good old castor oil. Then we'll see if he still feels like shouting."

Licata wasn't intimidated. "Nunzio, how dare you talk about me that way? You're a disgrace to your family."

Nunzio was about to hurl himself at Licata, but Jano stopped him. "Hold it, Nunzio. We can't lay a finger on the prince. But on *him*, we can." He pointed to Ciccio Vinciguerra, who had risen from the ground and still short of breath, was unable to speak. "He said that fascism has done more harm than good in Sicily. I heard it with my own ears. That's called *disfattismo:* defeatism!"

"But we're not at war. 'Defeatism!'" Licata repeated scornfully. "Worry about maintaining public order and don't go picking on some poor man." Prince Licata finished undoing the knots, and then took Vinciguerra by the shoulders and helped him walk as they started toward his car. "I'll take him home and pretend that none of this ever happened."

"Hey, he can't treat us that way!" This time it was Ginetto, the youngest of the gang, who spoke up.

The prince heard him and turned around. "Ginetto, grow up for once and go to work. Your parents are sick and tired of supporting you."

"Calm down, boys, let's all stay calm," Jano said with authority. Then he shouted to the prince, who had now reached his car. "Prince Licata, there's no room for mummies like you anymore." The five of them laughed uproariously at the jibe. Nunzio gave Jano a slap on the back, satisfied with how he had resolved the dispute in their favor. Ginetto and the others also exchanged rowdy punches to underscore their victory.

At that time, it didn't take much to make young troublemakers feel all-powerful.

Ferdinando Licata got in his Alfa Romeo and went back the way he had come, headed for Borgo Tàfile, where Rosario Losurdo's farmstead was located. Ciccio Vinciguerra needed protection, so Licata thought he should be moved from the Dell'Orbo estate, belonging to Prince Moncada, to the Castellana lands, belonging to Losurdo.

When they reached the farm, he found Losurdo negotiating the sale of some horses with two brokers who'd come from Marsala, on Sicily's west coast. Manfredi, his chief campiere, was helping Losurdo bargain. Seeing the prince arrive, Losurdo excused himself to his guests and went to meet him.

"Weren't you supposed to go to Trapani?" he asked the prince, surmising that there had been some mishap. Then he turned to Vinciguerra, who seemed more dead than alive. "Ciccio. What are you doing in the car with the prince?"

"*U patri* saved my life," the man said, getting out of the car.

"Ciccio never says a word, but when he does he gets in trouble," the prince declared as he approached Rosario Losurdo.

"What happened?"

"Jano and his buddies took him," the prince explained in a loud voice so that everyone around could hear him. "They tied him to their truck with a rope and made him run through the countryside of Salemi." Manfredi had also approached the group, though he remained a few feet away. The prince saw him and went over to him. "I'm sorry to have to tell you this, but your Nunzio was there as well." The prince raised his voice, something he rarely did: "He disrespected me, do you understand? Me! He urged the others to give me castor oil! Nunzio, your son!" He tried to calm down. "I held Nunzio in my arms, didn't I, Manfredi? What have these children of ours become! Who recognizes them anymore! They've lost all respect and dignity. And they make their fathers lose it as well."

Manfredi was mortified. He would have liked to disappear beneath the clods of soil if he could. *U patri* was right. Nunzio had lost respect for his elders. It was those revolutionary new ideas that the fascists had put in his head.

"Who knows what Jano and those other degenerates made him think he could become?" The prince had promised Manfredi possession of a plot of land in the Madonnuzza. Manfredi hoped with all his heart that the prince would not change his mind after what had happened.

But he was mistaken. Ferdinando Licata decided to take advantage of the situation to save a little of his own dignity. In fact, he took him by the arm and drew him away from the others to say in a regretful, albeit falsely so, tone: "I made you a promise a few weeks ago. And I was going to honor it when I returned from Trapani. But this incident really offended me. You can't be a benefactor to those who don't respect you."

"But *patri*, you know how loyal and grateful I am to you. Nunzio, unfortunately, has latched on to that Jano like a leech. Damn him for what he did to you."

"Let me finish. I know you, and I know how loyal you are to me. But these presumptuous usurpers are our enemy, do you understand what I mean, Manfredi? I can't stand by and allow them to eat my bread. Traitors must be kept at a distance. Them and those like them. I'm sorry Manfredi, but they've gone too far, enough is enough. Either your son falls back in line, or you and your family will have to clear out of Salemi."

Those last words came crashing down on the poor man's head with the force of a maul, making him stagger. Manfredi was not accustomed to begging and swallowed the ultimatum. "Don't worry, I'll make sure he listens to reason."

"Good." The prince left him and went over to Losurdo, who, though he stood aside, had overheard the entire conversation. "Our friend Vinciguerra will no longer go to the Dell'Orbo estate. He'll stay here with you. Replace him with someone else. I don't want what I saw today to happen to him again."

Losurdo nodded, and Licata went back to his car. "Let's see if I can manage to set off now." He started the car, leaving everyone stunned. Losurdo and the others followed him with their eyes until the dust vanished behind the curve.

Manfredi had still not recovered from the prince's outburst. As it gradually sank in that he would not be able to own that piece of land, his anger against his son Nunzio became more and more acute and his rage uncontrollable. Nunzio had to put an end to his dreams of power.

Because of him, the hope of a lifetime had dissipated like fog in spring. But perhaps all wasn't lost. The prince had made it clear that if he were to bring Nunzio back into the fold, he would reconsider his decision. No question about it: he absolutely had to force Nunzio to disown that group of fanatics.

He jumped onto the horse-drawn buggy and reached Salemi in time to see the truck arrive in town, back from its punitive mission against Ciccio Vinciguerra.

Manfredi stood up in the carriage, holding the reins of the mare taut.

"Nunzio!" he shouted to his son as he was getting out of the truck. Jano was not with them because he had decided to go and hang around Mena's farm. Nunzio recognized his father's voice and turned around.

"What do you want?" he said rudely.

Manfredi, despite his size, leaped from the buggy with uncommon agility. Still holding the whip in his hand, he approached his son and dealt him a sharp lash on the face, leaving a bloody mark on his cheek. Nunzio's three buddies immediately pinned the father's arms, but the young man gestured for them to let him go, and they released their hold.

"That was to remind you of the manners I taught you. They tell me you don't show respect to anyone anymore—you and your fine companions," Manfredi said, trembling with rage.

"Listen, old man, watch what you say. Otherwise I'll give you a taste of my wooden club." It was Ginetto who spoke with such cockiness.

"That's exactly what I mean," Manfredi had now softened his tones, hoping to get through to his son. "You're not like that. You can't fake a cynicism you never had."

"You, what do you know about me? I grew up under your strict rule, and you taught me to bow my head before everyone. Now it's other people who have to bow down to me. Which do you think is better? Eh, Papa? You were raised like a mule who puts up with being beaten. But the future is ours now." He laughed in his father's face and began singing the fascist anthem "Giovinezza," as his friends joined him.

"Because of you I can't have the Madonnuzza farm."

"The savings of a lifetime for a piece of land that even the lizards won't go near. Do you realize what a miserable beggar you've been your whole life?"

At that affront, Manfredi was about to strike Nunzio's face with his whip again, but this time the young man was prepared. Blocking his father's arm with one hand as he was about to swing, he slapped him with his other hand. Manfredi staggered, more from shock than from the actual force of the blow. He would never have believed that his own son would hit him. He stepped back. "Nunzio, my curse on you and your seed for seven generations to come. You are dead to me, to your mother, and to your brother." So saying, he climbed onto the buggy and rode away while the Black Shirts' battle hymns resounded behind him, brazenly bellowed by Nunzio's pals.

Nunzio, however, had fallen silent. He watched the buggy disappear down the lane, deeply disturbed by his father's curse.

Chapter 17

In small rural towns, where most social encounters took place at Sunday morning mass, rare family gatherings or religious feasts celebrating the patron saint, a movie in the piazza provided the occasion for young and old alike to experience an exciting collective dream.

The Fiat Balilla with the films and projector was due to arrive in Salemi in the early afternoon. During the winter, the projection was set up in the town hall, while in the summer months Piazza del Duomo served as an ideal setting, with the screen positioned where the Corso began. That day, however, it threatened to rain, so the town clerk decided to hold the screening in the municipal chamber.

Once the Fiat had parked in front of the town hall, a thousand arms volunteered to carry the sensitive equipment inside. Already half the town was gathered in the piazza to watch the ritual of mounting the screen and setting up the projector. To the kids, the cans of film, those curious round aluminum canisters with raised ribs, seemed like magic boxes. And the scraps of film that the projectionist sometimes had to cut to match the images to the sound were fought over by the children, occasionally setting off lengthy battles.

The movie screening had by now become a monthly highlight that few people in town wanted to miss. Many even came from neighboring villages, especially if the film was a love story. The movie announced for that afternoon was *Casta Diva*, a drama directed by Carmine Gallone and released several years earlier, starring Màrtha Eggerth, a Hungarian actress well known for the numerous films she had made in Italy.

All the girls in the area had obtained their parents' permission to watch the film, accompanied by a brother or a family friend. The movie was set in the nineteenth century and told the story of a great ill-fated love affair between the composer Vincenzo Bellini and a singer. The dramatic ending involved the death of the heroine, the chaste goddess of the title. Mena Losurdo had managed to get her father's permission to attend. She and her brothers, Michele and Donato, along with their mother, Rosita, had arrived in their buggy early so they could get the best seats.

Of course, every viewer had to bring his own chair, otherwise he would have had to watch the movie standing in the back of the hall.

As soon as the room was set up and the doors opened, the crowd of villagers began to flow inside in an orderly manner, carrying chairs and benches, which were arranged in front of the sheet hanging from the ceiling on a long bamboo rod. Everyone who entered greeted friends and family, and the whole audience responded ironically to the greeting, like a chorus. The boys gave one another big slaps on the head and then hid behind their neighbors' backs. Some threw spitballs in the air, which struck the heads of those in the front rows. Annachiara had also entered the hall with her daughter Ester and her son, Saro. The Black Shirts from the local fascist combat league, Ginetto, Nunzio, Prospero, and Quinto, also showed up, but nobody paid any attention to them. The magic of cinema was able to bring everyone together.

Jano arrived soon afterward. He had come without a chair; nevertheless, he found someone who reluctantly gave up his seat. His gaze wandered around the room until he finally spotted his prey: Mena was a few rows ahead and hadn't yet noticed him. Jano sat down, and then the lights went out, and the cheerful hubbub died down. Whistling and hissing were heard, but when the screen lit up, a perfect silence immediately fell over the room.

At the end of the first half the lights came back on and everyone stood up to stretch their legs, stiff from remaining stock-still. It was then that Mena turned toward the audience behind her, glancing around for some friendly face.

The girl was wearing a close-fitting, dark pullover sweater that accentuated her appealing curves. For an instant, her clear, intense gaze met Saro's, but she looked away immediately so as not to blush.

A few rows behind was someone who couldn't take his eyes off her: Jano. The young man shifted so she could see him, and then smiled. "Ciao, Mena, enjoying it?"

Mena noticed him and waved back. "I'm afraid it's going to end badly."

"You'll see, she'll manage to get him to marry her."

"Let's hope so. Bellini was a real dolt," she declared, referring to the character in the film.

Jano smiled at her characterization. Then the lights dimmed and went out altogether before the second half began.

When "The End" appeared on the white sheet, a lot of the women and girls tucked away the handkerchiefs they'd been using to wipe away tears over the protagonist's death. Even after the lights came on again, everyone in the room kept silent, as if hoping that the film might keep going, presenting a more satisfying ending. But then a young man began clapping, and everyone chimed in with hearty applause. People began flowing out of the room. It was not an easy matter, considering all the chairs and benches that had to be carried out.

Jano took advantage of the confusion to approach Mena. "You were right: she dies at the end," he said with a smile.

"All these movies end the same way," she said, her eyes still shiny, "If life were that way, it would be a perpetual tragedy."

"But you cried; tell the truth."

"Don't be silly. It takes more than that to move me," the girl lied brazenly.

"Like what?" Jano challenged, blocking her way and forcing her to stop, as people continued to flow around them.

But Mena sidestepped him and went on walking. "Jano, what's gotten into your head tonight?"

"Mena, I'd like—"

But he wasn't able to finish the sentence because Rosita, a few steps ahead, turned around and called, "Mena, hurry up! It's about to rain."

"I'm coming, Mama!" she called back to her mother. Then she turned to Jano. "What did you want to tell me?"

He touched her arm and said, "You look beautiful tonight and—"

But the legs of a chair slid in between the two, forcing them to separate. Jano was irritated and smacked the chair heatedly. "Watch where you're going, pipsqueak!" he shouted.

The boy who was holding the chair against his chest faltered, partly because he was carrying a second one balanced unsteadily on his head. "Oh, I didn't see you," Saro tried to apologize, throwing a mischievous glance at Mena.

Seeing his funny position, she burst out laughing. Then, leaving the two to face each other, she ran off to join her mother who was outside by now.

"You did that on purpose," Jano hissed in his face.

Saro tossed it off as a joke, however. "But I really didn't see you. Besides, Jano, you should get over your paranoia." So saying, he continued on toward the door, leaving Jano standing in the middle of the room, foaming with rage. Meanwhile, a steady drizzle began to fall.

The arrival of the movie in Salemi had brought all activities in the town to a standstill. Those who hadn't gone to the town hall for the showing were few and far between: mainly the elderly, those in poor health, and individuals who seized the opportunity to attend to matters that they didn't want anyone to know about. One of these was Nunzio, who had sunk into a deep depression after quarreling with his father. He needed to confide in someone who was very close; a friend—or something more than a friend. He took advantage of the film's screening, when Salemi's streets emptied for a few hours, to go and visit Tosco.

The former servant of Marquis Bellarato lived like a virtual recluse, in a beautiful, five-room house that had been a gift from the marquis at the beginning of their life together.

When he heard someone knock, Tosco felt his heart leap. No one ever came to his house. But deep down, he always hoped that Nunzio would remember him.

He opened the door, and when he saw the young man, he threw his arms around him, hugging him tightly. But Nunzio, as usual, brusquely pushed him away and went in, closing the door behind him.

"At last, you've come! It's been a month. I can't stand not being with you," Tosco whined as his visitor entered the dining room. Nunzio didn't answer him. He was silent, looking around at the antique furniture, the precious silver, the enameled watches, the ceramic knickknacks, the Liberty-style lamps: Tosco had filched them all from the marquis's palazzo, considering them his own, given that he was the natural son of the marquis's father.

The elder marquis had fathered him with one of his maids, who conceived while his wife was expecting Pietro. The two boys, nearly the same age, had grown up together. They'd played the same games, studied the same books. But although they were half brothers, Tosco became the servant and Pietro the marquis.

Pietro Bellarato discovered his deviant nature as the years went by and, unable to vent his brutality on women, he turned to his favorite plaything: Tosco. The young man, pathologically attracted to his half brother whose position he would have liked to be in, could think of nothing better than to satisfy all his most shameful desires, which was the ruination of them both. At little more than twenty years of age, Marquis Pietro Bellarato had become a kind of satyr, always on the prowl for new, transgressive experiences. He made his half brother dress as a woman, in his mother's clothes, or had him wear a horse harness and rode him stark naked. But soon enough they exhausted the range of perversions, and the plaything began to bore him.

So one fine day Tosco was set aside, like an old whore, though he hadn't yet reached twenty.

For Tosco, being rejected by his adored Pietro was the most traumatic moment of his young life. Several times he thought of suicide, but then, as often happens in such situations, he threw himself into the arms of the first one to come along. And the youths in town were merciless: they passed him around from one to the other, as if he were the town slut. They took advantage of his state of mental confusion, and one night they subjected him to an exceptionally brutal ordeal. He found himself at the bottom of a slimy pit, completely naked, not even aware of what was happening, because the ghastly wine they'd made him guzzle had completely muddled him. Then, like a distant echo, he heard mocking laughter from the edge of the pit and felt warm jets of an acidic liquid stream over his face, mouth, nose, every inch of his body. And his persecutors did not stop at that revolting act of cruelty. In the uncertain light of the moon, he glimpsed someone at the edge of the pit who, still snickering, had lowered his pants. But a commanding voice put an end to those scornful laughs and the pack, having now had their fill of nasty games, backed down.

A strong hand helped him pull himself out of the hole and led him to a nearby stream, where he could cleanse himself of all the affronts he'd had to endure. He stayed in the water for a long while. Then Nunzio, one of Manfredi's sons, took him back to the marquis's palazzo, where he was finally able to get some rest.

That night, strangely enough, Tosco found inner peace again. He started dreaming up a thousand tender fantasies about the one who would replace Pietro in his mind. Nunzio had been so kind to him, and he was so young. By means of countless subterfuges, they continued to see each other, although Nunzio, to avoid being teased by his buddies, behaved very coldly toward him in public.

"Have you eaten? Can I fix you something?" Tosco asked.

Nunzio's attention was attracted by a couple of leather straps with small bells attached, resting on a chair. He picked them up and tinkled the bells. "What are these?"

Tosco took them from him and hid them in a drawer. "Never mind."

"What are those bells? Who gave them to you?" Nunzio persisted.

Tosco took his arm. "Are you jealous?"

"Of course not! Come on, tell me. Is there someone else?"

"No, nobody. It's your friends' bright idea. Don't tell me you didn't know."

"I don't know anything about it, I swear."

"Your friend Jano gave them to me. I'm forced to wear them on my wrists and ankles every time I go out. He told me: 'So when people hear you coming, they can run away. Because you faggots are worse than the plague.' Now I only go out when the vegetable cart comes and I have to buy something. A good woman from the parish church takes care of the rest."

"I'm sorry."

Tosco went to hug him again. "I can't take it anymore. Help me. Don't abandon me!" His cry of despair pierced Nunzio' heart like a spear. And to think that he had gone to him seeking a little comfort. Then, as if reading his thoughts, Tosco looked up and wiped his eyes. "You're sad too. What happened to you?"

"The usual quarrel with my father. Only this time he put a curse on me."

"What did you do to him?"

"I didn't do anything. It was that bastard, Prince Licata, who went back on his word. He had promised my father a piece of the Madonnuzza estate. For my father, who never had anything in his life, owning that land would be the reward for a lifetime of hardship."

"The prince went back on his word? I can't believe it! Was it perhaps because of you?"

"Yeah, it's my fault, because I belong to the fascist combat league."

"That's the only reason? You must have affronted the prince in some way, for him to break his promise."

"We roughed up Ciccio Vinciguerra."

"Who?! *U pisci*? But he's of no consequence."

"When he talks, he says things against our Duce. We had to punish him."

"Ferdinando Licata is a tough bastard. But in times like these, no one is untouchable anymore," Tosco remarked. "You'll see, sooner or later he too will make a misstep, and then your father will be able to have his piece of land."

He hugged Nunzio and whispered, "Will you stay here tonight?"

"No. I only have an hour before the movie ends."

"Too bad. We'll have to hurry then."

Later, when the screening was over, Nunzio met up with Jano as he was heading home with Ginetto.

Jano was irritated and walked along in silence. When he was in that mood, his comrades knew it was wise to leave him alone. But Nunzio approached him just the same and said, "I need to talk to you."

"Nunzio, you missed the movie."

"Actually, I had things to do."

"With some gorgeous babe?" Ginetto butted in.

"I had a quarrel with my father."

"I know. Ginetto told me everything. That prince is becoming more and more of a pain in the ass."

"Him and his gabelloto," Nunzio added.

"Losurdo has one good thing going for him, though," Jano corrected him with an insinuating smile.

"Which is?"

"He has a daughter named Mena." He smiled at the thought of how beautiful she was. "So we don't touch Losurdo. And the prince is still too powerful. Let's not make our lives difficult."

"Easy for you to say. Meanwhile, because of your bullshit, I'm the one who's worse off," Nunzio burst out.

Jano clapped him on the shoulder, stopping him. "Hey, pal, I don't bullshit," he said, pointing a finger in his face. "If you don't like what we do, you're free to pull out. Just be careful you don't cross me."

"Come on, Jano, Nunzio's father is a fool," Ginetto interceded to soothe his companions.

"Ginetto's right. My father is a nobody. And I'm getting all worked up over nothing."

"That's better, my friend." Jano threw an arm around his shoulders. "All of us have one thing in common: our fathers, who are assholes." And with that, the three walked on and were swallowed up by the dark of night, laughing uproariously as if nothing had happened between them.

Chapter 18

Evening hours at Salemi's carabinieri station were interminable. After six o'clock, Brigadier Costanzo Felici and Vice Brigadier Rocco Trigona, together with two recruits, were forced to live as virtual prisoners in the small headquarters. Only rarely did they get to go out and mingle with some townspeople with whom they had managed to make friends.

The two shared a room, where they slept and rested up during their off-duty hours. A second room was occupied by the other two conscripted recruits. The adjacent kitchen had space for a large table, where they spent most of their free time, that is when they didn't have to be on call for Chief Brigadier Mattia Montalto. Costanzo Felici, a Neapolitan, served as the cook; he knew his way around pasta sauces and eggplant parmigiana like a five-star master chef.

That year, the old folks in Salemi said they couldn't recall ever having such a dry, stifling summer. Only late at night did the temperature make sleeping possible. That's why Costanzo Felici and Rocco Trigona had lingered at Mimmo Ferro's tavern that night, playing cards with some friends. It was very late when they returned to the station, a bit tipsy after having downed more than a few glasses of wine.

Before going to bed, Costanzo whipped up a mountain of spaghetti *al sugo* for himself and his colleague. The two recruits had already been asleep for some time.

While Costanzo was draining the pasta and Rocco, with earphones in his ears, was trying to find a music station on the crystal radio, a rock suddenly broke through the window and landed beside Costanzo. Startled, he dropped the enameled pot, burning his hand. Corporal Trigona, absorbed in listening to the music, didn't notice a thing. Only when he saw his friend move cautiously toward the window did he take off his headset.

"Costanzo—" he began, but he didn't finish the sentence because his friend gestured for him to keep quiet and turned out the light.

He joined Felici near the window with the broken pane. They peered out but found the street deserted. So Costanzo Felici headed firmly toward the door, followed by the vice brigadier. They went out into the little square, their automatics in hand.

It was four in the morning, and the streets of the town were sunk in deep silence. The brigadier motioned to his colleague that they should go back inside. They returned to the kitchen, and Felici bent down to retrieve the rock. Or rather the sheet of lined paper wrapped around the rock. They sat at the table and smoothed out the sheet as best they could to read the message. The writing was shaky and uncertain. But the message could be read clearly: "There is a surprise for *vossia* at Borgo Guarine."

"Do you think we should wake the chief?" Costanzo Felici asked, worried.

"Let him sleep—it's nothing," Trigona replied smugly. "An anonymous note."

"But here in Sicily, anonymous notes are like gospel, you know?" His own words convinced the brigadier to wake Montalto, who lived in a two-room house with his wife, Lucia, in the center of Salemi. They had been married for five years now, but had not yet been blessed with a son and heir.

When he got to the station, the brigadier showed him the anonymous note, and Montalto decided that they should leave immediately for Borgo Guarine.

———

The sky was beginning to grow light, transforming the night's darkness into a muted blue. That time of day reminded Chief Montalto of numerous stakeouts, patiently lying in wait to surprise bandits hidden on some farm. He'd spent so many nights out in the open, he had lost count. When they came in sight of the Guarine farm, a light mist hung over the entire countryside. An eerie silence surrounded the place. All they could hear was the dull thud of their horse's hooves on the dirt road and the creaking of the buggy's wheels. Trigona, the vice brigadier, drew in the reins, and the horse stopped just outside the farm's limits. The three men got out of the buggy with pistols drawn. They approached with caution, but one detail immediately caught the chief's attention: the door of the house was partly open.

He pushed it and went in slowly, with Brigadier Felici looking over his shoulder, while Trigona circled to the back of the house. As soon as he entered, Montalto felt his stomach tighten. Illuminated by the first glimmers of daylight, he saw two corpses on the floor, two men lying on their back. One was unrecognizable due to stab wounds. Montalto approached and turned the man's head. He was unshaven, and his clothes stank of ashes. The other was also in need of a shave and wore hunting clothes. Montalto's longtime experience suggested that they must be bandits. He entered the kitchen. There the spectacle was even more horrifying. The Brigadier Felici, who was following him, felt a surge of nausea. The floor was smeared with blood and littered with body parts. A cleanly severed hand lay in front of one of two beds. The chief walked around a large table toward a fireplace, where he'd noticed shapeless masses. The stump of a human body was lying halfway inside the chimney. Revulsion washed over him when he saw that it was the body of a poor woman, every inch of her flesh ravaged. Montalto still didn't know what awaited him in the bedroom. When he get there he saw on the floor the body of a child, perhaps five years of age, his skull smashed.

"Chief! In here, quick!" The vice brigadier's voice roused him from what seemed like a nightmare. Rocco Trigona had remained in the kitchen. What could he have found that could be even more horrific?

Montalto's attention was drawn to a movement in the cradle. He walked over and saw one infant dead and another little bundle of flesh flailing its arms. He saw that the baby's face was swollen. He took her in his arms.

It was a baby girl: the twin of the child lying disjointed on the bed. Finally, the infant coughed convulsively and, as if a stopper obstructing her throat had been released, began wailing desperately. Taking a blanket from the cradle, Montalto wrapped the baby in it and held her close. He then turned toward the kitchen and nearly collided with Vice Brigadier Trigona, who, hearing the crying, rushed into the room.

"Chief—a baby?" he asked incredulously.

"A little girl," Montalto said, showing him the infant he held in his arms.

"Come see what I found." Trigona led him to the small bed in the kitchen and lifted the covers, motioning for him to look underneath.

Montalto handed him the baby, whom Rocco Trigona held somewhat awkwardly, then bent down and saw little Jano sleeping soundly, as though he'd fainted.

Felici and Trigona brought Jano and his infant sister to Dr. Ragusa's house. Annachiara had had her first child, Stellina, a few months earlier and temporarily welcomed Piera, the newborn, as another daughter. She remained with them until she was weaned, whereupon the court gave her up for adoption to a couple in Catania. The doctor examined Jano, but the child hadn't suffered any physical trauma, and that same day, he was taken to a close family friend, not far from town.

Around noon, Montalto, who had remained behind to collect evidence at the farm where the massacre had taken place, was joined by Captain Lorenzo Costa of the Royal Guard and a couple of his subordinates. Soon afterward, Ragusa also appeared, summoned by Montalto to give a clinical account of the cause of death and above all to report on the atrocities the woman had suffered. In addition, the public prosecutor, accompanied by two of his deputies, arrived from Santa Ninfa.

Ragusa, after just a cursory look at the carnage, confirmed that following the killing of the man and children, the woman had been raped several times. What she had gone through was unimaginable. Besides being raped, she had been tortured with a knife and bore shallow cuts all over her body. The two men found in the doorway, however, had been killed outside the farmhouse and later dragged inside. The marks left by heavy boots were obvious. Outside a thorough search also identified the points at which they had been attacked and killed.

All the inhabitants of the neighboring farms came running when they learned of the tragedy. They all knew the sacrifices that Geremia and Rosalia had made to raise Gaetano Vassallo's children after Teresina, his wife, had died giving birth to the twins. That atrocious massacre added tragedy to never-ending tragedy. But who could have done something so heinous? The peasants, men and women alike, watched in silence the comings and goings of the experts, the carabinieri and detectives who kept going in and out of the farmhouse carrying exhibits and material evidence that might be useful to the investigation.

Hidden among the crowd was Gaetano Vassallo. Barefoot, in ragged clothes, with a filthy cap on his head and a long beard, he blended in among the numerous farmers crowding around the scene of the bloodbath. He was heartbroken but clearheaded as never before. Seeing what had happened almost made him howl in pain. His thoughts went back to a year before, when he had seen his wife die in his arms. Now this new horror was added to a sorrow that had not yet healed, and it tore at his heart. He would have liked to run into the house and hold his children tight, but destiny denied even that simple comfort to him.

He had to keep his nerves steady. He had to find out who was responsible for that butchery. Then he would take his revenge. Whoever was behind the massacre would curse the day his mother had brought him into this world.

He tried to catch a name, a clue, anything the carabinieri might say. But he couldn't afford to draw suspicion upon himself, so he wandered among the little knots of peasants, pretending to be curious, asking first one then the other what had happened. He also had to be careful to avoid meeting the eyes of anyone who might know him, even though in his beggar's disguise it would be hard to recognize him.

After that ill-fated night, Vassallo felt as if he himself were dead. Consumed by guilt for not having been able to help his loved ones, he abandoned any idea of revenge and disappeared. No one ever heard any more about him, and some speculated that he'd hanged himself because he could no longer bear the weight on his conscience.

———

Chief Montalto discovered the trap door to the cellar, which had previously been perfectly hidden by the cradle. He walked through the entire tunnel before emerging two hundred yards away in a cave in the nearby mountain. The soil in some places had been recently disturbed. Cigarette butts indicated that someone had been waiting there for quite some time. By the end of his search, he had formed a clear idea of what had happened.

"I think Vassallo came to visit his family with these two felons," he said to Captain Costa, pointing to the two outlaws lying near the doorway. "Someone set a trap for him, but he managed to escape through the tunnel and that 'someone'—more than one, of course—took it out on his entire family."

"I wonder who could have hated him so vehemently," Captain Costa mused. "In any case, I wouldn't want to be in their shoes now. If Vassallo finds out who did this, he'll skin them alive with his own hands," he concluded with a shudder.

"There is only one justice, and that's divine justice. But whoever did this will have to answer to human justice as well," the chief brigadier agreed.

"But who could have such a deep-seated grudge against Vassallo?" Captain Costa purposely went on wondering.

"Vassallo has many friends who protect him, but just as many enemies who hate him. That outlaw has a pair of files filled with reports and accusations. Still, such savagery has never occurred around here."

Montalto thought for a long moment. "Yes, it's very unusual. These are people who come from outside." The chief brigadier was beginning to come closer to the truth.

"I have an idea, however," Captain Costa offered, to lead Montalto onto the desired track. "I heard from an informer that not so long ago Rosario Losurdo, Prince Ferdinando Licata's gabellotto, went to ask a favor of someone: guess who?"

"Vassallo?" Montalto deduced.

"The very one! And remember Marquis Bellarato, who was killed so atrociously in his palazzo that went up in flames?" The chief, all too aware of the incident, nodded. "Remember the charred body found in the palazzo, alongside the marquis?"

"Of course, I was the one who conducted the investigation. It was the corpse of Salvatore Turrisi," Montalto said.

"Right. Naturally, you know that Turrisi was a member of Vassallo's band and that he was there to perform the favor that Losurdo had asked of Vassallo, most certainly as ordered by Prince Licata."

"In fact, the prince had a vested interest in the marquis's death," Montalto remarked.

"Because the marquis had gotten in the way of the purchase of a certain estate," the captain went on. "The motive fits perfectly. At that point, Vassallo must have blackmailed the prince, and he decided to have Vassallo killed. Losurdo was sent to do the job. But when Vassallo escaped, he reacted ruthlessly against his family."

Chief Brigadier Montalto shook his head. "I'm not convinced. Around here, we're all farmers and laborers. This is the work of professional cutthroats. No one commits such a reckless act of butchery, unless he's an outsider and a swine."

Chapter 19

That morning, the town clerk, Michele Fardella, himself brought Mayor Lorenzo Costa the notes he had found wedged under the knocker of the town hall door.

"Two more anonymous notes," he told his former superior in the Royal Guard, placing the double-folded sheets on the desk.

Lorenzo Costa continued to leaf through the newspaper, *Il Giornale di Sicilia,* and didn't pay any attention to the notes.

Every day, at least two or three anonymous messages arrived at the town hall, through the oddest channels. Sometimes people were unhappy with how things were going, other times someone was denounced for having stolen someone else's animals, or, more prosaically, a betrayed lover exposed the duplicity of a woman who had dishonored him. All in all, the notes aptly represented the theater of everyday life in Salemi and the surrounding area.

"Do you have any orders for me this morning?" the trusted Fardella asked.

"No, Michele. You can go," the mayor told him. "When you leave, turn on the radio."

He tossed the newspaper on the desk and picked up the two notes. The first was carefully typed and signed "a group of employees." "How conscientious," the captain thought. Then, ensconced in his chair, he began reading.

"Your Excellency, We would like to inform you that Sicilian Insurance Company has fired all of its Jewish personnel, but ironically enough has kept its manager. The law should apply equally to everyone, especially fascist law, and we request that Your Excellency will take appropriate measures, since this is an abuse and contrary to the Duce's wishes.

"The manager has always been a tyrant, and he is no longer wanted at this firm, otherwise we will alert the proper authorities. Our respects . . ."

"Bastards, another headache to deal with," the mayor fumed, slamming the sheet of paper onto the desk. One way or another, the issue had to be resolved. But he would think about it tomorrow.

He opened the second anonymous note. This one was just a few lines written by hand, but when he finished reading it he straightened up in his chair, alarmed, and carefully read it again.

"Open Salvatore Turrisi's coffin, and you will find a nice surprise. If you guess who the real corpse is, they'll dub you a knight. A friend."

The mayor ran to the window to try to call back Michele Fardella. But the town clerk had already disappeared from view.

He read the note one more time and then let his memory travel back nineteen years. He recalled the murder of Marquis Bellarato, which was the reason he'd been sent from Palermo to Salemi in 1920. He remembered finding a second charred body, that of Salvatore Turrisi. Lorenzo Costa cursed the Sicilians and their habit of hiding behind anonymous notes. His sixth sense told him that the matter was covering up something very serious.

What joke did fate have in store for him?

Jano had become obsessed with Mena. The girl was able to make him forget his animosities and smoldering rage, and her good humor, irony, and no-nonsense ways stirred feelings that he had never felt for anyone, not even his mother. Was that perhaps love? Her lovely face, the green eyes that contrasted with her long black hair, made him feel almost dizzy. He couldn't get her out of his mind. He absolutely had to have her as his wife.

Jano was musing on these sweet thoughts as he sat hunched beside the window of the truck that Nunzio was driving, headed toward Borgo Fazio. They had to pick up some furniture for the mayor there.

They hadn't yet said a word since leaving Salemi. Nunzio was whistling a catchy little tune to keep himself company. Jano was studying the landscape in front of him when he saw a buggy pulled by an amber-colored mare appear around a curve, coming in the opposite direction. He recognized Mena immediately; there wasn't a woman in Salemi who could handle the reins as capably as she could. In fact, as soon as the girl saw the truck coming toward her, in the center of the roadway, she slowed the mare's pace and directed her to the side of the road.

"Slow down, slow down," Jano shook Nunzio, who was lost in his own thoughts.

Nunzio braked and steered the truck to the edge of the road. "Stop. It's Mena."

Even before the truck came to a halt, after passing the buggy, Jano leaped to the ground and turned back to the young woman, who had stood up.

"Mena. What a surprise. I never thought I'd meet you here." He walked over to the buggy, resting his hand on the iron handhold for climbing up.

"I brought lunch to my brothers," she said coolly.

Without giving her a chance to react, Jano got into the carriage and took the reins from her hands. "I'll take you home," he said and then turned to Nunzio, who was watching from the window of the truck. "You go on, I'll see you later."

He was as happy as a child over that unexpected meeting. The truck drove off, and only then did Mena realize that she was left alone with Jano.

"We can't ride together. If my father sees me, he'll tear me limb from limb," the girl said firmly.

But Jano had already whipped the mare, who, with a sudden jerk, started trotting briskly again, sensing a more authoritative hand guiding her. The buggy's lurch made Mena fall against Jano, who smiled and put his arm around her waist.

"Hey, Mena, don't get me all roused up, though."

"Don't touch me." She made him move his hand. "You're really determined to make me lose my honor today, aren't you, Jano?"

He laughed heartily and cracked the whip, making the mare pick up her pace.

"Being here with you is a dream. Do you know you've bewitched me? I'm always distracted while I'm working, because I'm thinking about your eyes." He tried to slow the horse's trot now, not wanting that enchanted moment to end too soon.

"I didn't know you worked," the girl teased him. He fell for it. "I'm a big shot, what do you think? You won't see me ending up like these yokels. A wife of mine will be looked up to and respected like a lady." He reached out to put a hand on her shoulder.

Mena, however, drew away from him and moved to the far end of the seat.

"Come on, don't be like that." Jano took both reins in one hand and, with his right hand, tried to pull the girl toward him. "My intentions are serious." His eyes blazed with desire, and with a tug he managed to grab hold of her.

Mena became more adamant. "Listen, I don't like this. Get out, now."

She realized that Jano was about to overstep his bounds.

Jano stopped the horse in the middle of the road and then turned to the girl, trying to take her by the shoulders and put his arms around her.

"Mena, I'm crazy about you. I want to marry you. Please, don't say no."

He tried to kiss her neck, but the girl twisted free.

"Jano, stop, for the love of God!" She struck him with her fists, but Jano, stirred by the contact with her soft skin, could no longer control himself.

"One kiss! Just one kiss! Mena, you'll see, it will be beautiful. You need someone like me . . . You'll like it."

Mena tried to break away and get out of the buggy. She stood up from the seat, but Jano grabbed her by the wrist, forced her to sit down again and threw himself on her. Mena cried out frantically and clawed his face with her fingernails. He drew back, rubbing the scratches. Mena watched him, terrified, and began whimpering.

Jano stopped the bleeding with his hand and sat up, incredulous.

"Forgive me! I beg you to forgive me! I told you: you drive me crazy, I don't know what came over me. Mena, I beg you to forgive me." Sincerely distraught, he took her hand and kissed it humbly, continuing to ask for her forgiveness.

Mena was truly frightened. She dabbed her hand with the edge of her blouse, wiping away the traces of blood left by Jano. Then in a faint voice she said, "Take me home now. My parents will be worried."

Jano, without another word, took the reins and signaled the mare, who resumed her rhythmic trot. They did not speak the rest of the way. Jano was trying to find a way to salvage the regrettable situation. With a handkerchief, he cleaned away the blood that had clotted over the scratches. In the distance he saw the houses of Borgo Tafele.

Mena recognized the trees and clusters of prickly pear surrounding the farm before he did.

A few minutes later, they entered the courtyard of the farmstead. Nicola, one of Manfredi's sons, left the cart he was using to transport cow dung out to the manure heap and ran to slow the horse, grabbing the mare by the bit. The figure of Rosita appeared at the kitchen window. Spotting Jano and seeing her daughter's face, the woman realized that something distasteful had happened. She went to meet the two, while

Rosario Losurdo hurried back to the farm from the toolshed, where he had seen Mena's buggy returning, though driven by Jano.

Rosita was the first to reach the two young people. "Mountains never meet—" the woman said to Jano.

"—but sooner or later, people do," the young man said, completing the proverb.

Rosita couldn't help but notice the bloody scratches on his cheek. "Did you hurt yourself?"

"A branch along the way, nothing serious."

Meanwhile, Rosario Losurdo joined them, worried as well about the unusual arrival. "Mena, did you get lost?"

The girl didn't answer. Lowering her eyes, she went into the house, followed by Rosita. Nicola took the opportunity to lead the horse and buggy toward the barn.

His daughter's silence alarmed Losurdo, who stiffened and took a step toward Jano.

"Jano, where's your horse? Should I begin to worry?" Then he focused on the marks on the young man's face. "What did you do to your cheek?"

Finally, Jano decided to speak: "You know how highly I regard you and how much I respect your entire family. I've seen how you raised your children. I am honored to be a friend of Michele and Donato." He uttered the last lie with his gaze down, not to give himself away. Then he looked up and met Rosario Losurdo's eyes. "I'm in love with Mena, and today I'm asking you formally for her hand. I have a good job, and I can support her in excellent style—"

"Wait, hold on, Jano. Don't say another word," Rosario interrupted him. He was still concerned. "Answer truthfully. Did something happen that can't be rectified?"

"Not at all. I respect Mena. I want to marry her," Jano replied brazenly.

Losurdo was relieved. "Well, I find it odd that my daughter hasn't told you."

Jano went on the defensive. "And what should she have told me?"

"Mena is already promised," Losurdo lied.

That statement was like a blow to Jano—worse, an insult. "Already promised?" he stammered.

With that disclosure, Rosario Losurdo hoped to get rid of him forever. But Jano wouldn't accept defeat. "It's me Mena loves."

"I don't believe Mena would have led you on to that degree; otherwise

I'll have to straighten her out but good! A serious young man like you shouldn't be teased." By this time, Losurdo was enjoying himself, toying with him like a cat with a mouse.

On top of it, Jano had no sense of humor whatsoever, so he didn't realize that Mena's father was taunting him.

"I'm sorry, Jano, if for a moment or two you thought otherwise. But cheer up! A fine fellow like you must have a thousand young women eager to marry him."

Jano was no longer listening to him. He was so struck by the revelation that he hadn't yet recovered. "And who is he?" he asked.

"Who?" Losurdo repeated.

"Who's the lucky man?" Jano asked again.

"The fiancé?" Losurdo asked. Now he was the one in difficulty.

"That's right, who is he? Do I know him?" Jano persisted.

Losurdo didn't know what to say. He scratched his head searching for a response. Then he remembered the boy who had cut his hair a few days ago; the one his daughter never missed a chance to look for at church or in town. "Saro. It's Saro!" But the next instant he regretted saying the name. He'd gotten the boy tangled up in a mess that could have serious consequences.

"Saro . . ." Jano repeated the name as if hypnotized. His eyes betrayed an inner fury. He turned and left the farmyard, even forgetting to say good-bye to Rosario Losurdo.

Chapter 20

— 1939 —

When the gravedigger finally struck the wooden coffin with his shovel, he nodded to the people standing around the rim of the pit to let them know he'd found what they were looking for. He continued digging around the coffin and eventually managed to secure two ropes beneath it before climbing out of the pit.

The town crier, Ninì Trovato, and three other old men assigned to cemetery operations grabbed the four ends of the ropes and struggled to raise up the coffin. Each one pulled without paying any attention to the others, causing the casket to rise to the surface lopsided, and there was a moment when Ninì almost let the rope slip out of his hands. The coffin tilted alarmingly, so the gravedigger had to go and give him a hand. Marshal Mattia Montalto did likewise, helping the elderly man opposite Ninì. Finally, the coffin emerged from the hole and was deposited on the ground.

Curzio Turrisi, brother of the deceased, Salvatore, had also been invited to the macabre ceremony. Curzio was now a free man, having paid his debt to the law with eleven years of harsh imprisonment. Present as well was the public prosecutor Tommaso Amato, who had authorized the exhumation at the insistence of the mayor, Lorenzo Costa. Also in attendance were Jano, representing the mayor, and Michele Fardella, Salemi's town clerk, who was to draft a report of the exhumation and was in fact armed with a fountain pen and paper. Dr. Bizzarri, who had taken over Dr. Peppino Ragusa's medical post, had also been summoned.

The gravedigger took his crowbar and easily unhinged the lid. After some effort, and with Ninì Trovato's help, he lifted the lid and gave a quick professional look inside before stepping away. The marshal was the first to approach, followed by Jano and then Curzio Turrisi.

Although nineteen years had passed since the day of the fire, what remained of the corpse hadn't rotted away, but seemed mummified. The blackened trunk of the body charred in the palazzo's blaze could be glimpsed beneath the tattered clothing. The skull, with its jaw wide open, seemingly mocking those present, was covered by a black film similar to parchment.

Dr. Bizzarri, puffing like a locomotive with his 220-pound bulk, bent over the corpse. "Strange. Was he embalmed?" he asked, bewildered.

"No," Nini Trovato spoke up, "it's a phenomenon of this terrain. I've found other mummified corpses like that in this cemetery. Dr. Ragusa said it's a physiochemical phenomenon produced by microorganisms present in the soil here, which is composed of dry sand."

Dr. Bizzarri listened to him, curious. He nodded and then straightened up from the casket. Finally, he ordered the gravediggers to transport the mummy to the cemetery's chapel.

"But why this sacrilege?" Curzio asked Michele Fardella, who at that moment, as the mayor's representative, was viewed as the highest-ranking figure among all those dignitaries. "Can't you leave him in peace even in death?"

"It's the law. We received a tip. It may not be your brother in the coffin," Fardella told him.

"Who else could it be? And after so many years, who do you think will care?" Curzio persisted glumly, stepping aside while two gravediggers, having placed the body in a gunnysack, headed for the graveyard's chapel.

"Actually, I have no basis of comparison to determine if the identity is truly that of the dead man," Dr. Bizzarri said to cover himself.

The marshal spoke up: "We have Salvatore Turrisi's file at the station. There should also be a passport-size photo. I'll get it to you."

"What I need is medical records and fingerprints, Chief. I can't do anything with a passport photo, sorry to have to tell you."

"I'll make it available to you in any case," said Marshal Montalto firmly.

Poor Dr. Bizzarri conducted a thorough analysis of the cadaver's abject remains, but could find nothing that would corroborate the theory that the body had been switched, as the anonymous note had implied. The body's height matched that of Salvatore Turrisi. The bones were intact, meaning that the deceased had not suffered any fractures. This confirmed the fact, maintained by his brother, that Salvatore had never in his life fallen and had never broken so much as a bone in his little finger. The fire had completely obliterated his fingertips, making it impossible to analyze his fingerprints. All in all, the note had all the earmarks of a hoax.

Jano and Michele Fardella reported the negative results of the autopsy to Mayor Lorenzo Costa. He, however, continued to argue that the anonymous note was telling the truth. Otherwise why would anyone bring up something that had happened almost twenty years ago?

Through one of those mysterious twists of fate that often, unbidden, give our lives a sudden turn, Marshal Mattia Montalto, a few afternoons later, went to Dr. Bizzarri to bring him Salvatore Turrisi's file.

The doctor thanked him for taking the trouble, opened the file, and absently scanned the records concerning the activities of the outlaw Turrisi. Then he took the ID photo and glanced at it briefly. Salvatore Turrisi was smiling, the way people smile in all passport photos.

Dr. Bizzarri was visibly startled.

"Doctor, what did you spot?" asked the marshal, noting his surprise.

The doctor turned the photo toward him and pointed to the mouth.

"I don't understand," the marshal hesitated.

"Don't you see here?" He pointed to the teeth. "Turrisi was missing his upper left incisor."

The marshal looked at the picture and noticed a small black space between two of Turrisi's teeth.

The doctor stood up and went to get the skull of the exhumed corpse. He brought it to the marshal and showed him the teeth. "You see? This cadaver has all his teeth in place. Not a single one is missing."

Marshal Montalto studied the photo again. There was no doubt about it. It couldn't be the same person. "The anonymous note was telling the truth."

"One hundred percent," the doctor concluded. "These are not the remains of Salvatore Turrisi."

———————

The news shook the town like an earthquake. Word that the body buried almost twenty years ago was not Salvatore Turrisi spread with lightning speed to every corner of Salemi and the Madonie.

"So then who is the person we found charred in Marquis Bellarato's palazzo?" Lorenzo Costa shouted to Michele Fardella, Marshal Mattia Montalto, and a stunned Jano, all gathered in town hall. "And what happened to Salvatore Turrisi?"

"And who is Marquis Bellarato's killer? Did he die in the fire, or is he still at large? And who is the charred corpse?" the marshal added. "Turrisi at least had a motive. We have to start all over again or else drop the case."

"Don't even consider it. People must not get the idea that we allow crimes to go unpunished or let murderers go unidentified. The command from Rome was clear: order above all," the mayor barked.

The marshal dutifully awaited instructions, which were promptly given.

"Montalto, I want on this table, by noon tomorrow, all reports relative to the period of the fire at Marquis Bellarato's palazzo. Let's say, everything that happened in Salemi two months before and two months after the fire. I myself will review the case. It is a categorical imperative that we now give a name to this corpse who for nineteen years has lain in Salvatore Turrisi's coffin."

The marshal nodded slightly and left the room.

———

In the following weeks, Mayor Lorenzo Costa very carefully pored over all the daily reports compiled by Marshal Montalto nineteen years earlier. By the end of the second week, he had formed a clear picture of the situation. To sum things up, he called for his right-hand man: Michele Fardella.

"My dear Michele, I now understand what happened nineteen years ago," he began in a patronizing tone. "You may not recall, but just three days after the fire, the wife of a certain Nicola Geraci reported her husband's disappearance to the carabinieri. Nicola Geraci was a socialist, a representative of the red leagues of Petralia Sottana, a good-for-nothing. But now I'll tell you something that will make you fall off your chair," he went on in a melodramatic whisper.

"I remember Nicola Geraci: he was a typical politician who never stopped talking," Michele Fardella said.

"Geraci had had words with Prince Ferdinando Licata. At a meeting in the town hall, the prince convinced the peasants that being socialists wouldn't do any of them any good. Nicola Geraci couldn't stand for that, and in front of the whole assembly he threatened the prince that sooner or later he'd make him pay for it."

"You never openly threaten a big shot. He didn't know what he was letting himself in for," Fardella said.

"He was a marked man. And three days later he disappeared from circulation. He never returned home to Petralia Sottana, to his wife, who is still crying over him. The body was never found." He studied the clerk closely, to detect by any facial movement whether he had reached the same conclusions that he himself had.

Michele looked at the mayor. "Are you saying that the charred body, the one found in Marquis Bellarato's palazzo, could be Nicola Geraci?"

"I'm willing to bet on it."

"Nicola Geraci, a socialist . . . but what was he doing at the home of the marquis, who everyone knows hated the reds?"

"I don't know. But we'll find that out too."

"How?"

"I'm thinking of Prince Licata, *u patri*. Maybe we've found a way to get rid of him and get our hands on his estates."

Those last words made Michele Fardella's blood run cold. "Prince Licata can't be touched," he whispered.

"The interests of fascism are above the interests of the individual," the mayor reminded him. "If you think about it, Licata was the only one in town who had a motive for killing Marquis Bellarato and Nicola Geraci. The attorney was a spokesman for the socialist leagues of Petralia Sottana and was supporting the Farm cooperative in its bid to obtain land. Then, in that famous meeting at Salemi town hall, Licata cleared away any socialist pipe dreams the peasants may have had in their heads. Nicola Geraci threatened him and a few days later vanished from sight. The motive against Marquis Bellarato was known to all. The marquis, working on behalf of his cousin's cooperative, was competing for the award of an estate whose name I no longer even remember . . . *Baucina*, I think. Licata's cooperative had to come up with the balance on the option, otherwise it would lose its deposit since Marquis Bellarato had the money to obtain the land. And as coincidence would have it, on the very afternoon before the day the option was to expire, the marquis was killed, and the palazzo went up in flames."

"But what does Nicola Geraci have to do with it?"

"The fire was started in order to hide any traces," Captain Costa continued. "No one could have recognized the two charred corpses. But Licata's brilliant idea was to involve Salvatore Turrisi. *He* certainly had good reason to kill Marquis Bellarato."

"And Licata saw to it that the second corpse was identified as Turrisi thanks to the Saint Christopher medal," Michele Fardella said, completing the mayor's line of reasoning. "Exactly. Naturally, I'd like to know what happened to Salvatore Turrisi."

"The prince must have given him money and made him leave the country, to get him out of the way."

"Or else he must have had him killed, to eliminate any witnesses," the captain concluded. "His accomplice is Rosario Losurdo, his trusty side-kick, the gabellotto for his estate. We'll have to take care of him too, and then we'll be free to do what we want with their lands."

"But there are legal heirs," Michele Fardella objected.

"Fardella, you still haven't figured out what you can accomplish when there's a dictatorship willing to protect your ass?" He led him to the window. Through the panes, they could see the few hurried passersby, bundled up in their long, heavy overcoats. "If we play our cards right, we'll soon be *padroni*. We'll own this town and the lands surrounding it."

Mayor Lorenzo Costa knew that in order to implement his plan, he'd have to gain the support of Jano Vassallo, the operational arm of the fascist action squad. Nothing could be easier. Jano didn't have to be convinced of the goodwill and legitimacy of a mission, as long as it involved fighting and hell-raising. The mayor explained the strategy he had outlined to Michele Fardella and Jano agreed to the plan with predictable enthusiasm. He even found a way to improve upon it, by suggesting that Dr. Peppino Ragusa might also have been mixed up in the grand conspiracy devised by Prince Licata. Hadn't the doctor been the one to confirm the identification of the second corpse as that of Salvatore Turrisi?

"What do you have against Peppino Ragusa?" The mayor, who was no fool and was all too familiar with Jano's vengeful instincts, wanted to know the real reason behind that proposition, well aware that Jano never acted for the sake of justice.

"He's a Jew, and despite that he continues practicing his profession as a doctor."

"Jano, don't talk bullshit. Why do you want to involve Ragusa too?"

"All right, all right. A person can never lie to you, can he?" he said with a knowing grin. "It's because of Saro, his son. He's come between me and Mena. Do you know who I mean?"

"Rosario Losurdo's daughter. A beautiful girl. But she won't want any-thing to do with you once you go and arrest her father."

"Leave it to me, she'll fall for me, you'll see."

The mayor shook his head. Jano could be even more diabolical than him. "Okay. We'll arrest the doctor too, as an accomplice of Licata and Losurdo."

Jano's eyes glittered. "Good. What's our first move?"

"We'll wait until Dr. Bizzarri completes the autopsy on the corpse and identifies Nicola Geraci. After that, we'll go talk to the prosecutor."

———————

Dr. Bizzarri had never found himself in a bind. He'd asked the mayor for at least three weeks before signing a statement identifying the body. Marshal Montalto had offered his full cooperation, bringing him the files and photographs of people reported missing during that period in Salemi and the Madonie, among them Nicola Geraci. But the doctor was not a forensic specialist and had requested the assistance of a pathologist from the public prosecutor's office in Palermo. Mayor Costa had denied his request, however. He could very well do it on his own, he told him at a meeting in the town hall. And he had insisted that the doctor look for any resemblance to Nicola Geraci, in short, making it clear without beating around the bush too much that the corpse had to be identified as the representative of the socialist leagues of Petralia Sottana.

But Dr. Bizzarri was a conscientious physician and did not want to endorse a statement that he was less than certain of, based on his critical findings. That was why he asked his colleague Peppino Ragusa for help.

Ragusa arrived at the cemetery chapel with his habitual leather bag.

"Thank you for coming, Doctor." Bizzarri went to meet him, wiping his hands on a small linen towel. "You may think it odd, to say the least, that here I am having to ask for your assistance."

"Well, I'll admit I had a hard time believing it."

"Unfortunately, politics is an ugly thing. They ordered me to come here, and I never thought it was to replace a . . . Jew."

"But now you need that Jew."

"Dr. Ragusa, for me it's never been a problem. But these are times we've brought upon ourselves. I joined the party only because I needed to work. Is it a sin to work?" He held out his hand, even though the Council of Ministers had prohibited shaking hands as of June of that year, ordering the fascist salute instead. "No hard feelings, okay?" Bizzarri said with a smile.

Ragusa instinctively shook his hand, beginning to like the man.

"So then, what is this about?" Ragusa asked, approaching the altar on which the body of the mummified corpse had been laid; Bizzarri had seen to removing the clothing.

"I've never seen a natural mummification like this," Bizzarri said, touching the parchment-like skin still attached to the cadaver's bones.

"The ground here has bacteria that devour the fleshy parts of the body, mummifying it," Ragusa explained. "The process is also aided by the porosity of the soil, composed of dry, permeable sand, rich in salts, which protects the bodies against the process of decomposition. We've found others in the same condition."

"We have to try to identify who this body belonged to."

Ragusa bent down to look closely at the skull and skin blackened by the fire. Then, with Bizzarri's help, he turned over the corpse. He picked up his tools and began dissecting.

Based on the condition of the spinal column he established that it couldn't possibly belong to a young man of twenty-five, the age that Salvatore Turrisi had been at the time of the fire. The spinal column was that of a man of at least forty. Then there was the head: he found no traces of soot in the throat. This discovery left him taken aback.

"What did you find?" Bizzarri asked eagerly.

"It's what I did *not* find," Ragusa replied. "As you of course know, people who are burned in a fire inhale soot that should then be found in the pharynx, the trachea, and the lungs. There are no traces of soot where you would expect to find them."

"You mean he was killed before being thrown into the fire?"

"It's likely. That's what we're going to verify with a spectrochemical analysis of some bloodstains. Have you ever heard of fatty embolism?" he asked as he began scraping the remains of a bloodstain with a scalpel.

Dr. Bizzarri shook his head.

"About ten years ago," Ragusa continued as he inserted the blood traces between two glass slides that he then slipped under the microscope, "surgeons and pathologists realized that, following a trauma, bone fracture, or various injuries, some fat from the adipose tissue penetrates the blood vessels. Carried along by the blood, the fat reaches the right ventricle and from there the lung. As a result, it causes an obstruction of the small pulmonary vessels, which in many cases leads to vascular occlusion and therefore death. Sometimes the fatty embolism develops within a few seconds, always stemming from some form of external violence."

In the end, the analysis proved Ragusa's intuition correct: the man was first killed and then thrown into the flames.

But who was that corpse? Ragusa studied the photographs of Nicola Geraci at length, comparing them with the charred body. In fact, the size of the skull, the skeletal structure, the shape of the jaw and the height could correspond to those of the man found in the coffin. But Ragusa couldn't bring himself to endorse the identification.

"There is a high probability that this is in fact Nicola Geraci," he told his colleague at the end of the autopsy. "The decisive proof would be dental evidence. But there is no photo in which his teeth are showing."

"We also tried to track down his relatives. But the carabinieri haven't found anyone, not even his wife, who seems to have immigrated to Germany," Bizzarri explained.

"Under the circumstances, I don't feel I can sign a statement identifying him as Nicola Geraci. I'm sorry," Ragusa said.

"Still, you've managed to assuage my conscience," Bizzarri said, shaking his hand with gratitude. "And thanks for the lesson." His ruddy cheeks stretched into a broad smile.

———

The following morning, Michele Fardella entered Mayor Costa's town hall office and handed him Dr. Bizzarri's report.

Costa carefully read the statement and when he had finished, raised his head, satisfied. "Good, now we have scientific proof that the corpse is Nicola Geraci, and that he was killed before being thrown into the fire. The witness?"

"Jano is coming with our man."

"Do I know him?" the mayor asked.

"It's Prospero, the son of Corrado Abbate, Baron Adragna's steward. He's a smart one."

"But isn't he a member of the fascist combat league?"

"He's in the elite unit."

"I would have preferred someone outside the military."

"We can look for someone else if you want."

"It's too late now. If you've already filled him in, we'll manage to make do with this Prospero. The fewer people who know about this matter, the better it is for everyone," the mayor concluded. He stood up and went over to the window.

A few minutes later, there was a knock at the door. It was Jano, who came in followed by Prospero.

The young man froze to attention before the desk, while Jano sat down in a chair.

Costa went over to him and sized him up. "What's your name, *camerata?*" he asked, using the fascist form of address.

"Prospero Abbate. Son of Corrado and Maria—"

The mayor cut him off, clapping him on the shoulder. "Fine, fine. Sit down, make yourself comfortable."

The young man looked at the mayor and sat down in the chair next to Jano's.

Costa stood before him. "We are an invincible team," he began warmly. "We must therefore help each other without any ifs, ands, or buts. There is something you must do for us."

Prospero felt grateful for that request. For him, being of help to the mayor was a dream. He would have leapt into the flames if he'd been asked.

A few mornings later, Jano, Michele Fardella, Prospero Abbate, and Mayor Lorenzo Costa himself left for Marsala in the mayor's Fiat Balilla, purchased with the town taxpayers' money, to pay a visit to prosecutor Tommaso Amato, a man of confirmed fascist loyalty.

The prosecutor's private office was housed in one of the spacious rooms on the first floor of a small building on Via Egadi, north of Capo Lilibeo. The windows opened directly onto the sea, offering the prosecutor a breathtaking view. Attorney Amato, when he wasn't required at a court hearing, spent up to fifteen hours a day sitting in front of those windows, studying documents and codicils that helped him resolve claims and disputes that were almost always quite depressing. That magnificent sea, he said, was his torment: it was close at hand, but he could never enjoy it.

"Come in," he said when he heard a knock at the office door. He'd been expecting Salemi's mayor, and Costa was punctual as usual.

The mayor sat down before the prosecutor's desk, while Michele, Jano, and Prospero remained standing behind him. "Mr. Amato, forgive me for coming straight to the point, but I'd like to get back to Salemi by this afternoon," Costa began, opening his leather briefcase. "An autopsy on the alleged body of Salvatore Turrisi produced surprising results. It's all written here in Dr. Bizzarri's report," he said, handing him a file, which attorney Amato proceeded to leaf through.

"The body was identified as Nicola Geraci?" he asked, after reading the document.

The mayor nodded. "But there's something new."

"What else have you found, Mayor Costa?"

"This man," the latter said, pointing to Prospero Abbate behind him, "has some disclosures to make about who killed Geraci. Come forward, Prospero."

The young man stepped up to the prosecutor's desk as Amato settled back in his leather chair and studied him.

"What's your name, young man?"

"Prospero Abbate, son of Corrado Abbate and Maria Pellizzeri."

"Fine, fine," the prosecutor interrupted. "What did you see?"

"Well, it happened nineteen years ago."

"And how come you're only telling us about it today, my boy?" Although Prospero was a fully mature man, the prosecutor, from the perspective of his half century of life, viewed them all as boys. His gruff tone intimidated Prospero.

"Well, actually, I was afraid."

"Come, come, let's hear what you saw."

"On the afternoon when Marquis Bellarato was killed, I was at his palazzo."

The prosecutor leaned toward Prospero. "How old were you?"

"Nineteen years ago, I was eleven," Prospero replied firmly. "Sometimes the marquis invited us kids to the palazzo to give us some barley sugar. I was with him when Rosario Losurdo arrived."

"Rosario Losurdo has always been Prince Licata's gabellotto," Mayor Costa explained.

"I know who he is!" the prosecutor replied impatiently. Then he turned to Prospero and said sternly, "Go on."

"The marquis made me hide behind the drapes. I could hear what they were saying. I can't remember the exact words now, it was so long ago. All I recall is that Losurdo asked him to pull out of the competition to purchase the Baucina estate; that Prince Licata would remember the favor and would someday reciprocate. Losurdo raised his voice and threatened the marquis, who laughed at his threats. The marquis then got up from his chair and shouted at Losurdo that he would never pull out.

"After that," he went on, "Losurdo went to the fireplace, took an iron poker used to stir the fire, and struck the marquis a number of times. Before leaving, he set fire to the drapes with a smoldering log, then fled. I ran away before the rescuers showed up. I never told anyone about this." He fell silent and looked first at Mayor Costa and then at Jano, as if seeking confirmation that he had done his job well. The two ignored him, however.

The prosecutor sank back in his chair. He thought for a few seconds. Then he looked up at Prospero. "That day, was it raining or was it sunny?" he asked shrewdly.

Prospero was taken by surprise. He had hoped his task was completed. He looked around for backup. He didn't find it. "Well, actually . . ."

"How does that change anything, Mr. Prosecutor?" Costa intervened to help his man out of a tight spot. "Instead, he's made some very serious allegations."

"All too serious. Do you realize, young man"—attorney Amato turned back to Prospero—"that your words could cause people to be sentenced to death? And do you know that if it turns out that you made false accusations, you could end up in jail for more than fifteen years?"

"It's the truth, your honor," Costa interjected. "Before coming here, I took the trouble to verify his account. I should tell you that I discovered that Prince Licata, at the time, was head of a cooperative that was in line to purchase the lands of an estate. The same estate that Marquis Bellarato, in partnership with a cousin, was interested in. Licata's cooperative, however, did not have the money to pay off the balance on the option, which as it happened was due to expire the very day the marquis was killed. I ascertained that the marquis would have paid off his option to purchase the lands the following day. But he was never able to do so because he was murdered by Losurdo, Licata's right hand, I repeat, the very afternoon prior to the expiration."

"And why was the body of Nicola Geraci also found there? He was a representative of the socialist leagues of Peralta Sottana, it says here," attorney Amato asked, indicating the mayor's file. "What did he have to do with it?"

"Nothing, Mr. Prosecutor. I learned that Nicola Geraci, during a public meeting at Salemi's town hall, had seriously affronted Prince Licata, threatening him with death. Instead he was the one to die. The plan devised by Prince Licata and his gabellotto was flawless. He would get rid of the marquis and Geraci in one fell swoop. After the marquis, Losurdo killed Geraci as well and threw him into the flames at the palazzo. He was even indirectly helped by Dr. Peppino Ragusa, who apparently examined the corpses and established the identity of the second body as that of a certain Salvatore Turrisi. By doing so, he sidetracked the investigation. For that matter Turrisi also had a reason to hate the marquis. He went around saying that the marquis had unjustly accused him of killing a young shepherd boy. In fact, after that day, Salvatore Turrisi disappeared from town as well and was never seen again. Licata must certainly have paid him to leave the country and to cover his tracks."

The attorney thought the theory sounded plausible. But Prospero's testimony was false. The prosecutor's instinct never betrayed him. "These are grave accusations," he said. "I'll have to think about the matter, study the evidence. It means going after an aristocrat, a person highly esteemed and respected by the entire town. Accusing him of being the man behind two murders. You can't smear someone so lightly, based on a memory of something that happened nineteen years ago."

"Mr. Prosecutor, I would like to leave this office today with the arrest warrants." Costa, though he was younger than the prosecutor, exuded an undisputed authority. "As mayor, to insure public order, I ask you not to disappoint me. You know that in Rome there is only one thing *he's* a stickler for: order! I therefore request this authorization, to be able to carry out my command the best way I can. I myself will assume full responsibility for the consequences of such an act. You will not be involved in it; you have my word."

––––––––

The mayor returned to Salemi that afternoon with three arrest warrants in hand: one for double murderer Rosario Losurdo; the second for the man behind him, Prince Ferdinando Licata; and the third for the Jew Peppino Ragusa, for his complicity.

All the way back, he and his men thought about the most spectacular way to slam those three in jail, especially Prince Licata, *u patri*. For the town and the surrounding countryside, the arrest would be a signal of the party's extraordinary strength. Mussolini himself, when he learned of it, would congratulate them. Maybe he would even invite them to Rome. For all these reasons, Jano was against handing over the prince on a silver platter to the carabinieri at the local headquarters, who by law should be the ones to execute the arrest warrant.

"We did all the work, and Marshal Montalto will be the one to benefit from it," Jano grumbled for much of the trip.

In the end, he managed to extract the mayor's promise to allow the combat league to make the arrests.

Jano could already see himself on the front page of every newspaper in the realm.

Sometimes fools are content with little, and for Jano, who had never had anything in his life and who in one night had been deprived of his entire world, those arrests would serve perfectly well.

Chapter 21

Summer was over, and autumn was spreading its warm amber tones over the fields and woods.

At the station, Chief Brigadier Mattia Montalto was contemplating for the hundredth time the anonymous lined paper and the words that had alerted them to the massacre. He had attempted to gather handwriting samples from several persons in town whom he suspected might have composed the note. He was sure that whoever had written the tip-off must have seen the attackers; he was mathematically certain that there had been more than one. But it was difficult to determine whose writing it was, partly because he was not a handwriting expert.

Nevertheless, for some time now his suspicions had been pinned on a certain Michele Fardella, a charcoal burner who, tired of slogging away eight months a year in the forest cutting wood to make charcoal, had recently begun working for Captain Costa of the Royal Guard.

With the help of Salemi's schoolteacher, Montalto was able to leaf through the notebooks of all the children attending elementary school, one of which, it turned out, had a page torn out. It just happened to belong to Margherita Fardella, Michele's younger sister.

Montalto then had Vice Brigadier Trigona pick up Fardella and bring him to the station. It was the third time he'd been summoned, and Fardella, a quick-tempered type with little respect for authority, did not hide his resentment.

"Brigadier, if you have some accusation to make against me, say so. But stop treating me like a criminal!" he griped as he entered the station.

"Fardella, no one is accusing you of anything," Montalto said calmly. "But I am conducting an investigation, and it is my right to question you."

"So go ahead and ask me. What else do you want to know?"

Montalto held up the lined sheet of paper in front of him. "Did you write this note?"

Michele Fardella rolled his eyes to heaven. "My God, Brigadier, still the same old story about that note? I already told you the last time, it wasn't me who wrote it. I can't write, understand? Or even read."

"Fardella, you'd better tell me the truth. Because I found the note-book whose page you tore out . . ." He paused a moment to keep the suspect on tenterhooks. Then he concluded, "The notebook belongs to your sister."

Michele Fardella managed to remain impassive, but he lowered his eyes to the floor. Montalto understood that he would not say another word. If he talked, he was a dead man. Whoever had ordered that massacre would have no qualms about killing him.

"All right, then: if you won't talk, you'll spend a few days in a cell to loosen your tongue." So saying, he nodded to the vice brigadier, who took Fardella by the arm and led him to a holding cell.

———

As usual, word of Fardella's arrest spread within minutes. That evening, Chief Montalto, as he did every evening before returning home for dinner, stopped by the Circolo Vittorio Emanuele, the club where the town's prominent figures habitually met to rehash the day's events.

He found Baron Francesco Adragna there who, along with Don Antonio and Count Calogero Colonna, was listening to Vito Bonanno read aloud from the *Avanti!*, the official newspaper of the Italian Socialist Party.

As soon as Montalto entered the room, Bonanno stopped reading. "Chief, come in, sit down, listen to what that idiot Salvemini wrote."

"Who is he, one of your buddies, Don Bonanno?" Montalto joked.

"Actually, he's someone we'd gladly see hanged from a tree," Count Colonna explained.

"Listen to what he says; he tears everything down . . ." Vito Bonanno went back to reading the article:

"The Italian capitalist class is a recent phenomenon. In particular, the newly rich created by the war, whom the common people call 'sharks,' are coarse individuals, both intellectually and morally. These profiteers were not satisfied with making the workers see reason. Instead, they've decided to destroy the workers' organizations. The landowners have been even more brutal than the industrialists."

He stopped reading and turned to his companions, saying, "He's talking about us here." Then he continued:

"As a result of centuries-old tradition, landowners have been accustomed to considering themselves the absolute masters of their lands while treating the peasants like beasts of burden."

"The fucking bastard!" fumed Baron Adragna. Turning to Don Antonio, he added, "Pardon my language, Don Antonio, but they come up with some doozies, these anarchists."

"They too—" Bonanno began, but his reading was once again interrupted.

"He's still talking about the landowners," Baron Adragna clarified.

Bonanno went on:

"They too wanted to take revenge on the slaves who had dreamed of becoming masters and had rushed to join the fascist ranks. Fear of the social order being overturned is great for these landowners and fear is a bad counselor. The professional military men who organize and run the fascist squads have injected their mentality into the fascist movement, and with it a methodical brutality that prior to this year was unknown in the Italian political struggle."

Captain Lorenzo Costa of the Royal Guard entered the room in time to hear the last lines of the article. When Bonanno finished reading, he broke in, drawing everyone's attention. "These subversives will all end up hanged."

"Captain, would you like a marsala?" Baron Adragna went to the bar where he filled a glass with the fragrant wine.

"Italy needs stability and order. And only we can guarantee both," said the captain as he took the glass offered by the baron.

"Of course, to implement these assurances, someone may end up with a broken head," Count Colonna said, smiling.

Antonio Grassa, a liberal, was more caustic: "When you begin putting up with something, first it becomes tolerable and after a time even normal. We must be careful not to get too used to broken heads, otherwise one of these days we'll find our own broken."

"You gentlemen don't have to worry, because we are there for you," the captain assured them, sipping his glass of marsala. Then he approached Montalto. "Chief Montalto, if you will allow me?" the captain said, inviting him to step aside.

"Excuse me, I've been summoned," Montalto joked as he took his leave from the other guests and followed Captain Costa into one of the club's sitting rooms.

"Forgive me, Chief. I know you've arrested Michele Fardella. He's a good man, fearless. He hasn't done anything," Captain Costa insisted in no uncertain terms.

"I'm sure it was he who threw the note about the massacre into the station house," Montalto replied curtly.

"That old story again . . . I've told you what I think. I believe that Prince Licata and his gabellotto Losurdo are implicated in the affair. Why won't you listen to me?"

"Prince Licata would never do such a thing."

"He wouldn't, but his gabellotto would. Do you want to bet that Losurdo is hiding something? Why don't you search his farm?"

"On what grounds?" said Montalto.

"Come up with something. Don't take it out on Fardella. He can never tell you the names of those responsible for the massacre, because if he does, he's a dead man. Is that what you want?"

"Of course not. But if Michele Fardella witnessed the massacre, he also knows who was responsible for it," the chief brigadier insisted.

"Assuming what you say is true, Fardella will never talk," Captain Costa repeated. "Listen to me. Release him. I need people like him." He paused, then went on as if he had found a solution. "Tell you what, you give me Fardella, and I'll find you the one responsible for the massacre."

"Captain Costa, you're mistaking me for one of those gang leaders. I'm a chief brigadier. I can't make pacts like that. If we carabinieri could name a price for our actions, some would cost more, others less. But we pay for them all with a single currency: courage."

"Bravo, Chief, you've learned your lesson well. I respect your point of view. But I ask you for the last time: release Fardella; he doesn't know anything."

Montalto calmly adjusted his cap. "Fardella will be held for the time prescribed by law, not a minute less, not a minute more." So saying, he turned and, after saying good-bye to the other men, left the club.

Chapter 22

T he greatest delusion about violence is believing that it can defeat evil, whereas in reality it leads to more violence.

That was the case for Jano. Witnessing the massacre of his family had affected his mind like a drug, one that had intoxicated him and that he could not do without.

As bitter fate would have it, the person responsible for the massacre was the very man he most admired, Lorenzo Costa, the man who referred to him as his right hand, second only to Michele Fardella. If Jano had known the truth, the sorry circumstances of a lot of people in Salemi would certainly have been different. But the secret of that night in late July was guarded by only two people, bound together by a covenant of blood.

So though Jano was able to wrest permission from the mayor to have his combat league carry out the three arrest orders, the mayor demanded a pledge from him in return: he was to begin the operation the following day at dawn, to avoid any possible disturbance by the citizens. In short, he wanted the three accused men to be arrested with absolute discretion, without the drum-beating spectacle that Jano had in mind. He had to preserve order, above all else. With the arrest of the prince and his gabel-lotto, the social equilibrium would be upset and this could lead to all sorts of uncontrollable consequences.

Jano promised him absolute restraint until dawn of the following day. But Jano was untrustworthy, devious, and erratic. As mayor of Salemi, Lorenzo Costa knew it, but he also knew that to govern with a stick he needed men like Jano, and over time he had learned to tolerate his insubordination. Never would he have thought that Jano might disobey his orders in a delicate situation such as this.

Knowing what he was like, and to settle him down, the mayor suggested that he spend the evening with Carmela. At first Jano said he would follow his advice, but then, walking home, he thought about Mena . . . and then about Saro . . . and then about Peppino Ragusa, Saro's father.

It was eight in the evening. The wind that blew from the west at dusk had weakened, while a light, persistent rain, typical of spring, had begun to fall. It was the perfect time, since at that hour the families of Salemi would be sitting around the table for their one meal of the day. Surprise was assured . . .

The temptation was too strong. In an instant, he forgot the pledge he'd made to the mayor, retraced his steps and went to call his most trusted men.

———

Peppino Ragusa had taken his seat at the head of the table and was cutting a crusty round loaf of bread. Annachiara was seated opposite him, near the stove, while Ester and Saro sat at either side of the table. His wife had made a thick bean soup.

That evening, as was surely the case in all the other homes in Salemi, the main topic of conversation was the discovery, made a few days earlier, that the body of Salvatore Turrisi had been mysteriously switched in the coffin.

As Ragusa was taking a second helping of soup, three forceful raps on the door made them all jump. Annachiara, frightened, looked at her husband. It certainly wasn't the timid knocking of her husband's friends coming for their usual lessons, and besides, the lessons had been suspended.

Peppino Ragusa stood up to get the door, but there wasn't time because a violent mallet blow flung it wide open, and two thugs, Quinto and Cosimo, threw themselves at him, pinning him down. Ragusa struggled as hard as he could, but it was no use. An instant later, Nunzio and Ginetto came in, followed by Prospero Abbate and finally Jano. They were all in black shirts, under which they wore black turtlenecks. Saro rose from his chair and tried to help his father, but Nunzio hit him in the stomach with his club, making him double over in pain. Ester, screaming in terror, tried to embrace her mother, but Annachiara broke away to confront the man who had struck Saro. Nunzio however clubbed her right on her forehead. The woman slumped to the floor, her blonde hair bloodied, as her daughter ran to her. The sight of his wife bleeding intensified Ragusa's efforts. Despite being fifty-two, he was still strong as a bull. He spun around, making the two who were holding him lose their balance. Then he kicked out, striking the nearest man, Quinto, causing him to release his grip. Ragusa, meanwhile, had also shaken off Cosimo, caught unaware by such unexpected force. Head down, howling like a trapped animal, Ragusa hurled himself at Nunzio, who was still ascertaining the injury done to Annachiara. Ragusa rammed him in the belly, pushing him against the table and dealing him a counterblow to the kidneys that nearly made him pass out.

But Jano and Prospero were quick and began beating the doctor with their clubs. Ester wept and screamed at them to stop. Saro, on the floor, was writhing from the blow he'd received. He did not have the strength or the courage to stand up and stop the rampage. The two went on beating Ragusa, hammering away at every part of his body: head, shoulders, kidneys, legs, the head once more, and over and over again. Until Ginetto went over and grabbed Prospero's hand.

"Stop! Can't you see you've nearly killed him?"

Jano broke off as well. Like his cronies, he was exhausted by the exertions. They were all breathing hard, and Jano slumped down on a chair. Ester was dabbing at her mother's wound with the edge of her dress, revealing her leg. Jano, seeing her, became excited. He got up and took a step toward her.

Ginetto, who had not participated in the brutality, seemed like the only one who'd kept his head. "Let's go, before anyone comes."

Jano stopped and headed toward the door. "Take him to the truck," he said, pointing to Peppino Ragusa. Then he disappeared through the doorway.

———

Violence exhilarated Jano. It gave him the impression he could dominate others' lives; it made him feel like a god.

Later he knocked gently at Carmela's door. The woman opened it in her dressing gown and flinched at seeing the mask of hatred his distorted features wore.

"Well? You look like you've seen a ghost," he said as he entered.

"What are you doing here? Today isn't Saturday."

"Are you expecting someone else? Is that how you come to open the door, dressed like that? What would your husband say?" he asked coldly, pushing her into the room and closing the door behind him.

Offended, she tried to slap him, hissing "I'm not a whore!" But he stopped her wrist. "I'm just *your* whore," she whispered. His only answer was a slap that knocked her to the floor. The woman curled up, rubbing her cheek. "Bastard!" she spat at him.

Jano leaned over her, turning her over on her belly. He pulled off her dressing gown, and then grabbed the shoulder straps of her nightgown and tore it off with a quick tug, leaving her completely naked.

"You don't even sleep with panties on," he said admiring her round buttocks.

She turned around brazenly, hiding her nipples with one arm, but revealing the thick bush of dark pubic hair. Jano feasted his eyes on her soft, sinuous curves. Carmela was a magnificent example of a southern woman, with an amber complexion, strong hips, a narrow waist, round motherly breasts, and an inviting, plump belly.

The young man, now in his socks and undershirt, greedily devoured her most intimate parts, biting her until he made her scream out, not caring what the neighbors might hear or say.

———

That night was interminable for Jano. Despite the craving that filled him with fury and desire, he was unable to satisfy his lover's lust. He tried and tried repeatedly, numerous times, to enter her, but always failed miserably and sometimes even comically. Eventually he fell asleep, exhausted by the tension, the impotence, and an entire bottle of red wine.

That night was interminable for Peppino Ragusa as well. His face swollen, every part of his body aching, he spent the long hours on the floor of a cell set up in a room in the town hall, adjacent to the combat league's command center.

It was also interminable for the five Black Shirts who had been ordered by Jano not to let their prisoner out of sight. An hour before dawn, they would have to prepare to carry out the other two arrests.

But that night was interminable for some mysterious individuals as well, who roamed around town until it was nearly dawn and then disappeared under the cover of darkness.

———

A timid tap at the door made Carmela jump as she lay on the bed. For her too, it had been a hellish night, filled with remorse and rage over a fate that had taken her husband far from home and that had not even given her the comfort of a child. A rotten destiny that had led her to know a nasty character like Jano, who would be hard to get rid of.

When she heard another knock on the wooden door, this time louder, she shook Jano firmly in an attempt to wake him and bring him round from the alcohol he'd guzzled the night before.

Finally, the young man came to. His temples were pounding, but he managed to sit up, his legs dangling over the side of the bed.

Meanwhile, the knocking at the door continued.

Jano remembered that they were supposed to go arrest Prince Licata and his gabelloto, Losurdo. It was already dawn, and he dejectedly took note of his physical and mental states.

"I'll go make you some coffee," Carmela told him, slipping her nightie and worn dressing gown back on.

Jano got out of bed and dragged himself to the door. His mouth was furry, his head heavy, and he was furious at what had happened the night before with Carmela. Or rather what had *not* happened.

He opened the door, and there stood his five trusty companions in crime. He didn't notice that their faces were more haggard than his.

"A quick coffee, and I'll be right with you, comrades," he said absently. He started to go back inside, but Nunzio grabbed his arm and stopped him. "Jano, something terrible has happened," he said in the grimmest tone possible.

Jano broke free of his grip. "What are you talking about?" His guilty conscience led him to think, terrified, that all of Salemi had already heard about his breach of promise. "Who's going around spreading that crap?"

"What crap?" Nunzio was at a loss to follow his train of thought. Jano calmed down. "So what do you mean?" he asked warily.

"Something awful happened at the cemetery. The caretaker is still in shock. We have to hurry there." Behind him Jano saw the other four, their moods blacker than their shirts.

"Are you nuts? We have two arrests to make."

"First we have to stop at the cemetery," Nunzio insisted.

"Jano, get dressed and let's go, there's no time to lose," Ginetto urged. Irritated by their air of mystery, Jano lost his patience. "Enough! Will someone tell me what happened?"

The five imperceptibly stepped back, as if fearing to incur their leader's wrath. But no one dared say another word.

"The truck is ready and waiting. We have to get going, Jano," Prospero said, indicating the pickup a few yards away.

Jano was furious over the way they were acting. Carmela appeared behind him and handed him a cup of steaming coffee. "What's going on?" the woman asked predictably.

Jano drank the coffee and lit a cigarette. "You'll find out later. Today they'll be talking about us on the radio, you'll see." He gave her back the cup and followed his trusty Black Shirts to the truck.

––––––––

Salemi's small cemetery was on a hill not far from town. The road spiraled up through a wooded area of pines and evergreen oaks, circling the hill until it reached a clearing in front of the cemetery gate, whose architrave was carved with the words *Domus mortis*. The cemetery spread out for almost two and a half acres, and alongside the monumental tombs of Salemi's noble and most prominent families were graves with marble headstones, belonging to middle-class people; and those of the poorest individuals, recognizable by a simple wooden cross bearing only the deceased's name and dates of birth and death.

Jano had failed to get a single word out of his men to explain the reason for their detour. They would only shake their heads.

Prospero stopped the truck in front of the gate, and everybody got out and headed into the cemetery.

Jano still didn't understand. "So what are we supposed to look for?"

Finally, Nunzio got up his nerve. "Come on, Jano, take us to your mother's grave."

Jano balked. "What does this have to do with my mother?"

"Nothing to do with your mother, God rest her soul," Nunzio reassured him. "But let's go."

Jano stopped delaying. He walked briskly toward the low wall that marked the boundary of the cemetery to the east. By now light had overcome the darkness, even though the sun had not yet appeared on the horizon. The five men followed Jano, flanking him right and left. Jano spotted his mother's gravestone.

The headstone was where it should be, but a mound of fresh earth testified that someone had been digging there.

With his heart in turmoil, Jano approached the edge of the pit. He looked down and saw the wood of the coffin. "Bastards! Bastards!" he yelled.

"But everything seems all right," Ginetto said hastily.

"Yeah, let's close it up; some idiot had fun shoveling dirt last night," Nunzio added.

"Damn them! It's a sacrilege!" Jano kept ranting as Nunzio tried to calm him down.

Then Jano suddenly darkened. "Wait a minute," he said in a low voice. "The lid was disturbed . . .

It's been unhinged!" he yelled.

"No, how could they?" Ginetto tried to deny the evidence.

"Look, take a good look!" Jano pointed to a corner of the coffin, where it was obvious that the lid did not line up with the edge of the box.

"Over there, Ginetto, go see."

"But—" Ginetto tried to object.

Jano, in a tone that wouldn't take no for an answer, bound him to his duty: "I order you to go down there!"

Ginetto, with the help of Prospero and Quinto, lowered himself into the grave. He bent over the coffin. Reluctantly, he touched the lid, which was indeed only resting on the edge of the box.

"It was opened, wasn't it?" Jano, beside himself, shouted from above.

Ginetto gripped the edge of the lid with both hands and tried to lift it. As soon as he tilted it up, it slipped out of his hands, which were slimy from the damp earth, and slid to the side, revealing the interior of the coffin.

A horrific sight paralyzed Jano and his men.

A huge sow hacked in two and still bleeding had been placed over the skeletal remains of Jano's mother. The stench of rotting flesh made Ginetto puke, spewing vomit over the sow and the corpse.

The son's bloodcurdling scream resounded far off in the valley. His companions gripped him forcefully and held him down to keep him from bashing his head against the marble headstone in a fit of mad rage.

Lavinia Licata saw on the horizon the great cloud of dust raised by the wheels of the Black Shirts' truck. From that distance, she could hear them singing their infantile, seditious anthem. The men sounded as though they were out on a school field trip, and yet, armed with clubs and muskets, they were able to terrorize people. More so because their foolish actions were dictated by their immaturity rather than their aggressive natures.

When the truck came to a stop with a great screeching of brakes, Jano jumped down from the running board and headed resolutely toward the door of Licata's palazzo. He banged on the door several times with his club, while the other men joined him, taking their places around him. Ginetto, Nunzio, Prospero, Quinto, and Cosimo knew that they were making an arrest that would have all of Sicily talking about them for years to come.

"Prince Licata, open up!" Jano shouted at the top of his lungs. He was infuriated and had yet to fully vent his rage over the affront that had been done to him. A supreme offense for any human being, but unimaginable for a son in Sicily.

He continued banging furiously on the wooden door. The sound of a bolt sliding open was heard on the other side; then two burly campieri appeared. The older of the two was Bettino, whom Jano had already had the misfortune of meeting some time ago. The two men looked threatening, like a dark sky before a storm lets loose, and were armed with double-barreled hunting rifles.

"Take me to your boss, now," Jano ordered impatiently.

But Bettino, a good several inches taller than him, put out a hand to bar the way. Meanwhile, the other campiere had stepped aside to make way for Lavinia, who appeared behind them. The woman stopped in the middle of the doorway, and the younger campiere stood protectively beside her.

"If you are looking for my brother, I will tell you that he left last night for one of his regular trips to Europe. You will have to return in a year or so," she said very calmly.

"Are you fucking with me?" Jano had thrown all caution to the wind.

Offended by his language, the woman pursed her lips and turned to go back into the palazzo. But Jano, more enraged than ever, overtook her and, pushing her aside, broke into the house, followed by three of his men.

Bettino and the other campiere immediately reacted by cocking their rifles, but Lavinia, with an imperious wave of her hand, indicated that they should let them enter. Cosimo and Prospero remained outside, holding off the two campieri with their muskets, so they wouldn't move.

Jano and the three other Black Shirts searched every corner of the palazzo, but there was no sign of the prince. Lavinia had been telling the truth: evidently Licata had gone on a long journey, given that his clothes were gone from the closets.

Chapter 23

No one in town would ever have imagined that Ferdinando Licata, *u patri* of the entire community, would one day be forced to flee Salemi to avoid arrest or imprisonment. But the prince was despised by Mayor Costa and even more so by Jano, who basically viewed all aristocrats and those in power as the origin of his troubles. The young man would surely have subjected him to the infamy of the dreaded "box" in order to humiliate him and make him see who was now in command in Salemi.

Licata would never stand for such an affront. Consequently, after displaying his power to Jano by violating his mother's grave, he planned to leave for America that very night.

A Florio steamer sailed every two weeks from Palermo, headed for America. He would return once things had changed. After assigning his sister Lavinia blank power of attorney, the prince left Salemi with a heavy heart.

———

That same morning, Jano Vassallo hurried to Rosario Losurdo's farm. Prince Licata's gabellotto was third on the list of those he had to arrest. Now he was afraid he wouldn't find him. If Losurdo had learned from some friend that he was making those arrests, he too would have gone into hiding and would never be found.

Though he'd been warned by the prince, Rosario Losurdo had not wanted to abandon his lands. He had thanked the prince but told him that he would not budge from his farm. He had had nothing to do with the death of Marquis Pietro Bellarato nineteen years ago.

And so Losurdo was actually waiting for the Black Shirts to turn up, standing in the yard of his farmstead surrounded by his children and the peasants who helped him work his lands. The arrival of the combat league's truck was heralded by the sputtering of its old engine.

Jano climbed out and approached Losurdo, his five militiamen flanking him. Stopping a few steps away from the gabellotto, he surveyed the entire Losurdo family lined up in support. For an instant, his eyes met Mena's, but she quickly lowered her gaze.

Jano pointed his club at Rosario's chest and said, "Losurdo, I have to speak to you in private."

Rosario pushed aside the threatening club with a swipe of his hand.

"Follow me," he said, heading for the house.

Jano motioned to his men not to move and disappeared inside the farmhouse.

"The beauty of our land," Jano began, "is that here secrets fly like arrows. If an act of violence happens, no one talks and everyone looks the other way, yet it is instantly known to all with the speed of light."

"I don't have much time for you, Jano. Get to the point," Losurdo said brusquely.

"My dear Rosario, how much time you have depends on my mood." He pulled a legal document from his shirt and showed it to the gabellotto. "See this? It's a warrant for your arrest. For a crime that you committed nineteen years ago."

"Bellarato again? Jano, why are you all so determined to get me? First they tried to frame me for the slaughter of your family. Someone planted weapons from the massacre at my house. I did five years for that charge, but I had nothing to do with it, and you know it. Then the marquis's murder. I was in the fields when they killed him, and I can prove it. You should look elsewhere for your scapegoat, Jano."

"This time there's an eyewitness," Jano insisted. "Somebody saw you kill Bellarato with your own hands."

The new accusation infuriated Losurdo. "That's a lie! Why this persecution?"

"It depends on you," said Jano enigmatically, folding the sheet in four.

"What do you mean it depends on me? What do you have in mind? Whom do I have to betray?" Losurdo thought Jano was asking him to testify against Prince Licata.

"You don't have to betray anyone. Let's just call it a trade: I let you have your freedom in exchange for a favor."

"What kind of favor?" Losurdo asked suspiciously.

"These days it's not advisable to have your father-in-law in jail on a murder charge. For that reason, I'll spare you."

Losurdo was beginning to understand.

"Basically, I'm not asking you to do anything improper. You can continue to enjoy your lands, and we will be more than friends."

Rosario Losurdo went rigid. He clenched his fists to force himself not to beat the hell out of that cocky little shit in a black shirt.

"In fact, we'll be family! So, can I call you . . . Papa?"

It was too much for Rosario Losurdo. He went for Jano menacingly. Jano tried to hit him with his club, but Losurdo, despite his fifty years of age, was more agile and grabbed the wood as it was being brought down on him. He twisted Jano's wrist, forcing him to let go of it. Losurdo tossed it away and then grabbed Jano by the shirt, nearly lifting him off the ground. He was furious and could have strangled him.

"You vicious little sewer rat, I will *never* give my daughter to a bastard like you, I'd rather be hanged. Blackmailing son of a bitch! How much did that fake witness cost you? I'll give him three times what you gave him to make him testify that it was *you* who killed Bellarato when you were six years old!" Losurdo slapped him with such force that he knocked Jano off balance, causing him to hit his head on the table as he fell to the floor.

A moment later, the five Black Shirts burst into the room along with Michele, Donato, Mena, and Rosita. Nunzio and Prospero were the first to enter, and when they saw Jano on the floor, rubbing his head, they rushed to pin down Rosario.

Rosita screamed, "Leave my husband alone!"

The shouting grew louder. Michele, Losurdo's eldest son, put his hand on his *Sanfratellano*, and for a moment the knife's long blade got everyone's attention. He yelled, "Someone is going to get hurt! Watch out, I'm not joking!"

Fearing reprisals against his son, Losurdo roared, "Michele, put that knife away."

Cosimo leveled his sawed-off shotgun at Michele. "Do what your father told you."

Jano got up, refusing Quinto's help. "Calm down, nothing happened. Everybody calm down."

To make everything perfectly clear, Rosario explained his action to his family: "He asked for my permission to marry Mena. In return he would burn the testimony of a false witness who has accused me, saying he saw me kill Marquis Bellarato. But I had nothing to do with that murder. I will not sacrifice my daughter over such *infamità*—such vile infamy."

Jano went over to him. "Losurdo, today, here in front of everyone, I'm telling you that you will soon rot in jail, that Mena will be mine, and that I will become padrone, landowner, of the Castellana and Giovinazzo estates. Your family will be disgraced, and your wife will crawl on her knees to beg me for a crust to ease her hunger."

A desperate cry interrupted that grim scene. Mena fell at his feet, weeping forlornly. "Jano, have mercy! Don't harm us, I implore you."

Jano took hold of her and lifted her up. "Mena, don't despair, it's all right. Everything will be straightened out, don't worry. It's just that your father's head is harder than mine."

Rosita went to her daughter and snatched her out of his hands. "Jano, a curse on you," she pronounced angrily.

But Jano smiled and then turned back to Losurdo, who was being restrained by Nunzio and Prospero. "So, what's your final word?"

"You're despicable," Rosario Losurdo said sharply.

Jano ordered his men to put him in irons and take him to the truck.

The cellar of Salemi's town hall had been transformed by the mayor into holding cells where political dissidents could be detained along with those who had to be leaned on to extract a confession or some information.

Losurdo was locked up in one of these cells, which was located next to the one in which Peppino Ragusa had been jailed the night before.

The doctor had fallen into a pit of depression, unable to accept what had been done to him after his years of sacrifice to bring some small comfort to the citizens of Salemi.

He heard another unlucky soul being put in the neighboring cell. Then the bolt slid closed and the lock clicked. When the heavy footsteps had moved off, he put his mouth close to the wall that separated him from his prison mate.

"Peppino Ragusa here. Who are you?"

"It's Rosario Losurdo, Doctor."

"Rosario? What are you doing here?"

"The same old story about Marquis Bellarato. They say they have an eyewitness who swears he saw me kill the marquis. It's obvious it's all a frame-up. I'm innocent."

"Being innocent is a fine predicament, because generally you have no alibi," the doctor declared.

"I'll be able to show that I had nothing whatsoever to do with that murder. But I'm afraid for my family. I don't trust those buffoons and the way they handle their power. They don't even fear the carabinieri. By now they've supplanted them."

"Despite everything, however, we must not lose hope."

"But you, Doctor, why have they arrested you?"

"They accuse me of having issued a false statement in connection with my postmortem of the charred body found in Marquis Bellarato's palazzo. I identified it as Salvatore Turrisi, one of the marquis's campieri, whereas it's been ascertained that it was an attorney from Petralia Sottana, Nicola Geraci."

"For this they're going to try you?" Losurdo asked incredulously.

"They say I lied about the identification to sidetrack the investigation. But I acted in good faith. I had no wish to derail the inquiry."

The doctor moved away from the wall and slumped on the straw pallet, his head in his hands as he swallowed back tears.

On the other side of the wall, Losurdo bottled up his rage, and hearing the doctor's anguish, felt more pity for his fate than for his own. He released his anger by punching the door violently, nearly injuring his wrist.

That same afternoon, Rosita, accompanied by her son Michele and her daughter, Mena, climbed into the buggy and set out at a gallop for the carabinieri's headquarters. Montalto represented the law there in Salemi, and he would have to listen to her.

The marshal lived with his wife, Lucia, just above the station house. Lucia welcomed Rosita with a firm, compassionate embrace. News of the combat league's arrests of Losurdo and Ragusa had already traveled through the countryside.

Rosita confronted the marshal, coming straight to the point: "Marshal, lawfulness must return to Salemi. This morning Jano and those thugs of his came and took my husband, an upstanding man. You must do something."

"I'll speak with Jano myself, Donna Rosita, but take it easy now. Come and sit down."

Lucia brought a tray with liqueur glasses and a bottle of rosolio. She poured a little and handed the glasses to Rosita and the men. Mena was too young to drink.

"Those men are worse than wolves. They sink their teeth into your neck and never let go. Marshal, you have to take Rosario under your protection. You're the only one I trust."

Then Michele chimed in: "Excuse me, Marshal, but shouldn't it be you who makes arrests? What do the combat leagues have to do with it?"

"We had to make an agreement with them. The leagues handle politicos and dissidents. We carabinieri take care of ordinary crimes."

"Exactly, that's what I'm saying. Why are they involved in carrying out an arrest on a murder charge?" Michele, getting worked up, rose from his chair. "That's your job!"

"Yes, it's true, they've overstepped their bounds. I'll go and request that they hand them over to me. I promise."

"When will you do that?" Rosita insisted.

"As soon as I assemble my men." Marshal Montalto knew he was going to encounter trouble. "It's likely, however, that they had orders from Mayor Costa."

"Naturally, their worthy accomplice!" Michele spat.

Rosita spoke again. "Marshal, Jano must be stopped. He has his sights set on her"—she gestured to Mena sitting nearby, silent and frightened—"and he's created all this mayhem to extort Rosario's consent to marry her."

"So that's what it's about?" Lucia asked, stunned. "This young man is a disgrace to the whole town!"

"He's been buzzing around the farm like a hornet for some time now," Rosita kept pressing him. "Marshal, I'm afraid one of my sons might do something foolish."

"If I see him around the farm again, I'll shoot him," Michele threatened boastfully.

"Young man, you won't shoot anybody!" the marshal admonished. Then, approaching Mena, he asked, "Is what they're saying true?"

"Jano is a bully," Mena replied. "Once, when I went to bring lunch to Michele and Donato, he climbed onto the buggy. We were alone, and he tried to kiss me. But I made him behave."

"Scumbag!" Michele snarled.

"Easy now, let's not get excited," Marshal Montalto was now really worried. "I'll speak to Jano myself. But don't do anything on your own, or the results may be tragic. Listen to me, Michele. You're in charge of the family now. Don't do anything crazy."

The young man, who had only recently turned twenty-one, nodded, his head bowed as if accepting the responsibility the marshal had just placed on him.

———

After that first stop, Rosita continued on to the home of Dr. Ragusa.

As soon as Annachiara opened the door and saw her standing there, she burst into uncontrollable weeping. The two women held each other in a long, sisterly embrace. Annachiara could not stop sobbing. She was genuinely touched by Rosita's visit. Ester went to her mother and handed her a handkerchief, as Saro led Mena and Michele inside.

"Don't cry, Annachiara. I've already been to see Marshal Montalto. He'll set everything straight, you'll see," Rosita told her as she went in and sat down at the dining table.

"You don't know how much I appreciate this gesture of yours, Rosita," Annachiara said, wiping her eyes and smoothing back the blonde curls that had come loose when they embraced.

"We have to help each other. Those swine have it in for our men. But we'll give them a dose of their own medicine."

"We've lost everything. They treat us like lepers." Annachiara was about to burst into tears again.

Mena went over to Saro. "I'd like some water."

"Come with me, Mena."

They went into the big kitchen, and Saro picked up a glazed earthenware jug. He tipped it over slowly to pour water into a glass, but the pitcher was empty. He smiled at his oversight. "I'll go to the well and get some," Saro said.

"I'll go with you," Mena said simply.

Saro's heart jumped. They went out the back of the house and headed toward the well. Beside it stood a flourishing fig tree that in summer offered a pleasing canopy of shade known throughout the neighborhood.

"My mother is inconsolable," said Saro, his heart clamoring, taking the metal pail as Mena held the rope.

"Mine, instead, is like a man," Mena said with a smile. "If it were up to her, she would already have bumped off all the mayors and fascists in the surrounding area."

"I can't see your mother in the role of dark avenger," Saro smiled too as he lowered the pail into the well. "Are you like her?" he asked after a moment of silence.

But Mena didn't answer. She continued letting out the rope that Saro held firmly in his hands. "Saro, how old are you?" she asked him out of the blue.

"Me?"

"Do you see anyone else around?" she teased.

Saro's heart was about to burst. "Twenty-one," he said, as he began hauling up the pail full of water.

"And at your age you're not married?"

Not only was Saro still unmarried, but he was still a virgin. Despite the fact that all his friends had already been to the prostitutes in Marsala more than once.

Mena's question made him blush. "What kind of question is that to ask?"

"Answer me."

"No, I'm not married. Do you see any wife around here?" Saro playfully answered.

"Well, there could be," Mena murmured softly.

The rope slipped through the young man's hands, and the pail fell into the water with a splash. He almost lost the rope altogether. Mena burst out laughing, covering her mouth with pale, slender hands that had not yet been ruined by heavy farm work.

"Are you making fun of me?"

"I would never do that, Saro," she said, pronouncing his name with sincere fervor.

The two gazed into each other's eyes, not moving; enjoying that moment of intimacy. Mena was the first to break the spell: "Pull up the water."

Saro recovered the pail and poured water into the pitcher that Mena was holding; placing her lips on the rim, the young woman took a long drink. A trickle of water dripped onto her blouse and slid down her chest. When she was done she handed the jug to Saro, turning it around so that he could drink from the same place she had. Saro gripped the pitcher and drank, placing his lips exactly where Mena had rested hers, without once taking his eyes off Mena's green gaze.

"Let's go back now," the girl said and started out, followed by the young man.

Saro stored that meeting in his heart as one of the most intense moments of his life. Mena too would never forget it.

———————

The following day, Jano went to the town hall to report the arrests of Rosario Losurdo and Dr. Ragusa to the mayor. But Lorenzo Costa received him with an expression that did not bode well. Michele Fardella, the mayor's trusted shield, was also present.

"You disobeyed my orders," the mayor began, coming straight to the point. "I told you to make the arrests all together, at dawn."

"That's just what I did," Jano said, trying to appease him.

"No!" yelled Costa, banging his fist on the desk and rising from his chair. "You did not do that! You're a liar and, what's more, unreliable, since you don't follow orders!" When Costa got angry, he made the windowpanes tremble.

"It's unfair of you to say that."

"You couldn't wait until dawn, no! You had to hurry and arrest the doctor so you could have your little satisfaction over Saro, right? Couldn't you have waited?"

Jano, stammering, didn't know what to say to justify himself.

"You gave the prince a chance to get away! Losurdo would have skipped out too, if he wasn't the idiot he is." The mayor strode around the office as Jano, dazed, stood in the center of the room. He hung his head, annoyed by the presence of Fardella, who was laughing quietly to himself.

"Tell me, what am I going to do with you?" Costa asked as he walked over to him. "Go ahead, you may speak now."

"I arrested the doctor and Losurdo."

"That much I already knew. Tell me something I don't know," Costa was now having fun with his subordinate. He threw a knowing glance at Fardella, who responded with the same crafty look.

"They're in a cell. In the basement of the building."

"I already knew that too. I'm the mayor of this shitty town, and the least I can do is be aware of who is in my building."

"The prince left for Europe and will be back in a year."

"That's what they made you believe. Prince Ferdinando Licata is still in Sicily, and perhaps not too far from here." Costa always knew what he was talking about.

But the discussion was interrupted when someone knocked at the door. The figure of Montalto appeared unexpectedly in the doorway.

"Come in, Chief," Costa said amiably.

The marshal entered the room and got straight to the reason for his visit. "You're the very man I was looking for, Jano, and it's appropriate that the mayor be present."

"What's this about, Montalto?" the mayor said with a scowl. The marshal approached the desk to address Costa.

"We made a pact, long ago, when you were installed in that chair, concerning this young man," he said, indicating Jano, indifferent to the latter's reaction. "Do you remember?"

"Yes, I do."

"Not all that well, if I may say so. Because he was supposed to deal

only with dissidents and individuals sent into political confinement."
Montalto took a breath. "Not criminal cases. For those there are the carabinieri. Otherwise dissolve the *arma* and do as you please!"

"There's no need to raise your voice," the mayor said, keeping his
anger in check. "You can't win when you try to do someone a favor."
Then he started to explain in a conciliatory tone, "It was done because I
didn't want to involve the carabinieri in an awkward situation. You know
what it means to arrest an aristocrat around here, don't you?"

"What are you saying?" The marshal didn't understand what the
mayor was getting at.

"It means making an enemy of the landowners and other noblemen.
Everyone would have seen you as an aggressor—someone unsympathetic
toward power, toward maintaining the status quo. In short, I wanted
to insure that the unpopularity of the action would fall on the combat
league. And this is how you thank me?"

"Much too kind, Mayor. But you shouldn't have troubled yourself.
Now we must see that things are put right, and I've come here to inform
you that I will take the two prisoners into my custody."

"Not on your life!" Jano exploded, already tired of all the simpering.
But a look from Costa stopped him.

"I'm afraid that's out of the question, Marshal," Costa said, conveying
the same message, though with honeyed words.

"I'm sorry, Mayor, but I must insist. It's important to reestablish the
roles in this town." He glanced at Michele Fardella, who continued to
remain silent in the corner.

"The decision has been made, Montalto. I have already arranged for
their transfer to the district prison in Marsala the day after tomorrow."

"That was up to us to do."

"I've already told you: it's a very unusual case."

"Don't you trust the carabinieri, Mayor?"

"I trust no one but myself. And now, Marshal, if you have nothing
more to say, I have a lot to do."

Montalto knew he would not get his way, and he played his last card.
"Then allow me to escort the prisoners."

"Are you serious?" Jano said, but the marshal didn't deign to look at
him.

"Well?" Montalto insisted.

"I can't agree to that, Marshal. You already have too much to do here.
And now, good afternoon."

With those words, he abruptly dismissed him. The marshal snapped to attention, turned on his heel, and left the office.

"You see, these are your messes that I always have to clean up after," the mayor burst out as soon as the door closed behind Montalto. "We must not make enemies of the carabinieri. Otherwise people will side with them, and that's just what we don't want," Costa said irritably.

"Everything should have been done with the utmost discretion," Michele Fardella added.

"When we take Ragusa and Losurdo away in shackles, people will realize who's in command here!" Jano exclaimed. "Not with the utmost discretion, as Fardella says, but with the utmost fanfare. Everyone must see them with irons on their wrists, and everyone must know that it is the Black Shirts who are putting them in jail. That's the only way we will win."

The Duce could not have said it better. Mayor Costa bowed his head, and, for once, he had to admit that Jano was right.

"And now what you have to do, Mayor," Jano continued, "is draft a nice writ of seizure confiscating the lands of Prince Licata and his gabellotto, Rosario Losurdo. For the time being, we'll freeze them. They'll no longer be able to profit from them until the trial is over. And we'll be the ones to benefit from the taxes they receive from their tenants."

This time too, Costa and Fardella had to admit that the doggedly aggressive Jano was right.

———

History repeats itself because people never change. Marshal Mattia Montalto was an honorable, decent man. Injustice distressed him. However, with the abuse of power in those times, the law no longer served justice but, rather, the calculating individuals who had managed to secure the most profitable administrative posts.

The scene in Costa's office had a sense of déjà vu about it. Which was why he couldn't stomach the presence of a murderer like Michele Fardella alongside the mayor, the town's highest public official.

Chapter 24

Brigadier Mattia Montalto's determined opposition made Captain Costa of the Royal Guard throw all caution to the wind. He had to get Michele Fardella out of hot water. He was afraid his trusted man might confess something compromising about the massacre at Borgo Guarine.

So Costa decided to take action.

The following day, he met with ten of his most intrepid hotheads, at the combat league's base of operations.

"It is absolutely imperative that any subversive activity be nipped in the bud," he began in a stentorian tone. "I have heard from reliable sources that several groups of agitators here in Salemi are preparing to instigate an uprising against the Fasci. One of these groups is organized by Prince Licata." The young men looked at one another, incredulous. The prince was highly respected by all; how could he side with subversives? "That's exactly how it is," the captain continued, satisfied that he had made an impression on his men. "Prince Licata is a ringleader, but he can't be touched. We would end up making all his landowner friends our enemies, and that's something we don't want. So we'll strike his operational arm instead: Rosario Losurdo, his gabellotto. He was the one responsible for the Borgo Guarine massacre. It's time we made the bastard pay for it!"

A battle cry rang through the room, and everyone rushed to the racks to grab his club and pennants. But the captain again claimed their attention. "Stop! Hold on. This is not a punitive expedition, like the others. Losurdo is a tough bird. We must act shrewdly, devise a plan. Remember that he too is well liked by his men, and many campieri are willing to risk their lives for him and the prince. So, here's the plan I've come up with . . ."

Chief Brigadier Montalto was nobody's fool, and Captain Costa's insistence that he free Fardella had made him realize that the former charcoal burner must know something. Moreover, he didn't care for that dogged fury against the prince. He too was aware of Ferdinando Licata's ideas, but they didn't worry him. The prince was an honorable man. Lorenzo Costa, however, had targeted him, and seeing that the newspapers carried stories about fascist squads that went around attacking dwellings and local clubs, slaying civilians, Montalto decided to go to Licata and warn him.

The prince received him in the Hall of Globes. "Why are you so worried, Chief Montalto?" he asked, showing him to a seat in one of the parlors.

"Excellency, I don't wish to alarm you, but you should know that Captain Costa considers you guilty of organizing a subversive cell here in your palazzo," Montalto explained. Then he elaborated: "Actually, there are a lot of stories going around, and on the continent in recent months, a number of innocent people have been killed for much less. I wouldn't want some hotheads to do anything foolish."

"Are you afraid the action squads may attack the palazzo?" Licata asked point-blank.

"That's exactly it, Excellency."

Licata relaxed and smiled. "Then don't worry. I've taken my precautions, and I am well protected. In any case, thank you for your concern. Italy needs people like you: honest and loyal.

"We live in times of great upheaval. I hope this madness will end before long." With that, Montalto rose. "I don't wish to take up any more of your time, Prince."

"Tell me one last thing, Chief Montalto: Are you still investigating the massacre at Borgo Guarine?"

"Of course. The investigation has just begun."

"Do you have any suspects?"

"If an offender isn't caught within the first forty-eight hours following a crime, it becomes more difficult to apprehend him afterward. But I'm a patient man. Still, I must admit that I haven't yet been able to form a clear-cut idea of possible motives. In any case, an inquiry is under way, and there's the *segreto istruttorio*: the obligation to maintain secrecy concerning a preliminary investigation."

That said, the chief brigadier took leave of the prince with a perfect military salute.

———

The infamous squad went into action in the dead of night. Led by Lorenzo Costa himself, it was made up of seven of the most violent bullies associated with Salemi's fascist league: Abbate, Ioppolo, Amari, Busacca, Cotta, Garofano, and Modica, all gallows birds, destined to lord it over everyone in the territory of Salemi for many years to come. Four of them climbed onto an open wagon drawn by a handsome bay, and two others got on donkeys, while Lorenzo Costa and Antonio Ioppolo rode a pair of young black steeds. The grim band left Salemi at full speed for the long ride to Rosario Losurdo's farmstead.

Leaving their mounts about a quarter mile away from the farm, the eight-member action team approached on foot. Prospero Abbate, the most corpulent, carried with him a gourd shaped like a flask, which the poorest peasants used as a jug. The gourd contained ethyl alcohol. They reached the shed, and, at a sign from Captain Costa, Abbate poured some of the gourd's contents on the buggy and some on the woodpile. Then he lit a match and threw it on the stacked wood.

The fire's glow filtered through the windows of Manfredi's house. Used to always sleeping with his nerves on edge, Losurdo's chief campiere opened his eyes at the first crackling and realized immediately that the storehouse was on fire. He leaped out of bed, waking his wife. Then he ran out of the house and saw the flames rising above the shed, beyond the walls of the farm. He reached the gate and opened it, joined at that moment by Rosario Losurdo, rifle in hand. The gabellotto glumly watched as the blaze quickly devoured the roof of the shed.

"Gutless bastards," he muttered to himself, quickly running through his head the list of enemies he and Prince Licata had. The inventory was not short and was certainly incomplete.

Meanwhile, the peasants who worked the prince's lands came running from the nearby shacks and cabins. Some carried shovels; others, buckets and hoes. Manfredi ordered them to dig a trench as a firebreak to protect the farm. Unfortunately, they couldn't try to extinguish the fire with water, since, after a blistering summer, the cisterns were running low.

From a distance, under the cover of dense brush, Costa and his seven henchmen watched the farmers' rescue efforts as they belatedly tried to protect the farm from the flames. They saw Losurdo look around, searching among the night's shadows. But darkness was in their favor. When they were absolutely sure that they had fulfilled their mission, they crept out of their hiding place and returned to Salemi.

Prince Licata arrived at the scene of the fire early the following morning. With him were Chief Brigadier Montalto and two of his recruits. Manfredi and the other campieri who made up Prince Licata's small army were sifting through the still smoldering rubble with Losurdo, looking for some trace, some clue. They paid no attention to the charred remains of a dried gourd, so they never managed to find evidence that the fire was arson.

They were still rummaging among the ashes when the action squad's picturesque group arrived: a cart drawn by a gray horse, two donkeys, and two young colts, carrying eight Black Shirts. Captain Costa dismounted, followed by his men, armed with clubs and bad intentions.

"Captain. News here in Salemi travels more swiftly than the mistral," the prince greeted him with bitter sarcasm.

"News is as swift as vendetta, Prince Licata," Costa was quick to retort. "I see that you do not lack enemies."

The chief brigadier joined in the ceremonial pleasantries: "Costa, are you on a mission?"

"Brigadier, your friends are my friends. I respect Prince Licata. But not Rosario Losurdo, who welcomes godless subversives in his home," he said, turning to the gabellotto, who at that moment was armed only with a shovel.

"Captain, I remind you that you are on private land here!" Losurdo shouted at him.

"And I remind you that I represent the law. As does the brigadier," Captain Costa clarified. "In fact, we combat leagues directly represent the will of the people. You have a problem, Losurdo. Someone who's out to get you—probably the same person who set this fire—wrote that besides protecting vile agitators, you're hiding evidence from the Borgo Guarine massacre at your home. Is that true?"

Rosario Losurdo smiled. "Tell your Mr. Anonymous to come and tell me to my face. It's a joke, right?"

"I never joke when I'm working, Losurdo. If you say you're innocent, you won't object to having me take a look inside your house."

"How dare you!" the prince intervened, but Losurdo stopped him.

"It's not a problem, Prince. Let him go ahead and search; I have nothing to hide."

"Fine, then. Shall we begin?" The captain was persistent.

"On one condition, however—or, rather, two," Ferdinando Licata interjected. "I wouldn't want there to be any—how shall I put it?—sleight of hand. So before entering, you will be searched, and then each of you will be followed by my campieri."

"Agreed," Costa consented.

A few minutes later the captain's Black Shirts, after being thoroughly frisked by the prince's private guards, entered the area of the farm and began hunting for evidence of Losurdo's guilt. They divided themselves up into three groups: Amari and Busacca searched the barn and Manfredi's house; Cotta, Albanesi, and Garofano rummaged through Losurdo's residence; while Ioppolo and Modica began poking around the small chapel, now converted into a storeroom for household goods and harnesses. Each group had two campieri sticking to it like shadows, watching to see that it did not perform some conjuring trick, as Prince Licata had made sure to emphasize.

While some searched and others kept an eye on them, the families of Losurdo and Manfredi gathered in the center of the courtyard. Prince Licata, Captain Costa, and the brigadier, with his men, stood silent in another part of the yard, waiting for the search to be completed. A half hour, later a cry from the former chapel made all heads turn.

"Captain, hurry!" The voice was that of Antonio Ioppolo.

Captain Costa, followed by the prince and all the others, quickly rushed to the chapel door.

They entered the little church that was no longer consecrated. There were chests stacked up in a corner, a confessional, a pile of leather harnesses, an old plow, and, in the back, what was left of the altar. Ioppolo, behind the altar, motioned for the captain to come over. Stepping around the obstacles, the group approached. Prince Licata immediately spotted what had drawn the man's attention. Ioppolo had raised a stone slab from the floor, and under it, in a hiding place dug out of the earth, lay a cloth-wrapped bundle.

Licata looked at Manfredi, who had been tailing Ioppolo and Modica in their search. With a look, he asked him if everything was on the up-and-up. Manfredi nodded glumly. Captain Costa made his way through the men and stooped to examine the concealed hollow.

"There was a pile of crates and baskets over it. What made me suspicious was that the stone slab wasn't lined up," Antonio Ioppolo said, hoping for a pat on the head.

And the captain did not fail to applaud him. "Good for you, Ioppolo. Maybe it's what we were looking for."

He picked up the cloth bundle. He stood up so he could be seen by everyone, especially the prince and the chief brigadier, who, having been the last one in, was now trying to get close to Costa. "Give that to me, Captain."

The captain was all too happy to have Montalto make the discovery. He placed the bundle in his hands and waited for him to show them what it contained. The chief realized that he was holding a gun and another object—possibly a knife. He unfolded the undershirt they were wrapped in, and a Glisenti 1911 revolver appeared before everyone's eyes, along with a nasty-looking knife, its blade still specked with dried blood. Prince Licata went rigid. Only now did he realize that the whole production, the fire, the search and the discovery, were part of a trap that Captain Costa had staged. As he was following those thoughts, the brigadier's voice called him back to reality.

"Rosario Losurdo, what are these weapons doing on your farm?"

Despite all he'd been through and the hard life he'd endured since he was a child, Losurdo too was left speechless. He could only stammer, "I swear I don't know anything about it! That gun isn't mine."

The prince's thundering voice made everyone turn to him. "Chief Montalto, it's clear that those weapons were planted here by some rotten bastard who, I swear to you, will not have a long life!"

"Let's all calm down!" Montalto cried. "Anyone could have hidden this gun here. Now, though, Losurdo, you've got to come with me to the station. I have to draft a report, and I need your testimony."

"Chief Montalto, I have nothing to say. I don't know anything about those things."

"You can tell me in your statement." He nodded to the two recruits, who took hold of Losurdo and pushed him out of the chapel, followed by Montalto, who had rewrapped the gun and knife in the cloth.

Prince Licata drew close to Captain Costa. He towered above him, and now that he was truly formidable. "Costa," he whispered in his ear when no one could hear them, "pray to God that nothing happens to Losurdo, because otherwise you will be in my debt, and I have no compassion toward my debtors." Without giving him time to respond, he strode out of the chapel.

About a hundred yards away, hidden in a pigpen, Gaetano Vassallo, accompanied by Cesare, a young member of his band, had his binoculars trained on the gate to Losurdo's farm.

As soon as the fire had been reported to him, he had immediately wanted to go see for himself. He'd watched the arrival of Prince Licata, that of the chief brigadier of the carabinieri, and, finally, that of Costa with his Black Shirts. Now he saw Losurdo leaving the farm with irons on his wrists, escorted by two recruits and followed by the brigadier.

"They've arrested Losurdo," he whispered to the young man. "I don't understand what Losurdo has to do with the storehouse burning down."

Only later would Vassallo learn from the usual informers that Losurdo had been arrested because the weapons used in the massacre of his family had been found on his farm.

Chapter 25

L eaving the mayor's office, Marshal Montalto was pessimistic about Italy's future. He saw a nation in the hands of corrupt reprobates, where economic interests were the only ones that counted, while the principles for which he had always fought—justice, fair play, meritocracy, work as a mark of man's dignity—were now at the mercy of individuals who did not respect the most elementary rules of civil society. He had made a promise to the wives of Dr. Ragusa and Rosario Losurdo, but he had not been able to keep that promise.

His uniform was no longer worth anything. How could he appear before the citizens and enforce the law, if he couldn't make the basic rules prescribed by lawful authority be accepted?

On his way out, he met Saro. The young man was coming from the basement of the town hall, where he had asked to see his father. To no avail, however, since the Black Shirts had insolently chased him off, telling him to make a written request to the mayor.

"I'm sorry, Saro. I'm truly mortified," the marshal told him. "But the combat league will not hand over your father and Losurdo to me. They themselves will transport them to Marsala, the day after tomorrow. The hope is that the trial will begin very soon."

"*U patri* left, otherwise he would have been able to do to something," Saro said regretfully.

"With these people, not even *u patri* could do anything. They don't listen to anyone. They've lost touch with reality. They have their own principles. Either you follow them, or you're out."

The marshal's words were a chill wind for Saro. Throughout his life, following his father's principles, he had always tried to respect the rules, never deviating from the law—something which not many people in Sicily did, often preferring to take justice into their own hands. Unfortunately, most of the time the state was negligent, and laws in fact were made by the noble class, namely, the landowners and their guardians, the gabellotti and campieri. The music had changed somewhat since the fascists had taken over the government, but in the long run though the musicians were different, the melody was still the same.

That night Saro fell into the darkest despair.

In his heart he felt a fierce desire to be in charge and make things go the way he wanted and not how the Costas or the Janos of this world wanted them to be.

Then the image of Mena took shape in his thoughts. Beautiful Mena, with her emerald eyes, raven black hair, and a young, perfect body whose soft skin radiated a perceptible passion through every pore. What could he do for her? How could he help his father and Losurdo at that very difficult time in their lives?

These were the thoughts that kept him awake all night.

The images of Mena were warm and tender, but they came to him with a tone of reproach. Saro continued pacing around the room. Then he seemed to come to a resolution. It was a decision that would change his life irrevocably.

Before acting on it, though, he had to see Mena. It might well be their last meeting, but he wanted her to know how great his love for her was.

It was the middle of the night, and Salemi's streets were deserted. Saro hurried through them almost on tiptoe, not wanting to risk being seen by anyone. He headed toward the town's western gate and the path leading to Borgo Tafèle, a cluster of dwellings where Rosario Losurdo's farm was located. As soon as he was out of Salemi and on the dirt track, he began running, his course made easy by the fact that the trail was downhill. When he came in sight of the village, dogs from the various farms began barking as he went past, but nobody paid any attention. Finally, he reached the farmhouse. He knew exactly which window was Mena's bedroom.

Rosario Losurdo's arrest had thrown his family's lives into confusion. Rosita had tried to take the situation in hand, replacing her husband in everything: assigning work and dealing with everyday problems, big and small. Michele had quit guarding Prince Paolo Moncada's Dell'Orbo estate in order to stay close to his mother and help her at this difficult time.

His brother, Donato, continued his work as a campiere instead. Mena and Nennella took care of the housework.

Despite being exhausted by the time evening came, Mena was no longer able to sleep soundly. She woke up continually; every noise made her anxious, and she worried that someone would come and arrest her brothers as well.

All night long, she tossed and turned in bed, envious of Nennella, who shared the same room but didn't question things very deeply. The maid slept the sleep of the just, and a faint whistling came from her nose, like babies when they have a slight cold.

During the hours when she was not quite asleep, Mena also fantasized about Saro. She liked Dr. Ragusa's son very much. His behavior was always polite, not like certain ill-mannered louts in town who acted like they were from the mountains. She had replayed the scene at the well a thousand times in her mind, with a thousand nuances but only one ending: an intense, passionate kiss with her back pressed against the trunk of the fig tree, his legs thrusting between her thighs so that her groin could feel his.

But as soon as her imagination exceeded the bounds, she tried to dispel the image. She didn't want to have to confess those impure thoughts to Don Mario. But the nights were long, and sooner or later, just as she was falling asleep, when her focus was less alert, she pictured herself lying under the shade of the tree with Saro, who would kiss her and touch her breast and then—

Her eyes flew open. She'd heard a strange sound, a faint melancholy call, hoop-hoop-hoop, like that of a hoopoe bird. A hoopoe, at that hour of night? The sound was very close. Then a small pebble struck the windowpane. Mena got up and went over to it.

She recognized Saro and felt a quiver in her belly.

The young man motioned for her to come down. She nodded, took a large shawl from the chair, and joined him in the courtyard, praying that no one would wake up.

Saro was waiting for her outside the door, unconcerned with the possibility of being seen by anyone. Mena stepped out and, not saying a word for fear of waking her mother, let him know that he was crazy to be there at that hour. Saro was about to answer her, but she gently placed her hand over his mouth to keep him from talking. Then she took his hand and led him to the storage shed, which was a distance from her house and that of Manfredi.

When they got there, Mena finally said, "Are you crazy coming here at this hour of night? Do you want the campieri to shoot you?"

Saro's only response was to embrace her, burying his face in her long hair. Mena closed her eyes and touched her cheek to Saro's. She breathed deeply to impress his scent upon her memory. Finally, he broke away and kissed her on the mouth. She melted completely. At first his tongue played over her tightly shut lips, and then tried to make its way into her mouth. Mena was still a little resistant, but then her lips slowly parted, and Saro was finally able to slide his tongue between her perfect little teeth. When their tongues met, there was a burst of passion: they interlocked, sought each other, fused, and broke apart to reconnect once again. The two young people's excitement was at a fever pitch. Saro left the warm, moist haven of her mouth and moved down to her breasts, releasing them from her nightgown. His fingers squeezed the unripe little buds, and his tongue gently licked her nipples, which sprouted up like two plump shoots. Saro was insatiable, and Mena began to tremble with pleasure, completely carried away. She felt his engorged penis against her stomach. Instinctively she touched it, and then grasped it firmly through his pants. She pushed her hand down and then up. His member was swollen. Mena slipped her hand into his trousers and was finally able to feel it in all its fullness.

Saro's tongue had reached the soft skin of her abdomen and contin-ued moving farther down. Mena stopped him, however, and pressed his face against her belly. Saro continued to lick the silky skin below her belly button and could feel Mena's pubic hair brush against his chin. His ex-citement was at the breaking point. Mena let out a moan, stroked Saro's hair, and then pushed him toward her vagina: it was her consent to go all the way.

With the tip of his tongue, Saro started toying with her pubic hair. He bathed it with saliva and then very gently began nibbling at it. Slowly he pushed his tongue deeper and finally reached her most hidden core. As soon as the tip of his tongue touched her clitoris, Mena was wet; at the same time, tears of irrepressible joy ran down her cheeks. Then she let Saro know that the long-awaited moment had come. Saro rose up to kiss her soft lips again, as she directed his member between her legs. Saro patiently let her guide him, not wanting to cause her the least trauma. He simply remained motionless. Mena understood his sensitiv-ity, and, in her heart, she was grateful. She inserted his penis between her thighs. Her vagina was moist and throbbing, ready to receive that impa-tient, passionate organ she was clutching. Gently Mena slipped it into her most private recess, swollen and slick with longing. Then, when she was certain she was in position, she gave a few little thrusts with her hips. Saro was in an agony of desire. He would have liked to slam into her forcefully again and again, but he made a great effort to control himself and remained still. Mena, with her fingers, felt that he had reached the critical point. Once again she pressed her lips to Saro's, as if to thank him for his patience. She smiled sweetly at him, and then with a sharp thrust, sank completely onto the boy's body. She felt her hymen break, though the sensation was in her mind, and a gush of blood ran down their legs. They held each other even more tightly, and Mena began writhing her hips to prolong the moment of intercourse. Now crying and laughing, she was kissing Saro on the mouth and eyes, caressing him and gripping his buttocks to press him to her as tightly as possible. Saro was now free to fully release his passion, until then repressed; thrusting his hips, he drove his member into Mena's body, more and more forcefully, faster and faster, slowing down and then resuming with renewed fervor. Mena was now already at the point of orgasm, and with a last rhythmic gasp, Saro felt his semen flood the girl's belly as she climaxed.

They were silent for a long time, holding each other tight and cuddling. Saro was the first to speak. "I've made a decision. My father and your father don't have a chance. They'll be tried and sentenced for a crime they haven't committed. I've decided that tomorrow night I will try to free them."

Mena gasped in surprise. "But that's crazy. They'll catch you. How can you think of doing that?"

"I have a plan; I think it will work."

The girl was desperate. "You can't do it. Haven't you thought about me?"

"That's the reason I came, to tell you." Saro couldn't seem to find the right words. "You see, I really hadn't planned on what happened."

"You're already sorry?"

"No, no, Mena, try and understand. I love you. We'll get married. But first I have to free your father and my father. That's what I came to tell you. That I love you, but that if something were to happen to me, you have to wait for me because I'll be back and I'll marry you."

"Of course I'll wait for you, silly. I love you too, and I'll never love anyone else in my life. But for the sake of our love, I ask you not to do anything foolish. There has to be some justice, even in this world."

"No, there isn't."

"But what if something were to happen to you? I would die."

"Nothing serious will happen. But if I should have to go away for a while, swear that you will wait for me. Swear to me?"

"I swear." Their mouths met longingly for one last passionate kiss.

When the Black Shirts were forced to remain on guard duty at the town hall, which happened rarely, their supper was prepared by Tina, the wife of Ninì Trovato, Salemi's town crier. With two prisoners awaiting transfer, the combat leaguers had been confined to the building for several days now, to keep watch over them. After the arrest of Losurdo and Ragusa, Jano had ordered Tina to cook meals for them as well until the two could be moved to the prison in Marsala. So that night, Ninì's wife prepared five bowls ahead of time, two for the prisoners and three for the Black Shirts. For the prisoners, Tina always served up boiled potatoes with cheese, walnuts, and olives, while for the Black Shirts she alternated spaghetti with sardines, eggplant caponata, and *panelle*, fritters made with chickpea flour.

Generally it was young Pepè who brought the guards' meals to the town hall. Pepè was Ninì Trovato's grandchild, the only son of his daughter-in-law, Giuseppina, another of the town's grass widows. His son, in fact, had left for Germany in search of work years before and had never returned. Every month, he wrote a letter to his wife in which he swore he missed her and his son and asked her to give his parents his regards, but he didn't say much about what he earned, where he was living, or when he thought he'd be back. The fact remains that Pepè and Giuseppina lived at Ninì Trovato's house. Ever since the boy was little, each time his grandfather took his trumpet and drum to make a public announcement in the piazza, Pepè would mimic him, leading the way to the door with his hand to his mouth like a funnel, blaring out a *pe-pe-pe-pe-pe* that got on the man's nerves.

Pepè was fourteen now, but everyone in town still called him that, having forgotten his real name. That night, Tina arranged the bowls on a wooden breadboard, a *spianatora*, which she used for kneading bread and pasta dough. She covered the bowls with a cloth and helped Pepè balance it on his head, warning him to go slow and not to trip, or she would beat the living daylights out of him. Then she gave him her blessing and sent him off to the guard detail at town hall.

Pepè, mindful of his grandmother's threat, walked cautiously but took a shortcut to get there quicker. He went along a passageway that ran downhill under an arch and continued steeply toward the piazza and town hall. The narrow streets were lit only by lamps in the windows of the houses. Suddenly a shadow stepped out from behind an alley and blocked his way. The boy was startled and nearly dropped all the bowls on the ground. The man helped him keep the board balanced, and for a few brief moments, the scene, viewed from the outside, was quite comical. When they'd both managed to restore the board's stability, the figure said in a husky, contrived voice: "Pepè, leave the spianatora to me. I'll take it to the guards."

The shadow was hidden under a long black cloak, and at the sound of that somber voice, Pepè began to whimper, "Please, don't hurt me. I'll tell you everything."

"You don't have to tell me anything, you just have to let me bring the comrades their supper."

"You want my grandmother to beat me up?" Pepè whined even louder.

To put an end to the melodrama, Saro drew a razor from his cloak; the blade glinted in the glow of a lantern hanging on a nearby door. The boy's head seemed to withdraw into the collar of his jacket like a turtle's into its shell. "Would you prefer a little beating or having that tender throat of yours slashed?" He flashed the blade under the boy's nose, with a quick sleight of hand.

Pepè shrank back even more. "Take it, do what you like, but don't hurt me. Please." He handed over the wooden board, which Saro grabbed with both hands. "Now count to a thousand, and only then can you go back home. And don't tell anyone about this—not even your grandparents— or I'll come and snatch you from your bed while you're sleeping and hang you upside down from the fig tree."

"I won't say a word, sir, I swear. Not to anyone."

"Good, now count."

"Up to a thousand?"

"Yes, up to a thousand, and not one less. Can you count?"

"Of course. I aced arithmetic."

"Good for you. Now turn and face the wall and start counting."

Pepè obeyed and began to count. Saro quickly headed toward town hall. The small door to the combat league's quarters opened on the left side of the building. The guards' pickup truck, known throughout the area, stood outside in the courtyard. In an adjacent alleyway, in a recess formed by two houses, used by women to hang out clothes to dry, were two horses that Saro had managed to borrow from some friends who lived in Pusillesi, a nearby district of Salemi.

With the wooden board balanced on his head, Saro approached the door, his heart beating rapidly. He did not have a prearranged plan. He knew he had to improvise. His only hope was that his father and Losurdo would not panic and would help him at the crucial moment of escape.

He knocked firmly on the door, and a few seconds later, Quinto opened up. Saro was quick to get past the Black Shirt, struggling with the board on his head to avoid being recognized.

"Grub's here!" he called out cheerfully, entering the command room. He set the dishes on the table.

Cosimo and Prospero dropped what they were doing at once and fell upon the bowls.

"What did your grandmother make us, something good?"

"Pasta with sardines."

They took off the cloth and uncovered the pasta still steaming in the bowls. Without further ado, Cosimo and Prospero sat down and began forking up the spaghetti, stuffing themselves with huge mouthfuls.

"Let's go, hurry up," Quinto said to Saro, who had placed the board with the last two bowls back on his head.

Luck was on his side. Nobody had yet noticed the switch. Quinto led him down the stairs to the basement and stopped at the first cell. He put in the key, and only then did he realize that it wasn't the usual Pepè who'd brought the food.

"How come Pepè didn't come?" he asked suspiciously as he flung open the cell door.

"He's sick. *Nonna* Tina sent me."

The cell door swung open. Peppino Ragusa was standing in the doorway. His face was bruised, his eyes lifeless, but as soon as he saw his son, he couldn't help but exclaim "Saro!"

Quinto instantly knew that he had been tricked, but in less time than that, Saro had shoved the board with the bowls at his father, who, completely stunned, found himself holding it. From under his cloak Saro pulled out the *liccasapuni*, the soap knife he used to shave customers at the barbershop, and with a precise stroke slashed Quinto's face. The guard first moved to protect his face, then tried to stem the blood by pressing the palms of his hands on the long gash. Saro did not let up. Picking up the wooden board that had fallen to the ground, he brought it down as hard as he could on the unfortunate victim's skull, causing the guard to slump, unconscious, in a pool of blood.

Peppino Ragusa was a good man and would never have imagined that his son could commit such an act, and in cold blood.

Saro hurriedly retrieved the keys from the lock and then went to open the door of Losurdo's cell, succeeding on the first try.

Rosario Losurdo immediately took in the situation.

"The other two?" he asked Saro, seeing Quinto lying unconscious on the ground, bleeding.

"They're gobbling up pasta." He pointed upstairs.

"They might have heard. Let's go! You go up first; we'll follow you," Rosario said.

Peppino Ragusa had remained in his cell, unable to handle the situation. Losurdo grabbed him by the arm and forced him to come out.

Saro began climbing the stairs, his ears straining to hear the slightest suspicious sound. Behind him came Rosario and then the doctor. Besides a razor, the only weapon they had on their side was the element of surprise. They couldn't afford to lose that advantage.

Saro reached the door and slowly opened it partway. Peering into the room, he saw Cosimo still bent over his plate of spaghetti. He motioned the others to follow him, but as soon as he went through the door he was struck by something that felt like a mallet, which knocked the breath out of him. He'd been hit by a chair, and as he fell to the ground, the razor slipped out of his hands. Rosario, who was ready for anything, stepped in and rushed headlong at Prospero. Head lowered, he struck him in the chest, driving him against the wall. Turning, he saw Cosimo coming at them with a sawed-off shotgun. It was obvious that the guards had staged the ambush to catch them unawares, and they had succeeded to perfection. Cosimo shouted, "Stop or I'll shoot!"

Saro, turning a somersault, lunged for the razor. The sudden move distracted Cosimo long enough to spare Losurdo a blast from the shotgun. Cosimo, in fact, aimed the double-barreled gun at Saro, who hastily picked up the razor and threw it at him like a boomerang. The razor's entire length lodged in Cosimo's right hand, just as he was about to pull the trigger. It happened in a mere fraction of a second; in fact, the razor's impact on the guard's hand deflected the load of gunshot. Cosimo felt a sting like the lash of a whip and then looked at the back of his hand where the liccasapuni was planted. He pulled out the razor and as soon as it was out, blood began gushing from the wound.

Dr. Peppino Ragusa watched the scene as if it did not concern him. But he was stunned by Saro: never would he have thought him capable of such violence.

Rosario Losurdo, meanwhile, had rushed at Prospero, who had yet to recover from the blow to his chest. Losurdo grabbed him by the ears and banged his head repeatedly against the wall as forcefully as he could. At the fourth violent impact, the man slid from his hands.

Cosimo was beside himself with rage; holding the gun in his other hand, since the right one was out of commission, he took aim at Saro, but Rosario Losurdo came up behind him and charged him like a buffalo, butting him in the kidneys and sending him flying to the ground. "Let's go! Let's get out of here!" he yelled to Saro.

Ragusa, meanwhile, was helping Prospero. His physician's instinct led him to assist anyone who required aid.

Saro turned back, grabbed his father's arm, and forced him to follow him. "Papa, this is no time to be a missionary."

They reached the front door and staggered out into the fresh evening air.

"Let's take the truck," Rosario said, seeing the pickup parked in the courtyard.

"No, no. Look at the tires," Saro told him. "We have two horses waiting for us down there."

Rosario looked at the vehicle's wheels and saw that all four tires had been slashed.

"Nice job," he remarked.

"That's nothing, I also cut the brake line," Saro told him.

They reached the horses. Losurdo mounted the thinner one, and Saro and his father got on a handsome young bay.

As they rode off toward Calatafimi, they heard the cries of Prospero and Quinto. Then they heard the truck start up, but they never saw it appear behind them.

They'd made it. Saro was proud of himself. His father less so.

Saro had been able to arrange things with excellent judgment. He evidently had the makings of an organizer: he was quick to make decisions and knew what had to be done to achieve a specific objective.

When he'd begun planning the escape, the first thing that concerned him was not so much being able to rescue his father and Losurdo but where to hide them during the long wait for the ship's departure.

Saro had decided that they would flee to America, at least until Italy had come to its senses regarding the insane laws against the Jewish race.

In finding a safe place to hole up without arousing suspicions, he had been aided by a religious friend, a Franciscan friar who lived at the Sanctuary of Calatafimi, the mother church. The pious friars had sheltered entire families of dissidents and even mafiosi within their walls on other occasions. The sanctuary had been built around the year 1200, and, over time, to oppose pirates coming from the sea, it had been transformed into a veritable fortress, solid and sturdy. Saro thought it would make an ideal refuge, not least because it was just a few miles from the port of Castellammare del Golfo, where they would board a fishing boat that would take them to Palermo.

It was still night when they reached Calatafimi. They headed for the sanctuary and Brother Antonino himself, Saro's friend, welcomed them and led them into the safety of the monastery's walls. At that time, perhaps because of the concordat enacted ten years earlier, church properties enjoyed a kind of immunity, so they were considered the safest refuge for those trying to flee the fascist regime.

The friar asked no questions; he looked at the men standing before him, greeted them with a nod, and then said softly, "Follow me." He turned and walked to a staircase that descended into the church's crypt. The friar moved swiftly through the silent corridors, lighting their way with an oil lamp, until he came to a door and opened it. Before letting them inside, he asked solicitously, "Have you eaten?"

"Actually we didn't have time," Saro replied.

"I'll bring you something. Meanwhile, go in and get settled. There are some pallets available."

Saro entered the large room first and was amazed to see how many other people were in there. Everyone stared at the newcomers in absolute silence, frightened, waiting to hear their stories. One question was going through their heads: Were they friends or informers?

Saro explained that they were from Salemi and that they were waiting to sail for America. At those words, everybody relaxed; they were all in the same situation.

For several years now, the sanctuary had become a way station for Sicilians who had to flee Italy clandestinely.

In recent weeks, the monks had taken in two Jewish families: one from Caltanissetta and the other from a small village near Enna. These desperate, anxious people had brought just a few things with them—only the strictest necessities—in order to be able to move quickly.

Somewhat apart from the two Jewish families, so he would not be confused with them, was a certain Vito Pizzuto, a gabellotto from the Vicaretto estate. He had been hiding in the sanctuary for at least a month, to avoid capture by the fascist squads in Trapani, who had accused him of antigovernment activities.

Everyone in the room had but one goal: to escape from a cruel stepmother of a country and board one of the ships of the Florio fleet, which departed from Palermo, and which a man could sail on without close inspection—provided he tipped the crew well.

As far as personal documents were concerned, there was even a ready-and-willing organization connected with an affiliate at the Port of New York. It offered a one-way ticket, false papers, and the possibility of repaying everything in easy installments. Of course, the *cosca*—the Mob—would withhold what they owed, taking it directly from what they earned in jobs the organization itself procured illegally, thereby holding the naive immigrants in a double bind.

Could paradise itself be more well thought out than that?

In those days, hundreds of thousands of desperate individuals crossed the ocean that way, in search of a new life and a new world, where work would finally restore the dignity that was denied them in the land of their birth.

————

Meanwhile, in Salemi, Prospero and Quinto had crashed the truck into a stone wall on a curve along the road to Calatafimi. Jano joined them, along with Ginetto and Nunzio, and was blaming the two hapless men who could barely stand up, still in shock following the impact.

Prospero had tried to tackle the road at high speed, careening dangerously because of the four flat tires, and when he hit the brake to slow down, the pedal failed, and the pickup slammed violently into a low wall hidden behind a prickly pear.

Later Prospero, Quinto, and Cosimo were taken to Dr. Bizzarri's clinic. Awakened in the middle of the night, the doctor stitched and dressed their wounds, and then slumped exhausted into a chair a couple of hours later: "That was quite a beating, no doubt about it."

The words irritated Jano, who didn't like being duped. "If I get my hands on them, they won't live to tell it."

"In the meantime, they must be laughing about it, waiting for a steamer to America," the doctor commented.

"What makes you think they're leaving the country?" Jano asked suspiciously.

"Didn't you tell me you followed them on the road to Calatafimi?" the doctor asked, pouring himself a glass of wine that he'd taken from the medicine cabinet.

"So? What's that got to do with America?" Jano insisted.

"Well, they're waiting at the sanctuary for the ship to depart, which should be next week in fact, weather permitting."

"What are you doing, guessing?" Nunzio asked him.

"No. Everyone knows it. People who want to leave the country and have problems with the law go into hiding at the Sanctuary of Calatafimi and hole up until the evening prior to departure. Then they're taken to the port of Castellammare, and from there a fishing boat brings them directly to the ship as it's about to sail. A crewman allows them to get on board covertly, and that's that."

The doctor looked at the three men who were listening to him in astonishment. He realized that he had said too much.

"Don't tell me you didn't know! Everyone is aware of that trafficking; lots of people earn a good deal of money from it."

"Are you sure?" Jano still couldn't believe it was true.

"Of course! Last year around this time, Brother Antonino called me to attend a woman who was pregnant. She was about to give birth, and they were facing the voyage to Palermo. They were afraid she might pop the baby out on the fishing boat. I had to induce labor."

"Brother Antonino, you said?" Jano wanted to know.

"Yes, he's actually a Franciscan friar. He's the one who runs the whole operation. But really, you didn't know? I can't believe it." The doctor shook his head incredulously. "It must be at least two or three years that this has been going on."

"I *get it*, Doctor!" Jano was irritated by Bizzarri's prolonged account, which only underscored their stupidity.

"Maybe it would have been better not to tell you. But the cat is out of the bag now. What's done is done."

The doctor's revelation had rekindled Jano's hopes of being able to capture the three fugitives. But to begin with, he had to get his hands on the monk.

The following day, along with Nunzio, he went to Calatafimi. Consulting the registry records, he learned everything there was to know about the friar. Brother Antonino was a foundling; his parents had abandoned him at the Capuchin monastery in Salaparuta, and he had spent his entire adolescence and early adulthood there. The friars had raised him like a son; it was natural that at age twenty he would take his vows, mainly because he had always refused to leave the community, despite the fact that the good brothers had encouraged him to seek work outside the monastery's walls.

Jano couldn't figure out a way to lure him over to their side.

Nunzio had no qualms. "Let's take him and put him in the box."

"Are you nuts? Do you want me to get in trouble with the mayor? The Church would demand our heads in retaliation if we were to do such a thing."

"What if we raid the sanctuary?"

"It's not allowed. The churches are taboo for us."

"Then we have to come up with something devious."

"Yeah, something very clever. But what?" Jano agreed thoughtfully.

"For example, blackmail," Nunzio suggested. "Everyone has something to hide in his life. Brother Antonino is certainly no exception."

"All we have to do is find his weak point. Do you feel like tailing him for a while?"

"With pleasure," Nunzio replied.

Nunzio's theory, which held that every man has a skeleton in his closet, proved to be true.

The following day, he stuck closely to the monk, alternating with Gi-netto, whom Jano had called in to give them a hand. The three never left him, from morning, when he went out to celebrate Mass in the nearby chapel, till night, when he returned to the sanctuary for evening Ves-pers. Brother Antonino was a small, thin man with hollow cheeks and a thick, dark beard. He was always on the go. He went to the market to buy whatever food the monks did not produce themselves; he taught catechism to children about to make their first communion; in the after-noon he played soccer with a group of kids on the dusty field in front of the sanctuary, without taking off his cassock. When the game was over, it took him a good while to dust himself off as the kids stood around laughing; he liked to clown around with them. Sometimes he went out before dark, accompanied by an altar boy, to administer communion to some elderly person who was ill and couldn't get out of bed. Brother An-tonino's conduct seemed to run along the lines of a normal, exemplary ecclesiastical life.

Except that one afternoon, when Ginetto was tailing him, he went into a house with the altar boy, who was carrying the holy water, and stayed there beyond the usual time. Ginetto crept up to the ground floor windows, but there appeared to be no one inside. In fact, he noticed that the kitchen looked abandoned, its cupboards hanging open and the wood stove cold, its doors broken. "Maybe they're upstairs," he thought. The small fire escape was easily reached thanks to a pile of masonry de-bris stacked up against the house. Ginetto decided to attempt the climb, even though his weight would not make it easy. He grabbed the railing and struggled to haul himself up. He climbed over the railing without making a sound. The floor was littered with trash paper, shards of tiles, and crumbled bricks, suggesting that the house must have been aban-doned for a long time. He leaned forward to peer inside the room. On a rickety dresser without drawers he saw the holy water and the little prayer book. Then turning his gaze toward the center of the room, he saw Brother Antonino sitting on the edge of a bedspring; kneeling be-tween his legs was the altar boy. It looked like the monk was hearing the child's confession. He was holding the boy's cheeks in his two hands and saying something to him with great tenderness. Ginetto couldn't hear the words, however.

Then he saw him lift the boy's face and kiss him on the forehead. The child did not stop him; it was as if he were mesmerized. Then the friar bent the boy's head and pushed it down between his legs.

Ginetto had seen enough. He climbed down from the fire escape the way he had come. Now he had to run to Jano and Nunzio to tell them what he had seen.

A few minutes later, Jano, Nunzio, and Ginetto arrived at the abandoned house to take the monk by surprise, catching him in the act.

Luck was on their side, because Brother Antonino and the boy were still upstairs in the bedroom. They decided that Jano, being more nimble than Nunzio, would climb up the fire escape, while Nunzio would enter through one of the downstairs windows. Ginetto would stand guard outside so no one could get in, in case something unexpected happened.

The execution was swift. Jano smashed the window and rushed into the room while the friar was still locked in an embrace with the child, who was now completely naked. A few seconds later Nunzio came through the door. The monk was struck dumb. The boy began to cry. Jano picked up his tattered shorts off the floor with the end of his club and held them out to him. "Get dressed and go home."

The boy took the shabby pants and hugged them to his chest; he started to leave, but Jano blocked his way with his club. "What's your name?" he asked him.

"Alessandro," the child replied timidly.

"And your father?" Jano pressed him.

"Roberto Pizzi." He ducked his head, expecting any number of blows for what he had done.

Jano raised his club, like the barrier of a railroad grade crossing. "Now scram." The boy, still naked, bolted from the room.

"It's not what you think," the monk started to say as soon as the child had fled.

But Jano glared at him. "What shall we call it, Padre? 'New catechism'? You're not worthy to wear that robe."

"I can explain . . . I don't harm them."

But Jano interrupted him: "At least spare us your bullshit, Padre."

"I'd like to let him have it but good, so he'll remember this night," Nunzio broke in, eager to rough up the monk. But Jano stopped him.

"I'm good to them. Sometimes I give them food; to the family as well," the monk was still explaining.

"Should we hear what his father and brothers think about it, Padre?"

The friar bowed his head. He realized there was no way out. "What do you want? You should know, though, that I don't have much money. Just a few coins the faithful give to the Church."

That was just the offer Jano was waiting for. A nice trade. "I don't want your money, Padre, just some information."

The next morning, bright and early, Jano stood before Mayor Costa's desk to deliver his daily report. "I managed to find out where they're hiding."

"Well done, Jano; you're top-notch," the mayor flattered him. "Where are they?"

"At the Sanctuary of Calatafimi. But I have another surprise for you, Mayor. There are also two Jewish families hiding at the sanctuary, waiting to embark for America."

The mayor leaned forward in his chair. "Two Jewish families?" he repeated.

"Right, from Enna and Caltanissetta. I can hand them to you on a silver platter, Captain."

"Who knows how much they've paid to escape to America. Enna and Caltanissetta, you said—" The mayor was thinking about the value of land in those regions.

"You can confiscate everything they own," Jano read his thoughts.

"Right. Even if they've sold everything, I'll void the transaction." Costa saw the confines of his lands continuing to expand.

"But I must ask a favor of you," Jano said, pretending to be deferential, though he knew the mayor wouldn't be able to refuse him.

"I knew it. Whenever you offer a gift, there are always strings attached."

"I learned that Vito Pizzuto, one of Vicaretto's gabellotti, is also hiding in the monastery, waiting to leave for America. We should look the other way where he's concerned. We should insure his departure."

"And why is that?"

"Because no matter what, he's a man who's done good for a lot of people," Jano lied.

"It wouldn't be because you want to take everything he owns while he's in America, would it?" The mayor smiled, well aware of Jano's insatiable greed.

"Well! I can never hide anything from you, can I?"

"All right, agreed. You get the mafioso, and I get the Jews."

Toward noon, Brother Antonino entered the chamber where all the fugitives were gathered. He walked to the center of the room and said, "I have good news. The ship owner has finally decided on the day of departure: it's scheduled for next Wednesday, May 3. So you will leave here the day before, the night of May 2, understood?"

The fugitives embraced one another, happy to at last be leaving that forced confinement. They hugged and kissed and congratulated one another. For a few minutes, there was an air of joy and celebration that had been bottled up for so long. The wait had made them all more anxious in the last couple of days. They crowded around the monk, asking him a thousand questions: how they would leave, who would take them to the port, if they should make sure to bring water and bread for the voyage. But brother Antonino was nervous and evaded their questions, saying everything would be done in due time. Then he motioned Vito Pizzuto to follow him.

After making their way through a few corridors, they reached the wing of the monastery where the monks' cells were located. Brother Antonino came to a door, opened it, and led Vito Pizzuto inside. In the center of the simply furnished room, which held a bed, a small table, and some chairs, stood Jano.

The monk went out and closed the door behind him, waiting in the hallway.

Vito Pizzuto was meeting Jano for the first time, and the Black Shirt made him wary.

Jano approached him and gave the Roman salute. "We don't know each other. I'm Jano Vassallo. Don't worry, I'm here to help you," he said, sitting down. "Please, have a seat." He motioned Pizzuto to a chair. The man did so without a word.

"I've come to ask for your cooperation. Let's say we have a deal to make: I'm interested in the Jewish families and the three men who arrived recently."

The words alarmed Vito Pizzuto, because it meant that they had all been sold out by the friar.

"As far as you're concerned, we've decided to allow you to leave the country. Naturally, everything has a price. But I can spare you a long, distasteful stay in our prisons."

"What do I have to do?"

Jano pulled a folded sheet of paper out of his shirt pocket. He unfolded it and placed it on the table, in front of Pizzuto, along with a fountain pen, saying, "You have to sign here."

Vito Pizzuto read what was written there. Then he looked up at Jano, his eyes filled with hate. "If I sign, do I have your word that you will let me leave?"

"You have my word. I myself will escort you as far as Castellammare to see that you get on the fishing boat."

"And what's your word worth?" the mafioso needled him, given that in other times, he would have crushed him under his shoes like a cockroach.

"Sorry, you can't certify its reliability. Take it or leave it. I'll just say this: if you sign, you can go away and forget all about me; if you don't sign, you'll find yourself in the league's cell in Salemi this evening, accused of treason along with the others."

Vito Pizzuto cursed the friar who had sold him out to that fanatical fascist.

"It's to your advantage to trust me, Pizzuto."

The gabellotto had never had to bow to extortion in his life and was demoralized. Then he made up his mind: he had no choice, so he took the pen and signed the document.

Jano, satisfied with how things were going, checked the signature at the bottom of the sheet and refolded the paper in four before sticking it back in his pocket. "You should thank me, Pizzuto. When you return to Sicily, you'll find your lands doubled, I promise.

"But about us"—Jano stood up—"naturally, we've never seen each other. You mustn't tell anyone about our meeting, otherwise the whole deal is off, except for this." He tapped the sheet tucked away in his pocket. "The deal is also off if for one reason or another I don't manage to capture all the other prisoners, so mum's the word. If they ask you where you've been, tell them that . . . that you wanted to go to confession.

"And don't make such a face. You'll see," he said, though his voice held a note of derision. "I'll be an excellent gabellotto for your lands."

Jano went to the door and opened it. The friar, who had been waiting in the corridor, accompanied Pizzuto back to the dormitory where the fugitives were.

Unable to meet the mafioso's accusing glare, the monk bowed his head. He would have preferred to rot in hell than be thought of as a traitor— and toward a friend, besides, since Saro considered him one. But there was nothing he could do about it, so he went on with the deceit.

Finally, May 2 arrived. For the fugitives, the hours never seemed to pass. They had already packed their bags the day before. They were dressed from head to toe and wore many layers of clothing, especially the women and girls, who had put on two or three skirts, one over the other, along with several blouses and sweaters. It was hot, however, and as the hours went by, they gradually took off some of the garments, cramming them into bags or suitcases that were already stuffed with clothes and other things.

Saro did nothing but think of Mena and recall every moment he had spent with her. He felt a great sadness, but he consoled himself thinking that she would wait for him. He'd made her swear to it.

His father, on the other hand, seemed crushed by everything that was happening: Peppino Ragusa appeared to have aged ten years. He couldn't stand the thought of abandoning Annachiara and Ester. But Saro had managed to convince him to leave, promising that his mother and sister would join them in America within a month, as soon as they could send them money for the trip.

The whole time, Losurdo had not stopped pacing back and forth across the big room, stopping occasionally to talk with the men from the two Jewish families.

At eight o'clock that evening, they heard a truck stop in back of the sanctuary. Peering through the windows, they saw Brother Antonino motion the driver to pull up as close as possible to the door. The truck had its tarpaulins lowered and was driven by an unfamiliar man whom no one had ever seen around there before.

Shortly afterward, the friar entered the room and gave the long-awaited green light: "All clear! Let's go, quick."

They hurried through the monastery's corridors, excited over the departure they'd been dreaming about for days. Then they climbed into the truck bed, which was partially filled with fruit crates. Before stepping into the now empty corridor, Saro paused beside his friend the monk and clasped him tight to show his gratitude, despite the fact that the priest had demanded a certain sum from each of them.

There were twelve people in total. They settled themselves on the floor of the truck bed, and the monk lost a little time arranging the crates along the drop-down rear edge so that if they were searched, the fugitives wouldn't be visible from outside.

When Brother Antonino had finished, he blessed them in a low voice: "May the Lord be with you." He heard murmuring from behind the wall of fruit crates in response. Then he stepped down from the truck, pulled up the rear panel and secured it in place with the two side latches. Walking around to the driver's window, he waved his permission to take off.

Brother Antonino watched the truck disappear on the road leading to Castellammare del Golfo. Then he turned and went back into the sanctuary for evening services.

The truck rocked and swayed on the bumpy dirt road full of potholes. In back, the fugitives sat on the truck bed floor in silence and in absolute darkness. A mixture of fear and hope filled everyone's minds. Each time the truck slowed, they were terrified of having run into a roadblock, but the vehicle never stopped. Only Vito Pizzuto seemed calm, as if the others' fears did not concern him.

None of them could possibly know that, shortly after leaving Calatafimi, the driver had taken a side road which, instead of heading toward the sea, led back to Salemi.

About ten minutes later the truck seemed to grapple with a steep uphill climb. The driver shifted into low gear, and the engine screeched trying to make it over the rise. Saro, deep in thought, noticed the change in course. They were going up, he felt, whereas to get to the coast they should have been traveling downhill. He turned around to try to peek under the tarp. But the cover was stretched down tight, and he couldn't raise it.

"Do you want them to discover us?" hissed one of the Jews, seeing what he was doing.

"We're climbing?" Saro said.

His exclamation drew Rosario Losurdo's attention. "You're right. To get to the coast, from Calatafimi, it's downhill all the way. I must have traveled this road a million times in the buggy."

Saro finally managed to move the tarp aside, but it was too dark to see where they were. "I can't make out the road," he said, dismayed.

Losurdo changed places with him and peered out.

The truck was now slowly lumbering up the hill. Then it came almost to a stop. It was nearing a junction, at the crest of the rise. It passed a sacred niche with a picture of the Madonna. Losurdo shouted, "It's the crossroads of the Assumption! We're going in the wrong direction!"

Saro started banging on the cab, yelling, "Driver! You're going the wrong way!"

But the driver didn't answer. Instead, he turned onto a track that led downhill, and the truck picked up speed.

Inside the truck bed, there was great confusion. Panic had seized everyone, and they were all yelling and screaming to get off. Only Peppino Ragusa continued sitting silently on the wooden truck bed.

Those who stood up were pitched left and right, depending on the driver's sudden swerves to adapt to the road's curves.

Someone shouted, "We've been sold out!" And someone else: "They're taking us to Salemi!"

It was like a signal; some began moving aside the fruit crates so they could get to the rear panel. Distraught like the others, Saro tried desperately to unfasten the side of the tarp that was already partway open.

"Papa, stay close to me," he cried to his father, who continued to ignore him.

Meanwhile, one of the Jews had reached the tailgate and managed to unlatch the two clamps. The panel swung down, and as the truck swerved again, several crates shot out.

Saro finally managed to wedge himself into the opening under the tarp. "Papa, get up, we have to get out of here. Jump after me."

Ragusa looked at him with immense sadness. Saro squeezed into the space he'd created between the side panel and the tarp. Before leaping, he shouted to his father again, "Get up! Jump after me!" He let himself drop and rolled onto a soft pasture. He stood up and sprinted for cover behind a bush. He watched the truck continue its descent, but none of the others made their way out from his escape route.

Veering sharply to the right, the truck entered a cattle enclosure. The cows huddled in the corner began lowing, frightened. The driver braked suddenly, and the passengers went tumbling on top of one another. The chaos was at a fever pitch. At that point, everyone scrambled to find a way out, climbing over baskets and fruit crates. They jumped out of the vehicle and dropped to the ground. But as soon as they touched down, strong hands grabbed them and, cursing and swearing, made them all lie on the ground, facedown in the dirt.

A hundred yards or so back, Saro, hearing the cries, realized that they had fallen into a trap. He advanced cautiously so that he wouldn't be spotted. In the moonlight, he could make out the dramatic scene in the distance.

He again hid behind a bush. From that position he could see the truck. He saw Vito Pizzuto come out last, assisted by one of the assailants. Now he recognized them: they were the combat league henchmen under Jano's command. And it was Jano himself who helped Pizzuto out of the truck. The traitor led him around to the truck's cab. Now Pizzuto climbed in—on the passenger side.

Jano walked back to look at the fugitives, who were still lying face-down on the ground. Saro tried to pick out his father and Rosario Losurdo and recognized them by the clothes they were wearing. Then he saw the comrades randomly bludgeon their captives with their clubs, aiming at any part of the body and ridiculing them.

The driver restarted the truck's engine, and the vehicle circled around the corral to get back to the exit.

Jano was checking the identity of fugitives: he lifted each one's head, grabbing him by the hair.

Suddenly Saro heard him shout, "There's one missing! Saro Ragusa is not here!" Jano ran after the truck, which had already left the enclosure, yelling at the driver to stop. Then he ordered one of the comrades, "Go see if he's still hiding in there."

The Black Shirt—it had to be Ginetto—struggled up into the truck bed and disappeared inside the tarpaulin. He came out almost immedi-ately, shaking his head. The truck then moved on again and drove off into the night, this time toward the coast.

Jano and his acolytes, enraged, went back to the fugitives and began beating them savagely.

Saro, powerless to act, couldn't stand to watch. Tears of rage ran down his face. He saw Losurdo rise from the ground and attack one of the Black Shirts, trying to defend himself. But he was immediately sur-rounded by the others, who clobbered him as hard as they could. Rosario Losurdo's face was bleeding, his eyes swollen; one of the comrades struck him in the stomach using his club as a battering ram. Rosario dropped to his knees and fell facedown, hands pressed to his abdomen.

Saro cursed Jano, realizing that they had been sold out in exchange for Vito Pizzuto's freedom. He swore he'd come back, and then Jano would pay for all his crimes.

He stood a little while longer in the shadows, in silence. He saw his father clubbed as well. Peppino Ragusa tried to get up from the ground, but a blow to his head knocked him unconscious.

Saro couldn't stand watching the scene any longer. He hurried away, the painful cries of those hapless people ringing in his ears for quite some time.

Chapter 27

– 1939 –

The dock at the port of Palermo was packed with a shabby crowd decked out in its Sunday best. It was a humanity with a difficult past but with the faint hope of a different future. The people brought with them tablecloths knotted into sacks, which held all their earthly possessions, and baskets filled with cheese and salami; their shoes and boots hung around their necks so they wouldn't get worn out. Some who were leaving were recognizable by their dazed expression, fearful of the step they were about to take, while others seemed joyful, realizing that they were finally leaving behind the poverty they had known since birth. The relatives, however—those who were staying behind—were silent and sad. They knew that they would never see their sons, husbands, and brothers again, and they stood motionless, watching the frantic preboarding activities without a word.

Reports about "America" were fantastic. It was rumored that coins sprouted on trees and that land was freely given to anyone who would cultivate it. Land! Owning a piece of land was the dream of half the men who swarmed the dock at the port of Palermo. The other half hoped to make their fortune as laborers, while the women daydreamed about marrying some nice young man who had gone there before them.

Saro had traveled all night and a good part of the following day, sometimes on foot and sometimes hitching rides from passing trucks headed for Palermo. When he reached the port, he was assailed by a horde of solicitors, some wanting to sell him medicine to prevent seasickness, some promising him a job as soon as he landed in America, and some asking him to marry their sister—otherwise she wouldn't be permitted to leave. He was completely bewildered by the demands of those desperate petitioners, who were often joined by small-time con men and swindlers who, posing as health officials for the port or as customs officers, managed to cheat a fair number of naive souls out of their few coins in exchange for promises that would never be kept.

Holding the third-class ticket he had purchased, Saro was directed toward a long line of people who were required to undergo a preliminary medical examination. The doctors simply had to make sure that the individuals did not have lice or some contagious disease; then they sent them to a second line, where a boarding pass was issued to those who had passed the exam and had a ticket.

When evening came, the second officer finally gave the order to board the ship. Like a swollen river, people flooded to the sleeping quarters below deck, lugging bundles and parcels, shouting and shoving one another to grab the berths on the first level.

Saro did not join the charge and remained on deck, in a corner next to the hawsers and air outlets. Leaning against the railing, he watched the maneuvers of the sailors who were preparing to cast off the moorings of the Florio fleet's *Principessa Matilde*. When the siren blew its raucous whistle, Saro Ragusa felt a piercing laceration in his brain. It was as if his heart were being squeezed by a fist. For the first time, he became conscious of the journey he was about to make. For the first time he understood the meaning of *good-bye*: that he might never see his beloved land again, the land of his roots, his parents and his sisters, his friends, but especially Mena. Sweet Mena. With her he had experienced the most intense emotions of his brief life.

The second time the siren shrieked, the steamer began to move. It was Saro's first time on a ship. He was intrigued by it all, watching the sailors on the wharf and on deck casting off the hawsers, and the display put on by the tugboat that had started pushing the *Principessa Matilde* out of port. The dock was mobbed with relatives, and silence hung over the scene. Some wept quietly, others waved white handkerchiefs, but most of them were overwhelmed at seeing the vessel move slowly away from shore. Saro leaned his forehead on the railing and felt tears running down his face. He tried to suppress his emotion, but the tears were unstoppable. Then he thought of his mother. When he was little, before falling asleep, he often felt discouraged, and at those times, his mother would tell him to pray. "Prayer is the medicine of the poor," she whispered in his ear and began a litany that she made up on the spot to lull him with its sweet sound.

Though he was no longer a child, Saro began to pray.

He curled up in his shabby clothes, and sank into a troubled sleep.

Once the *Principessa Matilde* passed the Strait of Gibraltar and confronted the great ocean, it began to pitch and lurch, as unstable as a toy boat. Scores of third-class passengers fell sick, many vomited and were forced to leave their sleeping quarters and find a sheltered corner on deck. The wind blew fiercely on the open seas, and only the hardiest could withstand the intense cold, wintry despite the fact that it was late spring. People were irritable and in a bad way, while the crew was short-tempered and insolent. Everyone's mental and physical endurance were sorely tested.

Saro didn't know a soul and kept to himself, spending most of the time crouched in the shelter of the afterdeck. Because there was nothing to do, the days dragged by interminably. The only time there was a flurry of excitement was when meals were served in the large hall below the cargo hold. It was there that Saro met Titina, a young girl from the Noto area, who was looking, she said, for a soul mate.

Titina was petite but curvy, with full hips and ample breasts, which, squeezed into a laced-up bodice, turned the head of every man on the ship. She had her eye on Saro, and on the eighth day of the voyage, when he sat down to wait for the mess crew to come by with the soup, she took the opportunity to sit beside him and strike up a conversation.

"Where are you from?" she asked, nibbling a piece of bread.

Saro looked at her. She had pale-blue eyes, like the sky, but her hair and eyebrows were dark. "I'm Saro, and I'm from Agrigento," he lied, remembering Manfredi's stories: the campiere had told him that the thieves and informers in America were connected to the thugs back in Sicily. "And you?"

"I'm Titina, and I was born in Noto," she replied promptly. "Do you have relatives in America?" she continued.

"No. Just some friends."

"I have a fiancé, and I'm going to get married."

"Good for you."

"I don't know him. I haven't even seen a photograph of him. The parish priest in my town arranged it all. He told me, 'Titina, go to America, otherwise all the men here will go to hell.'" She laughed, showing a row of bad teeth, like those of an old man.

Everyone turned to look at the two young people because it was rare to hear anyone laugh on the steamer, and they all wanted to share in someone's happiness, even if that person was a stranger. But when they saw it was Titina laughing, they went on dipping their spoons into their bowls.

"What are you looking at, you slobbering old fools?" the girl yelled.

Saro felt uncomfortable. "Don't mind them, Titina."

Their soup arrived too, cold by now, and they began eating. But Ti-tina kept pestering him. "Where are you going to live?"

"I haven't made up my mind yet," Saro said patiently.

"My fiancé wants to bring me who-knows-where, but I want to stay in New York," Titina complained.

"The place doesn't matter. If you're happy with him, you'll be happy anywhere."

"I want to stay in New York," she repeated like a spoiled child.

Later, when the ship encountered a violent storm, all the passengers holed up in the third-class compartment. It was the worst moment of the crossing. People wailed and moaned. Not only the women—but even men who back in their villages had never shown the slightest weakness. The young ones cried incessantly, testing everyone's nerves.

They were a humanity crushed by poverty and hunger, ignorance and despair. For some a glimmer of hope remained, but every one of them, even in their abject squalor, possessed a sense of dignity that would make them struggle against life's adversities; never giving up until they breathed their last. That strength marked those individuals as a special breed, people who, although treated as an inferior class, could face the toughest conditions, showing an uncommon spirit of sacrifice and abil-ity to adapt.

But the future was still a thousand miles away from that foul-smelling hold filled with their cries, their suffering, and their despair.

At that moment, reality was something else, represented by a young mother who, on one of the berths, was trying to nurse her baby. But the baby didn't want to suck the breast milk and wailed continually. Then toward evening the cries grew fainter. The mother tried to make him take the nipple, but the child was no longer responsive to nature's stimuli. The woman hugged him tightly, as though wanting to protect him from death. They tried to take him from her, but she defended him with her nails, screaming that her son was sleeping and that they couldn't take him. That night she got up and said she was going to the toilet. Instead she climbed the stairs leading up to the deck. She clutched the defense-less bundle as if it were the most precious of gifts. She went outside while the storm was still raging. No one saw her and nobody was able to stop her—or maybe someone did see her but let her go to her fate in her immense grief. She never returned to the hold, and the following day she became a mere notation in the logbook.

Then one day, as if by magic, the storm subsided. A desperate people regained their vitality and optimism. Everyone went out on deck to enjoy the sun's tepid rays.

Saro, lying in his usual place, saw Titina in the distance, toward the prow; she was arguing heatedly with a man who was decidedly much older. Saro watched as she gave him a shove, and after that, the man walked away, heading for the quarterdeck. Saro then realized that the man was coming in his direction; that he was the one the man was after.

He stood up, while the man, angry as a bull, strode up to him and said without preamble, "Don't you talk to my fiancée again, got it?"

"Which one is your fiancée, pal?" Saro asked.

"Don't get smart. You know I'm talking about Titina. I saw you two yesterday. It isn't right for you to disgrace her."

"But Titina already has a fiancé. He's in America," Saro explained.

"That's the first suitor. If he doesn't appeal to her, Titina will marry me. And don't you come between us, you hear?"

"Look, buddy, I couldn't care less about your Titina. She's the one who's always bothering me. I already have a girl."

"How dare you disrespect her!" The man grabbed him by the lapels.

But Saro jerked free. "You're asking for trouble."

With lightning speed, the man took out a knife several inches long. "You're the one who's asking for it," he said, poised to attack.

Saro didn't want to fight; he spun around and started to run away. The man with the knife was about to chase him, but a young man nearby slammed into him with his shoulder and knocked him down. The two young men looked at each other. The rescuer was tall, with a pleasant face and a roguish mustache that made him look like a movie star. Tugging his blue checkered cap down even lower, he nonchalantly raised two fingers to his forehead and saluted Saro, who smiled by way of thanks.

Meanwhile, the man who had been knocked to the ground was fuming with rage. Now he didn't know whether to get back at "Mustache," who had intentionally shoved him, or continue chasing Saro. He got up and chose the latter option. Saro was almost at the stairs to the hold, out of the jealous fiancé's reach by now, when someone cruelly tripped him, making him fall to the ground. Saro turned around to see who the scoundrel was who had made him stumble, and was startled to recognize Vito Pizzuto sitting on a crate, well dressed, smoking a cigar.

Instantly the man with the knife was upon him, but the sound of a whistle had summoned several sailors and an officer. The sailors restrained the armed man before he could hurt anyone. The man tried to break free, squirming as forcefully as he could, but the sailors had their own methods; they clubbed him and knocked him out, and then dragged him to an isolation cell. The officer approached Saro to learn why the man was after him. He wasn't sure whether to throw Saro in a cell as well. Had the man maybe tried to rob him? Or perhaps it had to do with old grievances?

Saro wouldn't answer.

"If you won't answer me, I'll have to put you in lockup. That could jeopardize your entry into America. You're better off cooperating," the officer said patiently.

Meanwhile, a man was approaching, and as he passed, the crowd parted to let him through. His charismatic figure was known to all the ship's passengers, and it was curious that a first-class passenger would come to the third-class deck.

When Prince Ferdinando Licata got to Vito Pizzuto, the latter, recognizing him, rose to his feet as a sign of deference. The prince addressed him in a low voice with his typical intonation: "*Chi nun po' fari a buttana, fa a ruffiana*"—"If you can't be a whore, be a pimp." He gave him a long, smoldering stare meant to incinerate him. "What's your name?" he asked.

"Vito Pizzuto," the Mafia boss replied, aware of the prince's authority.

"I'll remember you," Licata said, continuing on his way.

Vito Pizzuto did not react. He lowered his eyes and disappeared among the crowd of passengers, who watched him go, muttering about the prince.

Ferdinando Licata approached the officer and said, "Lieutenant, the young man is my friend. I've known him since he was a boy. He's the son of a doctor in Salemi."

The officer, recognizing the prince, motioned to his sailors, who immediately let Saro go. Then he saluted the prince and went away.

Saro was surprised to see Prince Licata on the ship. He moved to kiss his hands, but the prince drew back and gave him his first lesson: "*Cu' iè ricco d'amici iè scarsu di guai!*"—"A man with friends has few problems."

Saro smiled at the thought of having Prince Ferdinando Licata as a "friend."

"Prince Licata, you too are going to America?"

Ferdinando smiled and responded with a nod. "Come, I'll show you around the ship."

———————

Then one fine day at last: "It's *la Merica*!" All the passengers spilled out on deck to finally see their dream. The reality was far superior to whatever they might have imagined. There was the Statue of Liberty. They stared at it, gaping, as the ship went past, astonished at its size.

But America was still far away for them. Only the first- and second-class voyagers could go ashore in Manhattan, along with Americans and crew members. All the third-class passengers were put on a small ferry that would take them to an island a quarter of an hour away by boat from the Port of New York. Before being allowed to enter America, that assemblage of desperate individuals had to pass through the Isle of Tears, the nickname given to Ellis Island.

Part Two

1939–1943

Chapter 28

— 1939 —

To enter America you could not be sick or malformed, you could not have any mental disorders, a criminal record or, worse, a history of being an anarchist. If discovered upon disembarkation, these "defects" led to automatic expulsion. Immigration inspectors admitted people who were able to work, who had enough money or a prepaid ticket to reach their final destination, or a relative or friend who pledged to assist the immigrant until he found his first job. The government wanted to make sure that the new arrival did not end up swelling the ranks of paupers and criminals. Immigrants who were sick would be quarantined on the island until they were well; pregnant women, until they gave birth. Many arrivals were returned home, amid the wailing, tears, and despair of friends and relatives who, more fortunate than they, had obtained permission to enter.

For an immigrant sponsored by a "guarantor," the stay at Ellis Island might last less than eight hours. In this case, he was not issued any permit or authorization, and all that remained of his having passed through the island was a line or two in the immigration register noting his particulars—name, place of birth, and so forth—and his work skills.

Saro was one of the lucky ones, leaving Ellis Island after only a six-hour stay. Later he learned that some of his fellow passengers had been detained for more than three weeks, and that a couple of them were put back on the steamer to be sent home.

Along with about a hundred fellow travelers, he was allowed to board the pilot boat that went back and forth between the Isle of Tears and the Port of New York, and twenty minutes later, he finally set foot on American soil.

Toward the end of the 1930s, roughly one hundred thousand Italians crossed the ocean to live halfway around the world. They were far fewer in number compared to those who had preceded them at the beginning of the century, but their circumstances had not changed. Those who decided to emigrate were almost always fugitives, adventurers, offenders hunted by the police. or simply people with no hope.

Vincenzo Ciancianna was pondering these thoughts as he stood leaning against a lamppost, watching the hundred or so immigrants disembark from the pilot boat, having gone through the humiliation of Ellis Island. For more than thirty years, he'd been a recruiter for the Bontade organization and by this time, he was quite adept at recognizing those who could be of use to the family.

He had drawn up a personal rating scheme for the immigrants, dividing them into four categories. First there were the *piagnistei*, or "whiners." They were the ones whose faces were awash with nostalgia for the country they'd left behind. Clearly, they already regretted the choice they'd made and would gladly have reboarded the ship to go back home. Though these were the easiest prey for the Mafia's recruiters, in the long run, they were also the most undependable.

Then there were the *cacasotto*: those who were "scared shitless." Afraid of their own shadows, these timid souls panicked as soon as they stepped off the ship's gangplank, fearful of an uncertain future and of the new life they faced. Compared to those in the first category, however, they were more confident, because they carried in their pocket a letter from the parish priest or from some relative asking an uncle or a cousin to help them out, at least in the first few weeks. The Mafia preferred to leave them alone, since, for better or for worse, they already had a protector.

The next group was the *sottopanza*: the "eager beavers," ready and willing to pitch in. They had embraced the adventure and couldn't wait to start working. Moreover, they knew that they would find waiting for them on the dock a relative or a fellow villager who would help them find lodging and a suitable job. The recruiters stayed away from them as well.

Finally, there were the *verdoni*: the "greenbacks," with money. These individuals gave the impression of knowing what they wanted, even though it was the first time they were setting foot on American soil. They were attentive to everything going on around them; they had an arrogant gaze and a certain air of defiance. These were the ones who had worked for the landed gentry, *gabellotti* who must have done something wrong at home and fled from the Italian justice system, hiding in the bottom of a hold to seek refuge in America. Or more simply, they were mafiosi from Sicily, Campania, and Calabria who had to get away from the fascist regime and needed a change of scene. These tough guys weren't tough looking for a stable job. For them, America was merely a land where they could survive. For them, America was a land waiting to be conquered. These were the ones the recruiters went after more doggedly to persuade them to join the organization.

Vincenzo Ciancianna immediately identified the whiners, who were always the most numerous. He approached them and began speaking in their dialect, though as the years went by, his language had become increasingly bastardized by the addition of American words. With his protruding belly and jovial face, a big cigar stuck in a corner of his mouth, Vincenzo gave the impression of someone trustworthy. He promised the newcomers a place to sleep and maybe even a job, if they wanted one. Of course they did! For those poor, bewildered souls, his offer was a godsend, like sunlight on a rainy day or music from heaven.

The rat holes in which they were made to live and the work they were forced to do would forever bind them to the "family," for which they would handle the most lowly, though necessary tasks, such as unloading smuggled goods that reached the harbor, well concealed in the holds of ships coming from Italian and French ports.

The Italian immigrants' plight was doubly difficult, because not only did they have to defend themselves against other ethnic groups, such as the Irish, who had arrived before them, but they had to endure bullying and extortion from Italian families that dominated the neighborhoods and made them pay taxes and duties for protection that they could well do without. They knew, however, that if they rebelled, life would become unbearable: they would risk suffering a series of injustices and . . . accidents.

A cluster of newcomers formed around Vincent Ciancianna. That big belly and friendly face attracted the whiners like bees to honey. They were all convinced that the jovial Italian had been sent by the Lord, never suspecting that he was luring them into a trap with no way out. Vincenzo took one look and decided who would become a stevedore at the port, who would be sent to the laundries, the railways, the gaming parlors, and so on. He gave them each an application that was already filled out—handing them to the illiterates as well—and told them to show up that evening at the designated address and show the paper to the person who would greet them. That's all they had to do; their hosts would see to getting them settled.

"This is *la Merica, paisano*, the land of plenty. So get going!" Vincenzo invariably ended with that phrase, and, as if by magic, a smile returned to everyone's face. They thought they had finally emerged from the nightmare of poverty. So then America truly was the land of milk and honey!

That illusion would last a few hours.

Saro too had joined the group of immigrants surrounding the friendly, well-dressed man. When it was his turn, Vincenzo Ciancianna studied him for a few seconds, pronounced him "Hotel porter," and rummaged through his bundle of requests to find the application.

But Saro stopped his hand, which surprised the man. "Actually, I was a barber in Salemi," he said hesitantly, letting go of the big-bellied man's hand.

Vincenzo looked at him, confused. "Barber? I might have something for you," he said and began searching again through the stack of requests for the one he was looking for.

The passengers belonging to the fourth category, the greenbacks, were usually important people. Sometimes there was even a *mammasantissima*—the head of a crime family—sent by Sicilian cousins to escape the persecutions of the fascist regime. The greenbacks had only two names committed to memory when they arrived in America: Miss Molly's, a tavern that stood on a street not far from where the ships docked, and Vincenzo Ciancianna or his stand-in. As soon as they stepped off the pilot boat, they were to have someone tell them where the tavern was, and then, once they got there, they were to ask the host if "so-and-so" had arrived.

It was at Miss Molly's that Vito Pizzuto ended up, and that afternoon he met the recruiter for the Bontade family: Vincenzo Ciancianna.

Though Vito Pizzuto was not a big boss, his ability to extort taxes was one of the testimonials that Tom Bontade valued most in his letter of introduction. The few like him who entered the families right away—there were never many of them—were given a certain sum of greenbacks on account.

There was no barbershop at the Baxter Street address on the southern edge of Little Italy; instead, to his great surprise, Saro found a funeral home. He pushed open the glass door and entered the shop outfitted with funeral apparatuses and accessories. A bald little man in a black jacket came toward him, wringing his hands. With a sad smile and a re-morseful air, he said in a kind of Sicilianized English, "My sympathy to you and your family."

Saro couldn't comprehend a word he said. Shaking his head, he told the man in Sicilian, "I'm sorry, I don't understand."

"Ah, but you're a paisano." The little man's manner changed immediately. He shook his hand warmly, and became less obsequious and more open.

"I'm from Sicily, from Salemi. I wanted to ask, wasn't there a barber-shop here?" Saro handed him the form that the man with the big belly had given him at the port.

"And I'm from Messina; we're practically neighbors." The little man peered at the sheet of paper. "Oh, Ciancianna sent you. Fine, fine . . ." He looked him up and down. "Are you a barber?"

Saro nodded.

"All right, let's not waste time. We'll put you to the test right now." He turned and motioned Saro to follow him.

The man led him into the back of the shop and then down a long corridor with doors on either side before finally entering a large, cold, dark room that smelled of formaldehyde. He switched on the light, and Saro saw three marble tables. The dead bodies of a very old woman and a middle-aged man, both naked, were lying on two of the slabs.

"Do they upset you?" the little man asked.

"Well, they don't look too good," Saro said ironically.

"Did you know that after death a person's beard and hair continue to grow? Would you be able to trim and shave the men and fix up the women? Maybe put a little makeup on them? Some lipstick and pow-der? Of course, you would also have to dress them for the viewing by the relatives."

"I can give it a try."

The little man walked over to a small wheeled table that held the tools of the trade: scissors, razors, brushes, combs, and cosmetics. "Okay, get to work. Show me what you can do."

He left him alone, and Saro immediately got to work shaving the male.

The funeral director came back after a half hour to check what Saro had done so far. The corpse's hair was now slicked with brilliantine, and his face was shaven and fresh. Saro had also had time to apply a little powder to him, to conceal the ashen hue typical of cadavers. The little man seemed satisfied with the young fellow's work.

"Okay, you're good; you did very well for the first time. You seem reliable. Follow me, I'll show you the rest of the place." He turned off the light, and they walked through the corridor again. "See, these are the rooms where we prepare the dearly departed." He opened one of the doors along the corridor.

The room was furnished with a bier, two wooden chairs, a large cruci-fix on the back wall, and several vases in which bouquets of flowers from the preceding funeral were arranged. There were no windows, and the room smelled like a morgue.

"You'll get used to it, you'll see. It's funny how sooner or later we all resign ourselves to death, whereas it's *life* we can't get used to . . ." He closed the door and continued down the corridor. "You'll prepare the corpses in these rooms. There are six of them. It's unusual to have six bodies all at the same time. I've only had it happen a couple of times, due to score settling in the neighborhood. When war breaks out among the gangs, it's a boon for us undertakers," he said avidly.

"This room"—he indicated a door they were passing—"has a win-dow. You can sleep here until you find another place." Then he pointed to a double door on the other side of the hall. "And that's the chapel. It's where we bring the bodies for the relatives to pay their last respects. If they're Catholics, we leave everything as it is. If they're members of other faiths, we remove the crucifix and put up whatever they want, okay?"

Unlike the other rooms, the chapel was nicely furnished. It had pictures of saints on the walls, a row of chairs, a little altar with a wooden cross, and a small cabinet on the opposite wall. The room was illuminated by light filtering through a stained glass window with an image of the Holy Spirit in the center.

They returned to the back room, which served as an office of sorts. A table littered with papers functioned as a desk and probably also as a place to eat, since a plate with the remains of a meal stood among the pa-pers. After sitting down, the little man came straight to the point: "These are the terms: I'll give you six dollars a week. But I have to withhold two dollars for the association. You'll pay me separately for the room, and there too I'll have to keep twenty percent for the association."

"What association?"

"You mean you don't know? The *Unione Siciliana*. The Sicilian Union. It's thanks to the *unione* that we can work in peace. What's more, we undertakers should be doubly grateful to the *unione*."

"Why is that?" Saro asked.

"The *unione* was created to offer immigrants a decent funeral and a grave on Sicilian soil. Immigrants may accept the sad plight of being a man without a country, but they all long to close their eyes beneath Sicily's skies. If that's not possible, since death often creeps up and carries us off without giving us time to prepare for the momentous step, they at least want to be buried back home. The Unione Siciliana is a kind of insurance. Those who join it are guaranteed a decent funeral and a ticket for the return voyage."

"And if one doesn't want to enroll in this association? I have no plans to die anytime soon."

"Oh, so you want the benefits without spending a cent? Tell me, how would you have found a job and a place to sleep, just like that? What do you think, that it's all a bed of roses here?"

"If those are the terms . . ."

"Either that or"—He made an eloquent gesture—"face the music."

"I get it. I won't argue, then."

"Good, it's better that way. Work starts at eight and ends at eight. Unless there's some unexpected overtime. For meals you can fix something in the kitchenette back here. Hurry up and learn English. You'll see, *americano* is a cinch. I think I've told you everything . . .

"Oh, my name is Enzo Carruba."

"When do I start?"

"You've already started. Now, there are two bodies waiting for you to. Restore them to life." He smiled at his own joke. "While you prepare the man, I'll go get a dress for the old woman. So heartrending, these poor people." He left, still smiling. Saro didn't know if it was because he was pleased to have found a worker or because he was off his rocker by now.

At that time, New York was dominated by five major Mafia families.

The Genovese family was the largest and most deeply entrenched in the territory, and could count on three hundred affiliates. It dealt in extortions, contracts, waste collection, the fish market, and control of the ports of Newark, Elizabeth, and Fulton. It had a widespread network of gambling centers, ran the money-lending and drug trades, and had a powerful influence on the masons' and carpenters' unions.

The Gambino family had two hundred affiliates. It was involved in gambling, usury, drug trafficking, the recruitment racket, urban solid waste hauling, food products transport, as well as the Teamsters union.

The family of Joseph "Joe Bananas" Bonanno could rely on one hundred affiliates and was active in gambling, usury, drug trafficking, and the slot machines.

The other two families each had about fifty or sixty affiliates.

The Lucchese family operated mainly in New Jersey, with interests in money lending, drugs, extortion, and construction racketeering.

The Colombo family, active in Brooklyn, Queens, and Long Island, was involved in gambling and extending loans at exorbitant interest.

From these five families another twenty-six evolved, each of which had jurisdiction over a specific chunk of territory.

It was Charles "Lucky" Luciano who, in the early 1930s, had called for such well-defined territorial areas to put an end to the family wars that had racked the syndicate in previous years. Still, from time to time, it happened that some boss who was overly greedy or too sure of his offensive capabilities overlooked the rules and invaded territories or activities that were not within his jurisdiction.

On the Lower East Side, two minor families, the Sicilian Bontade family and Brian Stoker's Irish clan, vied for the funeral racket and cemetery plots. The Bontades were better organized, but the Stoker family was more ruthless, having recruited the most vicious criminals from the Bronx and Queens, regardless of whether they were Irish, Puerto Rican, or Polish.

After several months, Saro had mastered the tasks of shaving, applying makeup, and dressing the corpses, and had acquired a fairly good command of the new language. Events in Salemi seemed far away; there was no place for looking back in America. His only regret had a name: Mena. Her memory remained fresh in his mind.

One morning he was restoring the facial appearance of a young girl whose family wanted her to be attired in the wedding dress that she had not lived long enough to wear. She had arrived from Italy with malaria, but the inspectors at Ellis Island hadn't noticed it and had granted her a visa. Unfortunately, the disease had already devoured her liver, and she passed away a few weeks after achieving her dream of coming to America and just ten days before her marriage to the man who had asked for her hand, and for whom she had braved the difficult ocean crossing.

Saro was proud of how he had made her up and laid her out. He considered her one of his best works. He had rouged her cheeks, applied lipstick, and powdered her face meticulously to conceal the pallor of death. The long white lace veil spilled over her shoulders onto the gauzy wedding dress.

Saro wheeled the casket, mounted on a trolley, from the makeup room to the mortuary chapel. He threw open the double doors and entered with the coffin, setting it in the center of the room, which had already been decked out with flowers. Shortly afterward, the family and the priest arrived, welcomed by Enzo Carruba.

The girl's mother and father burst into tears at seeing her so beautiful: she seemed to be still living and breathing. The other members of the family were also moved at the sight of the poor girl. The groom-to-be chose not to attend the ceremony since he had no ties to her, no sentimental bond or familiarity. It had been the parish priest who had decided on their union.

The officiating clergyman gave a brief sermon that did not console the family, and after a half hour of tears and wailing, it was all over. The relatives left the chapel to prepare for the funeral ceremony, orchestrated as only the Italians know how. Enzo Carruba was pleased with himself because everyone complimented him on how he had planned the service and how he had done up the ill-fated girl. The tip was appreciable, and it vanished quickly inside the pocket of the little man's jacket: that money was not taxable by the racket, unless someone was an informer.

When the family had gone, Saro was left alone with the deceased. He went to the cabinet in the back of the room to get a screwdriver to fasten down the lid of the casket, then proceeded to close it, after glancing one last time at the unlucky bride.

Suddenly he heard someone running down the corridor. He turned and saw a disheveled, panting man with a bushy mustache burst into the chapel, clearly in a panic.

"You have to help me! Stoker's men are after me. Hide me!" Saro judged from his accent that he must be Neapolitan.

"My *padrino* will reward you!" the man implored desperately, referring to his godfather. "Save me!"

Moments later, two Irishmen burst through the front door of the funeral home just as the girl's relatives were leaving. Enzo Carruba, though frightened, tried to block their way.

"Signori—gentlemen—please; there's a funeral."

The first of the two Irishmen, who seemed to be in charge—strong as a bull, with short red hair—stopped him with his left hand, while his right hand, hidden in his pants pocket, gripped a semiautomatic pistol.

"Who are you?"

"I'm Enzo Carruba," the undertaker replied, hoping his name would be familiar to him. But evidently Carruba had never buried any of that freckled individual's relatives, because the Irishman gave him a violent shove, knocking him to the ground.

"Don't be a hero, and you'll save us all a lot of trouble. Is there a back door to this place?" Freckles asked.

The little man shook his bald head. A grin lit up the Irishman's face as he beckoned his buddy to follow him, thinking that he had his prey trapped.

The two began kicking open the doors to the small rooms used for preparing the corpses, but it was as if their quarry had dissolved into thin air. Then they noticed the double doors of the chapel and heard noise coming from inside. Freckles motioned the other man to be on guard. Aiming their pistols, they tiptoed toward the chapel. Freckles shouted an order, and the two thugs hurled themselves inside, ready to shoot.

Saro spun around, raising his hands. In one of them he was gripping his ever-present razor.

"Stop! Don't move!" Freckles shouted, approaching with caution, while the other man searched the corners of the room looking for their prey. "Drop that razor and move away from there," he ordered. Saro stepped aside and dropped the razor, truly frightened.

"Don't hurt me; I'm only doing my job," he said, trying to appease the overexcited gunman.

Freckles went up to the coffin and, not taking his eyes off Saro, glanced at the purple drape that hung to the floor, hiding the wheels of the trolley. At that point the second man came over and stood on the opposite side of the coffin. Now both were ready to fire. Freckles grabbed the edge of the drape and quickly raised it, aiming the gun under the coffin. But there was no one there. The Irishman continued to look around for a possible hiding place. Except for the chairs, a small cabinet and the casket, the room held no other furnishings.

Freckles stared at the coffin and the body covered by the lacy white veil. He lifted the veil briefly with the barrel of the pistol to peek at the corpse's face, and seeing the red lipstick, he let the veil drop back in place. He turned to his friend, completely ignoring Saro from that point on, as if he'd never existed.

"Let's go look in the other rooms," he ordered his crony, and the two went back out to the corridor.

Saro hurriedly reclosed the coffin lid and secured it with the screws. After a few minutes six pallbearers arrived, followed by Enzo Carruba.

"Have they gone?" he asked Saro, who picked up his razor from the floor. They heard loud thuds as more doors were being kicked in.

"Hear that?" said Saro. "Quick, hurry up, load the casket on the wagon."

The six young men lifted the coffin, balanced it on their shoulders, and headed toward the front door where the hearse awaited them, adorned with a profusion of black plumes and ornate spiral posts bearing skulls, hourglasses, and every other icon meant to recall the transience of our existence.

The two coal-black stallions had grand ceremonial harnesses decorated with brass studs and blinders adorned with two silver skulls and long plumes. They began champing at the bit when they heard people murmuring; the driver had a hard time restraining them, reining in and pushing the hand brake all the way.

Some women were weeping, others prayed, children were yelling and slapping one another on the head. The dead girl's mother was on the brink of collapse.

Saro accompanied the casket to the wagon and then climbed up onto the seat beside the driver.

The six young men deposited the casket on the floor of the wagon with extreme care, a final earthly consideration toward the young woman who had gone forever. Then they arranged the wreaths and bouquets of flowers, brought by friends and relatives, as a last fond farewell on the lid of the coffin. The deceased girl's father's eyes were red, but he held back his tears. Her mother, supported by two of the girl's older brothers, was inconsolable and angry at destiny.

Enzo Carruba stood at the door of the funeral home rubbing his hands, satisfied that, despite the unplanned disturbance, everything was going smoothly. In a few seconds, the procession would leave for the cemetery.

But all of a sudden, violent pounding startled the people closest to the coffin. At every blow, the casket shook. Then some wreaths and bouquets of flowers began to fall off the top of the coffin. Stifled cries could be heard coming from inside the casket. After a number of thumps, a deep silence fell among the crowd. They all held their breath and strained their ears, even those furthest from the wagon. Two more violent knocks made the casket jiggle.

Immediately people began clamoring and jostling to get closer to the coffin, some exclaiming, "It's a miracle," while others, more skeptical, shook their heads. One man shouted, "She's alive! She's alive!" Then as if it were a signal, other shouts rose among the crowd:

"The Madonna performed a miracle!"

"Quick, open it, take the casket down!"

One of the relatives seized a long iron bar that a street paver was wielding to tear up cobblestones, and several men used it to pry open the lid of the coffin. The screws holding the wood shut popped out, and the lid flew off as though raised by a superhuman force, landing outside the wagon. Everyone plainly saw the bride sit up inside the coffin. Then a collective gasp arose from the group, a mixture of joy, tears, disbelief, and fear. Some applauded, while others fell to their knees. Children shouted wildly for joy.

Enzo Caruba had never seen anything like it in his entire career as an undertaker. Carmelo Vanni, wearing the bride's clothes, his lips painted red, and minus the showy mustache that Saro had quickly shaved off, took in deep lungfuls of air. Panic, triggered by claustrophobia, had left him breathless. But there was no time to lose.

Enzo Caruba had been making the sign of the cross, when behind him the two Irish killers appeared at the doorway, angry and frustrated at having their prey get away. "What's all this?" Freckles asked as he ran out, followed by his sidekick.

Not far away, he saw what should have been a corpse, in a wedding dress, standing in the middle of the coffin, with everyone shouting and raising their arms in prayer. It took him several seconds to take in what he was seeing.

Those few seconds were enough for Saro to yell to Carmelo Vanni to jump onto the seat. Then Saro gave the driver a shove, knocking him to the ground, and with a kick released the brake. He grabbed the reins and whipped the horses, who couldn't wait to get going. The two stallions lurched, and the heavy carriage rolled forward, amid the alarm of all the onlookers who didn't understand why the young bride was climbing onto the driver's seat.

Behind him, Saro heard several gunshots. He turned and saw the two killers pushing their way though the crowd to get to the hearse.

Carmelo Vanni, still ludicrously wearing the white dress, joined Saro, who tossed him the reins. Lithely leaning down from the seat toward the rings to which the horses' traces were harnessed, Saro pulled out his razor and with a sharp stroke cut the straps. Then he jumped astride one of the horses, holding the other by the reins so he wouldn't run away. The black stallions were spooked by the gunfire and all the commotion. Saro motioned Carmelo to get on, so the man screwed up his courage and jumped on the horse.

Behind them, all hell broke loose. Relatives and friends watched, incredulous, as the person they still thought was the former deceased nimbly leaped onto the stallion. Then everyone started running after the wagon, yelling for it to stop. Mixed in with the group were the two hit men, guns in hand; pushing their way through the crowd, they didn't think twice about shoving and tripping the poor souls who got in their way. The dead girl's mother fainted.

Meanwhile, the two black horses had come unhitched from the shaft. As soon as it lost the stability of the shaft, the carriage, which had picked up some momentum, lurched. The two front wheels suddenly swerved, and the hearse tipped over and crashed to the street with a great racket, shattering into a thousand pieces of wood and putty.

The two killers were knocked over and fell to the ground. Freckles swore and from the ground aimed his pistol at the fugitive disguised as a bride. A couple of shots rang out, but by now the target was too far away.

In desperation, Enzo Carruba's hands went in search of what little hair he had left on his pate, shiny with sweat. "I'm ruined, ruined," he muttered, slumping against the door frame of his fine funeral home.

In the distance, Saro and Carmelo Vanni galloped toward Columbus Park. When they reached the park, they separated, going in opposite directions.

Chapter 29

Ferdinando Licata had made the voyage in first class, so on arrival at the Port of New York, he had gone ashore along with all the other first- and second-class passengers, without having to go through the Ellis Island inspectors. Waiting for him on the dock was his niece, Elisabetta, his sister Lavinia's daughter, who had brought her seven-year-old child, Ginevra, to the port with her.

Licata recognized his niece immediately in the crowd. Unlike his sister, she was a little overweight, but she had the same magnificent face: aristocratic and strong willed.

Though the passing of the years had modified his temperament somewhat, Prince Ferdinando Licata was not a man who was easily moved. Yet at the sight of his adored Elisabetta, he was unable to swallow the lump that rose to his throat. He held her to him for a long time, murmuring, "Elisabetta . . . Elisabetta . . ."

The young woman closed her eyes, as though recalling the sensations and scents of her far-off land. Smiling to cover her emotion, she drew away from her uncle and introduced him to the little girl she was holding by the hand. "*Zio*, this is Ginevra."

The child was distracted by the confusion that surrounded them on the landing dock, intrigued by the huge ship tied up behind that grand gentleman with the graying hair. Leaning down to match her height, Ferdinando Licata gazed at her and then clasped her to his chest as well, pinning her arms at her sides. Elisabetta watched them nostalgically as all the lost opportunities, far from the warmth of a real family, flashed through her mind.

Ferdinando released the child from his embrace and, straightening up again, could not resist giving his niece another kiss.

"That one is from your mother." It was not intended as a reproach, but Elisabetta bowed her head to hold back tears.

"She told me to tell you that she prays for you—for all of you—every day."

"I should write her a letter. But there's so much to do here. I don't have a moment free," the young woman said in excuse.

"You don't have to explain, Elisabetta."

"Mommy's name is Betty," the little girl piped up.

"Oh, is that her name?"

"Uh-huh, Betty. Only I call her Mommy."

"All right, Betty it is . . . But her real name is Elisabetta," Ferdinando teased.

"No, Betty!"

"Oh, all right, Betty . . . But it's Elisabetta!" The prince laughed, as did his niece, but Ginevra crossed her arms and repeated stubbornly, "Betty!"

One would think that Ferdinando Licata had had a dozen children of his own. He could communicate perfectly with them.

"She's just like her grandmother. She resembles Lavinia in that painting in the parlor. She was the very same age," he said taking a better look at the little girl.

"Yes, I know, she has the same forehead and the same eyes as Mama."

"And the rest of the family?" Ferdinando asked, changing the subject.

Betty took her uncle's arm, and they started walking toward the exit. "Nico stayed at the trattoria. You know, we can't afford a cook yet, and he can't leave the stove."

Betty and Nico had arrived in New York in 1926, and for five years, they had worked more than fourteen hours a day, scraping together every penny for a dream they'd always had: to open an Italian restaurant. Lavinia opposed the plan from the start, considering Nico unworthy of her daughter. Proud like all the Leicesters, Betty left Italy with what little savings she had set aside, to show her mother that she didn't need her money, only her affection. She and Nico had started out in a basement location on Crosby Street, just south of Houston Street. Later they found an opportunity north of Houston, in an area that had formerly been inhabited by New York's upper middle class. However, due to its proximity to the burgeoning working-class neighborhoods of Little Italy and Chinatown, it had been abandoned by the well-to-do families, who gradually chose to move uptown. Little by little, the houses were occupied by immigrants: Irish, Germans, Poles, Jews, Ukrainians, and Puerto Ricans. The extreme density of diverse ethnic groups made the area one of the most explosive and difficult for the police to control, which was why commercial space there could be rented at bargain prices. Betty and Nico patiently sought a place with the right location.

Finally, in 1931, the opportunity arose. The venue was located on East

Second Street, and along with the restaurant, they rented a nice apartment on the second floor of the same building. They named the restaurant La Tonnara and finally decided to have a child. Ginevra was born in March of the following year.

Not that the sacrifices ended with the opening of La Tonnara. On the contrary, the debts were unrelenting, and Betty, up until the time the child was born, continued working mornings as a milliner in the hat company of a Polish man. In the evenings, she served meals prepared by her husband at the trattoria.

When Ginevra was born, an elderly neighbor took care of her during the hours when Betty and her husband were busy at the restaurant.

The early thirties was a tense time, not only for them but also for Americans in general, for the Great Depression spared virtually no one. The trattoria struggled to remain afloat, and only her enormous pride kept Betty from returning to her mother in Salemi.

La Tonnara was furnished with objects that recalled Sicily. A closely woven fishing net, a *tonnara*, covered the ceiling. On the walls were lobster traps and harpoons for deep-sea fishing. Two large specimens of stuffed swordfish heads near the doorway were a great marvel to those who had never seen anything of the kind. The walls were painted with imaginary fishing scenes. But on one side, near the entrance to the kitchen, Ferdinando Licata recognized the landscape and the village of Salemi perched on a hill. Surprised, he questioned Betty about it.

"A man from Salemi, Salvatore Turrisi, painted it," Betty told him. "We fed him for a month. Then he disappeared, as suddenly as he had come."

Ferdinando looked at the painting more closely. "Salvatore Turrisi . . . was a campiere. I didn't know he could paint so well, and I didn't know he'd come here to America."

"There are a lot of things you don't know—" She was about to add "about your people," but stopped herself.

"You're right. We persist in looking for certain qualities in others without realizing that they may have entirely other virtues, equally remarkable."

"It's a fault most of humanity shares," his niece agreed.

"Did you know that back home this Salvatore Turrisi is wanted for murder?"

Just then Nico came in. He was back from the market and had his arms full of bags. Ginevra ran to him. "Daddy, look who's come from Sicily!"

Nico set down the bags on the table and went to greet the prince with open arms. "Prince Licata! Welcome to America and to our humble home."

The prince embraced him. "Nico, call me Ferdinando here, or at most, Uncle. Otherwise the snot-nosed kids will make fun of me." They laughed and clasped each other again.

"You've done a wonderful job. Well done. I'm proud of you both," he said, indicating the room. "But the real masterpiece is this little *piciredda*." He opened his arms, and Ginevra ran to him. Then she pulled away and scampered off into a corner of the room: "Daddy, look what *zio* Ferdinando brought me." She came running back with a replica of a small Sicilian *carrettu*, showing her father the little cart like a trophy.

"And another surprise." She disappeared behind the kitchen door, reappearing soon afterward with a large Sicilian puppet almost as tall as her. "It's Orlando! For you and Mommy." She held it out to Nico, who gave her back the little cart and took the puppet. "*Mamma mia*, how heavy it is! We'll put it here, in La Tonnara."

They smiled, like a family content with the choices they'd made so far. It hadn't been easy, but in the long run, sacrifice and honest labor yield lasting satisfaction, and after years of hard work, Betty and Nico were now beginning to reap the first fruits of their efforts.

Saro ditched the black horse as soon as he reached Columbus Park, having eluded his pursuers.

Now his problem would be finding a place to sleep, for he couldn't go back to the funeral home anymore.

He decided to get as far away as possible from that area. He had to mingle with the crowds, disappear—and in such an immense city that would certainly prove easy. Saro began looking for businesses displaying the barbershop pole, thinking that if he was lucky, he might find a job. Or else he could go back to the port, where Vincenzo Ciancianna could direct him to some other work.

He was walking along the Bowery, beginning to get clear signals from his stomach that it was time to put something in it. A hot dog cart was parked on the corner of Bayard Street, giving off a faint smell of burning rubber. He approached and saw a man stuffing long rolls with strange, pale sausages that he had never seen before. Apart from the smell, they looked inviting and succulent, with that odd yellowish cream spread on top.

"Are they good?" he asked naïvely.

"Of course. They're hot dogs," the German replied.

"I have no money."

"Get lost, then; you'll scare away the customers."

"I can give you a shave and trim your mustache," Saro said, pulling out his razor so quickly it frightened the man.

The vendor fingered his rough beard. "Why not?" he thought. Business was slow, not many people around, so he agreed.

Fifteen minutes later, the German looked as if he were spruced up for a special date, and Saro was able to taste a hot dog. He sat in the shade of a doorway and savored it as though it were a five-course dinner. He was able to relax now that his stomach was no longer rumbling. Finally, a little peace after the morning's excitement.

He reopened his eyes, convinced that he had spent only a few seconds dallying with the image of Mena. But the light had changed completely, the hot dog vendor was no longer on the corner, and the sound of a band, composed of a bass drum and a trumpet, had rudely awakened him. The musicians were dressed in dark blue uniforms, and as soon as they finished playing, a woman, the third member of the group, started shouting something into a megaphone.

Saro pricked up his ears.

"As long as children go hungry, we will fight for them! As long as human beings are imprisoned, we will fight for them! As long as there are casualties of addiction, we will fight for them! As long as there are forced to sell their bodies, we will fight for them! As long as there are people in need of the Lord's light, we will fight for them!"

At each refrain, the bass drummer struck his instrument with resounding force. Small groups of children had formed in front of the musicians and were pretending to conduct their own orchestra, waving their hands in the air.

"Come!" the woman went on shouting through the megaphone. She was a plump, matronly lady with enormous breasts that swayed each time she moved. "The doors of the Lord are always open. A word of comfort could save your life. You, girl!" She turned to a young woman who stood beside a door, waiting for customers. "Forget your wanton life. Return to the straight and narrow. Think of your mother."

"And you think of your sister!" the woman retorted. "It's thanks to my mother that I know all the tricks of the trade!" She laughed coarsely and retreated into the shadow of the doorway to avoid being bothered again.

The matron did not give up and looked around for another passerby. Her gaze fell on Saro, who was still stretched out in the doorway next door to the prostitute.

"And you, brother"—she walked over to Saro—"turn your back on the siren called 'the bottle.' Look at the state that vice can reduce you to. Look, all of you!" Now she addressed the audience of children and a few curious adults. "Children, you might become like this poor young man if you start drinking: a drunk who can't even find his way home."

Saro stood up. "Actually, I was resting. I'm not drunk."

"That's what they all say. You're Italian, aren't you?"

"Yes."

"Well, then, you see, everyone knows that Italians like to drink wine until they become sloshed."

"But I *haven't* been drinking! How many times must I tell you!" Saro had raised his voice, sounding hostile.

A policeman approached the small crowd that had formed around them. "What's going on here? Are you threatening her?" he asked Saro harshly.

But the woman intervened, stepping between Saro and the cop. "Everything's all right, officer. He's one of ours. There's no problem, really."

Though still doubtful, the policeman saluted the Salvation Army lieutenant by touching his nightstick to his cap and walked away.

"Brother, come with us to the Outpost, become a soldier, enlist in the Salvation Army for the joy of the Lord." The woman was ecstatic. Saro looked at the man who was playing the bass drum. The drummer, thin as a breadstick, shrugged his shoulders; whispering so that the woman wouldn't hear him, he said to Saro, "It doesn't cost anything; plus you get to eat twice a day."

For Saro, those words were magical. He had found a place to hide as well as a way not to starve. They were right to say that America was a great nation.

He was taken to the nearby Madison Street Outpost. It was a large cellar; at one time, it must have been a warehouse for wines and spirits, since the walls seemed infused with a typical tavern aroma. He was welcomed by a lady in a blue skirt and white blouse with red military epaulets on which a star was pinned. She must have been around fifty, but wrinkles had not yet formed at the corners of her eyes. She had long blonde hair braided and wound around her head; the hairdo made her look like a granny who baked oatmeal cookies. Her face was still beau-

tiful, though, and her kind blue eyes seemed at odds with her pomp-
ous, militaristic manner. She greeted Saro with a broad, affected smile.
"Come in, brother. Welcome to our Outpost. Here we fight for all of our
unfortunate brothers like you."

She led him to a sideboard in a corner of the room, laid with sandwiches and bottles of orangeade and Coca-Cola. "Go ahead and help
yourself. It's easier to pray on a full stomach." She left him and joined
another group in civilian clothes. Shortly afterward, the two musicians
whom Saro had met on the street came up to the table. The bass drummer, reaching for a sandwich, noticed that Saro was having trouble with
his second sandwich. "You don't have to stuff yourself," he said, "they
never run out. It's a real gold mine. I told you."

"How long have you been with them?" Saro asked him, his mouth so
full he could hardly talk.

"A month, and I assure you I won't be too quick to leave. I'm a soldier
now," he said with some pride.

"But do you go around playing that drum all day?"

"Sure."

"It's not for me."

The woman who had received him came back. "Brother, what is your
name?"

"Saro. Saro Ragusa."

"I'm Captain Virginia. Come, let us go to the Altar of Thanks to pay
homage to the Lord." Without waiting for him, she walked to the center
of the room, where there was a kind of dais, and knelt down there. A few
people imitated her, and Saro, after wolfing down the rest of his sandwich, felt compelled to follow her, though the whole thing really didn't
appeal to him. He knelt down, and Virginia started singing a hymn.
Soon everyone present joined in singing, and the chorus could be heard
even out in the street:

As long as there are women who weep, I will fight.
As long as there are children who are hungry and cold, I
will fight.
As long as there are alcoholics, I will fight . . .

When they had finished, Virginia asked him, "Do you, Saro, want to
become a soldier of Christ?"
The question startled him. "Well . . ."

"Oh, Lord . . ." The woman raised her arms to heaven, quickly followed by everyone there, including Saro. "Thanks be to You for your
benevolent kindness, for having guided this lost sheep to the path of
light." Then she rose and, turning to Saro, said, "Now come and sign the
Articles of War."

He let himself be led like an automaton. At that moment, if he'd been
asked to jump into the fire, he would have done so. With his signature
at the bottom of a mimeographed sheet listing the twelve points of the
Salvationists' creed, the formalities were finally completed. Saro was now,
for all intents and purposes, a soldier in the glorious army. Those looking on applauded and started singing the "Hallelujah," but this time all
the trumpeters and bass drummers played in unison, rattling windows
throughout the entire building. At the end, they all flocked around Saro,
congratulating him on his decision. Some kissed him, and others heartily
shook his hand. Then Virginia claimed everyone's attention. She climbed
up on the podium of the Altar of Thanks in order to be heard and seen
better. "Gentlemen? Gentlemen, please!" She clapped her hands to call
the soldiers to order. "After having taken 'refreshment'"—she used that
word to drive home the point to her audience—"let us return to our joyous battlefields. And please, capture some other fine trophy for us," she
said, eyeing Saro with the satisfaction of a hunter who has just hung an
elk's head over the mantelpiece.

The small groups reassembled—bass drum, trumpet, and barker—
and spread out through the streets of the city to resume their mission of
conversion.

Saro had fallen in with a group, thinking to slip away unnoticed, but
Virginia stopped him, gripping his wrist and leading him toward a door.
"One moment, Saro. We're not finished with you yet." She took him
into a dressing room with a bench and a rack hung with a large number of uniforms: pants, blouses, and skirts, all regulation blue, except, of
course, for the blouses, white as snow.

When he left the dressing room a few minutes later, Saro was wearing
the uniform of the Salvation Army: blue pants and a white shirt with red
epaulettes, though without any stars.

A girl with fiery red hair, just back from a "war" expedition, was
munching a sandwich and saw him come out of the room. Sitting beside her was her group's trumpeter. They watched Captain Virginia come
out behind Saro and with great nonchalance walk over to the organ that
stood on one side of the room. She sat down on the stool and started

playing a melody of great emotional impact. The new aspiring soldiers were brought to the Altar of Thanks, for the initiation ceremony.

Meanwhile, Saro was approached by one of the organizers of the groups to be sent out on missions. The man had a clipboard that held a stack of papers with lists of names.

"You are soldier?" he asked and then waited for Saro to tell him his name.

"Saro Ragusa," he replied, somewhat annoyed by all the rules.

The lieutenant checked the register and didn't find his name. "You're a new soldier, right?" He wrote his name, date of birth, and work experience on one of the sheets. "Can you sing? Are you tone-deaf?" the man asked, lowering his clipboard.

"Of course I can sing. Italians sing and drink wine, everybody knows that," Saro said, smiling defiantly as he glanced around in search of agreement.

"Okay, there's no need to get offended. This is your first time out, if I'm not mistaken. Let's see which group I can add you to." He studied the list, searching for a team that would be a suitable match for a novice.

"Hey, boss—er, I meant to say, lieutenant." A female voice came from behind them. The lieutenant turned and saw the girl with the flame-red hair coming toward them. "Dixie and I are ready to go out again. He could come with us." She pointed to Saro, who was still disoriented by the day's overwhelming events.

Saro was now able to see her up close. She was quite tall, despite the fact that she was wearing a pair of flats. Her tight-fitting blouse showed off a perfect body. Her narrow waist and broad hips and shoulders lent her an athlete's appearance. Her breasts were small, a feature that gave her an aura of elegance and refinement.

"You're Isabel, right?" the lieutenant said, consulting his list again. "You're with Petrova and Dixie?"

Isabel nodded, still chewing her sandwich. She glanced at Saro without interest, and he was dazzled by her sea-blue eyes. Dixie and Petrova came over as well. Saro looked at the young man. The roguish mustache made him seem congenial from the very first glance.

"By the way," Dixie said, "this is Lieutenant Petrova." He indicated the Russian, a woman around forty, neither fat nor thin, but pleasantly plump. "And she's Isabel." Isabel was an explosive Irish concentrate. She threw him a disdainful glance. "And I'm Dixie."

"Dixie, tell me your real name."

"In Naples they called me Mimmo. But my name is Domenico. Here everyone calls me Dixie. As you see, I have an international name." He grinned broadly.

"Okay, then," the lieutenant concluded, adding Saro's name to the trio. "Saro, you're with Petrova's detachment."

———————

The souls they had to save were prostitutes, drug addicts, alcoholics, thieves, and common criminals, and since they had to go looking for them in their own surroundings, Broome Street, in the Bowery district, was one of the busiest streets where the Army's recruits made their rounds. Petrova was the barker, while Dixie played the trumpet and Isabel, the drum. Saro was assigned to take up the collection in a tin can. From time to time, some old man slipped a few pennies into the can. A drunk might stop to listen to Petrova's preaching, but when he realized that the gist of it was that he shouldn't drink anymore, he swore at her and hurried away. So did the addicts, whereas the prostitutes, unable to leave their station, made fun of her.

Every morning, in certain neighborhoods, there were at least a couple of deaths. They were those who had succumbed to an overdose, or others who had been consumed by cirrhosis.

Saro, overcoming his instinctive shyness, approached people he thought might be able to give a little money to charity, but the refusals were ten times greater than the donations. After a time, the wheedling and cajoling became frustrating for the Army's soldiers, which is why the captain advised them not to spend longer than an hour at a time out in the field.

The first days were the hardest for Saro, but then it was like his friends had predicted: "You'll soon get used to it, and then it will become a job like any other." Petrova's group continued to make its rounds on the Lower East Side, sometimes crossing into Little Italy. But Saro, with the excuse that he was Italian and didn't want to be seen by his friends, talked Petrova into staying on the west side of Broome Street. Actually Saro was fearful of having a nasty encounter with Stoker's men.

On the fourth day, he had another unpleasant encounter. Near Sullivan Street, in a blind alley, there was a garbage dump piled with cartons and trash cans. The alley was dark, but he could clearly see a petite young woman being shoved around by a man.

When he walked into the alley and approached them, Saro saw that the young woman's face was swollen, her lips smeared with blood. Saro recognized the woman. It was Titina, the girl he'd met on the ship.

"Titina!" he called, as the man stood with his arm half raised, poised to give her yet another smack.

Titina saw Saro in the distance but didn't immediately recognize him, lost like so many others in the fumes of alcohol. Still, he was clearly someone who knew her, so she ran to him to escape the man's rage. She looked up, one eye half-closed because of the swelling, "Help me! Help me!" she cried through her tears.

"Don't you recognize me? I'm Saro. We met on the ship."

It had only been a few months since they arrived, but in that brief time, Titina had seen a battalion of men tramp over her body.

"Oh, Saro. Of course I haven't forgotten you . . ." But she was interrupted by the bully.

He must have been no older than twenty-three, but he was strong as an ox. He pulled Titina away, shouting, "Hey, you, stay away from my woman!"

Then he grabbed her by the throat.

By now Saro was joined by the other three members of his group. Petrova stepped in with her usual sermon, but this time her timing was wrong. "Brother. Calm your rage. Don't do anything that will offend our Lord first of all," she spoke directly to the man.

His only response was to pull out a knife and, with a swift, imperceptible move, release the switchblade, brandishing it at the newcomers. "Keep away from me!" He gave Titina a violent shove toward the back of the alley, causing her to stumble and collapse on the mountain of cartons and packing straw. Saro was just as swift and gripped his ever-handy razor. The two men faced off for a moment, undecided whether to fight.

"Brothers, no! Not that!" Petrova cried.

Dixie intervened, grabbing Saro's arm. "Forget it! These people don't listen to reason."

"I know him; he's one of Stoker's gang," Isabel added. "These people aren't normal. Let's go, Saro, come on!"

Saro straightened up, lowering his guard, and so did his opponent. Petrova, Isabel, and Dixie went back to the drunk woman lying on the ground, while Saro stayed behind and watched Titina get up from the heap of cartons with the man's help. When she was back on her feet, the man took his suppressed anger out on her, ruthlessly punching her in the stomach and making her crumple. She spat blood and began whimpering, begging him not to hurt her again and promising she wouldn't drink anymore.

Saro bit his lips, outraged. In that brief episode, he'd witnessed humanity's worst side and had come to the realization that violence was the only weapon by which to survive in that infernal city. He would have to renounce all of his father's teachings: honesty, moral integrity, ethics—all rubbish that didn't get you very far in New York. Other values took precedence. Saro knew quite well what they were and vowed to himself that he would become a true American citizen, worthy of his new country.

Chapter 30

The Father, as everyone in the neighborhood now called Ferdinando Licata, was relishing sensations and emotions that he had never felt before. He had never known the meaning of a real family. The affection of his little grandniece, the quiet, hardworking life led by Betty and her husband, their genuine love, strengthened by the struggles they'd had to overcome when they arrived in a strange land, were making him change his prior thinking about family and more generally about the meaning of life.

The difficulties he had endured in recent months had blunted his iron will. The prince had never run from anyone or anything before. But now he was reassessing the old Sicilian saying "*Calati juncu, ca passa a china.*" "Bend, reed, until the flood passes" was not a show of weakness but rather of strength and character: The strength to be a great strategist and to know when to lead the retreat to avoid being vanquished; being able to wait for the right moment, even if it meant waiting a very long time.

Ferdinando Licata's life had experienced an abrupt change of direction. Before, he never would have thought of going to the market to do the shopping; that was something servants did. Now, to help the family, he took his niece's large bag every morning and went down to the street, mingling with the women and elderly men designated to perform that daily ritual. The first few times, he observed what the housewives of Little Italy did, and quickly learned the women's tricks of the trade. Now he could haggle over the price, add a fruit when the produce had already been weighed and the price set—"I'll take this; it has all the sunshine of Sicily in it"—and knew the names of the shopkeepers and fruit vendors. Before long, everyone came to recognize him. It took him a few more days to become skilled at choosing the best fruit. He felt the oranges one by one, examined a pear's stem, checked to see that there were no wilted leaves on the lettuce.

Sometimes, if he had to go shopping for just a few things, and Ginevra didn't have to go to school, he would take her by the hand, and they would go out in grand style. He was extremely proud of his grand-niece, partly because she resembled him and could be mistaken for his daughter, but mostly because she was so charming that the women in the neighborhood would stop to give her candy and sweets.

Like all children, Ginevra took advantage of the privilege of being a pretty little girl and would ask her uncle to buy her some cookies or cotton candy or chocolates. Whims that Ferdinando Licata, after first flatly refusing, invariably ended up satisfying, fully expecting another reprimand from Betty, who didn't want the child to grow up spoiled.

Later uncle and niece made a pact of *omertà*, secrecy, whereby Ginevra swore she would never tell her mother what he'd bought her.

––––––––––

La Tonnara was bringing in a rather decent income. Betty and Nico had learned to economize on the dishes they served, and at the same time, they cooked Sicilian specialties, drawing on the same spices and ingredients they used at home. Sicilians who came to the restaurant left with tears in their eyes, recognizing the flavors of their homeland. The trattoria was therefore a success: every evening, it filled up with customers not only from the neighborhood but also from other areas of the city.

But Ferdinando Licata's watchful eye noticed that Betty had become increasingly nervous lately and snapped over the slightest thing. Nico told her to be patient and not to worry. Ferdinando couldn't figure out what the problem was.

Early one morning, Licata understood.

He had gone to the market as he did each day to buy the vegetables and fish on the list that Nico made for him the previous night. When he returned, he came in the back way, through the kitchen door.

He heard agitated voices coming from the next room. One was Betty's. From time to time Nico's broke in, but there was a third person with an unfamiliar voice who seemed to be angry with them.

Ferdinando set the shopping bag down on the kitchen table and moved closer to the dining room door so he could hear the conversation better.

"You can't come to us and ask us for money to pay off your gambling debts," Betty was saying.

Nico tried to calm her down, holding her by the arm. "Betty, that's not the way."

"The money isn't for us. It's the insurance you've agreed to on your beautiful restaurant."

Ferdinando slowly leaned forward to see who was talking to his niece.

He saw a burly freckled guy with red hair standing in the center of the room; he seemed like an Irish boxer. At his side were two shady individu-als, hands in their pockets, looking menacing.

"You know where I'd like to shove your fucking insurance?" Betty went on, shaking a fist under the man's nose.

Ferdinando smiled. He had never heard Betty utter a vulgarity.

Nico stepped in. "We don't have the money. At least not right now."

But Betty interrupted him. "We don't have it now and never will. We're over our heads in debt. In fact—" She went to the table where the cash box was. She opened it and grabbed a stack of papers and bills. Then she went back to the burly man and threw them in his face. "Are you going to deal with these?" The bills and demands for payment fluttered through the air. The man dodged the papers and grabbed Betty's wrist.

She tried to free herself.

"Goddamn bitch!"

Betty spat in his face.

Nico stepped forward to release his wife from the bruiser's grip. The man let go of his prey and pulled the checkered tablecloth off the near-est table with a loud clatter as plates and glasses crashed to the floor. He wiped his face, furious.

Nico drew back, protecting his wife. "How long will you give us to get together the money?"

"But it's not fair!" Betty cried. "We've already paid you this month. Mr. Stoker already took our money. This is extortion you're demanding for yourselves, for your vices. Stoker has always behaved properly with us. He can't be asking us for more money. It's you; you're the ones who need it, right?"

Nico covered her mouth. "Don't listen to her. She's beside herself. Our daughter is ill," he lied, "and we don't have the money for an op-eration. That's the reason. However, we'll get you your hundred dollars, even if we have to go out and steal it. Just give me one week's time."

"Five days. Just five days." Without waiting for an answer, the boxer turned and walked out, pulling off another tablecloth and making the food Betty had prepared for lunch go tumbling to the floor.

As soon as they left, the young woman clung to her husband and burst into tears. "We'll never get out from under. It's a curse."

As Nico consoled her and urged her not to lose heart, Ferdinando Li-cata retraced his steps, picked up the shopping bag, and went out, and then pretended he had just come in.

Captain Virginia had decided that it was time to test Saro as a preacher.

So overnight Saro, Dixie, and Isabel found themselves working together on the streets south of Houston, at times venturing as far north as Greenwich Village. They got along together so harmoniously that one would think they were old friends. They spent only part of the day working for the Army, trying to collect a few coins. The rest of the day, they would hide out on rooftops, or occasionally drink beer that they'd bought thanks to people's charity.

One such afternoon, when they were out on Greene Street seeking donations, Saro decided to go into a bar for a beer. As soon as he sat down, his eyes steered him to a large billfold bursting with bills. Later he learned that the fellow sporting it, a resolute man less than five feet tall, was a citrus fruit merchant. The little fellow was just back from the outdoor market, and that morning he had been lucky enough to have a load of lemons at a time when all his other competitors had mainly oranges. Saro quickly realized that this was an opportunity he must not let slip away. He went out in search of his friends and told them about the overstuffed wallet.

"But we can't steal it! How would that look?" Isabel said shortly.

"We won't steal it," Dixie suggested enigmatically. "We'll simply make him give it to us."

"Oh, do you have hypnotic skills?" Isabel asked mockingly.

"No, I have a plan," Dixie added even more mysteriously, and explained what it entailed.

Shortly afterward, Saro returned to the bar. The merchant was still sitting at his place. This time a whore was keeping him company. She was stuck to him like a leech and was tickling his ear with her tongue when Saro approached. She looked him up and down and, seeing that he was from the Army, remarked, "No one around here needs redeeming, baby."

Saro kept a straight face. He leaned over and spoke in the merchant's ear: "I have a little proposition that could let you double the bucks you have in your safe box within seven days. Interested?"

The man looked suspicious.

Saro continued undeterred. "I can introduce you to a friend who is able to perform miracles like that. Naturally, it's not entirely legal—but money is money, right?"

He uttered the last words lowering his voice even further. The merchant turned to get a better look at him. There's nothing more reassuring than the whiff of illegality for those who want to make a lot of money, fast.

The little man sent the girl away and invited Saro to sit down in her place. He was still wary. "But you're from the Salvation Army. You don't do dirty business."

"That's what you think," Saro replied.

"Well, what's the deal?" the merchant asked, swallowing the bait.

Evenings at La Tonnara were different now. Ever since Betty had decided to improve the restaurant's tone, using cloth napkins and tablecloths, and spending a few more dollars on the table settings, adding candles or floral arrangements, there'd been a decline in the number of customers. The neighborhood people were uneasy with a trattoria that seemed to have the pretensions of an uptown restaurant. They began deserting it, and this became a source of contention between husband and wife, along with the looming ultimatum issued by Stoker's men. Nico had gone around to friends, and someone had referred him to a couple of loan sharks from Calabria, but, for now, at least, he was reluctant to enter the escalating spiral of usury.

One morning as he began preparing vegetables for the soup, he opened the drawer with the knives and under the silverware compartment he found a hundred dollar bill, folded in four. Who could have put it there? Betty came in at just that moment, and Nico instinctively slipped the bill into his pants pocket. But her constant contact with people had accustomed Betty to catch the slightest movement of those around her. "What was it you hid away so fast?" she asked her husband. Nico knew he couldn't hide anything from her and showed her the bill. "Did you put this in the silverware drawer?"

Betty went over and looked at the bill. "It's Uncle Ferdinando's, I'll bet." She took it from her husband's hands. "He must have heard us arguing with those bastards the other day."

"It would get us out of a tight spot," Nico said.

"Don't even think about it. Don't you understand that I don't want to have even more debts to pay?"

"Betty, those people don't ask twice."

"An agreement is an agreement. Stoker had nothing to do with it, I'm sure. Those guys gave it a try, but with us it didn't work; it's that simple."

She went into the dining area to speak to her uncle. The prince spent part of each morning sitting in the trattoria, reading books or newspapers.

Slapping the hundred-dollar bill on the table, Betty said, "This is yours, right?"

"I don't see my name on it. I don't think so. Where did you find it?" he asked, lying.

"*Zio*, don't pull my leg. You overheard the 'insurance' collectors, didn't you?"

"They're people who have to make a living. All in all, they protect the place from ill-intentioned characters, don't they?"

"What I had to pay, I paid. I won't shell out a penny more this month. I know how these things end up. This isn't Sicily."

She left the bill on the table and went back to the kitchen.

The deadline for the ultimatum arrived. That evening Betty and Nico were especially anxious, expecting something bad to happen. A boy whom they had never seen before came in at closing time and asked if there was an envelope for the Stoker family. Betty replied that there was no envelope for them.

Then nothing more happened.

The following days were a time of great tension. The third and fourth day following the ultimatum's deadline also came and went. More days passed without anything, and in the end, the episode was forgotten. Betty did not fail to say the fateful words that all women say to their husbands sooner or later: "You see, I told you so." And the matter seemed to end there.

With each passing week, as Betty had predicted, new customers came from the surrounding neighborhoods of Greenwich Village and Chelsea. They were middle-class people or starving artists, who nonetheless gave the place a certain local color, and they sang Nico's praises to their friends, raving about his spectacular bean and seafood soup with toasted croutons.

One evening, the lights in the restaurant suddenly went out. A chorus of surprise greeted the unexpected darkness, but the candles on the tables allowed the guests to continue dining.

A few minutes later, however, the crash of shattered windows was heard and four bandits immediately burst into the trattoria, knocking over tables and everything else that happened to be in their way: glasses, plates, bottles. People screamed, terrified. Some hid under tables, others remained frozen in their chairs, those who stood up were struck with gun butts.

"Don't move!" shouted one of the four, a guy covered with freckles.

Betty, who at the time of the break-in was entering the room with a carafe of wine and some glasses, stopped and crouched in a corner. Under their black kerchiefs, she recognized the two Irishmen who had accompanied the bagman a few weeks earlier.

The man who'd yelled "Don't move!" went to the cash box. He opened the drawer and grabbed a handful of dollars, sticking them in his pocket. He passed near Betty and glanced at her briefly. Then he began shooting at anything that had a semblance of decor. When he had vented his rage, he shouted again, "Nobody move!" Meanwhile, the other three grabbed the chance to seize the customers' wallets and some of the women's necklaces, but their loot turned out to be inconsequential.

As soon as Ferdinando Licata heard the trattoria's window break, he realized what was happening. In his pajamas, since he had gone to bed some time ago, he rushed downstairs and hurried into the restaurant to help Betty and Nico. But he was unarmed and could do very little against the bandits. As soon as he entered, the man nearest the door grabbed him by his pajama collar and sent him flying into the room. He lost his balance and tumbled to the floor.

"Hey, Grandpops, did you lose your way to bed?" Freckles taunted him.

Licata didn't answer him. But he got up without taking his eyes off the man. The thug noticed his resolve but went on ridiculing him, shoving him away with the butt of his rifle. "Stay in your place, old man." Then he grabbed a bowl of soup from a nearby table and poured it over his head. Beans, mussels, shrimp, and bits of bread trickled down onto Licata's pajama top. The man laughed. Licata stared him in the eye again; despite the dim light, the thug would never forget those dark eyes, that clear gaze.

"My friend, you've just started digging your own grave. And I'll see that you dig it with your teeth," the prince whispered so that only the man could hear it.

Just then a child's voice made everyone turn around. Betty's blood ran cold, as did the prince's.

"Mommy . . . Daddy . . . what's going on?"

Ginevra stood in the doorway, wearing pink pajamas, clutching a rag doll, and rubbing her eyes.

The man standing nearest grabbed her, held her tight, and covered her mouth. Frightened, the little girl struggled and started crying. Freckles went over and gave her a slap that knocked her out.

Ferdinando and Betty screamed and tried to run to the child, but guns pointed at their chests stopped them.

"Don't complicate things, Grandpops," one of the thugs told him.

The leader of the bandits, the freckled one, raised his voice to be heard by all the diners in the trattoria: "It's over. We're going now, and it will be as if nothing has happened. Don't move, and no one will hurt you. We'll take the child with us; that way, none of you will move. If I see anyone leave the place, I swear I'll kill her."

"No-ooo, please! Leave her here, I beg you! Take me! Take me!" Betty wailed. But there was no response.

The four men backed up, guns leveled, and went out with the girl.

As soon as the door closed behind them, Betty started to run after them, but her uncle stopped her: "Wait. They won't hurt her. They'll leave her somewhere, you'll see."

But it didn't happen. Although they went looking for Ginevra throughout the neighborhood, with the help of friends, acquaintances, and strangers, there was no trace of the little girl. Later that night Betty insisted on going to the police to report her daughter's disappearance and, of course, the robbery at the trattoria, even though Ferdinando advised her to leave the cops out of it.

Saro had set up an appointment with the lemon merchant for the following Saturday in the Wall Street offices of the Irving Trust Company. He told him that it was the office of his friend Marangoni. The role of Mr. Marangoni was to be played by Dixie.

Dixie didn't have an office, but Isabel had already taken care of that.

If the merchant had any doubts about the deal, they were immediately dispelled when Saro scheduled the appointment. Having an office on Wall Street and in the Irving Trust Company, moreover, one of the newest skyscrapers in Manhattan's financial district, meant that Marangoni was sitting on top of the world. The merchant assured Saro that he would not fail to keep the appointment.

Now it was up to Isabel. The Irish redhead hadn't been with the Salvation Army for long; like Saro, she had enlisted a few weeks earlier. Before that, she'd worked at a disreputable local club as a cigar-and-cigarette girl, going from table to table selling tobacco and other exclusive house specialties, including cocaine, to the customers. That was where she met and got to know Martin Fisher, the caretaker at the Irving Trust Company. He had just gotten divorced and, having no intention of going back to his exasperating ex-wife, had started going out every night looking for whores, to make up for all the nights he hadn't been able to.

Isabel had met him at the Strange Fruit, a club frequented by jazz enthusiasts. He offered to drive her home at the end of her shift. Isabel agreed because, all in all, with his potbelly, friendly smile, and gift of gab, Martin was good company and didn't seem dangerous. Still, Isabel made it clear that she didn't go with the first man who came along. She was not a whore—in short, he shouldn't expect anything from her. Martin had heard that refrain before and pretended to play along. But Isabel wasn't joking. When the moment came, she'd left him empty-handed.

Her behavior only heightened the newly single man's interest in her. Martin Fisher began going to the Strange Fruit almost every evening, and every evening he waited for Isabel's shift to end so he could take her home in his new Ford, the first gift he'd given himself after the divorce. He must have a good job if he could afford a car like that, Isabel remarked one evening. That's when Martin told her that he worked at the Irving Trust Company, the skyscraper completed just eight years earlier, and the pride of all Manhattan. Isabel gave an admiring whistle, but Martin Fisher was honest with her, explaining that he was just a custodian.

When Isabel quit her job at the Strange Fruit due to incompatibility with the owner, who demanded her services after hours, she couldn't find work anywhere, and in desperation, she enlisted in the Salvation Army. Although she'd lost touch with Martin Fisher, she knew where to look for him when the time came. So one day she went up to the forty-fourth floor, where he'd told her he worked, and, much to his delight, dropped in on him.

Chapter 31

The following Saturday, Saro met the lemon merchant at the Irving Trust Company. Johnny Scalia was his name; he was a second-generation immigrant, also of Sicilian origin. He still spoke Italian, though he mangled a lot of the words.

They entered the immense lobby and headed purposefully toward the elevators. There were few people around. It was not a workday, and those they met were executives or diligent employees who had unfinished business to complete or reports that had to be on their bosses' desks by nine o'clock Monday morning.

They rode up to the forty-fourth floor and followed the corridor leading to the offices of the National Blue Joy Company. Saro rang the bell, and shortly afterward, the door was opened by an elegant secretary in a black suit, her red hair done up in an austere bun. A pair of glasses perched on the tip of her nose.

"Good morning," Isabel greeted them. "Are you Mr. Ragusa?" When Saro said yes, she nodded. "Mr. Marangoni told me he was expecting you. Please come in."

"I hope it's not our fault you've had to work overtime," Saro said. "Have we ruined your weekend?"

"I spend Saturdays in bed."

"I don't doubt it," Saro joked. But he quickly added, "Forgive me, I like to tease."

"What I meant was that there's nothing I have to do. But once in a while, one can make exceptions, especially if Mr. Marangoni asks you."

"He's not a heartless boss, is he?"

"Not at all, he's always very kind. That's why one can't say no to him." With her index finger she adjusted the glasses on her nose. "Kindly make yourselves comfortable. I'll go and tell him you're here."

She walked off, hips swaying, down the long corridor, and Saro thought that Isabel was perhaps overdoing the role of perfect secretary.

Johnny Scalia had not let himself be distracted by Isabel's appeal and her clinging suit. He looked around the office: a large room with windows, which held about a dozen desks and several drafting tables. Mahogany doors marked the long corridor, and the overall impression was that of a sizeable firm.

"What are those drafting tables for?" he asked Saro.

"Drawing up plans. For those who request it, Blue Joy can also design casino interiors."

The merchant nodded, interested. A few minutes later, Isabel returned to the reception room. "Mr. Marangoni is waiting for you. Would you care for something to drink? Tea, coffee . . . ?"

"Nothing for me," the merchant replied.

"I'd like some coffee," Saro said. Isabel gave him a withering glance. Then she smiled briefly and beckoned them to follow her.

The executive's office was as large as the room that housed the employees. File folders, documents, and personal items were neatly arranged on an enormous desk. To one side stood a bronze statuette of a golfer, a testimony to the office occupant's enthusiasm for the game, and in the corner, a few boxes of Cuban cigars, a penholder, fountain pens, a large Art Nouveau table lamp, and a leather portfolio. The large windows offered a panoramic view of the New York Harbor.

As soon as they entered the office, "Mr. Marangoni" rose from his imposing chair behind the desk and, removing his cigar from his mouth, held out his hand to the merchant, who shook it, somewhat in awe. In his linen suit, which, like Isabel's, had been borrowed from the shop of a friend named Gallo, a *paesano* from Aversa, Dixie looked impeccable.

"Please, Mr. Scalia, sit down," he said, motioning to a chair in front of the desk.

The merchant seated himself, and Saro sat down next to him.

"You must forgive me for inconveniencing you on a Saturday, but, you must understand, I prefer to conduct certain business matters outside of regular office hours."

"I understand perfectly," the merchant replied.

"A cigar?" He leaned across the desk and opened the box of Havanas. The merchant took one out and busied himself lighting it.

Saro, though the invitation hadn't been extended to him, reached out and took two cigars from the box, slipping one into his jacket pocket and sticking the other in his mouth.

"Well, let's get down to business," said Dixie, taking a deep puff. "The sooner we get this done, the sooner we can go back to our families. Saturdays and Sundays are the only days I'm able to see my wife. Are you married, Mr. Scalia?"

Saro threw him a stern look, meaning don't overdo it.

"My wife died last year."

"Oh, I'm so sorry; I didn't mean to—"

"It's okay," the merchant interrupted.

"So, then, Mr. Marangoni," Saro spoke up firmly, "will you explain to Mr. Scalia what the deal involves?"

"Of course, it's simple. It has to do with slot machines. I should point out that there is nothing illegal about it—apart from the fact that these little machines have been slightly rigged . . . in favor of the casino management, clearly." He laughed heartily, and Saro joined him. Scalia, on the other hand, just smiled.

"Do you have a supply of these machines?" Johnny Scalia asked.

"Let me finish; then you can ask me all the questions you want," said Dixie, serious again. "There are about a hundred of these slot machines, already set up, in a gambling parlor uptown. I'll tell you the location once we've reached an agreement. They're also covered by a license. As I said, there's nothing illegal about it. I'm offering you a good deal."

"May I ask why you haven't offered it to a friend, if it's such a good deal?" the lemon merchant asked suspiciously.

"For that very reason."

There was a knock at the door, and Isabel came into the office carrying a tray with a cup of coffee. They all waited while she set the cup down in front of Saro and then turned to leave, giving Scalia one last chance to admire her curves.

Before she got to the door, Dixie said, "You're free to go now, Miss Parker. I'll lock up the office."

"Thank you, sir, and have a nice weekend." Then turning to the two guests: "Good day, gentlemen." With that, Isabel's role ended, and she left the room.

When the door closed, Dixie whispered to the merchant conspiratorially, "She already put out. She has an ass like marble and a pair of tits!"

The merchant smiled and began to settle comfortably in the chair. He nodded, puffing on the cigar. "Yeah, she's a great piece of tail. It's true, her ass is her best feature, with all due respect."

"Well, let's get back to business," Saro said.

"So where were we? Why haven't I offered this deal to my friends? Well, Mr. Scalia, for that very reason, because as far as my friends know, my line of work lies in another area, import and export and so on. They aren't aware that I'm involved in several gambling clubs. I'm forced to get rid of them because a friend of mine tipped me off that in a week I'll have the shipping inspectors underfoot. To get on their lists, you have to be completely clean, you know what I mean. So I need to dispose of them, and fairly quickly, which is why the selling price is very favorable; a real good deal, like I said."

"What would the price be?"

Dixie leaned forward, looking the man in the eyes. He had established a figure with his friends, but now he wanted to up the ante. "We're talking about almost a hundred machines with a license, already set up in a gambling parlor. There's nothing else you have to do except go and collect a mint every day."

"So, how much?" the impatient merchant asked again.

"Thirty thousand," Dixie proposed, "made out to cash."

Saro wheeled around. They had agreed to ask for fifteen thousand dollars.

The merchant slumped back in his chair. "Too much," he said, discouraged.

"But the price is negotiable," Saro interjected.

"Twenty-two," Johnny Scalia offered.

"Twenty-eight," Dixie countered.

"Twenty-five," Scalia proposed.

"Twenty-six," Dixie came back.

"Twenty-five and we close immediately," the merchant said resolutely.

"You'll recover the twenty-five grand in a month. Do you realize what a deal you got? Let's shake on it." Dixie stood up, followed by Scalia, and they shook hands.

"Where are the slot machines?"

"In Spanish Harlem, One Hundred Seventeenth Street," Dixie said. He opened a drawer and pulled out two typewritten pages and a license. He handed the two sheets of paper to Johnny Scalia. "I've already prepared a contract. See if it looks all right to you." He left the slot machine license in plain view on the desk. The merchant eyed the license, and carefully read one of the two pages. It was a statement by Marangoni that he relinquished the operation and ownership of all the slot machines set up in the gambling parlor located at 454 East 117th Street. Reading the document seemed to convince the merchant, who handed it back to Dixie. "Sign it," he told Dixie. Then he took out his checkbook from his briefcase and wrote out a check for twenty-five thousand dollars.

Dixie, meanwhile, signed the two copies of the contract and handed them to Scalia, who in turn signed both copies, giving one copy to Dixie and retaining the other for himself.

"Well, Mr. Marangoni," he said as he rose to say good-bye. "It's been a pleasure doing business with you. If you have other proposals, here's my card; just give me a call."

Dixie took the man's card but didn't have one of his own for the customary exchange. "Will do. You know where I work, so come and see me whenever you want . . .

"Only please don't mention who you made this deal with," he added. "Don't forget."

"Sure, sure." Johnny Scalia smiled, pleased to be complicit in their little secret. "You don't have to worry. By the way, congratulations."

"What for?"

"Still so young, and already you've been able to set up this great organization."

They stood up and the merchant noticed Saro. "Oh, I almost forgot the friend who introduced us . . ." He took two hundred-dollar bills from his wallet and slipped them into Saro's jacket pocket. "You deserve them, pal."

"That's very generous of you."

Johnny Scalia's feet were itching. He thought he'd just made the biggest deal of his life, and he couldn't wait to hurry over and claim it. "I know the way, my friends. Don't trouble yourselves." And with that, he opened the door and left.

Saro and Dixie both held their breath and didn't say a word until they heard the door close behind the merchant. Soon afterward, the door opened again, and Isabel appeared. The three friends joined in a single embrace, jumping for joy. Isabel waved the check, and Saro brandished the two C-notes.

"You were terrific, better than Errol Flynn. You look like him too." Isabel hugged Dixie and planted a kiss on his mouth.

"Hey, hey, what about me? Who baited the hook?" Saro asked, feeling left out.

Isabel broke away from Dixie and hugged him too. "You were superb." She gave him a kiss on the cheek. "But now we have to beat it, Martin told us we could stay till noon at the latest, then the cleaning crew comes in."

"We also have to return the clothes," Saro reminded them.

"And then, on to the Savoy! They play the most explosive swing in all New York there?" Dixie said excitedly.

Johnny Scalia raced as quickly as he could to East 117th Street in Spanish Harlem, with the contract and license safely in his pocket. He found a club, the Crazy Strass at number 454, but the doors were closed. Scalia knocked, hoping to get in, but a team of painters was renovating the place, and the foreman told him that they were working overtime because the place had to be ready to open Monday morning at ten. Scalia saw rows of slot machines lined up against the walls, along with pool tables and various devices intended to fleece the suckers who went there. He was encouraged when the foreman said that they were painting the place because a new manager was supposed to be coming in to take over the machines. Scalia smiled at the thought that the man he was talking about was himself, and for a moment he pictured the tons of coins he would collect each week. He offered the workers a drink at a nearby bar, and then said good-bye and went back to his deserted house. Two strokes of luck in just one week; he couldn't ask for anything more.

There was such a crowd that Saturday at the Savoy Ballroom in Harlem that they couldn't even buy tickets. Someone had spread the word that Duke Ellington himself would play there that night. Dixie suggested to his friends that they go somewhere else, since they'd never be able to get in.

They took a cab down to the Onyx Club on West Fifty-Second Street. To get in, all they had to do was say the watchword to the guy who looked out from the large peephole in the door.

"I'm from Local 802," Dixie recited, and to his great satisfaction, the door magically opened. "See that?"

"What does it mean?" asked Isabel, not at all impressed.

"It's the New York chapter of the Musicians' Union," Dixie disclosed. "I joined it. Someday I'll be able to play the corner in one of these clubs."

Isabel and Dixie seemed to be a steady couple for most of the night, even though he was captivated by the trumpeter's phrasing and watched ecstatically, not caring much about the girl's attentions. She got bored and asked Saro to dance, but he said he had two left feet and would rather sit than have the whole room make fun of him. Isabel laughed loudly, got up, and forcibly dragged him to the center of the dance floor. Even without heels she was taller than Saro. She put her arms around him and said simply, "Follow me." Fortunately, a languid blues number had started, and the two held each other close, letting themselves sway to the notes of "Mood Indigo" by the great Duke Ellington. When the last note faded away, the two lingered in each other's arms a moment, in the middle of the floor. Then they broke apart, looked at each other in silence and smiled. Out of the blue, Isabel kissed him passionately for a few brief seconds, and then stepped away and headed back to the table. But Saro stopped her as the other dancers were coming back to the floor for a new number, this time a livelier arrangement with a beat.

"What was that about?" Saro asked, completely bewildered.

"Nothing, I just wanted to feel if you gave me a thrill," she said.

"And did I?"

"What do you think?"

Isabel went to the table and sat down next to Dixie, who, unaware of what was going on, was accompanying the piece the orchestra had begun, drumming along on the tablecloth.

"This is 'Jumpin' at the Woodside' by Count Basie!" he shouted to Isabel as she sipped a martini. "Feel that rhythm." He continued along with the orchestra, beating out the tempo with his fingers. He didn't notice that Isabel's eyes had grown moist.

Saro, however, noticed a change in the young woman. He had never seen her display her feelings so openly. On the contrary, despite her magnetic allure, he had always imagined her as always in control and capable of concealing the slightest sign of weakness. He didn't know what to make of her emotion. Was it due to Dixie's indifference, or was he the cause of her mood?

––––––––

For Johnny Scalia, Monday took forever to come. Keyed up over the deal he'd made, he had read and reread the sale agreement, looking for some clause that might have escaped him at the time, but he found nothing. The license specified the number, type, and serial number of the slot machines, everything was according to law—or almost. Tampering with the mechanism that governed the winnings was a detail that the authorities no longer even paid attention to now. All of the slot machines in the country had been tampered with, so that kind of inspection would be highly unlikely.

At ten o'clock sharp, he was standing in front of 454 East 117th Street. He went in and made his way toward the gambling parlor's offices. The place was in perfect order, all the slots had a stool, the tables stood ready to welcome the patsies, the staff was bustling about. Someone came up to him and said, "We open in half an hour; we're still setting up."

"Go right ahead. I'm the new owner." So saying, he walked directly to the office, leaving the man puzzled.

Scalia knocked and went in without waiting for a response. He saw a sixtyish fellow in shirtsleeves sitting behind the desk. Raising his head from a mountain of papers he was sorting through, the man looked at him questioningly.

"Hi, I'm Johnny Scalia, the new owner of the slots. Are you the manager? Mr. Marangoni's done a great job sprucing up the place."

As Scalia spoke, the man with the rolled-up sleeves rose from his chair and came around to the front of the desk.

"*Ma chi minchia siete?*" he asked in a mixture of American and Sicilian, wagging his joined fingers under Scalia's nose in a challenging gesture meant to say "Who the fuck are you?"

"Weren't you informed by Mr. Marangoni?" Scalia's face was no longer cordial now.

"Who the fuck is this Marangoni? Who ever heard of him?" the man in shirtsleeves continued in the same harsh tone.

"His office is at the National Blue Joy Company, on the forty-fourth floor of the Irving Trust Company. I've been there myself. Look, just a second—" He pulled the license and sale agreement out of his pocket and handed them to the man. "You see? This is 454 East 117th Street. There, see the license? And this is the sale agreement for the slot machines."

The man read the two documents quickly, turning increasingly livid as he read. When he had finished reading, he looked up at Scalia who was beginning to feel uneasy.

"Everything is in order, I hope—" Scalia managed to say to the man, whose only response was to rip the papers to shreds. "*Now* everything is in order!" he yelled at the top of his lungs, tossing the pieces of the contract into the air like confetti. "Who sent you? Which family do you belong to?"

The shouts made the staff come running, among them two bouncers.

"A problem, boss?" one of the two asked.

"Ask him," he said, pointing to Scalia, who was now beginning to fear for his safety.

The bouncer turned to the lemon merchant. "What's your beef, buddy?"

"Saturday morning Mr. Marangoni sold me the slot—" But he didn't get to finish the sentence because the two thugs took him by the arms and forcibly lifted him up.

Scalia was on the verge of passing out and felt a vague infirmity spread through his body. He thought he was paralyzed, but when he fully regained consciousness he saw that he was propped up against the wall of a building. A passerby threw a coin into the hat at his feet. Still in shock, Scalia stared at the quarter, and the sight of it made him remember.

He hurried to his bank with his heart in his mouth, glancing at the clock as he went in. It was 10:40—maybe he was still in time. He spoke to the manager, who called over the teller. The teller's words were a cold shower for the poor lemon merchant: "Yes, a young man came in this morning; he was one of the first customers. I remember that he was well dressed, and he had a mustache like Errol Flynn. Given the amount of the check he cashed, I have a clear picture of him in my mind."

Scalia now raced downtown to the Irving Trust Company. He got into the elevator and asked the operator to take him up to the forty-fourth floor. "The National Blue Joy Company" he said.

"Forty-four, that is," the young man confirmed.

At the forty-fourth floor Johnny Scalia stepped out of the elevator and headed toward the office of the National Blue Joy Company, trying to stay calm. He was determined not to lose his temper. He would threaten to call not the police but someone who would do the job better than the cops. His heart was pounding.

He rang the bell at the imposing mahogany door. A middle-aged woman opened it: evidently another secretary. Scalia stepped into the corridor. The office was in full swing. Behind the glass, clerks and professionals were busily at work and did not look up from their desks or drafting tables.

"Is the red-haired secretary here?" he asked after looking over the place.

"So you don't like the color of my hair?" the middle-aged lady replied tartly. "May I ask whom you're looking for?"

"Mr. Marangoni," he said quickly.

"Mr. Marangoni?" the secretary repeated.

"Yes, Mr. Marangoni."

"Do you have an appointment?"

Johnny Scalia was beginning to breathe freely again. At least the man was there. "No, but tell him that Johnny Scalia is here, and he'll understand."

"Have a seat," she said, indicating the reception area, and went off down the long corridor.

Scalia watched her walk away and couldn't help but notice her big behind jiggling.

"What a difference," he thought, remembering the redhead from Saturday.

While he was lost in reflection, the secretary returned accompanied by a distinguished gentleman wearing an English tweed jacket and a bow tie. Seeing him approach, Scalia automatically rose from his chair.

"Good morning, I'm Robert Marangoni. Were you looking for me?" He reached out and firmly shook the merchant's limp, sweaty hand.

"Do you have a son, maybe?"

"I'm not married. But may I ask the reason for your visit?"

"I bought a batch of slot machines from you here, license and all."

At these words, the man turned on his heel and said to his secretary: "Regina, please take care of it." He strode off, extremely annoyed by that intrusion into his realm of geometries, curves, and angles.

"Do you realize what you're saying?" The secretary took him by the arm and led him to the door. "This is an architectural firm. We design bridges, buildings, tourist resorts. Don't you know that? Whatever possessed you to talk about slot machines? Mother of God, you hear all sorts of things nowadays."

She opened the door and shoved him out. Johnny Scalia felt a strong burning sensation in the center of his chest and leaned against the wall, waiting for it to pass.

Chapter 32

There was no need for the police to get involved in finding Ginevra because the morning after the raid on La Tonnara, a car dropped the child off a few blocks away on East Seventh Street, at the edge of Tompkins Square Park. The little girl was rescued by a woman who recognized her immediately, thanks to the photos that had appeared in the morning newspapers. She took her to the restaurant, where Betty, with a cry of joy and tears of relief, held her tightly in a suffocating embrace.

They brought her to the hospital, and the doctors were able to verify that she had not suffered any injuries of a sexual nature. However, the child was still clearly in a state of shock.

The damages to La Tonnara were substantial. The episode had demoralized the small family, which until then had lived in relative peace.

With their fears for Ginevra behind them, life resumed its normal rhythm. They had to pick up where they'd left off.

Ferdinando Licata offered to pay the damages sustained by the trattoria, but Betty refused her uncle's help. Ferdinando pointed out the danger of falling into the clutches of loan sharks: the couple would run the risk of ultimately finding themselves with an unwanted partner. Not to mention the fact that Stoker would be able to buy their debts from the moneylenders, and they would thus find themselves in his hands. This point made Betty reconsider her decision. In ten days, La Tonnara reopened to the public.

But people were afraid. Their regular customers chose instead to go to other restaurants in the area.

In the end, fixing up the trattoria had cost much more than paying the "insurance," as Stoker's people called the protection money.

Brian Stoker was the undisputed king of the northern portion of the Lower East Side, which many decades later would become known as the East Village. The Irish had settled in that part of the city when New York was a huge shantytown. His father had witnessed the city transform itself, and had physically helped build it as a bricklayer. Brian remembered him coming home at night to their hovel, having barely enough strength to gulp down the supper his wife had made before he collapsed on the horsehair mattress in a troubled sleep.

He worked as long as eighteen hours a day, eating a bit of bread and cheese to assuage his hunger around eleven in the morning, after the first six or so hours of work, and then not eating again until nine at night, before going to bed. The young Brian, seeing his father slave like a dog under such inhumane conditions, swore to himself that he would not end up that way. When he turned fourteen, before his father could force him to work at the construction site, Brian informed him that he had already found a job at the port as a dockhand for the Jeson family, who ruled the Lower East Side in those days.

Whatever the Jesons said became law. Woe to anyone who crossed them.

Brian began working as a drug runner for the top brass in the union and the police force. It was an easy job that earned a weekly income equal to what his father brought home in a month.

A few years later, when he became a bit stronger, they made him take part in a beating.

Over time Brian proved to be coolheaded and unconcerned about death, and was allowed to participate in "wet work," as the Irish called missions involving bloodshed.

Mama Jeson admired the young man with the icy gaze and held him up as an example to younger members of the family who may not have wanted any part in killing people.

From that time on, Brian Stoker's career continued on the upswing. His legendary ferocity kept other criminal elements away from the Lower East Side when even the police wanted nothing to do with such hood-lums. "Let them slit each other's throats," the cops said.

A couple of times, they tried to put Stoker in jail, but when the cases were about to go to court, the witnesses pulled out or said they didn't remember anything.

The Jesons realized too late that a snake like that, harbored in the family's bosom, would sooner or later turn against them. They therefore decided to do away with him, much to Mama Jeson's regret. But Brian hadn't been idly twiddling his thumbs. He'd managed to effectively work on the family's affiliates, bringing them over to his side, and one night he seized control, killing his benefactress, Mama Jeson, before the eyes of her husband and all the brothers. The sight of the woman being garroted, without any of them being able to do anything to save her, drove the younger children into shock and made such an impression on the others that the Jesons chose to disappear forever from New York.

And so in a single night, Brian inherited all of the Irish family's operations, including the cemetery plot racket, which became one of his leading ventures.

In recent years, he'd been trying to expand farther south in the Lower East Side, toward Chinatown, but had met strong resistance from the Italian Bontade family, under the protection of the Genovese clan.

Brian's son, Damien, was a rough draft of his father. He had acquired his ruthlessness and absolute amorality but not his cunning and skill as a strategist. He went roaring around the neighborhood in a fiery Buick as if he were a princeling. Whatever he wanted, he took, whether it was an orange or a young virgin. His father tried to keep him in check, but to no avail.

Damien didn't make a move unless he was flanked by Kevin and Hugh, the two bruisers who were also his best friends. Damien, more so than his father, was the real terror of the neighborhood because of his unpredictability, although Kevin—"Freckles" to everyone—was not far behind.

———————

But the three musketeers, as the neighborhood residents called them, made a mistake, and that mistake was the beginning of their downfall.

It was Kevin, who grabbed the handful of bills from the cash box during the robbery at La Tonnara and stuffed them in his pocket. When they got home and went to divvy up the loot, including the money and other valuables they'd taken from the trattoria's customers, they found a remittance voucher from Italy addressed to Ferdinando Licata. It was the equivalent of a hundred bucks, Kevin translated, handing the money order to Damien.

The next morning, they quickly took action. They stationed themselves at the side door of the local post office, and as soon as they saw the postman assigned to Avenue A leave the building on his usual rounds, they forced him into Damien's Buick and sped off toward their headquarters in the back room of Sullivan's Bar, a place that Damien had been able to commandeer with his usual wheeling and dealing.

They showed the postman the voucher and the address where it had been sent. From now on, each month he was to deliver it not to the address on the envelope but to Sullivan's Bar. To make him understand that they weren't kidding, they jabbed his hand with the point of a pocket-knife, but only just enough to elicit a few drops of blood. The poor post-man was absolutely terrified and stammered that he would do as they said. Then without further ado, they loaded him back into the car and dropped him off near the post office. All in all, the action took a half hour, but it was one of the most lucrative half hours Damien Stoker's crew had ever spent.

Too bad for them that the arrangement didn't last long.

When the money order didn't come, Ferdinando Licata went imme-diately to his contact's house. The man was a Genovese family accoun-tant, one of the channels through which American and Sicilian mafiosi communicated with one another to avoid federal controls. The clerk explained that there had been no change in the procedure that month: Lavinia, Ferdinando's sister, had deposited the sum with his counterpart in Sicily. The man had contacted him, telling him that the money had been deposited in their account and indicating the amount in code. He in turn had sent the voucher to Licata's usual address. That's all he knew.

"Don't worry, there must have been a sorting error at the post office," he tried to reassure Licata as he looked through a folder for the credit re-ceipt. "See, here it is, Don Licata." He handed him the slip.

"I'm not 'Don' over here," Licata said, snatching the piece of paper to check the date and remittance.

"By the way, just this morning, an envelope arrived for you." The man walked to a drop-front desk, opened a drawer, and took out a letter. "Here you are; it still has the scent of lemons," he said, trying to defuse the situation.

Prince Licata gave him a stern look, took the envelope, and opened it. It was from his sister. Lavinia wrote to tell him that Rosario Losurdo had been killed by poachers:

[. . .] He caught them hunting on our Madonnuzza property. Rosario did not hesitate to confront the outlaws, it seems there were three of them. He's always been a loyal friend of the fam-ily. He sacrificed his life for our land, may God rest his soul. The poachers have not been identified, but it seems they came from another province. Dear Ferdinando, you mustn't worry about me. Thinking of what you would have done, I entrusted the care of our estates to Manfredi. He is our new gabellotto. I believe you will approve of my choice.

The letter ended with the usual closing sentiments.

Licata folded it, deeply moved. His thoughts went to his faithful Losurdo. Then he thanked the Lord for giving him such a strong, decisive sister to depend on. He remembered the reason why he had come to the accountant's house. A terrible suspicion occurred to him: that the voucher had been intercepted by someone.

He headed to the bank and asked the manager to check if someone had withdrawn a credited remittance in his name.

The manager called over the teller, who remembered having recently cashed a payment order to a man who had the prince's proxy. Actually, Licata learned much later that the teller was on the Stokers' payroll. At the time, however, he had no evidence to make him doubt the teller, and he had him describe the man who had gone there in his place.

The Stokers had a trademark: their flaming red hair. As soon as the teller described the man, covered with freckles, eyes black as coal, Licata recalled Damien's two bodyguards.

The prince decided to go meet a man whom friends in Sicily had advised him to contact in case he needed help.

The man's name was Jack Mastrangelo, and although he'd lived in Brooklyn for ten years, no one seemed to know how to find him.

For three days, Licata drifted from one address to another, from one shop to another, in the sprawling working-class neighborhood where Mastrangelo lived. But people didn't know him, and if they knew him, they weren't talking and swore they'd never heard that name before. When he was about to give up and ask his friends in Sicily for help, Mastrangelo materialized as if by magic. He was a stocky man, his facial features disfigured by two long scars, one running from his mouth to his left ear and a vertical one up along his right temple. The wounds spoke volumes about his life.

Mastrangelo tapped him on the shoulder: "Were you looking for me, Prince?"

"Who are you?"

"Mastrangelo. Jack Mastrangelo." The man seemed annoyed.

"Oh, finally!" the prince exclaimed. "I've been looking for you all week."

"I know."

"I need your help."

It didn't take long for Mastrangelo to find out where Freckles lived: an elegant building on East Fourth Street, not far from the Bowery. One Saturday evening, Mastrangelo entered the second-floor apartment, followed by Ferdinando Licata. He turned on the bathtub faucets and let them run until the water reached the top. Then the two settled in to wait for their man. Mastrangelo hid in the dark entrance foyer, while Licata sat on a sofa in the living room.

In the preceding weeks, Mastrangelo had ascertained that every Saturday, without fail, some of Stoker's gang spent their leisure time in a gambling parlor in Little Italy, where everyone ended up getting drunk. That Saturday too, the script was identical, though with one variation: a particularly desperate whore who was looking for some quick bucks had accompanied Kevin back to his apartment, struggling to prop him up.

The woman opened the door, felt for the switch, and turned it on, but the lights didn't come on.

A figure emerged from the shadows, scaring her. "Who are you?" she cried in surprise.

"Take this and get out of here," Mastrangelo snapped, handing her a $5 bill. "If you open your trap, I'll come looking for you in that cesspit you live in, and you'll be sorry you were ever born."

The prostitute snatched the bill from his hand, let go of Kevin, and ran off. She never told a soul about what had happened. Freckles staggered forward, ending up in Mastrangelo's arms.

Mastrangelo dragged the man into the apartment and then toward the bathroom. Kevin was so drunk, he hadn't yet figured out what was happening to him. Mastrangelo pinned his hands behind his back with a pair of handcuffs, then threw him into the brimming tub.

Licata watched in silence from the bathroom door.

The sudden contact with the cold water startled Kevin, who finally seemed to awaken from his alcoholic stupor. He saw a man standing over him. He was about to cry out, but Mastrangelo plunged his head under the water for a few seconds. When he let him up, Kevin coughed and heaved in an attempt to take in some oxygen. After the third immersion, he realized that he'd better not try to call out.

"Who are you? What do you want?" he asked, coughing up water. "You're in very bad trouble, my friend." Mastrangelo grabbed his feet and pitched him underwater again. When he tried to kick out violently, Mastrangelo grabbed his balls and squeezed as hard as he could. Kevin, his head submerged, began to scream but the water immediately filled his mouth, nearly drowning him. With Licata's help, Mastrangelo quickly bound his ankles with a cord. Then he let him up for air. After he'd sucked in a lungful, though his breathing was still labored, he had enough breath to still threaten, "Do you know my boss is Damien Stoker? When we catch you, you'll be in deep shit."

Mastrangelo tossed a rope around the lamp fixture hanging from the ceiling. He slipped one end of it under the cord that secured the thug's ankles, forming a bowline knot as skillfully as any sailor. Then he grabbed the other end of the rope and yanked it tight.

Mastrangelo pulled with all his might, and the man was hoisted out of the bathtub, hanging upside down like a pig ready for slaughter.

"I want some information from you," Mastrangelo said sweetly.

"Lower me! I'm going to throw up."

"How did you manage to get Ferdinando Licata's remittance vouchers?"

But Kevin couldn't hold back the vomit and began spewing up alcohol mixed with water and everything he'd eaten that evening. His inverted position made matters worse for him. Some of the contents flowed into his nose and the rest covered his face, the stomach acid burning his eyes. He was in agony and thought he was going to die. He could barely breathe, he coughed and spat.

When he had settled down a little, Ferdinando Licata leaned close to his ear to make himself heard better and repeated Mastrangelo's question.

Finally, the reply came: "The postman—We forced the postman to deliver them to us—Now let me down!"

"One more question. The daughter of La Tonnara's owners: Did you lay a hand on her?"

"No! No! We didn't touch her, I swear!"

He was too quick to respond, and Licata didn't believe him. "Tomorrow is Sunday. You wouldn't want to be left hanging like that for a whole day. You know no one will come before Monday."

"What do you want to know?" He began sniveling.

"Which one of you touched her?"

"It was Hugh. And Damien too—a little. But they didn't rape her. I swear."

"That much I knew." Licata rose. His face had turned to stone.

The Roxy Club on West Fifty-Second Street, in the heart of the jazz district, was one of the most popular places in the city, and you could get in only if you were a regular customer's friend. The club was a restaurant, gambling parlor, illegal opium den, and brothel all rolled into one. It offered something for everybody, but its specialty was "Cloud Nine Pizza." Needless to say, its main ingredient was a generous sprinkling of cocaine on tomatoes and Italian mozzarella.

You were admitted by showing a ticket that was split in half. The half with the name of the invited guest clearly visible on one side was retained by a doorman in braided livery who determined who could enter. Once you were in the door, you could choose between the gaming parlors or the dance halls. But the restaurant was the favorite destination of all the guests. It was a large room with soundproof walls. From outside you couldn't hear any noise, but as soon as the door was opened, a great racket exploded from the room. There were numerous tables, and waiters and waitresses moved among the guests serving the Cloud Nine Pizza. The menu featured a few opium cigarettes as a starter. The drug provided a sense of euphoria, but those who were used to the cigarettes required something stronger, so they resorted to morphine injections. The din grew louder; inhibitory restraints were completely relaxed. Amid the uproar, a jazz band, crammed onto an elevated platform so it wouldn't take up table space, played swing at a dizzying tempo.

On the lead trumpet was Dixie, in his first engagement. A friend who'd heard him play during one of his excursions with the Army had asked him if he wanted to supplement his pay at a rather unusual club. Naturally, Dixie didn't wait to be asked twice. He quit the Salvation Army on the spot and joined the Roxy's orchestra, never dreaming that he was getting into a shady scene. Thanks to him, Saro and Isabel were able to get into the club. They handed the half dollar to the solemn doorman and were led directly into the restaurant, as indicated on the half of the ticket retained by the bouncer.

When they entered the dining room, they were struck by a deafening roar. At that moment, a woman in the throes of a drug-induced fit writhed convulsively on the floor. Some friends tried to calm her, but to no avail. Two of the club's bruisers then stepped in, one grabbing her unceremoniously by the legs and the other by her arms. They carried her out amid the general indifference of those around them.

The area downstairs, near the garage, was equipped with a first-aid station with nurses and a doctor. If their intervention failed, then the patient was put into a car and driven home or unloaded in some alley in the Bronx.

Isabel waved to Dixie, throwing him a kiss, as she and Saro found a seat in a corner of the room. It was their debut in the fashionable world of high society. Around them, young starlets fawned over well-to-do producers; alluring young men busied themselves catering to wealthy homosexuals. Big shots from Mafia families represented another type of customer, recognizable by the fact that they shamelessly flaunted scads of dollars and were surrounded by gorgeous, flashy young women.

The band started playing "One O'Clock Jump" by Count Basie, and most of the clientele leaped up and began dancing. Everyone seemed to be having a wild time, as if it were the end of the world. Whenever a section launched a solo—first the saxophones, then the trumpets, and finally the clarinets—the musicians stood up from their chairs and blared out the notes with every ounce of breath in their bodies.

When it was Dixie's turn, the simpatico Neapolitan ran through all the tricks of the trade, performing a brilliant solo, and he was rewarded with a standing ovation at the end. Isabel was as happy as she'd ever been in her life. She clapped her hands loudly, hopping up and down like a little girl, enthralled by Dixie's ability and the applause he received.

Dixie, too wrapped up in the acclaim of the crowd jammed into the room, didn't notice Isabel's enthusiasm. He showed his thanks by holding up the trumpet, the undisputed queen of his life. Saro looked at Dixie and then at Isabel, and realized that the Irish redhead was head over heels in love with their friend.

When the piece ended and the orchestra took a break, Dixie joined his buddies at the table. He was beaming. His life had suddenly taken a turn that he hoped would lead him to fame.

He kissed Isabel on the forehead and hugged Saro. "A crowning success! Teddy confirmed my gig for the entire season," he announced to his friends.

There was no way the trio would go unnoticed, especially given Isabel's presence: the long red hair loose about her shoulders, the sheer chiffon dress that barely concealed her breasts, the patrician facial features and pale blue eyes. She looked like a diva.

She didn't fail to attract the attention of certain individuals sitting at a table not far away. Among them was Johnny Scalia, the lemon merchant who still hadn't digested the trick they'd played on him a few weeks earlier. As soon as he spotted Isabel and recognized the other two as well, Scalia nudged the man sitting beside him. He pointed to the trio, and then leaned over and whispered in his ear, "It's them."

The man rose from his chair, and another individual sitting next to him stood up at the same time. They were clearly mafiosi, with their leather shoulder straps with guns under their jackets. The two gorillas began heading toward the trio's table when suddenly the shriek of a whistle sounded in the hall; everyone got up at once and began fleeing, running from side to side in the room like crazed rats, frantic for a way out.

Police in uniform along with plainclothes officers strode through the main door, shouting at everyone to calm down and take their seats again. But nobody listened to them, and everyone continued screaming, pushing, and shoving to get out.

At the sound of the whistle, Dixie just had time to tell his two friends not to panic. The first thing the manager had shown him, even before hiring him to play, was the escape route to use in case of raids of any kind, police or Mafia. Along with the band members, they disappeared under the platform that concealed a trap door leading to a long tunnel that brought them to a laundry room in a nearby skyscraper.

The following morning, Dixie got up early to buy the first edition of the *New York Herald*. A certain Tom Rice, the newspaper's music critic, had promised him a review the night before. An excited Dixie met Saro and Isabel for breakfast at a nearby coffeeshop and searched for the piece in the entertainment section as the other two looked on.

"Here it is." He folded his newspaper and began reading, "It's Tom's byline. 'Hundreds of people are on the dance floor or sitting at the tables or at the bar. Off in a corner there's a line of taxi girls: two coins for three dances. Rosy light spills down from the ceiling and there's pandemonium everywhere. But the vital heart of the room is up there, on the platform where the band members are lined up in two rows, stamping their feet rhythmically and sweating over their instruments. And when Teddy Hill's musicians start playing the final refrain of one of their war-horses, the dancers forget to dance and crowd around the podium. The first trumpet rises from his chair. It's Dixie, a fantastic young man from southern Italy, with a movie star's mustache, who blares out a long, long note managing to "split" it until the finale. Then he performs a series of dizzying scales, in the best Harlem tradition. The floor shakes and the room feels like a dynamo, the smoke-filled air rising in waves. It's music that even the deaf would be able to hear.'"

Dixie was thrilled by the article. Saro too was happy for his friend. The most tepid was Isabel, who felt she was losing him. They were toasting with cups of coffee, when three imposing figures surrounded their table.

The first of the three snarled, "Come with us."

"Is that an order?" Dixie asked.

"No, a recommendation," the man replied.

"We accept your invitation," Dixie replied amiably, rising. "Is it about a new gig?"

"Your next gig will be in a cemetery plot," the man said shortly.

————

Brian Stoker wasn't a fan of the telephone. He said it was a diabolic de-vice invented to harass people, and he wouldn't have one in his home. If someone wanted him, they had to phone Damien first. Then Hugh, one of his son's two bodyguards, would rush to his home to give him the message.

That Monday morning, the phone rang at Damien's place. An anony-mous voice said to inform Brian that he should go to Kevin's apartment because the man needed help, given that the blood was going to his brain. Damien immediately phoned Kevin, but the phone just rang. He began to worry. Together with Hugh, he raced to his father's house and persuaded him to accompany them.

They were forced to break down the door. The three men called out loudly, but no one answered. They searched the closets and looked under the bed, then Hugh went into the bathroom and saw his friend hanging by his feet from the ceiling fixture. Kevin still showed signs of life. Hugh called Damien, and together they got him down. He was in a state of mental confusion and in very bad shape. They had to get him to the hospital quickly if they wanted to save his life. Just then the phone rang. Damien went over and picked up the receiver, afraid of more bad news.

The same voice as before whispered, "This time I took pity. But forget about the territory between Fourth and Seventh streets, and First Avenue and Avenue A. If you respect this agreement, there will be no other accidents, like the one that unfortunately happened to Freckles. Let him tell you the details, if he still has any breath left."

Ferdinando Licata hung up the phone without waiting for Damien to respond.

Chapter 33

That same year, 1939, the family of Vito Genovese found itself without a boss. Don Vitone had been forced to embark hastily for Italy because of a scrape he'd gotten into a few years earlier, which the district attorney of New York, Thomas Dewey, had exhumed from the archives, determined to finally detain him.

Vito Genovese, Peter DeFeo, Gus Frasca, and Mike Mirandi had decided to fleece a naive building contractor in a poker game when the man was imprudent enough to reveal that his pockets were bulging with money. They swindled him out of $116,000 in Willie Gallo's gambling parlor in Brooklyn, in a fixed card game. But Gallo decided that, as owner of the place, he was entitled to a larger share. Of course, the other four wouldn't stand for it and chose to eliminate their overly demanding partner.

Two years later, the DA's office in New York reopened the investigation when Mike Mirandi, arrested for drug trafficking, was given house arrest in exchange for a confession about the murder of Willie Gallo.

When they learned that the DA's office was about to charge them because Mike "the informer"—as he was called from then on—had squealed, Genovese, DeFeo, and Frasca skipped town. Genovese left for Italy, and the other two disappeared somewhere in the United States.

So overnight the Genovese family found itself decapitated. A nephew of Don Vitone, Sante Genovese, took command.

And so it was to Sante Genovese that Saro, Isabel, and Dixie were brought following their discovery by the lemon merchant. Like most novices, Sante was considered a lunatic. An impulsive person with no moral standards, he didn't know how to find the middle ground and lacked the fine art of diplomacy. Coming before Sante for a judgment was truly risky. But our three friends didn't know that. At the moment all they knew for certain was that they were in the presence of the number two man in the Genovese family, the most important Mafia family in New York at the time, and this fact alone was cause for concern.

Next to Sante in the formal parlor of the Genovese home sat Johnny Scalia, along with other members of the family and a few bodyguards.

Mike Genna, the *consigliori*, as he was referred to in Sicilian, sat nearby in a corner.

As soon as Saro and his friends entered the room and saw the lemon merchant, their stomachs dropped.

"So then, do you know this gentleman?" Sante abruptly asked the new arrivals.

The three young people's eyes flew to Johnny Scalia. Dixie even went so far as to attempt a half smile by way of greeting.

Saro spoke first: "Mr. Genovese—or rather, Don Sante—we do know this man. He let the three of us cheat him out of twenty-five thousand dollars, fooled by the office we rented."

Sante smiled. "And what did you sell him?"

"A batch of slot machines, complete with license."

The boss shook his head. "Mr. Johnny Scalia is one of the family. He shouldn't have been disrespected like that."

"Don Sante, if we had known that, we never would have gone near him," Saro apologized. "But he kept flashing that big wad of bucks under our noses! In any case, we'll return every penny of it," Saro concluded.

"Can my friend go get the money?"

Sante Genovese nodded and ordered one of his men to go with him.

Dixie reluctantly left the room escorted by Genovese's goon.

"Don Sante, in our defense," Saro continued, "I must say that we would never have imagined that the great Genovese could be the *padrino*—godfather—to such a sucker."

For a moment, the boss was dumbfounded, unable to decide whether or not to take offense.

"You think you can be a smart aleck just because you're young?" he said, getting up from his chair and going over to Saro. "I never liked stray dogs—sooner or later they form packs and become dangerous."

"But dogs can also become attached to a master. Just throw them a bone every now and then," Saro suggested.

Sante ignored those words and walked over to Isabel. "I'm not sure what to do with you—though it's a real shame to waste such a tasty treat." He circled around the girl, and when he was behind her, he couldn't take his eyes off her cute little ass.

But at that point, he was interrupted by one of his men telling him, "Vanni is here."

"Who?" Sante had taken his uncle's place only a few weeks earlier and still hadn't learned the names of all the bagmen.

"Carmelo Vanni, the Bontade family's bagman."

Those words were music to Sante's ears.

Sante went to the door and opened it, and Carmelo Vanni spotted a young man in the room whom he immediately recognized. He could never forget him.

"Excuse me for butting into your business, Sante," he said. "But I happen to recognize that fellow over there. He saved my life, and I never had the chance to thank him. If it hadn't been for him, Stoker would have sent me to meet my Maker. Those bastards wanted to make off with our *pizzo*: the protection money for Enzo Carruba's funeral parlor. But that's Bontade's territory. Can I go in and say hello to him?"

"Business before pleasure, Vanni."

Vanni handed him an envelope containing the sum brought in by several rackets in Bontade's jurisdiction. Then he was given the go-ahead to talk to Saro.

Carmelo Vanni clinched Saro warmly, clapping him heartily on the back. "If you knew how hard I tried to find you! We can use sharp people like you." He glanced at Sante and quickly added, "With all due respect, Don—unless he's one of yours."

Sante was caught off guard and didn't want to let on that Saro was about to undergo endless retribution for having swindled one of his protégés. He therefore chose to simply nod yes.

"Good, good. You couldn't have fallen into better hands, my friend," Vanni said to Saro. "You know where to turn, though, should you ever have a problem. I owe you a favor."

He shook hands with Saro and then said good-bye to Sante Genovese. "See you next month, boss."

A few minutes later, Dixie returned with a bag crammed with the lemon merchant's money. He set it on the table and, with the gall that only he was capable of, turned to Sante with his usual half smile. It was never clear if it was meant as ridicule or whether it was simply his way of trying to win someone's favor.

"I have a personal favor to ask you, boss."

Sante Genovese looked at him suspiciously. Even he couldn't decipher that wry little smile. "Go on, out with it. What is it?" Meanwhile, he went over to the bag, picked it up and stashed it away in his safe: he had it coming to him to make up for the disturbance.

––––––––

After the phone call from the mysterious individual who had tortured Kevin, the Stokers tallied up the businesses in the area the caller had indicated, from which they extracted revenue. There were a couple of restaurants, three bars, some secondhand clothing shops, a laundry, a brothel: in short, a good portion of their income was cut off. Kevin was still in shock and said he didn't remember a thing, since he'd been drunk when he was assaulted and the apartment was completely dark. He had no idea who had roughed him up and how many they were.

Brian Stoker wasn't intimidated by a phone call. But he had to find out if it was a move by the Bontade family in response to their attempt to take over the funeral business in the Baxter Street area.

The Stokers would pretend to comply with the shadowy figure, leaving the neighborhood in peace for a time, but Brian decided that they would continue to keep their eyes open and discreetly monitor the territory indicated by the voice on the phone.

In the weeks that followed, the area adjacent to Tompkins Square seemed reborn. The Stokers, especially Damien, were only occasionally seen around and they had even stopped demanding protection money from the businesses in the district.

People in the neighborhood began greeting Ferdinando Licata with a certain deference. Even women stood aside to let him pass when he came by. At the fruit and vegetable market, he was allowed to go ahead of everyone, even though he refused the favor and preferred to wait his turn. And Michele, the owner, gave him much of what he bought for the trattoria free of charge, to Nico's great joy.

In short, word had it—who knows how such rumors are born—that the neighborhood's peace was due to his intervention following the robbery at La Tonnara and the kidnapping of his niece's daughter.

Licata wasn't pleased about this, because it put him in the spotlight; he'd much rather have been invisible.

Ferdinando Licata knew that the Stokers posed a threat to the entire community. The Bontades certainly weren't loved, either, but at least they had a code of honor that they respected. The Stokers had no rules, and this was not allowed in the Mafia culture. What's more, he knew that somehow his intervention had not gone unnoticed and that his name was on the lips of everyone in the neighborhood.

Licata had to confront a conflict that had gone on for a lifetime. But he already knew the answer. He maintained that it was better to dip your hands in blood than in Pontius Pilate's water.

He was consumed with finding a way to get rid of the two families or at least the Irish clan.

––––––––––

Dixie was aware of the fact that the Genovese family had a stake in many of the city's clubs and establishments. The day he and his friends had been forced to return the lemon merchant's stolen money, he'd had the nerve to ask Sante Genovese to recommend him to the manager of some club where he could play and thus help make ends meet. Sante smiled at the simple request. Because he was an avid frequenter of clubs where swing was played and admired the musicians' skill, he decided to help the unemployed artist. "At least you'll leave my businesses alone," he replied laughing, and he got him an appointment with his friend John Hammond.

Hammond, a young man of twenty-nine, was already considered a great talent scout in the music world. He knew all the dives and hole-in-the-wall joints where jazz was played. He could recognize a true talent after only three notes. The previous year, he had organized a concert called From Spirituals to Swing at Carnegie Hall, the august temple of classical music. Showcasing all the performers that he thought had something to say in the contemporary music scene, his review was an enormous success.

Hammond was able to place Dixie in several small combos to test his skills as a trumpeter. One of them was playing on Broadway at the Paramount Theater. On stage, renowned bands alternated with fledgling ensembles but invariably with top-notch musicians.

The night Dixie made his first appearance, the big band was clarinetist Benny Goodman's. The group he'd been put in, the Five Brothers, was led by a Sicilian named Giuseppe "Joe" Venuti, a jazz violinist with an open, likeable disposition. Dixie immediately found himself in sync with the man.

Saro and Isabel, thanks to their acquaintance with Sante Genovese, managed to get two front row seats. It was a gala evening, and they had spent a fortune to rent their outfits. Isabel was dressed in a smooth red silk dress that harmonized perfectly with her hair, which she had swept up in an elegant chignon. The dress had a modest front with a white collar that lent her a schoolgirl appearance, but her back was completely bared by a sexy plunging backline that dipped nearly to her waist.

For the first time in his life, Saro was wearing a white tuxedo. He felt ill at ease and feared he looked ridiculous, but thanks to his ability to adapt, after just a couple of hours he was sporting it like a second skin.

Isabel was euphoric. "I feel this will be the night of my life," she told Saro as they went to their seats.

"Actually it's Dixie's night—if he doesn't hit a bum note," her friend said.

"It's *our* night," the gorgeous redhead replied enigmatically.

Saro's heart skipped a beat. "Our?" He wasn't sure who she meant.

"Yes, ours: mine and Domenico's," Isabel explained, staring at him with those huge blue eyes that sparkled with joy. "I'm going to ask him to marry me."

Saro darkened and slumped in his seat. "I thought marriage proposals were made by men."

"Maybe in your country. In Ireland, it's we women who choose."

Immediately the image of Mena materialized in Saro's mind. He had promised her eternal love, but he was irresistibly attracted to Isabel's northern beauty. Perhaps it was her uninhibited ways that enticed him, whereas Mena was so reticent about her feelings.

A drum roll called him back to reality. John Hammond appeared on stage and promptly introduced Benny Goodman and his orchestra. The curtain parted, and there was prolonged applause from the audience when Goodman came on after the orchestra's opening.

Afterward, other bands and smaller groups took turns. Presented for the first time that evening were the three best boogie-woogie pianists, whom Hammond himself had discovered pounding away on the keys in Harlem dives. They performed a new version of "Honky Tonk Train Blues," literally making the theater shake. From that night on, a new dance craze exploded across America, and, some years later, the stepped-up tempo would accompany entire European nations as they danced to celebrate their liberation from Nazi-fascist tyranny.

Following the wild notes of the three pianists, the appearance of the Five Brothers did not generate the same enthusiasm.

Bandleader Joe Venuti decided on the spot to change the repertoire, adding some uptempo selections with a strong beat and extensive riffs. Playing with him and Dixie were several talented musicians, including saxophonist Joe Bishop, who also played in the Woody Herman Orchestra. They performed a number of infectious rhythms, making the band an overwhelming success. Dixie held his own in the company of those veteran soloists, and he too received his fair share of applause during the performance.

At the end of the set, Isabel and Saro joined their friend backstage to congratulate him. Tom Rice, the music critic from *New York Herald*, had arrived before them and was raving about Dixie's talent.

Isabel gave Dixie a hug and kissed him on the cheeks. Dixie, elated, held her tight and kissed her deeply on the mouth. His tongue thrust in, in search of hers, and Isabel, who had been waiting for just this moment, returned his kiss passionately.

The kiss was so ardent and prolonged that musicians and friends turned and applauded the sudden outpouring. The two broke apart, as if dazed by their outburst, and blushed, intertwining their fingers and squeezing their hands tightly together as one.

Saro went to his two friends. He was happy for them, but his joy was merely an outward show. "Well, congratulations twice," he said to Dixie. Witnessing the passion that had exploded between the two, he felt a bitter wind blow though his heart. He was about to leave, but Dixie stopped him. "Hey, wait, we'll go drink a toast together, as always."

"Thanks, but I don't want to be a third wheel," said Saro.

"I have one desire: to share this evening's success with my two dearest friends."

"Well, now you only have one left," Saro smiled, looking at Isabel. "Someone here has become something more than a friend."

"Did you hear that, Isabel? He says you're no longer my friend."

The Irish redhead looked at her hero blissfully and nodded, as she gave him another kiss on the mouth.

"Let's go get drunk! This time the night won't be long enough for us!" Dixie cried, and the three left the theater arm in arm.

Chapter 34

When Prohibition ended in 1933, organized crime, which had built its financial empires on the alcohol trade, was forced to find a new substance to replace the one that had become legal. And what better choice than strictly prohibited narcotic substances? The Mafia soon became the biggest dealer in the drug market, transforming drug addiction into one of the worst plagues of all time.

Years earlier, in May 1929, in a luxury hotel in Atlantic City, New Jersey, mobster Frank Costello was able to bring together the elite figures of the American Mafia. The meeting ended with the founding of the Cosa Nostra. Salvatore Lucania, known as Luciano, a purebred Sicilian, did not take part in that Atlantic City conference because his violent, unprincipled character was not viewed well by the Italian Mafia communities in America. Nevertheless Luciano was an invaluable element in the new organization, and Costello, as the intelligent strategist he was, was well aware of it. In fact, only Luciano was capable of establishing ties with French and Italian drug traffickers. Already by the end of the 1920s, he'd been able to build a sophisticated organizational structure that imported large quantities of drugs from production sources, sending them into big-city neighborhoods via pharmaceutical companies and foreign chemical industries. In those years, there were not yet laws against the misappropriation of heroin and morphine from shipments intended for therapeutic uses. Thanks to this trade, Luciano managed to accumulate an immense fortune which began to bother some of his enemies.

Five months after the meeting in Atlantic City, Luciano was seized at the intersection of Sixth Avenue and Fiftieth Street by three killers who forcibly shoved him into a high-powered black car that then headed toward the outskirts of Brooklyn. They drove the car into a dilapidated warehouse. Legend has it that Luciano's only words were "Do what you have to do, but hurry up about it."

He didn't get his wish. He was subjected to every kind of torture. The three thugs hanged him upside down, suspending him from a hook on a hoist. They bound his wrists with wire. They ripped off his expensive suit and lashed his entire body with a belt. Then the most sadistic of the three had fun carving his skin with the tip of a knife. One of the others used his face as a punching bag, rearranging his features. It was sheer butchery. Thinking they'd killed him, the three left him there.

But they'd miscalculated Luciano's mettle; he was rescued by a vagrant and taken to a hospital, where he kept his mouth shut. From that day on, Salvatore Lucania became "Lucky" Luciano to the world.

Luciano disappeared for a few months, well concealed in a hideout protected by friends. He waited for his wounds to heal, for his bones to knit, and for the bruises to fade, and then he returned to take up the reins of his organization that, in the meantime, had not missed a beat. The huge drug profits, greater than any other illicit trade, even allowed Luciano to buy off government officials. The New York market was his, but he had been skillful enough to subdivide it into twenty territories, each under the jurisdiction of a family that regularly paid out a tenth of its earnings into his coffers.

Luciano had been able to organize the distribution of drugs with the ability of a great strategist through a close network of relationships that could not be traced back to him. And, in fact, prosecutors in New York were never able to accuse the biggest drug trafficker of all time of dealing in narcotics.

The drug market represented a significant percentage of the Bontade and Stoker families' incomes as well. The two families were often in dispute over the simple fact that their territories bordered each other's. The Bontades, who in turn were under the Genovese family, controlled part of Little Italy, while the Stokers held sway farther east and north in the Hamilton Fish Park neighborhood.

In the past, a turf invasion by one or the other families would be settled with a good round of bullets. But after the establishment of the Cosa Nostra in Atlantic City, resolving disputes individually was expressly forbidden. The first paragraph of the Atlantic City pact stated that any dispute must be governed by an executive committee.

The entire workings were well known to Ferdinando Licata, who had decided to play his hand in that very territory.

Licata had not been with a woman since he'd arrived in America. Now he was beginning to feel the desire for one, so one Saturday he announced to Betty that he would be seeing some Sicilian friends that evening, and she shouldn't wait up for him.

Licata knew where to go. A Neapolitan *guappo*, a cocky tough guy introduced to him by Jack Mastrangelo, had recommended a girl at the

Blue Lemon in Chelsea, well equipped with everything: coke, a luxurious room, and a pair of tits that would make Hedy Lamarr envious. But what interested Licata even more was the fact that the young woman hated her boss, Lucky Luciano.

That Saturday evening, Ferdinando Licata put on the most youthful outfit he had, dabbed on some cologne, and went to the Blue Lemon. The setting was like millions of other clubs: red velvet armchairs, discreet private booths, café tables for dining, lounges for watching the show. The girls were first-class: there was nothing vulgar about them, and their plainly visible curves would have made a dying man leap out of his sickbed.

Ferdinando Licata took a seat at a distance from the stage. He asked the waiter for a bourbon—and Marta. The man went away and shortly afterward, the young woman materialized beside him.

It was true. Marta's breasts proved as enticing as the Neapolitan had promised, and that night, in the girl's alcove, the prince was able to uphold the honor of Sicilian males.

"My compliments, Prince. Italians never disappoint. A girl could be in danger of falling in love with you," the woman flirted.

Though he knew she was just playacting to please him, the prince was flattered by it. "Love is nothing to be scared of. Would you be afraid to fall in love with me?" he teased her, encircling her waist with his strong arms.

But she released herself from the embrace and straddled him, immobilizing both his wrists. She leaned over him, so that her breasts brushed against his face. "You haven't yet told me what line of work you're in."

"I work at being wealthy," he said with a crafty smile, trying to lick a nipple.

"You make it sound easy. Will you teach me how?"

"Sure, I'll give you my card before I leave. There are people with millions in the bank who don't know how to invest their money. I have the ability to increase their capital a hundredfold in just a few days."

She pressed against him and began sucking his earlobe. "I'll call you Croesus, then. Whatever he touched turned to gold."

"Well, my gold is drugs." He whispered the last words and smiled at seeing Marta's face. "Disappointed?"

"No, I'm surprised. I never would have thought . . ." Marta turned over on her side. The magic was over.

"They've given me a lot of money. A hundred thousand dollars, I have to buy some stuff, and I'm scrambling to find the right dealer. So far I've only come up with small fry. I need one dealer who can provide all the goods at once. That's how I always play it safe with the law."

"A hundred grand is quite a lot of dough."

"One deal, and it's done. That's why I only want to talk to a distributor. But I want premium goods, I'm willing to pay a higher market price, but it has to be top-quality stuff—and I have two weeks' time. If I can't find it here in New York, I'll go looking for it in Chicago.

"Now you know why I'm so rich. But remember . . ." he said, putting his finger to his lips.

All the same, he knew that type of woman perfectly well, and was fully aware that she would relay everything to her pimp, who in turn would inform the middleman who was in direct contact with the family. A tip that juicy might be worth an extra share of drugs for everybody. Fernando Licata decided it was time now to move out of his room at La Tonnara and rent a room somewhere so that his niece and her family wouldn't be associated with his new activities.

The bait pitched by Ferdinando Licata was immediately sniffed out by one of the big shots in the Bontade family: "big" in the true sense of the word, because Big Jordan in his youth had been an Olympic rowing champion. Over the years, his body had turned into a mass of lard, probably as a result of performance-enhancing drugs consumed in large doses during his years of competition. Over six feet tall and weighing 330 pounds, he looked like a lumbering giant or, worse yet, a frightful fairytale monster. Big Jordan's cousin Joe Cooper, on his mother's side, was one of Tom Bontade's bodyguards. And Tom held him in high regard because, since the time they were kids, they had never lost touch. He was a kind of brother to him.

Marta, the peppery French girl, was the only one who could satisfy Big Jordan's libido. It was during one of the long, exhausting nights devoted to the peculiar erotic rituals necessary to awaken the big man's desire that little Marta told her client what she had learned from Licata.

"He wants a hundred thousand dollars' worth of drugs?" the giant repeated, his interest piqued.

"That's right. But he wants to make one single purchase. He does that to cut down on the risks," the young woman said, and then went back to business.

Big Jordan told Cooper about the tip, and together they informed Tom Bontade.

The bid was quite unusual. Furthermore, proposing a price that was drastically higher than the going rate violated all the rules. But the deal was too attractive for Bontade to pass up. One hundred thousand dollars was a considerable sum: one-sixth of a full year's sales. But where to find twenty kilos of cocaine in less than two weeks?

In underworld circles, news like that travels at the speed of light. Within a few hours, the request to purchase a huge amount of pure cocaine made the rounds of the families in New York. To meet such a demand, it would be necessary to combine the supplies of two or three families.

The Bontades were approached by the Stokers. They too had heard about the exorbitant request and wanted to form an alliance with their perpetual rivals.

Hugh, one of Damien Stoker's bodyguards, met with Cooper, and together they arranged a meeting between their respective bosses: Tom Bontade and Brian Stoker.

Chapter 35

On Second Avenue at Tenth Street, there is an open space with a dense stand of elm trees. At the center of this tiny grove is one of the city's oldest churches: St. Mark's Church in the Bowery, an architectural jewel. Isabel, seeing it the first days after she'd arrived in New York, had dreamed of one day getting married there, and now the dream was coming true.

After three days of passion, never once leaving the house, she had asked Dixie to marry her. They were good together, the sex was great, they were made for each other, and they couldn't turn down their good fortune. Dixie thought it over a moment and then pronounced it an excellent idea. A few days to arrange the paperwork, and by the following week, the priest at St. Mark's was blessing their union.

It was a bitter pill to swallow, but Saro served as their best man. Beaming with joy after the ceremony, the two newlyweds said good-bye to their friends and left on their honeymoon in a car that Tom Rice had lent them. They drove to nearby Coney Island, where they spent the most intense and passionate few days of their lives.

Saro spent those same days languishing with a bottle of cheap whiskey in an attempt to numb his senses and rid himself of the sense of guilt that cropped up whenever he thought about Mena. The image of the young woman he'd left behind in Sicily was still vivid in his mind. She had promised to wait for him, and Sicilian women are capable of growing old and still honoring a promise they'd made. But now Saro was no longer sure he could keep *his* word.

Since he'd arrived in America, he'd had no news of the girl. At first, when he was bitterly homesick, he had written to her at least once a week. Then he'd gradually taken more time between letters. Why had Mena never responded? Had something happened to her? Or maybe she no longer believed in their love?

These and other worries plagued him from the moment he opened his eyes in the morning until he went to bed. Like all young people, he hoped for a life rich with satisfaction, but fate had not been kind to him since day one, when he'd been rejected by his parents. Ever since he'd found out, he'd felt a great sense of guilt, taking upon his shoulders the sins of those two young people who had decided not to recognize him as the fruit of their love. But misfortune was not yet finished with him.

Chapter 36

There was a rule in the Mafia that when it came to profits, all personal grudges had to be set aside.

Tom Bontade and Brian Stoker decided to forget the "misunderstandings" that had divided them until then, agreeing to a truce that would last at least until they had concluded their deal with the outsider.

The two heads of family met on neutral ground, at a lounge in Bensonhurst, Brooklyn. Both patriarchs had witnessed numerous skirmishes in their lives and knew when it was time to stop the violence and call on diplomacy in their common interest: namely, dollars.

The meeting was arranged by Sante Genovese, who appointed his own consigliori, Mike Genna, as moderator.

"Sante Genovese has specifically asked that all hostilities be suspended during negotiations," Genna began, setting his glass of whiskey on the table. "Our brothers in Sicily want to see if Cosa Nostra can be trusted. They want to know if we are together, if we are a unified body. Luciano, from prison, told them that trade with Sicily can be extended throughout the States because the families are united. For that reason, he doesn't look favorably upon your disagreements."

Though Genna personally represented Sante Genovese, he was careful to measure his words, because the two men before him embodied two of the leading families of New York, inspiring fear and commanding respect. Genna wanted to shout at them, "Enough of your crap! Thanks to you, business has fallen off in recent months because people are afraid and because the police are breathing down our necks!" But he knew he couldn't express himself freely, so he exhibited all the declamatory arts for which he was well known.

"Mr. Genna, we've already smoked the peace pipe, if that's what you're worried about," Tom Bontade, the eldest of the three, said with a wry smile. Brian Stoker nodded.

"Good. Forgive my frankness, but I am an ambassador here relaying someone else's words and thoughts. Let's move on now to the actions that must be taken. Sante asks me to tell you that if the amount of stuff you have is not enough, he will arrange to provide you with part of the shipment from his own supplies. What should I tell him?" He waited for the two to respond.

Tom Bontade was the first to speak again: "As far as I'm concerned, I need three kilos to fill half the consignment."

"We're okay," the Irishman said with undisguised pride.

That surprised Genna. "May I ask how you happen to have such a supply, Mr. Stoker?"

"The Puerto Ricans are helping us. We're in talks with them. They procured ninety percent of what we were lacking."

"'We're in talks' means it's not yet a sure thing, right?" Genna pressed. "It means we have to guarantee the delivery. One of them wants to be present at the exchange."

"But the Sicilian doesn't want to deal with more than one seller." Genna grew concerned.

"Don't worry, I'll guarantee it myself out of my own pocket," Brian Stoker assured him. "The overseer will stay with me while someone else physically makes the exchange."

"It will be one of my men," Tom Bontade declared.

"Is that okay with you?" Genna asked Stoker.

"If you're there to watch, it's fine with me," the Irishman said flatly.

The agreement was finalized. Now they could contact the Sicilian and set up the exchange.

Marta knew the Sicilian's phone number and promptly passed the information on to Big Jordan.

After firming up the arrangement between Bontade and Stoker, Genna phoned Licata to introduce himself and suggest that they meet a few evenings later for a game of poker. The prince declined the invitation. He would send a trusted friend, Jack Mastrangelo, in his stead.

While these events were taking place, in another part of the city Saro was going to meet his bitter fate. His senses dulled by alcohol and his morale at a low, he wandered aimlessly through the streets until he came to Chelsea. He was intrigued by the amusing sign at the Blue Lemon and went inside in search of companionship.

He stopped at the bar and asked the young man who was making cocktails, "Do you have a 'Juicy Woman' for me too?" The drink was advertised as the house specialty.

"Sure thing, pal, we never run out of her," the bartender replied with a phrase he repeated at least three hundred times a day.

He brought him a glass and poured a mixture of bourbon, gin, and vermouth, garnished with an olive. Saro drank it in one gulp and felt the fire in his stomach. He saw one of the girls from the club and pointed her out to the barman. "Give one to her too." Marta moved away from the bar and approached him.

"Lovesick? Or were you fired?" she asked him, taking the glass the bartender had placed in front of her, but not drinking.

"Lovesick? What is love anyway? Have you ever known it?"

"We've all known a little love in our lives," Marta replied patiently. "At least from our mother."

"My mother didn't even want to see me when I was born," he told her, motioning to the young man behind the bar to serve him another fiery mixture.

"Then you're in big trouble," said Marta, starting to look around again. "You'd better knock back that rotgut and go to bed. You'll see, things will look different tomorrow."

A Gary Cooper–type came over and took the glass out of her hands. "What's a doll like you doing in a place like this?" He took a sip of the cocktail and gave the glass back to the woman. "Can I buy you a beer instead of this crap?"

Saro felt humiliated. He knew he was in bad shape, but he couldn't let that bully get away with it.

"Hey, buddy, the young lady is with me," he said, getting in his face.

But the man shoved him aside with unexpected force. "The young lady can be with whomever she likes."

"Now, don't fight," said Marta, stepping between the two. "I already told you, handsome," she said to Saro, "go home and sleep it off, okay?" With that, she turned to the tough guy and took his arm. "Where to, pal?"

"Call me Joe."

"Okay, Joe. Let's go to your place, or are you scared of your wife?"

"What's my wife got to do with it? We'll go to your place, of course."

"Hold it! The young lady was talking to me!" Saro again tried to insist, but he knew he was making a fool of himself.

"And now she wants to fuck with me! Get away, you filthy dago," he hurled back at Saro, calling him one of the offensive names the Americans had given the Italians.

Marta led the man out of the club before something nasty flared up.

The girls who worked at the Blue Lemon had the use of several rooms upstairs, which the owner made available to them in exchange for half of what they earned. The rooms were reached by a service stairway. That way, public morality was safeguarded, or so they said.

Marta and the tough guy went to the building's alley and climbed the metal staircase. The man, following her, massaged her shapely behind with the excuse of giving her a push to boost her up. Marta laughed, enjoying it, and the client laughed too as he touched her again, this time pushing his middle finger into the crack of her buttocks.

Saro followed them out just in time to witness the scene. They seemed like a pair of happy lovers.

He was depressed, and his loneliness suddenly formed a lump in his throat.

He watched the two close the door behind them, and it was like dying. He doubled over with rage and impotence. He cursed his fate, railing against the entire world, but especially against that vulgar tough guy and that whore who had refused to stay with him. He raised his head, his vision clouded by the alcohol he'd consumed. He stared at the door and began climbing the metal steps.

———

In 1926 an article written by an anonymous crime reporter had appeared in *Collier's* magazine, observing that the greatest contribution to crime was developed in that generation: "It is nothing less than a diabolical engine of death . . . the paramount example of peace-time barbarism [and] the diabolical acme of human ingenuity in man's effort to devise a mechanical contrivance with which to murder his neighbor."

The writer was talking about the Thompson submachine gun, known by gangsters as "the Chicago Piano," or "the Chopper," The "Tommy gun," its other nickname, was invented by Brigadier General John T. Thompson, who served as director of arsenals during the First World War. The commander had developed it for use in trench warfare, but the first models didn't appear until 1920, well after peace had already been established. Because of its firing potential, it had been boycotted by both the army and the police, but for the criminal world, it was a radical step up and soon became the regulation weapon for every gangster.

The Thompson weighed just under nine pounds and was so easy to use that anyone could fire it. It had a firing rate of one thousand .45-caliber bullets per minute. At a distance of 450 yards, it could pierce a three-inch-thick wood slab, and at closer range, it was capable of breaking through a wall. It could even be purchased by mail, in unlimited quantities. The law required the seller only to record the buyer's first and last name, which most of the time turned out to be that of some eighty-year-old woman who knew nothing about it. The gun caused a great deal of bloodshed from Chicago to New York, leaving a trail of notorious massacres.

Later on, in the thirties, when the gun law became more restrictive, Thompsons could be obtained only through the black market at a price of $2,000 apiece.

That's how much Jack Mastrangelo, Ferdinando Licata's trusted man from Brooklyn, had paid.

This time Mastrangelo had arranged to meet two small-time hoods from Harlem at Pelham Bay Park in the Rodman's Neck section of the Bronx, a perfect place to practice with those guns because there were no houses for miles and the road hadn't been used much in years.

It was the second time that Mastrangelo was meeting the two hoods. The first meeting had been to get to know them, to see if they were up to the task he had for them. He concluded that they were a couple of low-level punks, but vicious and unprincipled enough to handle the job.

Mastrangelo arrived ahead of time and hid the car behind some bushes, a mile from where they were to meet. Then he approached the spot, making a wide detour, two Thompsons slung over his shoulder.

At the spot where he'd told the two hoods to meet him, there was a corroded sign for a discontinued bus stop.

Mastrangelo took cover behind a tree and waited patiently for the pair to arrive.

Twenty minutes later, he heard a car approaching in the distance. A rusty Ford appeared around the curve, carrying three men. There were only supposed to be two, and that insubordination riled him. He recognized the third young man: Abraham Solo. He had nothing to fear from him; he was a hothead like the other two. Driving the car was Gabriel, the eldest of the three, known as "Spike," and beside him sat Cornelius. The gate-crasher, Abraham, whom he'd met during a robbery at a grocery store, was in the backseat.

When they got to the intersection, Gabriel pulled off the road and stopped the car, raising a huge cloud of dust. Once it had settled, Mastrangelo, from his hiding spot, saw the three get out of the car and stretch their legs.

After making sure they hadn't been followed, he emerged into the open.

"Our agreement was that only two of you would come," he said as he walked closer, the two Thompsons across his shoulder.

"Come on, Jack, don't talk crap. Two, three, four, what's the difference?" Gabriel said, approaching him. "Abraham can be a big help to us."

Abraham grinned. "A big help, yeah."

"Well, that's your business," Mastrangelo said, taking the two guns from his shoulder and handing one to Gabriel and the other to Cornelius.

"Momma, this is super stuff!" Cornelius said, gripping it, pretending to fire a round at his buddies.

"Let's move and get off the road; somebody could come by," Mastrangelo said with a sigh, heading toward a nearby hollow. They walked about a hundred yards, and he said, "Here, this is fine. Watch out for the recoil. You have to grip the handle tight with your left hand, or you could end up killing one another. And don't keep your finger on the trigger, otherwise you'll use up the magazine in a few seconds. Fast bursts is what you want. There's no need to aim. Come on, try it. Shoot at that tree."

The two guys first did exactly the opposite of what Mastrangelo had told them: they held down the trigger the entire time and didn't grip the handle tightly enough. The magazine ran out, and they'd hit everything except the tree.

"Goddamn idiots," Mastrangelo muttered. "Those magazines cost thirty bucks apiece on the black market. Want me to charge you for them?" He snatched the Thompson out of Cornelius's hands and gripped it correctly. "I said short bursts. Short! Otherwise you'll run out of cartridges too fast. Also, you have to hold the gun tightly. Your hands must have a firm grip on it. Make believe you're holding on to a colt you have to break in!" He dropped the empty magazine and put in a new one. Then he pointed the weapon toward the tree and began firing short bursts. The blasts sent huge splinters flying off the trunk. Mastrangelo's aim was perfect: he always hit the same spot, until the trunk was completely sheared off, and the tree crashed to the ground.

"I want to try too," Abraham said, but Mastrangelo handed the Thompson back to Cornelius.

"No, Abraham, not you."

The next attempts were better. A half hour later, having used up all the magazines, the two Harlem punks were ready for the mission. "So, Jack, now you gonna tell us what we have to do?"

"All in good time. I won't tell you anything now because otherwise you'd go blabbing it all to your girlfriends, and within an hour everybody would know. It's a very delicate mission; that's why I didn't want any busybodies in the way. This operation will decide your life for the next twenty years. But if any of you talk and let something slip, I swear I'll make you eat your tongue. Now go back to Harlem and pretend nothing's going on.

"Look me straight in the eye," he barked. "If you open your mouth, I swear I'll cut out your tongue. Mastrangelo's word."

"What about the pay?" asked Gabriel, the tough negotiator of the group.

"You'll know soon enough. I told you, you'll be sitting pretty for the rest of your fucking life."

Jack Mastrangelo had made himself clear, and not one of the three talked about the job they were about to do for the Sicilians.

Chapter 37

In the early hours of dawn, the streets and sidewalks of New York offered up the remains of the killings that had occurred the night before: dishonest drug dealers, addicts who had overdosed, gamblers caught cheating, unfortunate prostitutes. No one would have paid any attention to them if it weren't for another stratum of humanity that lived one step lower, who in the morning went rummaging in the garbage looking for a bone to strip clean or an umbrella to mend.

When an old beggar woman snatched up a cardboard carton that could be sold for a few pennies, she discovered Saro's body, huddled in a fetal position. He looked dead. The old woman continued poking through the garbage cans in the alley. She was used to such encounters in the early dawn and thought maybe later she'd notify her friend at city hall, a policeman who sometimes handed her a quarter for a glass of warm milk. Suddenly she was startled to see the "corpse" turn over, gasping in pain.

Saro opened his eyes and looked around. He saw the old woman beside him, bundled up in a black wool garment, watching him, stunned. "And they say there's no such thing as miracles. Good thing you woke up, sonny boy, or you could have ended up in the dump, you know."

Saro didn't get it. Then he looked at his hands: they were totally covered with dirt and caked blood. He peered at the knuckles. They were bloodied and bruised, as if he had punched through a plaster wall. He fingered his clothes. They were torn to shreds in a number of places, and there were large bloodstains on them as well. He couldn't think straight. His head was crawling, as if he were in the grip of a hangover. He tried to get to his feet but fell back on the pavement. The old woman had meanwhile moved away, dragging her bag of cartons and useless trash.

Saro tried to recall what had happened the night before, but he blanked out at the recollection of climbing the metal steps.

Then he began to remember: the steps led to the room of the girl he'd met at the Blue Lemon. The fog was slowly lifting from his numb, befuddled brain.

Ferdinando Licata's plan was moving along smoothly. The Bontades had scraped together drugs from every distributor they knew, and the Genovese family had provided the remainder. In return for that favor, Sante had asked them for 90 percent of the proceeds on the amount loaned. The Stokers, however, had not yet solved their problem. They had placed themselves in the hands of a gang of Puerto Rican drug dealers who controlled the Bronx and had promised to deliver by the end of the month, but they were already a week past due.

When the call finally came, Mastrangelo picked up the receiver and asked, "Who's this?"

"Our cousin left, and she's fine."

Mastrangelo stood up. He recognized the voice of Fryderyk Marek, a Polish member of the Stoker family. "When will she get here?"

"Tomorrow evening at eight, at the station I told you about," Marek said, and then hung up.

Mastrangelo had managed to bring one of the Irish family's members over to his side. Years earlier, before he was affiliated with the Stokers, Marek had killed a heavy-handed policeman during a brawl in a bar in Queens. Mastrangelo, who had a knack for being in the right place at the right time, had saved him from the other cops who'd arrived on the scene, hiding him in a safe place until things calmed down. Fryderyk Marek was eternally grateful to him.

Mastrangelo, intolerant of any form of control, had always lived as a maverick, unlike his peers, who, as soon as they were old enough, joined neighborhood gangs. In working-class slums where as many as ten persons lived in two rooms, in tenements where dampness and the stench of sewers permeated the halls and apartments, in garbage-strewn courtyards where swarms of flies and packs of rats encamped without regard for humans, in places where people froze in winter and sweltered in summer, it was easy for men to take their animosity out on those who were weakest: namely, their wives and children. That's why kids, as soon as they were a little independent, preferred to stay away from that institution called "the family." The neighborhood gang was a means of escape, offering freedom as well as an outlet for brimming energies. What kids sought in the gangs were thrills, adventure, coarse jokes, some preliminary attempts at gambling, their first shoplifting experiences, vandalism as an end in itself, the rituals of collective smoking and excessive drinking, an initiatory sexual romp or two with some emancipated girl, and, ultimately, bloody confrontation with other gangs, to demonstrate their physical prowess. The gang signified a bridge of passage between street pranks orchestrated by a group of buddies and organized crime.

Mastrangelo represented the exception: he had always been a loner, didn't like the herd, didn't want to be ordered around by anyone, and didn't care for any type of rules. To avoid commitment, he systematically failed to keep appointments, and the end result was that no one spoke to him anymore. On the other hand, he had little to say, did not communicate well with others, and gradually accomplished his goal of being left to himself. But to survive on one's own without supporters in a city divided into gangs would have meant succumbing, so in order to get by, he made sure he had a lot of "friends." He had managed to spread the word that he was a kind of benefactor, like Robin Hood.

In actuality, all Mastrangelo did was store up debts of gratitude that would sooner or later be presented for payment.

Years earlier, he'd succeeded in hiding the Polack from the cops, so now he'd asked Marek to tip him off about the arrival of the stuff from the Puerto Ricans. The Pole had hesitated a little but couldn't refuse a favor to someone who had saved him from the electric chair.

Marek first informed Mastrangelo and, immediately afterward, the Stoker family. At that point, Brian Stoker phoned Tom Bontade and arranged to meet him late the following night.

As soon as he received the call, Mastrangelo drove to Gabriel's and Cornelius's apartment in Harlem.

After passing through a room filled with women, children, and wailing babies, he gave the two men the Thompsons concealed in violin cases.

He explained the plan to them step by step. They were to make their move the following evening, around eight, protected by darkness. A gang of Puerto Ricans was to deliver a shipment of pure cocaine to a freighter, the *Paraguay Star*, moored at Pier 97 on the Hudson River. Gabriel and Cornelius would find a rowboat at the dock. They were to use it to reach the stern of the cargo ship, where a friend on board the vessel would lower a rope ladder. They would climb aboard and remain hidden until the Puerto Ricans arrived, at which point they would have to improvise. He didn't know where the exchange would take place. Almost certainly in the captain's quarters. The job was easy because no one would be expecting the surprise: that was their trump card. They would make a clean sweep, taking out everyone there. They were to spare no one. After that, all they had to do was take the suitcase full of coke and return to their hiding place in Harlem. Upon completion of the job, Mastrangelo would meet them there, providing them with new passports and three tickets to Rio de Janeiro, Brazil. The flight's stewardess would let the suitcase pass through as hand luggage. Once they reached Rio, prior to landing, she would give them an address and the number of a bank account. They were to bring the goods there, sell them, and then deposit 25 percent in the account and split the rest among themselves. Finally, he advised them to stay away from Puerto Ricans for the rest of their lives.

As Mastrangelo explained the details of the plan, Gabriel and Cornelius glanced at each other, amazed. They never dreamed they'd be able to aim so high. They were pleased with themselves and at the same time proud to be held in such high regard by this guy.

"Any questions?" Mastrangelo asked at the end of his long speech.

Gabriel tried to disguise his elation. "How many Puerto Ricans will there be? And who are the people the stuff's supposed to go to?"

"Not more than five Puerto Ricans and the same for the Stokers."

"We gotta kill Brian Stoker?"

"No, he won't be there. Bosses never get involved in these matters."

The two men looked at each other, a little worried. It wouldn't be a piece of cake.

"Did I get it right: twenty-five, seventy-five?" Cornelius asked to confirm the percentages of the shares.

"You got it right."

"And how much stuff is there?"

"A suitcaseful," Mastrangelo said, and almost burst out laughing at seeing the look of astonishment on their faces.

––––––––––

When Saro's mind had cleared sufficiently, he realized he was in a blind alley off Lafayette Street, quite a distance from where the Blue Lemon was located in Chelsea. How had he gotten here? Who had brought him here? Was it possible he couldn't remember anything about what had happened? Disordered thoughts raced through his mind along with sudden flashes of horrible images of blood and battered faces. Lost in his nightmares, he heard water gushing from a hose behind him. In the alley, a waiter was hosing the pavement near the back door of a restaurant. When he had finished, he dropped the rubber hose and went back in, leaving the door ajar. Saro waited a few seconds before picking up the hose, turning on the spigot, and sticking his head under the jet of cold water, hoping to clear it that way. He washed his blood-smeared hands, took off his jacket and used it to dry himself, and then threw it into a bin: it was too tattered to wear anymore; people would take him for a beggar.

He started walking, going up Broadway to make his way back to the Blue Lemon. The last clear image he had in his mind were the iron steps in the club's inner courtyard. Marta had entered the apartment with that crude show-off, and the man had followed her in. He remembered per- fectly having seen the two of them joking, laughing. Saro also recalled having had a few drinks too many, and he remembered being furious at having let that guy make off with the girl. It aggravated an old wound; it was too much like the memory of Isabel with Dixie.

When he reached the intersection of Seventh Avenue and Nineteenth Street, near the alley that led to the back of the Blue Lemon, he found two police cars blocking the way. There was the usual cluster of curious onlookers and police officers coming and going. Saro approached the crowd and tried to see what was going on in the alley. Inside the court- yard stood a black van from the morgue.

"What happened?" he casually asked a guy next to him.

"They killed two people," he replied, trying to stretch his neck to catch a glimpse of some exciting image.

"They slaughtered them," an angry woman corrected him.

"Who was it?" an old man asked naively.

"They'll never catch them; it's the Mafia," the usual know-it-all con- cluded.

"Who was killed?" This time it was Saro who asked the question.

"A girl from the club, poor thing," a young woman the same age as Marta replied.

"Poor thing, my ass," a man retorted. "She was a whore. She got what she deserved."

"The cops said her john was killed too. A great big guy," the know- it-all said.

"And how would you know?" the girl asked.

"A cop told a reporter," the man snapped.

Saro felt his head spin. He suddenly felt nauseous. He stepped back from the group of people and moved off to avoid arousing suspicion. But a policeman noticed him and came over.

"Hey, buddy, you okay?" he asked him.

"I'm okay, I just have a slight fever."

"Naturally, walking around in shirtsleeves like that. Go on home!" the policeman barked.

"I will, thanks." Saro took a few steps and disappeared around the first street corner, hiding behind it. He leaned back against the wall and started crying. He began to remember.

He had flung open the door, entered the room, and saw the tough guy undressing Marta. As soon as she saw him, she went over to him, shouting something. He remembered clearly that she wasn't wearing a bra, but still had her skirt on. Then Saro hit her. At that point, the memory became patchy. Her face was swollen from being punched. The guy had tried to stop him but was struck full in the face by a heavy bronze horse head. A stream of blood began gushing from his broken nose. The woman rushed at Saro digging her nails into his chest. Saro instinctively fingered the right side of his chest, which was still sore. He unbuttoned his shirt and saw three scratches, still bloody, scoring the skin. Marta was punched again and collapsed on the floor; her screams immediately faded and became a death rattle. From behind, the john tried to lift Saro by circling his waist with both arms, but this time a whack bashed his head in. He sagged at Saro's feet like an empty sack. Saro stared at the bloody poker. He looked at his hands: they were covered in blood. He rubbed them on his jacket to try to wipe away the traces of that madness. Then everything suddenly went black, and he sank into a troubled sleep in which he persistently relived those moments that would forever change his life.

Saro was desolate over what had happened. But how could he go back in time and change his future and that of those two poor people? It was too late now. He had crossed the fine line that separates the few decent men from the majority of evildoers. Saro cursed his fate and the day he was born.

Chapter 38

Pier 97 on the Hudson River was the first dock for passenger vessels after the enclosed piers. Gabriel parked the Ford on Twelfth Avenue facing south and left the keys under the dashboard panel, as Mastrangelo had advised him to do. He said that in the heat of escape you might lose them, so it was better to leave them there.

The first shadows of dusk had already fallen. Darkness worked to their advantage. Circles of light from the few electric streetlamps barely illuminated the area, leaving vast dark pools all around. Cornelius and Abraham got out of the car first and went to get the guns in the trunk. Gabriel joined them, grabbing his violin case and heading toward the pier.

Several cars and vans were parked in front of the dock, while to either side the transport companies' sheds were lit up, with people still inside, since shifts at the port often went until ten o'clock at night.

The freighter was moored head in, with its right side to the dock. Two gangplanks extended from it. They would use the forward one for their escape. The three friends casually headed for the end of the dock, near the stern. They looked out over the water and spotted the rowboat tied up not far from the freighter. Cornelius, the most agile of the three, climbed down first. He held the boat steady for Gabriel and then Abraham, each of whom held a violin case. Once they were in, Cornelius began rowing.

All they could hear around them was water lapping nearby against the sides of the vessel and the distant sounds of ship maintenance. Cornelius rowed around to the stern of the *Paraguay Star*. Abraham was the first to spot the rope ladder in the darkness.

Cornelius rowed toward it with slow strokes. Everything was going along perfectly, just as Mastrangelo had said. Gabriel grabbed one of the wooden rungs of the rope ladder, and Cornelius slung his violin case over his shoulder and began to climb. They had decided that Abraham would be second, and Gabriel would go up last. All three made their way up, painstakingly hoisting themselves up at each rung. They were strong and athletic, with solid shoulders and arm muscles as brawny as those of wrestlers, but climbing a rope ladder is extremely difficult unless you have the training of a trapeze artist.

Cornelius was breathing hard when he reached the railing. He looked around and didn't see anyone on deck. The *Paraguay Star* was a cargo ship, with its enclosed areas grouped around a central smokestack. It belonged to a British company and had come to New York expressly to be examined by a government commission in charge of an expansion program for the US Merchant Marine fleet. The upper deck was illuminated by a row of lights, and the central tower was lit as well.

Abraham was struggling to make it up, with Gabriel, below him, urging him to move it.

Meanwhile, Cornelius had climbed over the railing and was crouching in the shadows. Just in time, because a sailor came up from below deck, lighting a cigarette. He passed a few feet away from Cornelius, but didn't notice anything. Cornelius waited until the crewman was out of sight, and then ran and hid behind a huge wooden crate.

Several minutes later, Abraham's silhouette appeared and immediately behind him, Gabriel's.

Cornelius poked his head out from behind the crate and waved to get their attention. The two men tiptoed over to join him. Everything was going according to plan.

––––––––––

A few minutes before eight, the Stokers made their way on board. They came up the forward gangplank. Old Brian Stoker wasn't with them, and Fryderyk Marek was also absent, having pleaded sick due to a bad toothache. Except for them, the gang was complete: there were the inseparable Hugh and Kevin, Roy Foster, the boxer-bagman with his usual dark crew-neck sweater, and Lee Edward and Tony Russo, two brawny young men. Bringing up the rear was Damien Stoker, carrying a leather bag. That night, he was extremely uneasy. Damien had brought only partial payment—a truly ridiculous sum. The Puerto Ricans certainly wouldn't give up the cocaine. Brian, his father, had advised him to play a certain ace up his sleeve if push came to shove. His father's idea didn't really appeal to Damien, but he would do as he was told.

The ship's captain went to meet the group and invited everyone into the *Paraguay Star's* mess room, the only indoor space that could hold two dozen people.

Shortly afterward, the Puerto Ricans arrived in two black Dodges.

Their leader was a certain Segundo, the right arm of Armando Diaz, the acknowledged boss of trafficking that originated in South America. Behind Segundo came Juan, the man carrying the suitcase containing ten kilograms of pure coke. They were accompanied by three mean-looking thugs.

The five men strode up the forward gangplank. A sailor led them directly into the mess room where Damien and his men were waiting for them. The captain of the ship had chosen to retire to his cabin.

Segundo entered the room and went over to Damien. "I kept my word, man. Ten kilos of first-rate cocaine. You can make fifty thousand doses by cutting it. Show him the goods, Juan."

The man set the suitcase on the table and pulled out a packet; he opened it and placed it on the tabletop. Damien went over and tasted the white powder. He nodded, as if to say "Excellent" and then stepped back. The man put the packet back in the suitcase and closed it up, leaving it on the table.

Damien hesitated, and this did not go unnoticed by Segundo. Alarmed, he asked, "What's up, Damien?"

"Don't worry, Segundo, everything's okay."

"The money?"

"I brought you an advance on the amount I'll earn from the sale of the stuff. All I'm asking for is twelve hours. It's a quick transaction, with only one buyer. A one-shot deal for all of us." So saying he picked up the leather bag and handed it to him.

Segundo grabbed it but didn't open it. "How much is in it?"

"Five grand. That's all I could scrape together. But I assure you, you won't regret it."

Juan looked at his boss and knew immediately what he had to do. He snatched the suitcase of cocaine off the table and got safely out of the way, standing behind the three gorillas who instantly drew their automatic weapons from their jackets, aiming them at Damien and his men. Damien motioned to his men not to react.

"What kind of fucking stunt is this, Damien? The terms were clear."

"Calm down, Segundo. Tell your men to take it easy. I have no intention of creating trouble. The terms will be respected. But in twelve hours."

"Man, you're soft in the head if you think I'm going to leave you my coke without payment in return."

Segundo was adamant, and Damien knew he'd have to play the ace up his sleeve as his father had suggested. "Segundo, you have nothing to lose because I myself will be your insurance."

"What are you talking about?" the Puerto Rican asked, pausing in the doorway of the mess room.

"I'll come with you . . . let's say as a hostage? We'll wait for the transaction together. Then when Roy Foster brings the rest of the money, we'll shake hands, and we'll all be happy and have lots of bucks in our wallets."

Segundo carefully considered the offer—and in the end gave in. "Deal. I leave your men the stuff, and you come with us. But if your father is pulling a fast one, I'll send you back in pieces, in a suitcase."

"You won't regret it, pal," said Damien. And with that, he took the suitcase with the ten kilos of coke and handed it to Foster, the bagman. "You know what to do with it," he said. At the same instant, the three Puerto Rican gorillas surrounded Damien and took him in custody.

"Let's go," Segundo ordered, "this whole thing stinks of a scam." He was about to leave the room when Cornelius's tommy gun shattered the glass of a porthole.

Gabriel, with the second tommy gun, was behind the door that opened directly onto the main deck. Abraham, meanwhile, was to open fire with a short-barrel .38 from the passageway leading from the upper deck to the mess room.

Suddenly the room was overwhelmed with rapid sprays of machine gun fire. Having learned his lesson, Cornelius fired in short bursts. Gabriel threw open the door, and there stood Segundo. He fired without aiming, but Segundo was faster than him and dropped quickly to the floor. The bullets flew over his head and struck two of his men who were right behind him. At the first volley of shots, Damien had the presence of mind to plunge through the frosted glass wall on the only side of the room that the three intruders had not been able to protect. Segundo followed him, but a bullet struck him in the thigh, and he fell back on a pile of rope. He saw Damien run and hide behind the cargo crates. Though limping and bleeding from the gunshot wound, he kept up his pursuit, while behind him the tommy guns spewed out their grim litany of death.

Segundo managed to stop Damien before he reached the forward gangplank. He jumped on him, wrapping his arms around his legs. Damien toppled to the ground, kicking violently to try to free himself from the Puerto Rican's grip. But Segundo wouldn't release his hold. He got up, pinned Damien to the ground with his knee, and punched him between the eyes. "You backstabbing scum! Rotten bastard!" he yelled, pounding on Damien's face, which was now a bloody mask.

"I didn't sell you out—" the Irishman tried to say. Segundo kept clobbering him, consumed with rage. If he didn't want to die, Damien had to do something. He felt the pressure of the semiautomatic at his side and with a last-ditch effort managed to grab it.

Meanwhile, the machine guns had stopped crackling. Gabriel wandered among the corpses piled up in the mess room. Abraham joined him, followed shortly afterward by Cornelius. They couldn't believe their eyes. They had pulled off a bloodbath without suffering so much as a scratch. It had all gone down like that guy Mastrangelo had predicted.

Gabriel went over to the leather bag, opened it, and saw several packets of bills. Cornelius, meanwhile, headed for the other bag. The guy who looked like a boxer, the one with the crew-neck sweater, was still clutching it to his chest, despite his death rattle, instinctively trying to protect it. Abraham approached him, stuck the .38 to the man's temple and fired. Cornelius was finally able to tear the suitcase away from him. He opened it and saw that it was crammed with bags of cocaine. His jaw dropped in astonishment as he showed his buddies the contents. The two smiled.

At that instant, they heard a gunshot coming from outside. They raced out of the room and were just in time to see Damien run down the gangplank and hurry away from the ship.

Cornelius tried to center him in the gun's crosshairs, but it was dark, and his outline soon merged with the shadows surrounding the port. Gabriel reached out and lowered the barrel of Cornelius's tommy gun. Police sirens could be heard in the distance, coming closer and closer. The ship's captain must have notified them on the radio transmitter. The three men, with two bags and the instruments of death stashed in the violin cases, calmly left the ship, and then silently vanished among the stacks of goods on the dock and headed toward the Ford.

Behind them, they'd left the corpses.

They had to drive through much of Manhattan to get to their hideout. Mastrangelo would be waiting for them there. They would be given passports with their new identities and tickets for the flight to Rio, where they would lie low for a few months. Later they could have their women join them. That devil Mastrangelo had thought of that too. The three men still couldn't believe the good fortune that had befallen them.

Their hideaway was located uptown near a large maintenance yard for buses and trucks. Gabriel and his pals had set up their base of operations in one of the sheds no longer used by the workers. This is where they hid the goods they stole and the weapons they used for their jobs.

When they got to the hideout, they found Mastrangelo waiting for them. He had been listening to a radio quiz show, having fun answering the host's questions about the movies and beating the contestants to the punch. Mastrangelo was a fanatic film buff and boasted that he knew almost all the lines of *Little Caesar* and *The Beast of the City* by heart. Edward G. Robinson was his idol.

When he heard the sound of the Ford's engine, he stood up and went to the door.

The three newly initiated killers were revved up, the adrenaline still pumping. They were laughing and acting like braggarts, feeling invincible and untouchable. They knew they had pulled off something more momentous than the Saint Valentine's Day massacre. Too bad no one would ever associate their names with the *Paraguay Star* bloodbath.

Gabriel threw open the door, beaming.

"Should I assume everything went according to plan?" Mastrangelo asked, still standing in the middle of the room.

"It was child's play," Gabriel said, setting the case with the Thompson gun on the floor. Then he went to get the whiskey bottle and took a long swig.

Cornelius came in next.

"How many did you kill?" Mastrangelo asked.

"Five, ten, who knows? We took out so many you couldn't even count them." Cornelius set his violin case down next to Gabriel's.

The last to enter was bulky Abraham. He held the two suitcases by the handles, like a schoolboy coming home from school. He was happier and more satisfied than all of them: from that day on, everyone had better show him some respect, or else.

"The plan you worked out was perfect. Not a single hitch. Do you have the passports?" Gabriel asked.

"Sure." And with that, Mastrangelo slipped his hand under his jacket and pulled a .45 Special out of its holster. Not losing a fraction of a second, he aimed first at Abraham, the only one who was armed, and then at Gabriel, and finally at Cornelius.

The three shots rang out sharply in rapid succession, and the three men slumped to the floor like sacks. Mastrangelo bent down to make sure they were dead, and then straightened up and took the two bags from Abraham's grip. He stuffed the wads of bills into the suitcase with the cocaine packets. Then he picked up the machine gun cases and went out into the night.

He took the Harlem River Drive south to Ninety-Sixth Street and then proceeded to Carl Schurz Park, where he tossed the two guns into the putrid waters of the East River. Then he broke up the two violin cases and threw the pieces in two different trash bins. He had done away with all the evidence that could connect him to that night's killings. All he had to do now was go to Grand Central Station and leave the suitcase with the stuff in a locker.

Now came the easiest part of the script Ferdinando Licata had written.

Chapter 39

The meeting with the Stokers had been set for a half hour before midnight in the discreet offices of the Dirty Rat, a club south of Houston, on Broome Street. The place was in a neutral zone, under the jurisdiction of the Genovese family; the two affiliates, the Stokers and the Bontades, had no choice but to accept the boss's hospitality with good grace. Besides, at that hour, the club was still full of customers, and their movements wouldn't attract attention.

Tom Bontade had been right on time. He'd brought his most trusted men with him for the delicate transaction: there was, of course, Big Jordan, and then Vincenzo Ciancianna, along with Bontade's bodyguards Barret and Cooper. And for the first time, he'd decided to try out Vito Pizzuto, the Sicilian who had recently joined the family.

It was now midnight, and there was still no sign of the Stokers.

"Those goddamn Irish Micks have never been reliable," the elder Bontade muttered to himself.

He asked one of his men to call Brian Stoker. But Cooper reminded him that Brian had no phone in his house.

Bontade cursed the Irishman's ridiculous, antiquated mentality. "Call that maniac son of his then. Actually, no, *you* do it, Vincenzo. You're more diplomatic. Go on."

The two men left to make the call. Tom Bontade had a bad feeling. If the Stokers didn't show up with the rest of the stuff, the deal could fall through, and Sante Genovese would raise hell for having been fucked with.

It was a few minutes past midnight when a club attendant knocked at the office door and let in Jack Mastrangelo. Nobody in the room appeared pleased by his arrival.

"Don Bontade, is something wrong?" he asked, approaching the elderly family boss.

"Everything's okay, Mastrangelo," Bontade said, moving to a table that held several liquor bottles and some glasses. "You want a drink?"

"I'm not here to spend the evening chatting. Do you have the stuff?" he asked the boss directly.

Bontade had to swallow the man's arrogant tone. He poured whiskey into two glasses. "What's the hurry, Mastrangelo? Let's enjoy life. Business shouldn't spoil our pleasure." He handed him the glass, and Mastrangelo, forced to take it, set it on the table without touching a drop.

"So you don't have the stuff," he accused in a tone that left Bontade no alternative but to answer him.

"Only half of it. I'm waiting for the other half to arrive."

"That wasn't the deal, Bontade." He deliberately chose to demean him by avoiding the deferential "Don." "My client hates glitches and people who don't honor their word."

"My word is law. My share is in that bag. It's the Irishmen's share that's missing. I can't vouch for them. However, sooner or later they'll arrive with the rest of the goods. Come on, calm down. You just have to wait a few minutes. That's not asking too much, is it?"

"I'm sorry, Bontade, but my client's instructions were clear. I'm not to go ahead with the transaction if I see something I don't like. For all I know, a gang of cops might even come through that door. Naturally, I don't have anything incriminating on me. The money is stashed else-where in the city."

"No cops will be coming through that door. Be patient a little longer, Mastrangelo, and we'll bring this great opportunity to a successful conclusion, you'll see." Bontade moved closer to Mastrangelo, who pretended to be uneasy. He took a few steps back, toward the door.

"Take it easy, Mastrangelo, no one's going to harm you," Bontade continued, genuinely concerned about having frightened him.

"I'm sorry, I'm really sorry, but my client was very clear about it. Our agreement is off."

He backed up as far as the door. Barret and Big Jordan barred the way out, but Bontade motioned to them to let him go. "Sure you don't want to think it over, Mastrangelo?"

"No."

"When the second half of the stuff arrives, I'll contact you, okay?"

"Okay," Mastrangelo opened the door and went out, while Bontade cursed the Stokers for causing one of the most lucrative deals in recent years to go up in smoke.

He hadn't yet finished railing against the Irishmen, when suddenly one of them materialized in front of him.

It was Damien, raging, pointing his gun at Bontade. He'd stormed into the room through the back door together with the Pole Fryderyk

Marek and Boy Richard, an Irish kid who couldn't have been even sixteen.

"Sicilian bastard!" he yelled before pulling the trigger. But Big Jordan tackled him, knocking him to the ground. The bullet only grazed Bontade.

At the same time, Barret drew his revolver and began firing wildly at the intruders, who dropped to the floor to dodge the bullets.

The Pole, who wasn't as motivated as his boss, dived out the door, while Boy Richard tried to return Barret's fire from behind a metal file cabinet. Meanwhile, Vito Pizzuto had rushed to Bontade's aid, helping him retreat toward the door. Vincenzo Ciancianna, the only unarmed man in the room, huddled under the table.

Big Jordan was locked in a hand-to-hand scuffle with Damien, but his bulk didn't favor him. He gripped the Irishman's automatic with both hands, while Damien pounded away at his face with his free hand. But Big Jordan could take punches better than Jake LaMotta.

When Boy Richard, seeing his boss in trouble with Big Jordan, moved out into the open to help him, Barret took the opportunity to shoot him in the side. The kid fell to the floor, gasping. Damien, meanwhile, despite Big Jordan's efforts, was able to direct the barrel of the gun at the big man's head. A moment later he fired a shot that ripped into the giant's flushed features, hitting him square in the face. Big Jordan fell on Damien with his full three hundred pounds. As Damien struggled to get out from under the ton of lard, Tom Bontade, seeing his lifelong friend on the ground, bleeding, snatched the gun from Barret's hands. He rushed at Damien with an enraged roar, shooting him several times in the chest, until the magazine was empty.

In the final moments of his life Damien continued to spew out hatred, the feeling that had accompanied him throughout his existence. "Traitor . . ." he murmured to Bontade. "You wanted it all for yourself . . . You destroyed my family . . . but someone will avenge me." With those words on his lips, he exhaled his last miserable breath.

Bontade was dazed and still beside himself over his friend's death. He bent over Big Jordan. All he could determine was that he'd been killed instantly. He turned to Vito Pizzuto, who stood beside him.

"What could he have meant?"

"If I understood right, somebody bumped off his family. He talked about revenge. Boss, we need to get out of here now. The place will be crawling with cops before long."

Tom Bonrade understood Damien's last words after reading the following day's newspapers. The late city edition of the *New York Times* featured coverage of the bloodbath aboard the *Paraguay Star*, stating that a
battle to the death between rival mobs had almost completely extermi-
nated the Stoker family and a gang of Puerto Ricans. According to police, the journalist reported, it was a settling of accounts that ended with
both gangs being almost completely wiped out.

Bonrade, however, knew the truth: someone must have gotten wind
of the deal that was under way and had contrived that ambush to make
off with the cocaine and the money. Two birds with one stone, as they
say. But who knew about the arrangement? Only the two families. What
rotten bastard could have betrayed his own blood and brought about
such carnage?

Tom Bonrade decided to go talk to Brian Stoker. He would go alone,
without bodyguards. Brian would have to listen to him, because Tom
Bonrade was now more than certain that someone was acting to destroy
his family as well as the Stokers.

That morning, Ferdinando Licata learned from reading the newspapers that Mastrangelo had indeed carried out his plan. He had ordered
Mastrangelo not to contact him for at least two weeks following the incident.

After three passionate days in Coney Island, Dixie and Isabel had returned to Manhattan, and had found lodging at a friend's modest hotel
on the Lower East Side, just across from Seward Park. Dixie started playing at a club in Chelsea, while Isabel went back to the Salvation Army. It
was the easiest job she knew and left her quite a bit of free time, as long
as the others in the unit didn't keep a close watch on her and report her
to their superiors.

Dixie was enjoying greater and greater success in the bands he played
with, but his and his wife's schedules didn't coincide anymore. When
Isabel left the house to go to the Army's Outpost, Dixie, having just returned a couple of hours ago, would be sleeping soundly until at least
noon. Then when she came home in the evening, her feet sore from long
hours roaming the streets, he would be getting ready to leave.

Isabel wasn't happy. She absolutely had to break that cycle.

Returning with her fellow soldiers one day from yet another mission
in search of souls to redeem and bellies to fill, she asked Captain Virginia

if she could leave early that day because she wasn't feeling well. She had stomach cramps, and the cold weather made things worse. Virginia understood. Once a month shifts were relaxed a bit for women, so she gave her permission to go home to bed. Isabel thanked her with a contrite face and, without even taking off her uniform, hurried back to the hotel.

"I'll go to bed," she thought cheerfully, "but for a different kind of relaxation." She was already looking forward to being with Dixie, and she laughed at the face he would make when he saw her. It had been almost two weeks since they'd been together.

She ran up the stairs, as excited as on a first date. She slid the key in the lock and turned it slowly. She heard the spring lock click and opened the door. It was just a little past noon; she might still find him in bed. Isabel took off her jacket and began unbuttoning her Army blouse. She continued down the corridor. Dixie wasn't in the kitchen, nor in the living room. She was in luck, she thought. So she moved on to the bedroom, where the door was ajar. She took off her blouse and stood there in her slip and blue skirt. But all of a sudden deep sighs made her blood run cold. She froze, straining to hear. The sighs were moans of pleasure. She pressed her hands to her mouth to keep from screaming. In an instant, her joy turned to despair. The moans were growing more and more intense. Dixie's voice was unmistakable. How often she had taken pleasure in the sounds of his coming. Now he was doing it with someone else. A strangled cry of collapse and climax put an end to the act.

Isabel finally found the will to push open the door. Dixie whirled around. The woman covered herself, pulling the sheet over her head.

Isabel stopped feeling sorry for herself and displayed her Irish temperament. She rushed at Dixie who, naked as he was, tried to hold her off.

"You crummy piece of shit, goddamn you and the shitty Italian family you came from! How dare you! How could you bring this bitch into our bed!" She tried to strike him with her fists, but Dixie was adept at dodging her punches.

"Hold on, Isabel, it's not what you think! Calm down! Let me explain!" Dixie was dodging the objects that Isabel had begun throwing at him.

"How long has this been going on?"

"For a while. But it's not important—"

"What do you mean, it's not important!" Isabel yelled. "It may not be important to you, but it is to me! You have absolutely no moral scruples. How did I ever fall in love with a monster like you! I hate you, I hate you!" She burst into hopeless tears. He tried to kiss her, but Isabel drew back in disgust. "I told you not to touch me! You make me sick! In our bed . . . I never want to see you again! Get out! Better yet, no, I'll go! This room makes me want to puke."

And she walked out of the apartment and out of his life.

Chapter 40

Contrary to all the rules that had always governed his life, old Tom Bontade paid a visit to Brian Stoker alone and unarmed.

The elderly Stoker was surprised to see him. For a moment, he thought he had come to kill him, but Bontade quickly reassured him.

"I'm here as a father, to talk as one father to another. Let's leave the wheeling and dealing that have poisoned our lives outside the door," Tom Bontade began, extending his hand.

The other man approached him. "I'm shaking the hand that killed my son," he said, his spirit broken.

"That's why I'm here. I want to understand what happened. Someone wanted to turn us against each other."

"And he succeeded perfectly," Stoker concluded.

"Right. He wiped out your family, making the blame fall on us Bontades. But I swear on my honor that I had nothing to do with it."

"Only you and we knew about the transaction," Stoker said bluntly.

"Someone must have leaked it. But it wasn't us, I swear to you."

"I believe you, Tom. Still, my son is gone now. I had to bury him."

"A father should never have to bury his child. I know what that's like." The recollection of his son who'd been killed in a shoot-out with an enemy gang had never left Bontade. "It's a memory you can't erase. You'll carry it with you forever."

"I feel old, I don't want to live anymore," Stoker said bitterly.

"Old age is sad not because joys cease, but because hopes end. As long as you have a child, you hope to see him settled down, with a promising future. But when he's taken from you . . . everything comes crashing down. Your life is over."

"I'm going to tell you a secret, Bontade. A decision I just made tonight: I'm going to retire. I have a nice nest egg set aside, which will allow me to live like a king to the end of my days. I'm going to Florida, to the elephants' graveyard, and I'll end my days there. I'm leaving New York." Those words were heavy as boulders. The feisty Brian Stoker never thought he would have to say them.

"But you can't give up right now. Don't you want to find out who played this loathsome trick on us?"

"I made my decision. It's final."

Brian Stoker was adamant. Reaching that decision had cost him great sacrifice. Above all, a sacrifice of pride. During his life, he had always struck back, blow for blow; he had never retreated, even at the riskiest moments. But now he had reached his limit.

Without Damien and the men who formed his team, the person responsible for the slayings would certainly seize the territory before he could organize a new force.

Tom Bontade, on the other hand, wanted to go back over the stages of the deal to try to figure out who had set the trap. He was now certain that scoring the cocaine was merely an excuse to wipe out the Stoker family and finance the new family through the sale of the drug.

Bontade obtained Stoker's permission to question the survivors of his group. Only Fryderyk Marek was still alive. Tom Bontade questioned him, but the Pole was clearly of no help.

Still, Bontade had waded through lies too often not to know when someone was telling the truth or lying, and that Pole, who had saved his own hide in two shootings, wasn't telling the truth. He ordered Barret, Cooper, Carmelo Vanni, and Vito Pizzuto not to let Marek out of their sight in the following weeks.

The four men organized surveillance shifts around the clock, and at the end of the first week, their efforts were rewarded.

Fryderyk Marek left his house on Rivington Street on the Lower East Side one morning and got into a taxi.

Maintaining a discreet distance, Vito Pizzuto and Barret tailed him to Bensonhurst. There Marek entered a little Italian café. As they passed in their car moments later, Pizzuto and Barret saw Jack Mastrangelo frowning as he spoke to Marek, evidently chewing him out about something.

So Mastrangelo was the man who had conducted the negotiations on behalf of a mysterious client, and the Pole had been the informer who tipped him off that the Stokers were about to trade ten kilos of cocaine. When they reported the results of their surveillance of Marek to Tom Bontade, the old boss recalled that it had been Big Jordan who'd told him about the deal. He'd heard about it from his hooker. A certain Marta.

She was the only one who could make him get it up. But how had Marta known about the offer?

"I should have thought of it sooner," Bontade reproached himself. "You have to find the hooker. We'll ask her about her recent clients, not her regulars; our man is on that list. The one who orchestrated this whole production." Cooper was familiar with Marta's girlfriends. He had personally accompanied Big Jordan to her place on more than one occasion, taking advantage of the opportunity to do it with one of her coworkers.

The girls told him that Marta had been attacked by a maniac the week before: some guy had killed her john and beaten her up, leaving her in a coma for several days. She was now at St. Vincent's Hospital in critical condition.

Barret had a cousin who was a paramedic at St. Vincent's. He asked him to do him a favor and let him see the girl. Barret's cousin was initially a bit reluctant because he didn't want to get mixed up in his relative's affairs, which he knew weren't totally on the up-and-up. But when handed a ten-dollar bill, he managed to silence his conscience, and during his shift he let Barret into the poor girl's room.

Marta was unrecognizable, her face purple from profuse bruising. A bandage covered her forehead, and another supported her jaw. Her eyes were so swollen that the irises were barely visible through the slits. Her nose was also bandaged, and the skin around her ears and eyebrows bore numerous stitches.

Barret, disguised as a nurse, approached and pretended to adjust the IV drip. Then he bent over her to see if she was awake. He saw her pupils flash. He realized that she was terrified by his presence.

He moved close to her ear and whispered, "Marta, some friends are asking me if you remember the name of the man who told you he wanted to buy a batch of coke. Do you understand what I'm saying?"

The girl didn't move, but her eyes never left him.

"Can you speak?"

Marta made an imperceptible movement with her head, and Barret realized that it was a "no."

He saw a notebook and pencil on the bedstand. "That must be how they communicate with her," he thought.

Barret placed the pencil in her hand and held the notebook for her. With a great deal of effort, Marta finally managed to write "Ferdinando Licata."

The name didn't mean anything to Tom Bontade. But Vito Pizzuto knew him.

"I know the big bastard," he said, stepping forward. "It's Prince Ferdinando Licata; he owns half of Salemi. He fled from Sicily too; we were on the same ship. Good for the prince; he's managed to adapt to our way of life," he added mockingly.

Cooper entered the room of the apartment that Bontade used as an office and meeting place, went over to the boss, and handed him a newspaper. Bontade read the banner headline: "Gangland-Style Killing." The morning papers had published news of the discovery of three corpses in a shed on the bank of the Harlem River, killed execution style with a bullet through the head. Their description matched those of three men seen by an eyewitness leaving the *Paraguay Star* around the time of the massacre. The authorities believed them to be associated with the slayings, even though no weapons had been found in the shack.

The scenario was becoming increasingly clear to Bontade. The three had evidently been used as hired guns; then the one who had enlisted them must have also killed them. In order to understand whether the Sicilian prince was responsible for the two mass executions, he had to go back to Brian Stoker. What had occurred had all the appearances of a vendetta.

When Tom Bontade went to see Stoker for a second time, the old man was getting ready to leave for Florida.

Bontade approached him with open arms, as if to embrace him.

"So you've come to say good-bye?" Brian Stoker asked.

"Life can be understood only if you look back at it in perspective. We were at war for all these years, when we could very well have lived in peace, without bothering each other."

The two men embraced. They actually seemed like two old friends, even though one of them had killed the other's son. "I may have found out who set us against each other," Tom said, breaking away.

"As far as I'm concerned, it's too late," Brian said dejectedly.

"Still, I have to make him pay for it. Does the name Ferdinando Licata mean anything to you?"

Brian Stoker mentally reviewed the people who had run up against his family in recent months.

"Licata . . . Kevin spoke to me about him. He's the old guy at La

Tonnara, a restaurant run by some Italians. We had some problems with those people, and one night we had to teach them a lesson. Water under the bridge. All our troubles started there. Kevin was tortured, then we started getting threatening phone calls—threats against the Stokers. Then that massacre . . .

"My time has come, my friend."

When he got home, Bontade met with Vito Pizzuto alone. "Why do you hate Prince Licata so much?" he asked.

"When we were on the ship, he insulted me in front of my friends. You don't disrespect someone like me. He called me a pimp."

Bontade felt like smiling but restrained himself. "They say a mosquito's sting itches less after we've managed to crush the mosquito. Licata has to die."

Pizzuto smiled.

"Prepare a plan," said his boss. "But you have to hurry if we want to take over the territory vacated by the Irishmen."

Ferdinando Licata had actually been established for some time in the territory to which Bontade referred. After the disappearance of the Irish gang, and particularly with Damien's death, the residents of Tompkins Square and the surrounding neighborhood had begun to breathe freely again. Mothers allowed their daughters to go out without being escorted by their fathers or older brothers; shopkeepers had lowered the prices of goods, now that they were no longer harassed by the Stokers' demands; and restaurant owners were able to smile again, released from the disagreeable presence of Damien and his buddies. And when Ferdinando Licata ran into some neighborhood friend who had benefited from his actions, he was greeted with the old title of Father. In fact, the older people continued to address him in the original dialect: "*I nostri rispetti, Patri.*" "Our respects, Father."

When he'd decided to enter the fray, the prince had moved out of his room at La Tonnara. He'd done so to relieve his niece Betty of his presence but, most of all, because he didn't want to involve her in his new activities. The apartment he had rented near Tompkins Square Park was not far from the restaurant. Not a day went by that he didn't see his beloved grandniece, Ginevra.

These were extremely busy days for him and Mastrangelo, because together they were organizing the structure of a solid "family." This meant searching for loyal "soldiers," which was the hardest task. It meant gaining people's acceptance by creating an image of absolute efficiency, so that they could replace the previous family crime seamlessly.

The last piece of the puzzle he needed to put in place was selecting a right-hand man. But Jack Mastrangelo already had someone in mind.

Chapter 41

For days and days, Isabel wandered through the city looking for help. Friends, acquaintances, companions, no one paid enough attention to her despair. They were all too busy finding food, a bed, a woman, a job. Everyone was running and had no time to stop and commiserate with a brokenhearted woman.

Isabel asked everyone for support except the one person who might have sympathized with her: Saro. She didn't have the nerve to go see him. A friend had even told her where he lived. She'd passed by his door many times but continued on her way so as not to have to swallow her pride. "Pride, the inevitable vice of fools," Isabel thought.

But one day she got up her courage and, instead of walking past, entered the door on Great Jones Street. She climbed the stairs to the top floor and knocked on apartment 4B.

The radio was on, broadcasting a performance by Cab Calloway's orchestra from the Apollo Theater in Harlem. But voices could also be heard, and soon the door opened.

Saro certainly didn't expect to see her and froze with the door partly open. With the most impish smile she could muster, Isabel gave him a wave. "Hi there, Saro."

The young man kept staring at her, stock-still, as though hypnotized.

"Aren't you going to ask me in?" Isabel was still gorgeous, despite the days she'd spent sunk in depression. "You know, things didn't work out with Dixie."

Saro continued to gaze at her, captivated. Then his expression gave way to consternation.

"Won't you even say hello?" Isabel went on, not understanding his dismay.

She heard footsteps behind Saro, and a female voice asked: "Saro, sweetie, who is it?" A girl appeared in the doorway: thick black hair; dark, unwavering eyes. She came up to Saro and took his arm. Then she saw Isabel. "Who is she?"

This time it was Isabel who was left nonplussed. Saro helped her out of the awkward situation.

"No one. The lady has the wrong address." So saying, he sadly closed the door in her face.

After a few seconds, Isabel walked to the stairs and burst into tears. No one wanted to have anything to do with her anymore. She felt faint and leaned against the wall, weeping uncontrollably, releasing her despair.

"That girl was desperate," Agnes said to Saro, going back to the kitchen.

"How can you say that? You barely saw her."

"You're forgetting my outstanding sixth sense," she smiled ironically.

"Then tell me the winning lottery numbers, Miss Sixth Sense." Saro went to her and put his arms around her from behind. He tried to hide his sadness.

Suddenly the music stopped, and the radio announcer said gravely: "We interrupt this performance to bring you news of Chancellor Adolf Hitler's speech to the Reichstag in Berlin earlier this morning." Seconds later, all of America learned the details of the Führer's speech.

Agnes turned and instinctively clung to Saro, as if seeking protection. As the announcer spoke, the Führer's guttural voice, shouting forcefully in the background, aroused her fear. "What does it mean?" she asked, looking into his eyes.

"It means war has broken out in Europe. But we don't have to worry. America won't get dragged into their bickering."

Saro was right. That day, Friday, September 1, 1939, Hitler launched his Panzer tanks and his Stuka dive-bombers against the Polish cavalry. In less than three weeks, German armed forces—the *Wehrmacht*—reached the Polish capital of Warsaw, leaving the other European nations astounded by the speed and efficiency of its military action. Political analysts were also left stunned by the destruction wreaked on cities by air raids. Entire villages disappeared, and cities crumbled under the aerial bombardments. This was just a taste of what would happen in the following years.

New York, unlike Warsaw, continued to be the lively city that everyone knew. The Führer's speech didn't worry the people there all that much. In general, the American public said that Europe was remote, far way across the ocean.

A few days after the news of the invasion of Poland, Little Italy was observing the anniversary of the martyrdom of Saint Ciro, the patron saint of emigrants from Marineo, a small village in Sicily. The Sicilian community that had made its home in the area around Elizabeth, Bleecker, Houston, and Prince streets had long ago decided to commission a statue of Saint Ciro similar to the one they had left behind in Sicily. When they had collected enough money, they ordered a Sicilian metalsmith to fashion it in solid silver, since back in the mother church of Marineo, the urn with the statuette safeguarding the skull of the saint was silver. Sent to America, the statue turned out to be a perfect replica of the original.

Ever since those early years of the century, each year between late August and the first week of September, Little Italy came alive. The streets were filled with an endless succession of colorful stalls, with booths selling mussels, sausages, and cotton candy for the kids. Windows were decorated with Italian flags as well as the Stars and Stripes, and archways of leafy branches or strands of tiny lights festooned the dark streets. The congregation had an altar built for the occasion, on which the saint's statue was placed. Two additional platforms were used for the bands providing the music. In the afternoon and evening, local residents could listen to passages from operas and watch plays in dialect, and stories performed by Sicilian puppets. Later the bands would play popular songs so that people could dance.

But the moment most awaited by everyone was Monday, the final day of the feast, when the solemn procession began at dusk. Before the long journey began, people would attach bills of different denominations to the statue, each according to his means. This devotional practice enabled the congregation to maintain the statue and to offer support to destitute families. After this moment of reverence, the silver canopy was hoisted onto the shoulders of a team of statue bearers, who had earned the privilege by paying big bucks. The life-sized effigy of Saint Ciro, covered with bills, escorted by the band, and followed by thousands of faithful devotees, then wound through the streets of Little Italy for a good two hours, amid general excitement. Everyone made the sign of the cross when the saint passed by. Many women, mostly the elderly, walked barefoot behind the shrine. Impromptu choruses lifted their voices in more or less spontaneous prayer, in dialect.

At the end of the procession, around midnight, was the start of the long-awaited fireworks, when everyone's thoughts drifted back home to the relatives and friends they'd left behind, in some cases forever.

This was the setting in which Vito Pizzuto decided to carry out his revenge against Ferdinando Licata. He met with Tom Bontade and laid out his plan, but the boss had doubts about the negative impact that it could have on the entire community.

Basically Pizzuto wanted to fill Saint Ciro's statue with sticks of dynamite, and use a rifle shot to set them off the moment Prince Licata approached the figure of the saint.

"The time to trigger the detonator will be when the prince affixes his offering to the saint's statue," Vito Pizzuto explained. "The silver shards should be lethal. Naturally, others may be injured. But our explosives expert will make sure the blast's discharge occurs in the area right in front of the statue, where the prince would attach his money," Pizzuto conveyed the plan with the coolness of an accountant.

"But an attack on the statue of Saint Ciro will make all the inhabitants of Little Italy despise us," Bontade declared.

"It's a risk we have to take. Anyway, it's safer to be feared than loved," Pizzuto concluded.

Tom Bontade pondered the proposal for a few minutes. He didn't like the idea of destroying the statue of Saint Ciro. It had cost the Sicilian community a great deal of sacrifice, and to blow it up like that seemed like a betrayal. Licata could also be killed with a shotgun blast, though it wouldn't have the same impact on the population that by now had adopted him as "Father."

"I'll give you an answer tomorrow morning, Pizzuto." With that, he sent him away, wanting to be alone.

Chapter 42

That year, 1939, the festivities of Saint Ciro were coming to a close on Monday, September 11. Thousands of people thronged the sidewalks of Little Italy.

Mingling with the crowd, dressed in his Sunday best, was Ferdinando Licata. He stood out, partly because he towered over everyone by a good several inches, and partly because in his Prince of Wales suit, he looked particularly elegant. The prince was holding little Ginevra by the hand, though from time to time she asked to be picked up so she could see over the wall of legs at her eye level. Behind them, Betty and her husband, Nico, were walking hand in hand, like a couple of sweethearts. They too were dressed in the finest clothes they owned, and smiled happily at the acquaintances they met. They had closed La Tonnara for the procession and allowed themselves a day off. Betty had never been so happy in her life. After the disappearance of the Stokers and their demands, people had begun frequenting the restaurant again; it was finally financially stable, and Nico was even thinking about hiring a cook to assist him.

Also circulating in the crowd were Tom Bontade and his trusted bagman, Carmelo Vanni. Barret and Cooper, the two bodyguards, didn't take their eyes off them, and rudely shoved aside any men and even women who were unfortunate enough to get in their boss's way. Bontade and Vanni, both in dark pinstriped suits, glanced around continually, as if looking for someone who hadn't yet arrived.

Agnes, Saro's new flame, stood in the doorway of a candy shop waiting for Saro, who soon emerged with a cloud of cotton candy. She took the wooden stick from him with a playful smile, kissed him on the cheek, and sank her mouth into the sweet airy fluff. They both stood on the doorstep in order to see over the heads of the crowd, prepared to watch the procession.

The Mass had ended, and the band began playing a solemn hymn. The twelve bearers, all wearing red cassocks, made their way through the crowd that pressed close to the statue of Saint Ciro.

They hoisted the pallet to their shoulders, whereupon the band stopped performing the sacred hymn and began playing a more rhythmic piece to accompany the procession. The priest stepped down from the platform where he had officiated at the Mass and took his place at the head, followed by a group of altar boys, devout women, and two other deacons. The procession then began.

The shrine with the silver saint followed the cortege, and behind it came the band and then the crowd of emigrants.

It took two hours for the procession to pass through the neighborhood's streets. The press of people forced the bearers to slow their pace. Litanies alternated with choruses, ancient hymns, and Hail Marys. After two hours, they returned to the starting point, where platforms had been set up. The band took its place on the stage, and the musicians were finally able to sit down. The priest ascended the outdoor altar, and Saint Ciro was positioned on a stand just below it. The donation ceremony would now begin, the final ritual before the start of the fireworks.

Suddenly spontaneous applause rose from the crowd. Several women cried out, "Viva Saint Ciro!" A man with his hands cupped in front of his mouth shouted, "Saint Ciro, allow us to go back one day!" It was like a signal, and many others voiced the same wish. Meanwhile, a line of people formed in front of the statue: men, women with sleeping babies in their arms, children, teenagers, and old people—many of them holding a one-dollar bill, some a five-dollar, a few even a ten- or a twenty-dollar bill. Some managed to pin the bill on the saint's statue, others dropped it in the basket placed at its feet.

From his position nearby, Tom Bontade turned and in the darkness saw the burnished gleam of a rifle barrel on the fire escape of the building behind him.

On the top floor of the building, Roy Boccia, a former sniper from the Great War, was focusing the crosshairs on the head of Saint Ciro's statue. Beside him stood Vito Pizzuto, who, with binoculars, was keeping an eye on Ferdinando Licata. The prince, still holding his grandniece's hand, had lined up to make an offering to the saint along with everyone else. Little Ginevra clutched a one-hundred-dollar bill in her hand, and few people in the square had failed to notice the generous donation.

Saro and Agnes had moved and were now standing beside a tree, the better to watch the offerings to the saint. Saro spotted Isabel standing near the statue. She wore a green dress that displayed her curves and a kerchief over her red hair, as was customary for women when they entered a church. Saro noticed that she looked forlorn. At that moment,

Ferdinando Licata passed by. Saro recognized him immediately and pointed him out to Agnes.

"See that man holding the little girl's hand? That's Prince Ferdinando Licata."

"I know who he is. Everyone here calls him Father."

"He's a friend of mine," Saro boasted. "He's from the same town as me, from Salemi. On the ship, he saved me from the brig, telling the officer I was his friend."

"He saved you from the brig? Can it be you're always in trouble?"

Saro smiled, and she planted a kiss on his mouth.

The atmosphere of the feast, the excited shouts of the crowd, the sweet sounds of the Sicilian dialect, brought back memories of his Salemi during the feast days of Saint Faustina: *tombola* in the piazza, the procession, the fireworks. The smiling faces of Stellina, Ester, and his beloved parents, Annachiara and Peppino, paraded before his eyes. And Mena. He missed them all and felt sad because he hadn't heard from them in quite some time.

Meanwhile, Ferdinando Licata and his grandniece were moving closer to the saint's shrine. There were still two more people in front of them.

Tom Bontade turned around and glanced at the fire escape again. The timing was right.

Vito Pizzuto's military field glasses were trained on Bontade. The boss couldn't see him, but he knew Pizzuto was watching him. A little farther down, Pizzuto spotted the unmistakable figure of Licata.

He murmured to the former sniper, "Do you have him?"

"He's mine," was the terse reply.

Vito Pizzuto focused the binoculars on Tom Bontade again, who had turned back to the statue. Next to his boss he also saw the unsuspecting Carmelo Vanni. No one except for him, Bontade, and Roy Boccia knew what was about to happen.

Boccia was the best in the business, both as an explosives expert and as a sniper. Placing the detonator in the saint's hollow head and the stick of dynamite in the statue had been a breeze. No one would ever have imagined an attack on Saint Ciro's statue.

Tom Bontade turned back to Pizzuto and nodded his head imperceptibly. It was the agreed-upon signal.

Bontade had withheld his decision of whether or not to make the strike until the last moment. In the end, he decided to go ahead with it.

By now there was only one person ahead of Licata and Ginevra. The prince picked up the child so she could reach the statue more easily. Their one-hundred-dollar bill had to be exposed, according to the rules, so Ginevra had to try to pin it to some surface that was still free. Finally, it was their turn. Licata held the little girl out toward the silver statue. Betty and Nico were watching the scene from several yards back. The people nearest to them saw the denomination of the bill and started clapping, followed by the hearty applause of everyone in the square. Cries of "*Evviva San Ciro!*"—"Long live Saint Ciro!" —rose again. Someone else shouted, "Long live the Father!" when suddenly the saint's head was struck a clean blow, and an instant later, an explosion ripped the statue's silver plating in two.

A burst of flame struck the people standing in front of the effigy. Ferdinando Licata, with Ginevra in his arms, was hurled a dozen yards back by the explosion's shock wave. Millions of splinters poured down like a rain of lacerating needles on those pressed around the statue. Screams and moans rose up to heaven, like a tragic Greek chorus. The crowd reeled, panic-stricken. After the first few moments of confusion, everyone started calling the names of their loved ones and running in all directions, trampling children and old people who had been knocked to the ground by the blast. Nico had instinctively thrown his arms around Betty to protect her, but then his mind flashed an image of his daughter leaning out toward the statue.

Many people were on the ground, their faces bloody. Recovered from the shock, Betty looked toward the altar and the saint's shrine: the place where she had last seen her daughter. But there was nothing there anymore except demolished platforms and some bills still fluttering through the air. The statue was now a shapeless lump of silver. When Betty began to realize what had happened, she screamed her daughter's name with every ounce of strength she had in her.

She raced to look for her among the weeping, suffering crowd.

Saro, who with Agnes had been a distance from the explosion, didn't run away like most people did, but ran toward the altar. Agnes huddled beside the tree and burst into tears, like many of those who had escaped injury. Reacting instinctively, Saro headed for the spot where he had last seen Isabel.

"Isabel! Isabel!" His cries joined those of other people wandering around frantically in search of relatives and friends.

He recognized the green dress. She was on the ground, still as a mannequin. He bent over her and lifted her up. Cradling her head gently in his arm, he brushed aside her thick red hair, charred by fire. To his horror, he saw that Isabel had been struck full-on by the flames and shards of silver. Her face was reduced to a pulp, oozing blood everywhere. She had been wounded in the chest as well.

Saro looked around desperately for someone who could lend a hand.

"Help! Help me!" he yelled to draw someone's attention. A man with his clothes in shreds heard him. He left a woman who was moaning a few feet away and came over.

"I'm a doctor," he said. Seeing Isabel's condition and not having his instruments with him, he placed his fingers on the artery of her neck. Then he shook his head and walked away to aid the other wounded.

Saro cried out, anguished. He pressed her tightly to his chest. "Isabel! My love . . . Isabel, don't die on me!"

Close by, Agnes heard Saro and went on crying, not only because of the tragic incident but because she knew she had lost the man she loved. Dazed and in shock, she wandered off.

Another cry rose from the center of the square. Betty had managed to recognize Ferdinando and the remains of little Ginevra. From a distance, Nico saw his wife throw herself on the ground, hysterically pounding her fists on the pavement. Frantic, he ran to her. He didn't dare look at the amorphous mass of blood, flesh, and shreds of clothing beside her, which must be what was left of his poor baby girl. He bent over Betty and hugged her, covering her with his body, as if to protect her from that horror.

Tom Bontade drifted through the square, offering comfort to those pleading for help. He tried to be seen by as many people as possible, hoping he would be remembered as the first to go to the aid of the injured.

Up above, on the fire escape of the building facing the statue, Roy Boccia disassembled the rifle and put it back in its case. Beside him, Vito Pizzuto took the time to observe the results of their plan, pleased with how things had gone.

Ferdinando Licata was lying on his back, his face mangled and bloody. His hands gripped tatters of the child's torn-off garment, while the rest of her little dress was impressed on Ginevra's charred skin, racked by the blaze and peppered with silver shards.

Betty frantically shook off her husband. She didn't know how to pick up the child, afraid to hurt her.

But Ginevra could no longer feel any pain.

A few minutes later, the first fire trucks arrived along with ambulances from nearby hospitals. The paramedics and physicians attended to the survivors first and then saw to the dead.

Caring hands removed Isabel's corpse from Saro's arms. They placed the young woman on a stretcher and then slid it into the morgue's black van.

Saro rose like an automaton, feeling drained of all volition. Not far away, he recognized Prince Ferdinando Licata from the bits and pieces of his clothing, and went over to him.

Two paramedics had laid a stretcher on the ground beside the prince. A fireman, with all the sensitivity required by the situation, tried to force Betty to move away from her child to allow the paramedics to see to her. But Betty struggled as hard as she could to stay where she was, becoming hysterical. One of the male nurses had to inject her with a sedative. In the meantime, his colleague gently gathered up the little bloody bundle of flesh and bones and placed it on the stretcher. He called a policeman over to help him, and together they carried the remains of the tiny body to the grim black van.

Only after they'd taken away the little girl did Saro realize that Ferdinando Licata was still alive, his eyes showing signs of movement. The prince seemed to want to speak to him. His state was appalling. The nose was gone, his mouth had become a hole, his skin was completely scorched. Saro bent down to him. Their eyes met and for a few seconds seemed to communicate intense emotion.

Pulling himself together, Saro shouted, "He's alive! Over here, quick! Doctor! He's alive!"

Two physicians were attending to an elderly lady. One of them left the woman, picked up the first aid kit from the ground, and ran over to him. He bent over Licata and immediately saw that there was no time to spare. "Quick, a stretcher! A stretcher and an ambulance!"

Two nurses came running from an ambulance with a stretcher. They laid him on it and brought him to the ambulance, which set off, siren screeching, for Columbus Hospital, on Thirty-Fourth Street.

Tom Bontade, the engineer of the slaughter, had been comforting a distraught woman in the center of the square when he saw Ferdinando Licata being loaded into an ambulance, not the morgue van, and realized in terror that the prince had not died in the explosion.

Chapter 43

The attack made a huge splash all across America. The Italian community was outraged that such a sacrilege had been committed. There could be no forgiveness for whoever had brought about such carnage. City authorities interpreted the act as a renewal of warfare among New York's Mafia families, and citizens clamored for an iron fist against the perpetrators.

Ten days after the attack, Ferdinando Licata was declared out of danger and transported to Bellevue Hospital. The explosion had completely destroyed his face, and he was bandaged up like a mummy. The only openings were holes for the eyes and a slit for his mouth, which he couldn't move.

In addition to his bandaged face, Ferdinando Licata's torso was in a cast due to the blow he'd received from the shock wave, which had hurled him onto the pavement. Ginevra's little body, absorbing the brunt of the explosion's force, had saved his life. The prince had sustained no internal injuries.

Four weeks later, he was able to speak and was permitted to receive visitors. One of the first to go and see him was Nico, Betty's husband. With a heavy heart, he told him about Ginevra. The little girl had been killed instantly, and the coroner, perhaps to lessen the pain of Nico's grief, had told him that she could not have been aware of anything. Ferdinando asked about Betty. Nico bowed his head. He found it difficult to speak. He told him at once that physically she was all right, she had not been injured. Her wounds lay elsewhere; the child's violent death had shattered her.

Ferdinando turned his head toward the window, so Nico couldn't see him. He knew his niece and her strong-willed nature. Betty didn't want to see her uncle. He had carried a curse from Sicily, an infection that doesn't spare anyone and mows down women, children, husbands, brothers, and fathers alike.

————

In the days following the attack, Jack Mastrangelo, acting on Licata's behalf, began moving into what had been the Stokers' territory, enlisting several Sicilians of proven loyalty. The prince had wanted them preferably from the Salemi area.

Mastrangelo spoke to the police commissioner conducting the investigation and got him to agree to place Ferdinando Licata under protection, since those who had planned the attack would surely try again to kill him. To reassure the public, the commissioner agreed to have Licata's hospital room placed under armed guard. Four policemen were assigned to protect the prince's life, each working six-hour shifts.

Ferdinando Licata's renown as a just and generous man skyrocketed. The tragedy that had struck his family earned him the compassion of the entire population of Little Italy and that of all Sicilians in America.

As soon as the prince was able to speak, Jack Mastrangelo went to Bellevue Hospital almost every day for new instructions from *u patri*. One afternoon, he was pleased to be able to bring the prince some good news. Mastrangelo sat down beside the bed. "I carried out all of your orders, *patri*. We're in command of the territory. No one put up the slightest resistance. The guys are on the ball and happy to work for you. They're impatient for some action."

"Well done, Jack, you did a good job." Ferdinando Licata spoke slowly to make himself understood, since his jaw was still partially obstructed by the bandage.

"Think about getting better, *patri*. Everything is under control out there."

Licata moved his hand on the sheet and touched Mastrangelo's arm. "I want Saro. It's time to talk to him."

"Okay, I'll bring him here as soon as possible."

In the weeks following the attack, the New York police department called all its available police officers back to duty. Leaves, vacations, medical visits, and business travel were suspended indefinitely. Surveillance in the district doubled, and numerous monitoring operations and searches were set in motion. There were weeks of intensive activity, with a constant flow of cars and vans carrying suspects and dubious characters to various police stations. But despite the extraordinary deployment of police officers, investigators were unable to identify the perpetrators and masterminds responsible for the Saint Ciro massacre.

The intense police activity was paralyzing the economic dealings of New York's crime families. Each day that passed meant countless dollars of lost revenue, while expenses continued to mount. Sante Genovese was furious with Tom Bontade. "Without saying a word to me, he goes and plans that fucking screwup!" he raged to anyone who went to see him. "If it weren't for my uncle who protects him, I would already have had him bumped off," he kept ranting. "An idiot like that will ruin us!"

Sante Genovese was afraid war would break out again between the old and new families, as it had in the twenties. Lucky Luciano's orders had been unconditional: any conflict between the families had to be evaluated and ruled upon by the top-ranking Cosa Nostra bosses; solutions adopted unilaterally were prohibited.

Sante knew that nobody would be able to stop Prince Ferdinando Licata. Sooner or later he would avenge the killing of his grandniece and his own attempted murder.

Tom Bontade's days were numbered, but how long would the blood feud last?

Sante Genovese had to put a stop to it at all costs. He had to reconcile them, no question. He had to get them to sit down at the negotiating table. Tom Bontade had to give Licata something to settle the score, and then everything could be resolved with a handshake.

If Bontade wouldn't agree to a truce with Licata, then Sante would threaten to tell Lucky Luciano everything, since he still held the power of life or death over the Cosa Nostra families, even though he'd been locked up for some years in a maximum security prison.

Jack Mastrangelo, as promised, brought Saro to the prince's bedside. Struggling to speak, *u patri* told Saro what he wanted from him. He knew he was a good kid and that he'd worked hard in America, though without much luck. He wanted to give him the chance he'd been missing until then. Saro would become the right-hand man to Mastrangelo, who would now become Licata's consigliori.

Mastrangelo was more astonished than Saro. He wasn't expecting that investiture from the prince. Him, consigliori! He didn't think he was worthy of the honor.

"You're the only person on earth whom I trust unreservedly," Licata told him. "I've seen how you work, and I've come to know you, Mastrangelo—or, rather, Jack. You have a few years on you by now; you can't keep being a maverick. It's time you settled down."

Mastrangelo didn't know what to say. The scars on his face trembled with emotion. Essentially that was what he'd always dreamed of: to be the consiglieri of a big boss. He didn't know if he should kiss the prince's hand in gratitude. He'd never done that in his life, and he didn't want to start now.

Licata seemed to read his mind and closed the subject: "It's all right, I understand." Then he turned back to Saro.

"As for you, I know there's a dark hole in your life."

Saro looked up and met the prince's eyes behind the bandages. Was it possible he knew about the Blue Lemon?

"Don't worry, you're among friends. We'll never betray you. Instead, you should thank Jack Mastrangelo for getting you out of trouble."

"What trouble?" Saro asked innocently.

"Poor girl. You went off like a maniac," Mastrangelo remarked.

So they knew everything, Saro thought, bowing his head.

"You battered them mercilessly," Mastrangelo went on undeterred.

"I don't remember anything about that night," the young man mumbled, trying to justify his actions.

"You were filled to the gills with alcohol."

"What happened?" asked Saro hesitantly.

"I was going to see one of Marta's coworkers; she has a room on the same floor. I heard the scuffle—or, rather, the bloodbath—the door was open. You were like a lioness who's had her cubs taken away. You wouldn't stop! Then you collapsed on the bed, nearly comatose. Marta was on the floor, and so was her client. So I picked you up, loaded you in the car, and dumped you far away from there."

"I can't thank you enough—"

"Don't worry, you'll have plenty of time to pay off your debt. You're one of us now; you heard what *u patri* said, right?"

"It's an honor for me."

"Okay, enough of these compliments; let's get to work," said the prince. "I've had word from Sante Genovese that Tom Bontade wants to talk to me."

To avert another war between the families, Sante Genovese had persuaded Tom Bontade, with arguments he could not ignore, to apologize to Ferdinando Licata for what had happened and to compensate him and his family for the loss of the child by giving him total control of the slot machine business.

At first Bontade refused to submit to Sante's insistent urging, but as soon as Genovese threatened to get Luciano involved, he quickly became more reasonable. He agreed to offer Licata an apology, but, he objected to handing over the slots, which seemed an excessively harsh punishment for his family.

They reached a compromise: Bontade would renounce his interests for two full years, and then he would be allowed back in, for a percentage to be decided with Licata.

Bontade had no choice but to accept the terms.

Sante Genovese told him that he would get in touch with Licata and establish the details of the peace offering. Genovese stressed that the interests of the families had to be upheld above all other considerations. "That fucking attack," he repeated again, "was a bad idea. It stirred up the police and paralyzed our business. And all for what?"

The reproach stung Tom Bontade more than the failure of the Saint Ciro attempt. Nevertheless, he had to agree to be completely amenable to anything that the *Cupola*, the top-ranking circle of Cosa Nostra bosses, might order him to do.

Chapter 44

Mike Genna, Sante Genovese's consigliori, was charged with setting up the meeting between representatives of the two families.

Since Ferdinando Licata was confined to bed, he would be represented by Jack Mastrangelo and Saro Ragusa. In keeping with Mafia rules, Tom Bontade, as a family boss, could negotiate only with someone of his own rank; therefore he would send Carmelo Vanni and Vincenzo Ciancianna to the meeting.

All week long, Genna ran back and forth from family to family, attempting to mediate and trying to pin down the fine points of the agreement. He had arranged for the meeting to be held in a restaurant in Greenwich Village, but at the last minute, Mastrangelo had it moved to La Tonnara, the trattoria owned by the parents of little Ginevra, who had been sacrificed by Bontade's senseless fury. It was a gesture of respect that the Bontades owed the Licata family.

Vanni reluctantly agreed to the demand, but he insisted that before entering, his men be allowed to search the place for any hidden guns.

When the evening chosen for the meeting arrived, Bontade's men, under the watchful eye of Mike Genna himself and members of Licata's team, began searching the trattoria.

Barret and Joe Cooper, who were Carmelo Vanni and Vincenzo Ciancianna's bodyguards, entered the place and carefully checked for possible hidden weapons, even searching the sole waiter.

After a good half hour of thorough probing, they agreed that the place was clean.

It was okay for Carmelo Vanni and Vincenzo Ciancianna to enter. They were frisked in turn by the two soldiers sent to protect Mastrangelo and Saro Ragusa: Lando Farinella and Bobby Mascellino.

Mike Genna invited the two groups to sit at a table that had been specially set for them. He took his place at the head of the table, while Jack Mastrangelo and Saro sat down to his right. To his left were Carmelo Vanni and Vincenzo Ciancianna, who, despite the others' dark faces, kept up a cheerful patter.

"So, what are we eating tonight?" Ciancianna began in an attempt to break the mood of uneasiness and suspicion, as he settled his impressive bulk in a chair.

The bodyguards stationed themselves behind the families' respective representatives.

Genna, taking the role of moderator seriously, began by saying, "Our thanks to our hosts this evening, Prince Licata's niece Betty and her husband Nico."

Mastrangelo interrupted to point out the woman's state of mind. "The *signora* has not gotten over the death of her daughter. Nevertheless, she's provided us with a cook and a waiter, so we would have everything we need."

"I remind you that the purpose of our meeting here is to resolve all the differences that may still divide your two families. I represent the Genoveses and thus indirectly Mr. Luciano. Please keep the tone within proper bounds," Genna advised patiently.

"And now let's eat," the jovial Ciancianna concluded with a hearty laugh.

Nico had prepared typical southern Italian dishes that could easily be reheated. The menu included lasagna, eggplant parmigiana, zucchini frittata with potatoes and prawns, and, finally, ricotta and spinach calzones. All accompanied by catarratto, a white wine with a bouquet of orange and prickly pear that recalled Sicily's beautiful lands.

The waiter brought the wine first. Mike Genna tasted it and then nodded for him to serve the others as well. Next came the lasagna, at which point Carmelo Vanni started unburdening himself.

"Tom Bontade sends word," he began, cutting a steaming wedge of lasagna, "that he is sincerely sorry for what happened at the feast of Saint Ciro."

Mastrangelo replied, "Prince Licata accepts Bontade's apology."

The script had to be performed through to the final lines. Everyone knew what he had to say and how the others would respond. Mike Genna had spent the previous week shuttling back and forth from one family to the other to calibrate the apology and pardon word for word. Nonetheless, the rules required the one who had done wrong to express his regret in a ritual that had been repeated almost identically for decades.

"Unfortunately, there was a mishap—a variable that was impossible to foresee," Carmelo Vanni went on. "We never would have thought that the prince would use his niece as a shield."

"Let me clarify," Mastrangelo broke in, his patience wearing thin already, "Prince Licata did not use his niece as a shield." Then addressing Mike Genna directly: "I would point out, Mr. Genna, that this was not supposed to be the spirit of this meeting. Is Vanni now insinuating that the prince is a coward and that he hid behind a little child? If those are his intentions, we won't listen to any more of it."

Genna stepped in, trying to tone things down: "Of course not, Mastrangelo, I'm sure they weren't Vanni's intentions. He just meant that there was an unforeseen circumstance, represented by his niece." Having said that, he spoke directly to Vanni: "Let's not digress. Say only what there is to say."

"I felt it was important to point out, though, that, if a mistake was made, it wasn't our fault," Vanni insisted.

Vincenzo Ciancianna looked up from his plate. Vanni's attitude was clearly confrontational.

"Carmelo Vanni, do I have to go on listening to your bullshit?" Mastrangelo set his fork down on the table, imitated by Saro.

Genna promptly intervened. "Gentlemen, let's calm down. Let's enjoy this fine meal, and let's stick to the subject. Go on, Vanni."

"Tom Bontade is sorry about the accident," Vanni continued solemnly.

Vincenzo Ciancianna relaxed and started in on his second portion of lasagna.

"He calls it an accident, does he?" Mastrangelo muttered sarcastically. "Let's call it what it was: murder. Let's say that Tom Bontade is sorry for killing a little seven-year-old girl!"

"That's it, enough! Stop it! We can't continue like this," Genna said heatedly, rising to his feet. "Let's go back to the reason why we're gathered here. I promised Sante Genovese I'd get you to make peace, and I'll do it even if I have to blow your goddamn brains out." The antagonists finally fell silent. Genna sat down again. "Let's go, Vanni. For the last time, let's hear Bontade's apology and his proposal."

"You got it," Vanni said quickly. "Bontade, as a testament to his good will and to put this *accident* behind us for good—"

"No way!" Mastrangelo exploded, turning to Mike Genna. "He's still fucking with us!"

With those words, his hand smacked the glass of wine, which went tumbling to the floor. It was the agreed-upon signal. Mastrangelo's guard Lando Farinella dashed to the wall where a fishing rope hung, grabbed it and yanked. Barret and Joe Cooper, Bontade's bodyguards, were focused on the glass, which cost them dearly. The large fishing net plunged from the ceiling, falling heavily over the table companions.

Saro and Mastrangelo had quickly sprung away from the table to avoid the trap. Mike Genna, Ciancianna, and Vanni, however, were caught by surprise. In the blink of an eye, Saro seized a harpoon from the wall, used for catching swordfish, and Mastrangelo grabbed an oar, while Barret and Joe Cooper were still trying to disentangle themselves from the net's heavy mesh.

Vincenzo Ciancianna instinctively leaned back, but the legs of his chair gave way, and he crashed to the floor.

Bobby Mascellino, Mastrangelo's other bodyguard, snatched a second harpoon from the wall, while Mastrangelo swung the oar and with its full force struck Carmelo Vanni's skull. Cooper, who by now had managed to free himself from the net, lunged at Mastrangelo with his bare hands. Saro raised the harpoon, ready to strike Cooper, who noticed it and swerved at the last moment. But Saro aimed again, hurling the barbed spear right through him. Without loosening his grip on the rope, Saro pulled on the harpoon to have it rip through the man's guts, but Cooper lunged sideways, seizing the spear with both hands, and knocking Saro to the floor.

Mastrangelo was quick to raise the oar and bring it down on Barret, who was still struggling under the net, and struck him with the sharp edge of the blade, smashing his skull and spattering the walls and floor with blood. Joe Cooper was still on his feet, trying hideously to pull the spear out of his chest, though obviously it was hopeless. He kept on with a strength born of desperation, releasing bits of gut along with blood. Saro, still on the ground, watched in horror.

Mike Genna had finally managed to disentangle himself from the net, beneath which only the moans of Vincenzo Ciancianna could be heard. Bobby Mascellino did not hesitate. Despite the fat man's innocuous nature, he threw the harpoon, aiming straight for the heart. A second later, Ciancianna lay still under the fishing net.

"What the fuck were you thinking?" Genna shouted, stunned by the slaughter. "This was all premeditated, right?" he yelled at Jack Mastrangelo.

"Blood for blood," Licata's man replied calmly. "The offense is avenged. Tell Genovese. Prince Licata is now at peace with himself and therefore with all those who want to be at peace with him."

"I'll tell him! But that's a hell of a way to act!" Genna was genuinely shaken. "You Sicilians sure are melodramatic! Was it really necessary to cause all this carnage?" Genna, careful not to step in the pools of blood, sidestepped Cooper—who was still staggering around the room, stunned, with the harpoon stuck in his stomach—and walked out of La Tonnara.

Cooper's agony went on a bit longer, but since they didn't have pistols or other firearms with them, they were forced to wait until he expired on his own. When he finally did, they breathed a sigh of relief and began cleaning the place up. Then they took care of getting rid of the four bodies, which disappeared at dawn in the concrete foundation of a new tenement building under construction in the Bronx.

Chapter 45

Shortly before Christmas 1939, the doctors at Bellevue Hospital performed delicate reconstructive surgery on Prince Licata's face, particularly the nose and mouth, 90 percent of whose surface had been destroyed.

The plastic surgery procedure was extremely complicated and the recovery time would be long, according to the physicians' prognosis. Ferdinando Licata asked to be moved to a secure hiding place, where he could spend the long period of convalescence surrounded by nature's greenery.

Jack Mastrangelo personally took care of finding a safe haven for him. He didn't tell anyone where it was, not even Saro. He thought it should be a place far from the East Coast, and preferably in another country. His own past led him to choose Vancouver, British Columbia, on the Pacific Ocean. Mastrangelo knew it well, having hidden there himself for two years a long time ago.

Once he had arranged for the prince's transport by plane, he rented a house at Sunset Beach. St. Paul's Hospital was just a short distance away, so the prince would be able to receive excellent medical treatment and have any further operations there if necessary. "The only thing you didn't find me was a girlfriend," the prince joked when they reached their destination.

Ferdinando Licata spent the entire next year and most of the following one there.

He passed his time listening to the radio and reading the newspapers. The prince was quick to grasp the importance of the media. He realized how crucial it would be to own a newspaper or at least enjoy the benevolent complicity of a sympathetic journalist. That was when he decided it was time to "stick an oar" in the world of journalism, as he told Mastrangelo and Saro.

He ordered his two lieutenants to approach a reporter from the *Sun* to "convince" him to be on their side. The *Sun* was the oldest and most influential newspaper in New York City, distributed on every street corner by an extensive network of newsboys. Until that time, most newspapers were circulated only by subscription, thanks to the perfect efficiency of the US mail. The *Sun*—not aimed exclusively at the business elite but also at clerks, laborers, and the general population—offered articles on local news along with tabloid sensationalism, thereby achieving great publishing success.

Promising to hand him some front-page news, Jack Mastrangelo approached an editor of the *Sun* and made him a tantalizing offer: promising to double his salary starting immediately. The young reporter, Luke Bogart, wasn't naive; he knew he was signing a promissory note, but how could he turn down a bundle of tax-free dollars?

Twenty-three months after the Saint Ciro attack, the surgeon removed the bandages from the prince's final operation and handed him an oval mirror. Licata observed his new features. Present at the ceremony, in addition to the surgeon and his assistant, were Licata's only two friends in America: Jack Mastrangelo and Saro Ragusa. The tension that had filled the room until then dissolved in a flash, because the prince then smiled.

"Well done, doctor. It's as if you gave me a second life. I'll have to call you dad."

The men smiled.

The surgeon was clearly pleased. "For me it is indeed an honor to be your friend—even more so your father." He turned and left the room.

Licata called Saro to his bedside. Mastrangelo stood back a few steps. They were now alone in the room of the Canadian hospital.

Ferdinando Licata took another look in the mirror. "A man who contemplates revenge must keep his wounds open."

"*Patri*, we have two bills to collect on," Mastrangelo reminded him.

Licata nodded. "It's time to cash in." Then he turned to Saro, looking directly into his eyes. "Jack has been watching you all these months, and he's told me that you work well together. You have the makings of a leader because you keep your head at critical times and quickly reach the right decision. At the same time, you're able to handle your men generously and without favoritism."

Saro was embarrassed by all that praise, feeling unworthy of it.

Licata got out of bed, took off his hospital gown, and, with Mastrangelo's help, began putting on the clothes he'd worn when he checked into St. Paul's Hospital.

"I'm furious at those butchers who kill women and children in cold blood," he said as he slipped on his silk shirt. "We'll sweep away all the rot defiling the streets of New York; we'll restore the old values of our forebears. War should be waged by soldiers, not civilians. As of today, anyone who lays a hand on a woman—or worse yet, a child—in our neighborhoods will be sorry he was ever born."

He sat on the chair to recoup his strength. "Here's what I have in mind." He motioned the two to come closer. "We'll operate on two fronts. The first is New York. And I'll handle it. We already control the Stokers' territory. The next step will be to eliminate the Bontades. By combining the two territories, we can be a real family, on a par with those that now dominate the city. The second front will be Sicily. And you, Saro, will deal with that."

Saro glanced at Mastrangelo, who remained impassively behind him. Licata noticed it. "Jack is one of us. He will remain our consigliori. I know him well, and he doesn't like to be conspicuous. Being in command doesn't interest him. But his experience will be invaluable to us. The three of us must act as one man. You'll pretend to be the boss, while I'll be the subordinate. I'll never appear openly. You'll be the one to give the orders, but I'll be the one calling the shots. Our adversaries mustn't know who's boss and who isn't. We must disorient them, and by the time they try to react, we will have already sidelined their best men. Now listen to me carefully. Here's the plan . . ."

———

The Clinton Correctional Facility, a maximum security prison nestled in one of the valleys of northern New York State, was considered the Siberia of penitentiaries in the United States. Residing in one of its cells since 1936 was Lucky Luciano, ever since lady luck had turned her back on him, as he put it.

Luciano's misfortune had a name: Thomas Edmund Dewey. He was the district attorney of the county of New York, a brilliant lawyer and esteemed politician, so well regarded that some years later he was nominated as the Republican candidate for president. Dewey was a moralist and the sworn enemy of every lawbreaker in the city. His fight against the Cosa Nostra was carried out not in the name of morality alone but also had utilitarian objectives. The stream of dollars produced by the Mafia had helped fatten labor unions, and from there a considerable number of Democratic politicians. If he could stop that flow of money, he would also dampen the Democrats' extravagant political campaigns.

Dewey had cut his political teeth in the United States District Court for the Southern District of New York, where he'd become familiar with the strategies of the rank and file. At the head of a seasoned group of assistant prosecutors, he had achieved significant results by putting gangsters such as Dutch Schultz out of play, and in Luciano's outfit, he'd sent Lepke Buchalter, the only foreigner in the family, to the electric chair.

But how to bring down Luciano and his organization? Thomas Dewey was familiar with the Mafia mentality. He knew that among Sicilians, the price of betrayal was death. He knew that he would never gather evidence against the kingpin as far as drugs were concerned. Except for his early years of apprenticeship, Lucky Luciano had never touched a packet of heroin or cocaine as an adult, in order to avoid having some informer point a finger at him. Dewey had an idea: women have a unique sensibility and way of thinking. For them, feelings take first place on the scale of values. *Omertà*, the code of silence connoting a sense of belonging and honor, has no meaning if a woman has been deceived, betrayed, or cheated. So he attacked the Cosa Nostra boss in the prostitution arena.

He began grilling the girls and madams in Lucky Luciano's stable. He accumulated volumes of testimony given more or less spontaneously. The girls all came from poor families. It wasn't easy to persuade them to testify against their employer, because almost all of them had been shamefully seduced by Luciano himself. The script was the same for each of them: A dinner of mock turtle soup, lobster, and champagne, and then an almond cake or a simple orangeade would send the candidate for whore into a dreamworld. When the girl awoke, she found herself in a brothel. There it was up to the madam to control her dream life. The rest was routine.

When Dewey was confident that he had assembled a powerful set of indictments and, above all, that the young prostitutes would not retract their testimonies in the presence of the "big boss," he snapped on the handcuffs and hauled Lucky Luciano into court. The man who was rumored to have killed dozens of enemies with his own hands would be brought up on the most paltry of charges: exploiting prostitution.

Thomas Dewey devised a legal strategy that caught George Morton Levy, Luciano's attorney, off guard.

The prosecutor treated each proceeding as a separate case. He called his first witness, a blonde Romanian woman whose presence suggested a glimpse of faded beauty. Ileana Romy stated that she had been the madam of a house.

"What do you mean by 'house'?" Dewey asked.

"A place where men who want to can meet prostitutes. I used to charge a dollar and a half a session for the use of the room."

"How many girls lived in the house?" the prosecutor continued.

"About a dozen in all."

"Can you tell us what happened on October tenth of last year?"

The woman was visibly nervous and kept looking over at Luciano, who by contrast never met her gaze, sitting motionless the whole time, as his lawyer had advised. "They were three Italian guys; I had never seen them before. They said Lucky wanted a percentage for the organization, otherwise he'd shut me down."

"And what did you answer?"

"That Lucky could shove it up his—I mean, that I had no intention of paying."

A few in the audience chuckled, and the judge restored silence.

"What happened then?"

"They returned the next day, and without even saying a word began scaring the clients and smashing the furniture. Then they beat up the girls and me."

"After these events, did you pay the organization?"

"There was no need to, because I had to close the business. They took away all the girls. I know they went to work for him." She pointed to Luciano who sat there, unmoving. "I went back to walking the streets, thanks to that gentleman."

The testimonies of the other women followed the same drift, more or less. Luciano's lawyer, Levy, wasn't worried because it added up to a mountain of allegations without any real legal construct. Allegations of crimes that were already beyond recall. Charges made by bona fide human wrecks; troubled girls who were a little batty due to the frequent use of drugs. But then a certain Cokey Flo Brown, a black girl barely twenty-two years old, was called to testify.

Dewey asked her right away, "What is your profession, Miss Brown?"

The girl wasted no time beating around the bush: "I'm a prostitute."

"Do you have a pimp?"

"Until two years ago I worked on my own—until a certain Nick showed up."

"Nick, who?"

"Nick Montana. Naturally, it wasn't he who came, but his henchmen."

"What did they ask you for?"

"What all the bosses ask for: I had to pay him a share of my earnings."

"And you agreed?"

"I had no choice. Montana's gang disfigured girls who refused, scarring them with acid. They came with the bottle, to show me."

"Was Montana part of Salvatore Luciano's racket?"

"Not on your life! He belonged to another family."

"What happened next?" Dewey was leading her smoothly. It was like watching a student recite her lessons.

"What happened," the woman said, looking toward Luciano, "was that after about four months, that guy over there came to my house."

"Your Honor, please have the record show that the witness has indicated the defendant Lucky Luciano," Dewey added.

"So ordered," the judge granted. "Have the record reflect the prosecutor's request," he told the stenographers.

"Go on, Miss Brown. Lucky Luciano came to your house, and what happened?"

Luciano looked up and was about to protest, but his lawyer gripped his jacket, forcing him to sit still.

"Luciano told me that starting that day, I had to pay the percentage to him personally. He told me not to be afraid of Montana because he had already settled things with him. He told me a pile of crap: that he was about to form a union to protect us; that it would be to my advantage to associate with him."

"What did you do after that? Did you personally hand over a portion of your earnings to the defendant Lucky Luciano?"

"That's right; personally and regularly, every month."

A buzz rose in the courtroom. Luciano, who until then had remained calmly detached and somewhat disdainful, lost his head and yelled that it was all a bunch of lies, that it was the first time he'd ever seen that woman, and that he had never taken so much as a dollar from a prostitute.

The police had a hard time restraining him. Five of them managed to bring him under control and drag him out of the courtroom. The photos that appeared in the newspapers deflated the myth of the cool, composed man capable of withstanding every storm.

The strategy devised by the district attorney paid off: when the verdict was read, the jury found Luciano guilty on no fewer than sixty-two counts of indictment.

The judge, in accordance with the jury's express will, ruled that just punishment for him could be no less than thirty years and no more than fifty. For once, truth had been upheld by lies: the deposition of Cokey Flo Brown had been engineered by the prosecutor himself. Dewey had spent days and days persuading her to help him. He had given her a lot of money to break down her defenses. Finally, Brown had agreed. It was a great deal of money and would enable her to start a new life elsewhere in the world. But then, two days before her testimony, fear of the Cosa Nostra's long arm, which could reach her even at the North Pole, made her think again, and she'd announced to Dewey that she was no longer willing to testify. The prosecutor had been devastated, realizing that all the statements given thus far would not be enough to convict Luciano. It took another $5,000 to make her reconsider her decision.

Insiders realized immediately that her entire testimony was an act of perjury. Anyone who has had any dealings with the Cosa Nostra knows that no *padrino* would ever compromise himself by acting as bagman and collecting from a prostitute. Least of all Lucky Luciano, the boss of bosses.

Dewey had played an empty hand, bluffing shamelessly. But fortune sometimes smiles on those who are daring.

Given the sentence, Lucky Luciano was out of commission forever, or so Dewey thought. He was sent in handcuffs to the Clinton Correctional Facility, the maximum security prison in Dannemora, New York. In 1936 Luciano was thirty-nine; if he behaved himself, he would be released before his sixty-ninth birthday.

———

Saro and Jack Mastrangelo had listened carefully to Ferdinando Licata's plan, marveling at his acumen. The plan was complex, but flawless in its details, even though it required a certain amount of luck. "But how can you achieve impossible goals without a dash of good fortune?" Licata asked.

In fact, the prince's strategy was extremely ambitious: ultimately its aim was to bring New York's prosecuting attorneys to the negotiating table with the Cosa Nostra bosses, specifically with the convict Lucky Luciano. Though such an undertaking seemed unthinkable, Licata had some aces up his sleeve.

Saro immediately got to work.

As previously decided, he would act the part of the boss, and in that capacity, he paid a visit to Sante Genovese, along with the inseparable Jack Mastrangelo.

Don Vitone's nephew Sante had been following the young man's activities. Welcoming him to his home, in the living room where Saro had first met him, Sante greeted him warmly, this time embracing and kissing him as if he were one of the family. He congratulated Saro, saying the young man had come a long way. Carmelo Vanni, the Bontades' deceased bagman, had shown good instincts when he recommended him. They talked about Lucky Luciano. By now he'd been rotting in that prison for six years. True, he enjoyed every comfort and was still able to run the Cosa Nostra's *Cupola*, its top-ranking bosses, buying off anyone who tried to oppose his decisions. But he was beginning to champ at the bit. Several times, through his friend Meyer Lansky, the Jewish gangster, Luciano had asked Genovese to find a way, on the up-and-up, to get him out of there.

Saro explained that he had come to solve that very problem. He proceeded to describe his plan to Sante in detail.

Following the Japanese bombing of Pearl Harbor in December of 1941, several months earlier, America had entered the war, not only against Japan but against Germany and Italy too.

It was a unique opportunity. And the Cosa Nostra bosses couldn't afford to miss that train. They had to take a chance and force New York prosecutor Thomas Dewey to come to an agreement about Lucky Luciano. But how?

Sante Genovese couldn't answer that question. "You want to kidnap the prosecutor and make an equal exchange? We thought of it, but it's too risky," Genovese concluded.

"No, no kidnapping. Luciano would be against that," Saro said.

"Then what is this brilliant idea?" Sante asked, intrigued.

"It's simple. We'll carry out various acts of sabotage at the Port of New York and on warships bound for Europe. We'll bring the war effort to its knees. We'll spread the rumor that the sabotage is the work of Nazifascist secret forces operating on American soil. We'll see to it that word reaches the ears of the military command that our organization, owing to Lucky Luciano, could neutralize those subversive groups. After all, everyone knows that the waterfront is in the hands of the Anastasia brothers, who are notoriously devoted to Luciano. At that point, Luciano will have to intervene personally. Once this happens, we'll ask the authorities to return the favor. That's the idea. We'll perform the acts of sabotage ourselves, after getting the all clear from the Anastasias. What do you say?"

What could Genovese say, except that it was worth a try? Just to be sure, however, he informed Luciano of Saro's plan, and the boss readily consented. He liked the idea that the Cosa Nostra could even have a hand in the war. Finally, he was beginning to see a glimmer of hope for his future release.

Chapter 46

H istory doesn't report it, and the few who knew about it may have forgotten, but there was a time during the winter of 1942 when residents of New York feared they would see invading Nazis, as well as Japanese troops, set up operations amid the trees of Central Park.

Throughout the city, but particularly along the docks, accidents and incidents of sabotage occurred that were attributed to the special forces of the Third Reich's secret service.

One of the first, most disturbing episodes occurred in the shipyards of Navy Pier 88.

For some weeks workers had been toiling to convert the French cruise ship the SS *Normandie* into a transport carrier for American troops.

The *Normandie* was the fastest transoceanic vessel at that time, able to complete the Le Havre–New York crossing in just four and a half days, thanks to a speed of over thirty knots. The *Normandie* had docked in New York on August 28, 1939, a few days before the Nazi invasion of Poland, and had been laid up in port since Europe went to war. Once the United States entered the war, the US Naval Command requisitioned the *Normandie* to convert it into a troop carrier. The vessel could transport up to twelve thousand combat-ready troops at a time, at a speed so fast it wouldn't even require an escort of torpedo boats. It was renamed the USS *Lafayette*.

On February 9, 1942, Saro Ragusa and his friends lingered at Petrosino's Café on West Fifty-Fourth Street near the Hudson River piers. Present at the table, besides Saro and Mastrangelo, were Carmine Mannino, Tommaso Sciacca, and Alex Pagano. Having done his military service in Friuli, Italy, with the fortifications unit of the US Corps of Engineers, Carmine Mannino knew all about mines and explosives in general. They had taught him how to bring down a bridge with only three charges and how to place active and passive obstacles in a given territory. Saro had accompanied him on his inspection during a twenty-minute walk along the pier, which had enabled Mannino to determine which locations the blast could damage most easily and thus where he should position the charges.

During lunch, they talked about everything except what they were about to do. Parked outside the restaurant was Saro's brand new Packard 120-C Touring sedan, its roomy trunk packed with sticks of dynamite. They were in high spirits and laughed each time Tommaso Sciacca, the group's clown, cracked a joke. They seemed like a group of old friends enjoying a get-together. Only Alex Pagano, the youngest of them all, was silent and gloomy. He had left his girlfriend back in the old country. His older friends told him, "Forget about Irene! Go lay some woman. Irene has probably already dumped you by now." But the more they insisted, the more angrily he vowed that Irene would never leave him because they really loved each other.

It was past two o'clock in the afternoon, and they had to get a move on because in thirty minutes the whistle would signal the end of the first shift at the port and the start of the next. It was the moment when they could blend in with the other workers. The shift supervisors had already been advised. If they spotted an unfamiliar face, they were to simply look the other way and not ask questions.

Saro urged his pals to speed it up. Carmine ordered another ice cream and ate it in the car, on their way to the port. The dynamite was inside three black leather bags. Carrying them, Carmine, Alex, and Tommaso looked more like three undertakers going to dissect a corpse than three dockworkers.

"You could have chosen three bags that were less noticeable," Mastrangelo criticized.

"I took the first ones I could find," Tommaso said in excuse.

"Go on, get going; there's the second whistle," Saro broke in.

Saro and Mastrangelo stayed in the car and waited for the three to go off and mingle with the other workers entering the shipyard of the former *Normandie*.

Once the charges and detonators had been placed, the three would have to leave the pier and get away using public transportation.

Around three in the afternoon, New Yorkers were still at work when, from the upper windows of skyscrapers, they saw a column of smoke rising from one of the docks at the port. In a flash, the news spread throughout the city: a fire had broken out on the *Lafayette*, the cruise ship that was being altered for troop transport.

Fire engines and ambulances raced to pier 88. From other docks along the port, pilot boats, tugs with water cannons, and tankers rushed toward the ship, which was now engulfed in flames.

The main fire originated in the center of the vessel, in the spacious first-class lounge. But it wasn't the only outbreak. Saro's men had done a skillful job, placing four explosive primers that would be triggered one after the other in four different areas of the ship, in such a way that the sabotage would be passed off as a simple short circuit. Since the ship had been in the process of being overhauled, it was quite plausible that some careless workman might have left an open flame or forgotten to turn off his soldering iron.

Over time the various commissions investigating the incident never reached a decisive conclusion on the cause of the blaze and the newspapers referred to it as an unfortunate accident.

Throughout the afternoon, rescue teams flooded the vessel with water and foaming agents. The result was that during the night between February 9 and 10, due to the weight of all the water used to extinguish the fire, the *Lafayette* slowly rolled over, coming to rest on its port side. The ship remained that way, with one side semisubmerged, until the end of the war—a grim testament to the lengths a Mafia organization would go to achieve its objectives.

Prince Licata's plan did not end with that first major show of force.

In late February, Saro, with the help of some explosives experts who had served in the Italian Army before fleeing to America, had thirteen Liberty merchant ships mined beneath the waterline. The ships were due to set sail for England, carrying troops and war equipment. As soon as the vessels left New York Harbor, they were shaken by thirteen explosions that split them in two and caused them to sink in just minutes. It was a mass execution for sailors and soldiers; only a few were rescued because no one had time to put on a life jacket. Eight hundred crewmen perished in the flames or were drowned.

An obsession with spies spread throughout the city. To stem the panic, the authorities were forced to take extremely unpopular measures. They sent thousands of Italian, German, and Japanese immigrants into internment camps, insisting that spies and saboteurs may have infiltrated those groups.

That did not solve the sabotage problem, however. In addition to the 71 merchant ships sunk in February 1942, another 49 were lost between

March and April, while in May no fewer than 102 Liberty ships were attacked by German U-boat submarines or sabotaged by the Mafia.

Naval officials were in a panic. The navy's chief of staff, Lieutenant
Commander Charles Radcliffe Haffenden, was no longer so sure that it
was German U-boats sinking the Liberty ships in US territorial waters.
In all those months, US Navy torpedo-boat destroyers had been able to
identify only one of them. It was possible, however, that the city was
swarming with Nazi saboteurs, or so they thought. But where had they
come from? When had they landed in America? Was it conceivable that
they couldn't be found? The few spies that the FBI had caught up until
that point had all been executed, after summary proceedings that were
well publicized in the newspapers and on the radio. Where were they
hiding, those covert forces that constantly defied surveillance and freely
held sway over the Port of New York?

The answer began to appear in the Navy Department's morning reports: those forces were the Mafia.

Commander Haffenden, with the help of New York City's new district attorney, Frank Hogan—the man who succeeded the cunning
Dewey in 1941 when he stepped down from the prosecutor's office to
become a candidate for governor—decided that it was time to engage in
direct discourse with the port's union bosses in order to get through to
the Cosa Nostra.

He never thought he would ever do or say such a thing in his life, but
the war effort took priority over any moralistic considerations.

———————

After the slaughter at La Tonnara, Tom Bontade had barricaded himself
in his house in Beechhurst, a residential area of Queens. He had lost his
most trusted men in the war with Ferdinando Licata. The only senior
men he had now were Vito Pizzuto and his henchman Roy Boccia. In
the last several months, Bontade had thought more than once of retir-
ing permanently from the business, but he didn't want to give in and let
the interlopers win. He had enough money to rebuild a team of soldiers
ready and willing to do anything he asked. But the problem wasn't in
finding a handful of violent individuals, for the city's streets were filled
with them. The thing hardest to come by these days was loyalty. For the
moment, the only man he could rely on besides Boccia was the Sicilian
from Salemi who'd been the last to join the family: Vito Pizzuto.

Pizzuto, for his part, was aware that he served a boss who was now getting by solely on his past. He still had control of the territory, but how long could he hold on to it if he was no longer seen in circulation? Pizzuto's only regret was that he had failed in his attempt on the prince's life. He had even tried to locate Licata's hiding place, to finish the job he'd started, but no one would help him. The fact that the prince hadn't been seen around after so long could mean that he'd managed to survive, but it could also mean that the explosion might have damaged his spinal cord, paralyzing him. If that were the case, then his power was actually hanging by a thread, and all Pizzuto had to do was sever it to seize control of what Licata had aggressively taken from Brian Stoker's family.

Vito Pizzuto was looking for a way to find out the truth about Licata. Everyone knew that the interests of the family were now controlled by Saro Ragusa, with Jack Mastrangelo as consigliori. The three men had formed a kind of invincible trinity.

Perhaps the weakest link in the chain was Mastrangelo. Little was known about him. He lived alone in a nondescript apartment in Bensonhurst. He had never been seen with a woman—though not with a man, either. He had no children. He was a silent type; you never saw him shooting the breeze just for the sake of talking. If he said something, it was always about the job and what had to be done.

Mastrangelo was difficult to approach and appeared to be extremely loyal to those who placed their trust in him. He had never fought for any family in particular, preferring to work as a free agent.

Among the families, he was rumored to have accumulated immense wealth over the years. Mastrangelo spent only the bare amount necessary to live. He didn't gamble, didn't do drugs, didn't visit whores. So not even money could be his weak point.

Roy Boccia, who was mulling over the situation with Bontade and Pizzuto, said, "You know something, Vito, I don't buy all this virtue. Every one of us has a hidden skeleton in the closet. We just need to find out what his is, and we'll have him in our grip."

Pizzuto nodded. And so they decided, on the spot, to dig up Jack Mastrangelo's secret.

For four whole weeks, Roy Boccia, alternating with seven other bloodhounds from the Bontade family, didn't let him out of his sight. Boccia, a real expert in this type of operation, had divided the men into five daily shifts. The first four were four hours each, with the last one ending at ten o'clock at night. The overnight shift started at ten and ended at six at the following morning. With such an undemanding schedule, they could go on for months that way.

Boccia knew from experience that once the second month rolled around, good news could come any day. So far, they'd accumulated a folder of reports a stack high, and Mastrangelo appeared to be the simple, unremarkable man that everyone described. But one day, a Sunday, Boccia's prediction came true.

That day, Ben Eleazar and Aldo Martini, two of the family's new recruits, were on duty. Eleazar was a Jew from Greece, and Martini came straight from Lombardy, near Milan. Jack Mastrangelo generally spent Sundays at home alone, stretched out on the couch listening to the radio or dozing. This Sunday, however, he got dressed and in the early afternoon drove off in his car. At first they thought he was headed to the airport, but he ended up in an exclusive area in Queens near the Whitestone Bridge. As Mastrangelo neared Francis Lewis Park, he slowed down, as if to make sure he wasn't being followed.

At some distance behind him, Ben Eleazar told the Italian at the wheel to slow down. Traffic was minimal, and it would be difficult to go unnoticed. The area, with its magnificent homes surrounded by trees and manicured gardens, was evidently a refuge for the city's upper middle class.

Ben and Aldo were excited at the prospect of having perhaps hit the jackpot. Boccia had promised a substantial cash bonus to whoever uncovered Mastrangelo's secret.

Jack Mastrangelo stopped in front of one of the most imposing edifices, with a massive three-story central portion and two-story wings extending in a semicircle at either side, like welcoming arms. A garden with abundant flower beds, exotic trees, and a broad drive lined by ancient oaks lent the grounds an air of classical restraint.

A few nuns were busy caring for the garden. The lawn was meticulously tended, and the walkways were bordered by perfectly trimmed hedges. Aldo Martini noticed a crucifix and the statue of a saint near the gate.

Mastrangelo parked the car, entered the garden, and walked down the oak-lined drive that led to the main entrance. The massive door opened, and a nun came out, greeting him with a polite smile.

They saw Mastrangelo disappear inside the institution.

"So that's his secret," Ben said.

"Could it be a son or a daughter?" Aldo Martini wondered.

It was neither. Aurora was Jack Mastrangelo's niece, the daughter of his sister, Elena, who had died thirteen years earlier, killed by her companion. Today was the girl's twenty-first birthday. Unfortunately, she was unable to celebrate with a carefree party like others her age. A form of catatonia had struck her thirteen years ago, when she witnessed her mother's murder.

The mother's boyfriend, a hopeless alcoholic, had been home alone with the girl. She was only eight at the time. When Elena came home after her shift at the factory, she caught him raping the girl. He had one hand over her mouth to keep her from screaming while he touched and abused her vilely with his other hand. At the sight of that appalling scene, Elena rushed at him and smashed a pot of basil over his head. The man fell to the ground, unconscious, as the woman desperately embraced the child, her protection too late. The man regained consciousness, however. His vision blurred by alcohol and the violent blow, he grabbed Elena by the neck and began tightening his grip, squeezing and jerking her brutally. The woman's only concern was for the little girl: she continued to try shielding her, but by holding the child, she couldn't defend herself. She died choked to death, her daughter gripped tightly in her arms. The girl kept shrieking, but by then her vocal cords were worn out, and only a muted sound came out of her mouth. The man felt the woman's legs go limp and let her go. Elena fell on top of the child, who had stopped screaming. She had also stopped struggling. Aurora had ceased to exist. The long nighttime of her mind began that day.

"Catatonia," the doctors pronounced. "It's a psychiatric syndrome characterized by motor, emotional, and behavioral abnormalities, which may stem from both physical and psychic pathologies."

That was the terse explanation they gave Mastrangelo. His sister's lover was accorded the judgment of partial insanity, because he had committed the crimes while under the influence of alcohol. He was sentenced to eight years. When he was released from prison five years ago, he tracked down the girl at the institution and phoned to pay her a visit. Mastrangelo was notified by the nuns, however, and intercepted him before he reached his destination.

The two scars marring Mastrangelo's face were a souvenir of their meeting. His sister's boyfriend was never heard from again.

Elena had always asked her brother to look after the child if something were to happen to her. It seemed like a premonition.

Mastrangelo had promised her at their mother's grave that he would never abandon Aurora, and that promise was for him an obsession.

He had willed all of his real estate holdings to his niece. And if something were to happen to him, the nuns, according to the will's instructions, would receive a handsome annuity to continue caring for her for as long as she lived.

Mastrangelo went to visit his niece every two or three months, but that Sunday was special. In the garden behind the institute, Mastrangelo approached the girl as she sat on a blue canvas chair.

Ben and Aldo were able to observe the scene from behind the massive wall.

"There," Aldo whispered, watching Mastrangelo bend down to give his niece a kiss on the cheek. "That's his weak point."

Chapter 47

A week after Aurora's twenty-first birthday, Jack Mastrangelo went out early one morning to meet with Saro. As usual, he stopped at the nearby Italian café to have breakfast and read the sports pages while sipping a cup of espresso.

As he was reading the New York *Daily Mirror*, Roy Boccia came in and sat down at his table. Mastrangelo lowered the newspaper and recognized the Bontade family's henchman. With great control, he raised the paper again.

"Boccia, you got the wrong table," he said, pretending to go on reading.

"You're just the man I was looking for, pal."

This time Mastrangelo folded the paper. "Are you tired of those Bontade clowns?"

"I came to offer you a deal."

"I don't do business with people like you." Mastrangelo took a sip of espresso, while the waitress poured coffee into Roy's cup.

Boccia waited until she had walked away. "This time I bet you'll make an exception. We need your help."

"What the hell are you thinking? All of New York knows who I'm working with. What do you want from me? I hate melodramatic gangsters."

"We want you to come over to our side."

Mastrangelo didn't bat an eye. He remained unfazed and continued speaking quietly. "You see, you ugly son of a bitch, the difference between you and me is that sewer rats of your kind run after cheese, no matter what kind it is, even if it stinks. I choose my cheese, and it has to be top quality."

"Too bad for you, pal, but this time you'll have to swallow whatever cheese we feed you, or else."

"Or else what?" Mastrangelo mocked.

With his usual twisted smile, Roy Boccia slipped his hand into his jacket pocket and pulled out a white card that he slid across the table, placing it under Jack's saucer.

Mastrangelo stared at it and had a terrible feeling. It was the back of a photograph. He reached out and turned it over.

The photo showed his niece, Aurora, in a setting that was certainly not the elegant establishment where she was supposed to be. Aurora had been photographed in a cellar, sitting on a chair. Behind her was a man, with an idiotic grin, caressing her thighs with both hands.

"It took a lot of effort for us to find her, but in the end it was worth it, don't you think? The boys can't wait to have a little fun. It's a rare experience, fucking a halfwit."

Mastrangelo slammed down his espresso cup, shattering it in his rage. He would have liked to crush Boccia's skull with his bare hands. "Bastard," he hissed. "You have no honor. No one has ever laid a finger on one of our women. If you so much as touch a hair on her head, I won't rest until you beg me to kill you. You have no idea what I'm capable of."

"Easy, Jack. We know you care about your niece. That's why no one will hurt her. But it all depends on you."

"What do you want?" Mastrangelo roared.

"Nothing impossible. You just have to bring Ferdinando Licata and Saro Ragusa to us at a place we'll tell you."

"When?"

"All in good time, Jack. But meanwhile, you mustn't let them find out. Otherwise your little niece—what's her name, Aurora? Well, Aurora might suffer some physical injury."

"Boccia, I'm telling you again, you better not touch her."

"Or what?" the mobster challenged.

Mastrangelo strode out of the place, leaving Roy Boccia to ponder the hazards of going up against someone like him.

Tom Bontade now had Licata and Saro Ragusa in his grip. Together with Roy Boccia, Jack Mastrangelo devised a plan that he carried out a few days later.

Mastrangelo would inform Prince Licata of the arrival of a large quantity of plasma and medical supplies earmarked for the war in Europe. The containers of plasma for transfusions were at one of the docks in Red Hook, Brooklyn, in warehouse 82, waiting to be shipped out on the next Liberty ship departing for Great Britain. If they acted quickly, the goods could be diverted to a different destination. Saro would have to deal directly with the chief cargo agent, who would personally see to replacing the containers with a shipment of unfinished leather that had been left in the warehouse for over two months. A mix-up of consignments was more than plausible, and when the hospital staffs went to open the containers expecting to find plasma, they would have the unpleasant surprise of discovering tons of smelly skins. It would be impossible to trace the original shipment, particularly since the agent would make sure that the bill of lading disappeared.

Saro and his men were supposed to show up at the dock the following night with no less than $12,000. The batch of plasma was worth at least ten times that. Licata consented to the deal, and on the night set for the exchange, Saro Ragusa went to the designated dock.

He was accompanied by Jack Mastrangelo and Carmine Mannino. Saro would get there first to verify the goods, then Ferdinando Licata would come with the money. This way, they would avoid any surprises.

The warehouse was shrouded in darkness. With extreme caution, Saro, Mastrangelo, and Mannino entered and started walking toward the center. Mountains of jute bales and wooden crates were piled up along the walls. Lit by a ray of moonlight, they saw someone in the middle of the warehouse, waiting for them. It wasn't a familiar face. Hidden among the bales were Roy Boccia, Vito Pizzuto, and three of their men: Angelo Bivona, Fabio Zummo, and Salvatore Di Giovanni.

Saro went up to Ben Eleazar, while Jack Mastrangelo and Carmine Mannino stayed a few steps behind.

"You're empty-handed," said the man who'd been waiting for them.

"I have to check that everything is okay. My boss is nearby. When I give him the signal, he'll arrive with the dough. If everything is okay, you have nothing to worry about. Are the others hiding?" Saro asked, looking around.

"If you've complied with the terms, you have nothing to fear," Ben told him.

"Okay. Where's the merchandise?"

"Follow me." Ben went to a stack of pallets loaded with cartons. "Drugs and Plasma" was written on all the boxes in large letters. He turned to Saro.

"Here are the fifty pallets. Which one do you want to check?"

Saro pointed at random to a half-hidden container. Ben pulled down the carton Saro had chosen and pushed it toward his feet. Saro broke open the box and verified that the bottles of straw-colored liquid were inside. The labels plainly indicated that it was plasma.

Saro signaled to Mastrangelo that everything was in order. Mastrangelo left the warehouse and lit a windproof match, waving it over his head.

"Now you can bring your friends out," Saro said.

"All in good time. First we see the money." Ben Eleazar knew he was convincing in bargaining talks; that's why Tom Bontade had chosen him to conduct this delicate negotiation.

The imposing figure of Prince Ferdinando Licata appeared, silhouetted against the warehouse's sliding door. He had a leather bag in his hand, similar to a doctor's bag.

"Don't move, *patri*!" Saro yelled. Then he turned to Eleazar. "Okay, friend. Either you bring out your gorillas, or this meeting ends here."

"Easy, everything's okay! We just wanted to be sure you hadn't called in the cops. Okay, guys. You can come out."

As agreed, only Angelo Bivona and Fabio Zummo came out of their hiding places. Both appeared unarmed.

Seemingly reassured, Prince Licata marched into the warehouse with long strides, heading toward Saro and Ben Eleazar.

Mastrangelo and Mannino let the prince pass, remaining in their places a few yards away from the hangar's sliding door.

When the prince reached Saro and Eleazar, he handed them the bag, saying, "Here it is." Ben grabbed the leather bag and stepped back.

A voice resounded behind him. "We're not here for the dough."

Vito Pizzuto emerged from a crate behind Ben. At the same instant, Roy Boccia and Salvatore Di Giovanni sprang out from behind some bales of jute, to the rear of the prince, pointing two Thompson guns at him. Angelo Bivona and Fabio Zummo grabbed the magnums from under their jackets and leveled them at Mastrangelo and Mannino. The two put their hands up, as did Saro Ragusa. Only Licata kept his hands down.

"I'm sorry, Prince, but Tom Bontade sends word that one of you is one too many here in New York."

"Pizzuto, Pizzuto, you've been looking for trouble ever since I've known you," the prince replied disinterestedly, as if the situation had nothing to do with him.

"Licata, we're not in the old country here, among peasants. You should adapt to the times." Staring at Licata, Vito Pizzuto saw a cool, cunning look in his eyes. "These street sweepers replaced sawed-off shotguns years ago here."

"*Comparuzzo mio*, my dear friend," Licata addressed him in a tone dripping irony," your ancestors taught us everything we need to know. You'll see, old sawed-off shotguns are irreplaceable when it comes to certain jobs."

Meanwhile, Angelo Bivona and Fabio Zummo had moved close to Ben, keeping the men with their hands up in their sights.

Vito Pizzuto ordered Ben, "Cuff them."

Ben handed the leather bag to Fabio Zummo, but at that instant Vito Pizzuto noticed the prince's eyes flash.

"Wait," Pizzuto drew his Colt and worriedly said to Zummo: "Check that the money is in there."

Zummo fumbled with the bag's clasp. Finally, he managed to release it.

If Vito Pizzuto had been an attentive observer, and if the other men hadn't spent too many years away from Sicily, they would have realized that a family boss would never personally carry a bag full of money. The fact that Prince Ferdinando Licata brought the cash for the deal could only mean two things: either there wasn't so much as a dollar in the bag, or it was bait for a trap.

As soon as Zummo snapped open the clasp to show his boss the bundles of money, a primer triggered a detonator that in turn exploded two sticks of dynamite.

Licata, Saro, Mastrangelo, and Mannino dropped to the ground, shielding their heads with their arms. The blast blew away Fabio Zummo and Angelo Bivona, who was standing beside him. Ben Eleazar was saved from the burst of flame thanks to Bivona's body, which shielded him, but the subsequent shock wave flung him against the sacks of jute, knocking him unconscious for several minutes.

A moment after the explosion, the men Licata had stationed outside burst into the warehouse: Lando Farinella and Bobby Mascellino. They rushed in through the sliding door, through which the prince himself had entered. Meanwhile, Tommaso Sciacca and Alex Pagano came charging through the back door. The four men were armed with shotguns, Colts, and Berettas. They blasted away at Vito Pizzuto, Roy Boccia, and Salvatore Di Giovanni. The fire was so intense and they were so taken aback that Di Giovanni surrendered immediately, but one last shotgun blast hit him squarely in the chest after he'd already put up his hands. In the confusion, Roy Boccia was able to escape from the warehouse. Ben was lying next to the bale of jute, still unconscious, while Vito Pizzuto was hiding, crouched behind a pile of crates, where Alex and Tommy found him.

Mastrangelo raced out to find Boccia. But after looking everywhere, he had to admit sadly that the man had managed to get away. Mastrangelo returned to the warehouse. Now his niece was really in danger. Their plan had only been half successful.

Pizzuto was dragged before Licata. He knew he still had a few more cards to play and was disdainful. "You thought you were smart, right Mastrangelo? Now what are you going to tell your little Aurora? Aldo Martini specializes in sexual sadism."

"Tell me where you've got her!" Mastrangelo shouted.

"You'll have to torture me, but it will still be too late to get her back untouched."

Mastrangelo punched him repeatedly in the face, bloodying his nose. Licata motioned to Tommy to stop him. Then he ordered them to tie Vito Pizzuto to the chain of the cargo winch.

Mastrangelo went over to Ben, who was still in shock following the explosion. "Where did you hide her?"

Ben shook his head. "You should have thought of that before. Now it's too late; you can't save her."

Tommy and Alex made Vito Pizzuto hold out his arms and tied them to an iron pipe so that he couldn't bend them anymore. Then they hooked the cargo winch's chain to the ends of the cable and slowly hoisted the man until the tips of his shoes cleared the ground.

Vito Pizzuto grew serious. "You don't scare me, Licata. Bontade will give you a dose of your own medicine."

Licata paid no attention to him. He focused on Ben Eleazar, an individual whose calling was not to become a hero. The prince was counting on that. "It will all be over soon, Ben. But it depends on you."

"I won't talk, you bastards!" Eleazar spat out as Tommy and Alex tied him up like Pizzuto.

"You don't have to talk right away—but in a little while. First you'll see what we have in store for your friend. At least afterward, if you decide not to cooperate, you'll know what to expect."

The two ends of the chains of the second lift were hooked to the pipe to which Ben had been tied. Tommy hoisted him just enough so that his feet came off the ground.

Ben Eleazar and Vito Pizzuto now swayed side by side in the middle of the warehouse, both with arms outstretched, looking like two men sentenced to be crucified.

Licata asked Farinella, "Lando, did you bring the box?" Then he went over to Pizzuto. "I want to see the terror in your eyes. It will remind me of all your pathetic crimes."

Farinella soon returned with a cardboard box. Licata pulled a pair of leather gloves from his jacket pocket and put them on, deliberately taking his time.

Ben looked from Licata to Vito Pizzuto to the mysterious box and was genuinely worried.

Licata rose on tiptoe and whispered something in Pizzuto's ear. The man then began struggling and kicking, swinging the chains that held him suspended. Tommy and Alex held his legs still.

Licata opened the cardboard box. Meanwhile, Saro came back with some duct tape. He cut off one piece to gag Ben Eleazar. Then he got another piece ready for Pizzuto.

Ferdinando Licata put his hand in the box and caught one of two rats that were madly scrambling for a way out.

Vito Pizzuto, terrified by what the prince had whispered in his ear, began screaming. Licata took advantage of his open mouth and stuffed the rat down his throat. Pizzuto's scream turned into a grunt. Three of them couldn't hold him still. Tommy and Alex pinned down his legs, while Saro began binding his mouth with the duct tape. Pizzuto snorted, his eyes bulging with the effort to eject the animal writhing in his mouth. Blood began trickling from his nose. The rat's long tail hung out below the tape, whipping the air frantically. Ben Eleazar was more horrified than his pal who was being tortured.

"Take a good look," the prince said to Eleazar. "In a little while, it will be your turn." Vito Pizzuto was making sounds that had nothing human about them. He thrashed about as if he were having convulsions. Licata ordered the men to let go of him. The body jerked as if struck by a lightning bolt. The unfortunate victim continued writhing like a man possessed, then they all watched with horror as the tail disappeared into the mouth and the neck swelled as the animal passed through the windpipe and on down to the stomach. Blood flowed from Pizzuto's ears, eyeballs, and even the lower parts of his body, soiling his pants. Several more very long minutes of agony went by until he finally died.

Saro stepped up to Ben Eleazar who was about to faint and removed the duct tape from his mouth. All he had the strength to gasp was, "She's in a safe house in Greenpoint. On Nassau Avenue. It's the truth, I swear."

As they were untying him, police sirens could be heard in the distance. Something they hadn't expected.

Mastrangelo took off with Carmine Mannino and Alex Pagano, dragging Ben Eleazar along with them.

Ferdinando Licata took another way out with Tommy Sciacca, Lando Farinella, and Bobby Mascellino. Saro, meanwhile, took care of planting dynamite in the car that Vito Pizzuto had driven in to come to the meeting. He wanted to leave evidence for the police that the explosions at the port and on the Liberty ships were the Mafia's doing—in particular the Bontade family, and not the work of subversive pro-Nazi cells.

Saro just had time to close the trunk of the car and sprint away from the warehouse, heading for Commerce Street. But police cars coming down Van Brunt Street spotted him and cut him off, pointing a wall of guns at him. Saro put his hands up, with the expression of a peeping Tom who's been caught ogling the girls in a public bathroom.

Fortunately for him, he was many blocks away from the warehouse where Pizzuto's tortured corpse was later found.

No one would be able to incriminate him, except for Roy Boccia and Ben Eleazar. But neither Boccia nor Eleazar would ever testify against him because they knew that sooner or later they would wind up in the Hudson River with their feet stuck in a bucket of cement.

Ferdinando Licata's savagery and extreme brutality, concealed beneath his refined, magnanimous ways, became legend—not only among New York's families but also along the East Coast.

Chapter 48

Once he'd realized that they had fallen into a trap, Roy Boccia had taken advantage of the confusion to beat it out the back door of the warehouse. He had to reach Aldo Martini right away, to tell him to get the girl out of Greenpoint; it was no longer a safe hideaway. But first he had to inform Tom Bontade.

Roy Boccia knew that Aurora was his life insurance. As long as she was their prisoner, Mastrangelo and the other family members would never risk putting her in jeopardy by attempting anything reckless.

Alex Pagano, driving the Lincoln, was speeding toward Greenpoint. On the seat beside him was Jack Mastrangelo, while Carmine Mannino sat in back with Ben Eleazar.

When they reached Nassau Avenue, Eleazar told them to keep going, almost until Lorimer Street. At 59 Nassau Avenue, he told him to stop. The hideout was in a two-story red-brick building in a state of total neglect. A fire had destroyed it the year before, and the walls were still charred. While waiting to be demolished, it had become a temporary shelter for bums and delinquents. The place where Aurora was kept, Ben told them, was in the basement.

Jack Mastrangelo jumped out of the car with Alex Pagano. Carmine Mannino took out a pair of handcuffs and fastened one end on Eleazar's wrist and the other to a hook specially welded to the floor of the Lincoln near the drive shaft. He closed the doors and locked them, and then followed Mastrangelo and Alex, who had already disappeared behind the partly open door.

The hallway was impassable. Piles of masonry debris, stacked up boards, and jumbles of electrical cables blocked the way to the staircase leading to the basement. Mastrangelo decided to go in through the back door. There the destruction caused by the fire was less visible. Followed by his two companions, Mastrangelo headed for the stairs. He had drawn his Colt and was alert to every sound coming from the building's dark corridors.

He heard voices and saw the gleam of a flame illuminate the shadows at the end of the hall. He signaled the others to watch out. Alex and Carmine had also drawn their automatics. They flanked him, and the three advanced slowly.

Now the voices were distinct. Mastrangelo was ready to jump out into the open. He motioned the others to cover him, and then sprang around the corner of the hallway, yelling "Don't move!" At the same time, Carmine and Alex dropped to the ground with guns drawn. But the scene that met their eyes was not what they expected: two vagrants were boiling water for coffee over a fire that they had made with some wooden slats. In a corner of their makeshift shelter were the remains of two mattresses and a water bucket. On the ground Mastrangelo noticed a small link chain. The bums were frightened by the sudden raid, but then, reassured by Mastrangelo that they weren't cops, they went back to what they were doing. The one with the white hair and beard took the pot of hot water off the fire and set it on a wooden box. Then he opened the lid and poured in some coffee powder. Meanwhile, the other man rigged up a couple of improvised stools. The older man sat down and began stirring the mixture with a chopstick. Mastrangelo went over to him.

"Sorry, buddy, but we only have two cups of the good china," the elderly vagrant said with a trace of irony.

Mastrangelo ignored it. "Was there a girl here?"

"A lot of them come by: Miss America, Miss Florida, Miss Give-it-to-me." It was clear the man enjoyed teasing.

"I'll repeat the question just one more time, then—"

But Mastrangelo was interrupted by the other bum. "Yeah, there was a girl, and she was taken away about twenty minutes ago. There were two men with her."

———

Roy Boccia had managed to whisk away Aurora a few minutes before Mastrangelo and the others got there.

He'd had just enough time to call Bontade and ask him for instructions. Bontade thought it wiser not to keep trying to intimidate Mastrangelo. The guy had revealed the extortion to Licata despite the threats against his niece, seriously endangering the girl's life. He thought it was more expedient to continue holding her as a hostage to keep Mastrangelo's anger in check.

But since they didn't have another hiding place lined up, Bontade told him to bring her to his house, at least until they were able to come up with a better arrangement.

When police cruisers surrounded warehouse 82, all they found was a car parked not far from the site of the shooting. The cops ascertained that the car belonged to Roy Boccia, a member of Tom Bontade's family. The trunk was ajar, and inside they found a large quantity of explosives. The bomb squad was immediately called, and the police commissioner alerted the New York County District Attorney's Office.

When Frank Hogan arrived at the scene, police agents had already discovered Vito Pizzuto's tortured body. Hogan was led inside the warehouse and could see what the poor guy had gone through. Even someone like the district attorney, accustomed to violence, was horrified by such cruelty.

Hogan issued a warrant for the arrest of Roy Boccia: he would have some explaining to do about the presence of dynamite in the trunk of his car. Hogan concluded that perhaps the Bontades were responsible for the attacks at the port.

It was all coming together just as Licata had hoped.

Hogan was asked to open a channel of communication with one of the big shots in the syndicate to ultimately reach the families that "governed" the waterfront, in order to resolve the issue of sabotage.

Frank Hogan had learned of the arrest of Saro Ragusa, a young Sicilian who his informants indicated was the head of the family that had replaced the Stokers gang on the Lower East Side.

Saro had been arrested not far from warehouse 82, where Vito Pizzuto had met his atrocious end. But there was no evidence against him that could connect him to that murder.

Hogan decided to question Saro, perhaps with the remote hope of being able to establish a direct line to the families who threw their weight around the port. It had been Charles Haffenden, commander of the B-3 Naval Intelligence Unit, who led him onto that track, with the idea that the Italian Mafia could be responsible for the attacks. Haffenden, called back to duty when the war broke out, had circulated information throughout the port area. Although Haffenden had been one of the first to realize that the explosions on the *Normandie* might have been caused by the Italian Mafia, no one wanted to consider that theory. The idea of sabotage perpetrated by Nazi-fascist spies was more plausible and reassuring.

So when District Attorney Hogan decided to interrogate Saro Ragusa, he also summoned Haffenden, and the commander of the B-3 willingly accepted the invitation, hoping to be able to corroborate the information reported by his agents.

"The car with the dynamite belongs to a certain Roy Boccia. There's no record on this Boccia in our files," Hogan told Haffenden.

"Was Boccia the bodyguard of the man who was killed?" Haffenden inquired.

"Right. They ran into a trap, but he managed to get away," Hogan said. "I put the places he frequents under surveillance, including Bontade's house."

Saro's struggles for survival in the American metropolis had matured him fast. By now the shy, insecure young man, timid with women, was a past memory. His rise in the underworld had been meteoric. He was now spoken of with respect and was considered one of the few of the new generation worthy to sit with the assembly of family bosses.

Saro, locked up in a holding cell, was informed that the district attorney and the commander of the B-3 Naval Intelligence Unit had come to see him. He figured that a visit by those two in full regalia had to be the result of Prince Licata's plan.

Commander Haffenden came straight to the point. He told Saro that they wanted to engage in a collaborative effort with the Italian families willing to give them a hand against the saboteurs operating at the port. The United States was at war, and any alliance was appropriate in order to defeat Nazi brutality. They asked Saro if he could provide them with union cards so they could place intelligence agents of the third district on board the trawlers. Plus they wanted to be informed of any suspicious activity, such as unusual fuel and provisions purchases, since they suspected that enemy submarines approaching the American coast were resupplied by support vessels operating in the area. In short, they wanted to put a stop to the acts of sabotage that were defeating the plan to furnish military aid to Great Britain.

Saro replied that there was only one person powerful enough to authorize such a collaboration, and it certainly wasn't him. It was Lucky Luciano.

Although he had now been imprisoned for six years in Dannemora, Luciano continued to direct and control the syndicate. He was the one they had to speak to.

———

That first meeting with Saro in a holding cell at the police precinct in Manhattan was followed by many others that took place instead at Haffenden's private office, in a suite at the Hotel Astor on Broadway. District Attorney Frank Hogan gave the green light to deal with Lucky Luciano but offered the commander a word of caution: he advised him not to contact the gangster directly, but to do so through his defense attorney, a Russian Jew by the name of Moses Polakoff.

Commander Haffenden followed the prosecutor's advice and summoned Polakoff to the Hotel Astor. As was his way, he came straight to the point and told him plainly that Luciano should not expect a sentence reduction or a retrial in exchange for his help. They were relying solely on his patriotism as a recent American citizen, not realizing that Lucky Luciano, unlike his relatives, had never applied for American citizenship.

———

Luciano's closest accomplice was also his best friend: the Jewish gangster Meyer Lansky. Polakoff sent for him as well as Saro Ragusa, who had been released for lack of evidence against him.

The three met at Longchamps restaurant on West Fifty-Eighth Street to discuss whether to give a thumbs-up to the authorities' request. Lansky was the most hesitant because he didn't want to give his friend Lucky any false hope. But Saro was able to convince him that it was the only way to go if they wanted Luciano to be released. Polakoff asked him how he could be so sure, given that Haffenden himself had told him that Luciano's help would not lead to any immediate payback.

Saro disclosed that, on the contrary, Frank Hogan had assured him that, when the time was right, the DA's office would take Luciano's help into account—provided that the acts of sabotage were stopped.

A few hours later, Saro reported the outcome of the meeting to Licata: he had managed to convince Lansky that any help Luciano gave the military authorities could not be considered "collaborating with the police." It was a matter of stopping acts of sabotage against the American armed forces.

Licata smiled. The plan was working perfectly. But they had to proceed step by step.

"We'll get Luciano released from Dannemora with our next move," the prince declared.

Saro contacted the attorney Polakoff again and told him to ask Haffenden if they could resume talks.

Meanwhile, forty-nine freighters had been sunk in April 1942 alone. While the public and the press believed that U-boats were the major cause of those disasters, in reality most of the sabotage was the work of the Cosa Nostra's covert teams.

Polakoff, meeting Haffenden in his office at the Hotel Astor, argued that it wouldn't be a good idea for him and his associates to show up at a maximum security prison like Dannemora. The guards would notice the irregularity. Therefore, he requested that Lucky Luciano be transferred to a less restrictive prison.

Haffenden relayed Polakoff's request to Frank Hogan, who agreed to it.

The Great Meadow Correctional Facility in Comstock, near Albany, was chosen. Lucky Luciano's transfer was carried out with the utmost secrecy on May 12, 1942. Three days later, Saro, attorney Polakoff, and Meyer Lansky were finally able to meet with the Cosa Nostra's capo.

Saro Ragusa was introduced to the boss by Lansky himself. Shaking hands with Lucky Luciano crowned Saro's ascent into the firmament of the Mafia.

Luciano shook his hand vigorously, as he usually did. "You're sharp, kid," he said. "They told me this was your idea."

Saro smiled at him. "Well, let's say someone inspired me. But yes, the idea of sabotaging the *Normandie* and the other convoys came from me." Licata had insisted that his name not yet be revealed.

Luciano then gave the go-ahead for an antisabotage operation.

From that day on, men from New York's families patrolled every inch of the docks at the city's ports. Extended strikes that would have caused a slowdown in the transport of military aid to Great Britain were averted. A cell of Greek Nazi-fascist saboteurs was stopped and charged with supplying fuel and provisions to German U-boats. Eight other real Nazi saboteurs of German origin were captured as they were coming ashore in Long Island.

All in all, following Luciano's orders, the sinking of Liberty ships and the acts of sabotage on the docks ceased completely in just a few weeks.

It was considered a great victory for the Cosa Nostra families because for the first time the organization had been officially recognized by the establishment—in particular, by the New York County District Attorney's Office.

Chapter 49

Aurora lay on a mattress thrown on the floor in the basement of Tom Bonrade's house. The cellar was lit by several narrow windows, which afforded a glimpse of part of the garden surrounding the house.

In her confused mind, Aurora was trying to make sense of the situation she was in, but only off and on was she able to distinguish good actions from those that involved some violence toward her. By now the happy moments were lost in the darkness of memory. Her life consisted only of unpleasant sensations that made her fearful and caused her throat to tighten in panic. But she couldn't express those feelings in any way. She knew she was imprisoned in a body that did not respond to her mental impulses. A body that had now become alien to her and that she would have gladly shed. Now and then she remembered the "good" times, associated with the funny man with the scars on his face who came to visit her and brought her flowers or chocolates. They were unforgettable moments. But what was she doing in that dark room now? Everyone had forgotten her. That man no longer came to bring her chocolates . . . *Aurora is all alone . . . Aurora is all alone . . . Aurora is all alone . . .* She repeated those words endlessly, then suddenly, as if miraculously, a tear fell from her eyes and rolled down her pale cheek.

After so many years, it was the first sign that Aurora was regaining consciousness. Unfortunately no one was there to witness it.

Meanwhile, upstairs they were arguing about her fate.

Roy Boccia was now wondering whether they should get rid of her as soon as possible.

Tom Bonrade, more wisely, believed that they should use the young woman to hold off Mastrangelo and his hounds instead.

"We could exact a peace agreement with them, in exchange for the return of the girl," the old family boss concluded.

"They're treacherous as rattlesnakes," Boccia contended. "We already landed in a trap once before, when Genovese himself demanded a truce between us. You know how that turned out. How can you still trust them?"

"I don't want to end up like the Stokers. I don't want to have to leave here. I want to buy time to beef up our ranks and get back what was taken from us," said Bontade. "But we have to find another place to hide the girl. This is the first place they'll come looking for her."

"Okay, boss. We'll keep the girl, and we'll stand up to those bastards." Roy Boccia had no choice but to accept his boss's decisions.

They had to hurry and find another safe hideout where they could stash their prisoner.

Tom Bontade's residence, on Tenth Avenue in Beechhurst, Queens, consisted of two large buildings with steeply pitched red tile roofs. Bontade lived in the building on the right, while his bodyguards and other family men occupied the one on the left, which had many rooms.

For more than a week, naval intelligence agents under the command of Charles Haffenden had been stationed in an uninhabited house across from Bontade's retreat. The stakeout was part of a much broader intelligence operation organized in collaboration with the families who had gone along with Saro's and Meyer Lansky's invitation.

Since a car belonging to one of Bontade's men had been found packed with dynamite, the investigators were certain that his family was involved in the attacks. For seven days, the agents watched to see who entered and who left the estate.

With their powerful binoculars, they could see Bontade pacing from room to room like a caged lion. It had been weeks since he'd left the house.

The agents had not yet spotted Roy Boccia, for whom they had an arrest warrant. They waited patiently for him to arrive to consult with his boss or come out of the house. But they had no evidence that he was actually in the villa.

Finally, that morning, they saw some movement at the door of the dwelling on the left. Boccia came out and headed swiftly toward the garage to the right of the main building. He got into a two-door Chevrolet Street Rod and drove off toward the Cross Island Parkway.

As soon as they spotted Boccia, Haffenden's agents left three of their men to continue the surveillance and took off in two of their black cars to follow the Chevy.

Haffenden had ordered that Boccia be stopped away from the villa so that Bontade wouldn't know of his arrest.

As Boccia was approaching the entrance to the highway, one of the two Fords passed the Chevrolet and, with a spectacular maneuver, skidded to a stop sideways across the road. Boccia was forced to come to a screeching halt. Meanwhile, the agents in the other car slammed into the Chevy's bumper to disorient the gangster. They jumped out of their cars and surrounded him, ordering him to surrender. They then dragged him bodily out of the driver's seat and made him get into one of the Fords.

Other motorists witnessing the scene observed the episode with some satisfaction. If the police performed an arrest, it meant one less criminal on the streets, and that was sorely needed in those years.

Boccia's Chevrolet, driven by an agent, made a quick maneuver and fell in behind the Ford that sped off in the direction of Church Street in Manhattan, where the naval intelligence unit was headquartered.

In a suite at the Brevoort Hotel in Greenwich Village, Ferdinando Licata's latest refuge, a meeting was taking place between the prince, Jack Mastrangelo, and Saro Ragusa. Mastrangelo was desperate over the fate of his niece. He had grilled Ben Eleazar, who really didn't know anything more than what he'd already told him. Only Roy Boccia and, of course, Tom Bontade would know where the girl was. They had to get their hands on Boccia.

Mastrangelo had put out the word among his informers, but they'd all reported that they hadn't seen him for some weeks now. Mastrangelo had no way of knowing that Boccia had been secretly arrested by the B-3 intelligence team.

Then Ferdinando Licata came up with an idea to flush Bontade out from hiding. It was time to use his journalist friend, Luke Bogart from the *Sun.*

Roy Boccia was brought to the soundproof basement of naval intelligence on Church Street. Charles Haffenden himself wanted to interrogate him and—to avoid any obstruction on the grounds of civil liberties—had even sidestepped notifying Hogan, the district attorney.

Boccia felt trapped. He could try to send Saro and Licata to the electric chair declaring that he'd seen them kill Vito Pizzuto, but he also knew that if he turned them in, he would be finished with the other Cosa Nostra families. The code of silence, *omertà,* among the Mafia is the cornerstone of its power.

Haffenden wore his naval commander's uniform for the interrogation session. He entered the windowless room, lit by two metal lamps hanging from the ceiling.

Boccia was sitting in the middle of the room on a wooden swivel chair. When the door opened, he looked up and saw Haffenden coming toward him with a steely look. Seeing the determination in those eyes, he knew he would have to endure the man's questioning to the death.

"Well, Roy Boccia, at last I get to meet you. You're the one who sank all my ships, correct?" As usual, Haffenden was blunt.

"I don't know what you're talking about," Boccia said confidently.

"I hate wasting time. So I'll appeal to your intelligence, if you have any." Haffenden paced around him. "We found I don't know how many pounds of dynamite in the trunk of your car—the same type used for the sabotage attacks."

"But I never carried dynamite! I swear I didn't," Boccia objected.

"All right, let's move on to something else. Were you present in warehouse eighty-two when Vito Pizzuto was killed? Or are you going to tell me you didn't even know him?"

"I knew him, yeah."

"Good, that's better. So, were you there?" Haffenden pressed him.

"No. I beat it out of there when the shooting started."

"So you didn't see anything? You didn't see who did that to him?"

Boccia hesitated a few seconds before answering, and Haffenden knew he was about to lie again.

"No," was the gangster's predictable response.

"Let's get back to the dynamite. What were you going to do with all those explosives? Why were you carrying them around the city? What was your next target?"

"I swear to you, I don't know anything about that dynamite. Somebody must have planted it in my car to frame me. I'm telling you, I know nothing about it."

Haffenden had no patience, but he had all the time in the world. Complacently, he told the killer, "Whatever you say. But understand that no one knows you're here—not even the DA's office. I can even keep you here for life, if I feel it's advisable. At least until you decide to talk. I'll see you in two days."

With that, Haffenden left the room. Shortly thereafter, Boccia was thrown into a cell where the sole amenities were a stinking bucket and the faint glimmer of a hooded bulb. Boccia sat on the floor, leaning against the wall with his head in his hands, and cursed the day he had gotten in Saro Ragusa's way.

A few days later, a disturbing piece of news threw the entire Cosa Nostra organization into a panic. On the third page of the *Sun*, a headline blared: "Tom Bonrade's Family Wiped Out." The subhead explained that a mysterious outbreak had killed one of the bosses of the Cosa Nostra, along with all his family and some of his bodyguards. The bodies showed no sign of bullet wounds, nor traces of any violence. The mysterious deaths may have been due to ingestion of a poisonous substance. The article that followed described how the bodies of Bonrade and his three bodyguards had been found. A macabre element concerned the fact that Bonrade had been surprised by death while he was still talking on the phone. The reporter then recounted the gangster's eventful life in minute detail, up until the final weeks, when he'd lived virtually barricaded in his home for fear of being killed. Evidently all the precautions were of no use. The article was accompanied by photos of young Bonrade and of the villa where the deaths took place.

The news spread quickly. Phone calls were exchanged among the foremost bosses of the families of New York and the entire East Coast. Some drank a toast, and others worried about their safety. A few, more daring or more interested in the facts, ventured out to northern Queens, where Bonrade's home was. They expected to find a sea of police cars, but Tenth Avenue was nearly deserted. The only people around were a few passersby, a mother pushing a baby carriage, some cleaning women on their way to take the bus home—life went on like any other day.

A friend, however, went up to the gate of Bonrade's estate and rang the bell. Aldo Martini, the recruit from Lombardy, went to answer. When he recognized the man, he stepped out to meet him in the driveway of the main building.

"Bob, what are you doing here?" Martini asked.

The man was taken aback, not knowing what to think. "Are you all okay?" he asked, confused.

Like any superstitious Italian, Martini grabbed his crotch: "What the fuck do you mean, Bob? Do I have to touch wood?"

In reply, the man handed him the newspaper. Martini scanned the front page full of news about the war in Europe. He looked up at him and said, "So?"

"Read the third page," the man said.

Aldo Martini turned the page. The headline made his blood run cold. Then he felt like laughing. Except maybe there *was* something to worry about. He ran inside the house to show the article to Bontade.

Tom Bontade's rage frightened his own men. They had never seen him lose his temper like that. Even in the most difficult moments, the Mob boss always managed to remain cool and composed. It was clear that the length of time he'd spent in the house had frayed his nerves.

Bontade wondered what powers had arranged the publication of a piece so patently false. He immediately phoned the newsroom to retract the story.

From that day on, however, Tom Bontade doubled efforts to protect his person. Security became an obsession for him. He barricaded himself inside the house and had anyone who entered, even the most trusted bodyguard, searched thoroughly. Even his food was tasted by his consiglieri before it was served to him.

Ferdinando Licata had put him on the ropes. Terror was his constant companion.

All Jack Mastrangelo had to do was wait patiently for Bontade to make a wrong move.

Chapter 50

The war in Europe had escalated dramatically following the Battle of Britain, the French occupation, the bombing of Pearl Harbor, and the United States entry into the conflict. The brutalities in the Warsaw ghetto and the rest of Poland, the slaughter in North Africa, and the atrocities committed in Russia had plunged the world further into the depths of barbarism.

Then slowly luck seemed to turn against the Nazi dictator. Russian general Georgy Konstantinovich Zhukov trapped three hundred thousand German troops in Stalingrad, condemning them to certain death or surrender.

In Italy, meanwhile, the population's discontent, particularly those factions hostile to the monarchy and to the regime, finally made its voice heard. Fascism no longer enjoyed the general consent of the people. As a result, a series of diplomatic exchanges began between Great Britain and the United States to determine how best to intervene in order to facilitate Italy's break with the German alliance. The British were more intransigent with the Italian government and, in particular, with the Italian monarchy. Unlike their British cousins, the Americans were more understanding. President Franklin D. Roosevelt knew that a majority of the more than six million Italian-Americans had voted for him, and he didn't want to displease them.

British strategists believed that it would be more productive to get Italy out of the war as quickly as possible, by seeing to it that the angry demonstrations of the antiregime activists grew to such an extent that the Germans would be forced to occupy the entire Italian peninsula with troops drawn from the European arena. They would then have to replace the Italian troops now stationed on the Russian front, in France, and in the Balkans.

The early months of 1943 were given over to organizing the invasion of Italy, which was to get under way in Sicily. The island was chosen because intelligence sources had reported that the population was strongly opposed to the fascist government and that a separatist group, composed of noblemen and large landowners had already set to work to form a powerful anti-German movement.

Operation Husky, the military's code name for the invasion of the island, was conceived during the Casablanca Conference of January 14, 1943.

Naval intelligence was aware that the fascist regime had persecuted Mafia families. Many bosses had been forced to immigrate to America to avoid arrest or imprisonment.

Lieutenant Commander Haffenden thought that they might be just the ones to help bring about a favorable outcome to the landing. Recalling the invaluable help they'd received from Lucky Luciano and his associates at the time of the sabotage attacks at the Port of New York, he thought that Saro Ragusa might once again be of help to him by interceding with high-ranking Italian-Americans of the Cosa Nostra.

Haffenden knew that the Sicilian and American Mafias worked hand in glove, doubly bound by blood ties and business connections. And so, once again the highest official of the US Navy's secret services B-3 unit decided to fall back on the young Ragusa.

When a date was set for the meeting, Licata called together the most influential heads of New York's families to decide jointly how to have Saro handle the difficult negotiations with the B-3 director.

Sante Genovese, Frank Costello, Joe Adonis, Meyer Lansky, Vincent Mangano, and Saro Ragusa—not to mention Polakoff, Lucky Luciano's attorney—all met at Licata's hotel suite.

No introductions were needed, since the prince was renowned among the city's Italian community, though he still put on a show of being powerless and unassuming.

Licata informed the Cosa Nostra bosses about the new opportunity that was being presented to them. Though it still wasn't public knowledge, Licata knew that the Allies were planning to land in Sicily and from there begin their invasion of Italy. With that in mind, to facilitate military operations, they wanted to ask the local populations for support. In his opinion, it seemed like an opportunity to restore Luciano's freedom, and one that should not be passed up.

"How do you mean?" Costello asked.

"They need logistical support. They know that the Mafia has been persecuted by the fascist regime, so they're counting on the fact that the entire organization will be ready and willing to assist the American friends who've come to liberate Sicily from the dictatorship. Someone representing all of us must go and parley with Don Calò in Villalba and convince him to side with the Allies—maybe even sabotaging German and Italian positions. If you still agree today that Luciano is our supreme capo, the decision as to whether or not to help the American troops must be left up to him." Licata's words were received with nods of assent by almost all the participants.

"But what's in it for us?" Sante Genovese asked.

"First, the respect of America's top command," Saro said before the prince could reply. "But above all, in exchange for a vital contribution in time of war, we'll request some form of pardon to free Luciano."

"Exactly," Licata confirmed. "We will insist to the lieutenant commander that only Luciano has the authority to meet with Don Calò in Sicily. No one else. That way, they'll have to let him out of jail, and that will indeed be a great victory for us all."

The group unanimously approved the resolution. Saro would meet with Admiral Haffenden, confident that his back was covered by the consent of the leading families of New York.

Meanwhile, Jack Mastrangelo continued his desperate search for his niece, Aurora. None of his usual informants could give him the slightest clue. Bontade had not contacted him again. Licata's ploy, the phony story in the *Sun,* had not produced any reaction except to make the family's boss continue to shut himself up in his Beechhurst house. Mastrangelo was itching; he wanted to deal with the situation head-on, but Licata urged him to be patient. Sooner or later Bontade would slip up.

Her forced immobility, the darkness of the cellar where she was locked up, the untrustworthy faces she saw around her, the endless thoughts that chased through her head with no explanation, had once again plunged Aurora into utter apathy. She slept and ate what little her captors managed to give her.

Bontade, meanwhile, became more hysterical every day. He didn't like having the girl down in the basement. Also, he didn't know whether to attribute Roy Boccia's disappearance to a betrayal, in which case he would make him pay for it, or to his having been captured by the police. He had his men bring him the *New York Times* and the *New York Post* every day to check if Boccia had been arrested. But no report appeared in the newspapers. He decided to wait a few more days; then he would see to getting rid of the girl one way or another, which in his mind meant kill her and dump her in a garbage truck.

———————

Lieutenant Commander Haffenden received Saro Ragusa and attorney Polakoff in his private office at the Hotel Astor, where he conducted his most delicate business.

Haffenden wasted no time in explaining his plan. It was more or less what Licata had predicted.

He told the two of them that his division had been working for months to identify all the Sicilian emigrants who had returned to Italy in recent years to visit their relations. They'd already contacted about a hundred of them and had them hand over photographs, postcards, books, official Italian documents, and anything that could help authorities form an idea of the islanders' mentality. Some had described industrial installations, government buildings, military strongholds, and routes linking the villages to one another—secondary roads that Italian and German troops were often unfamiliar with. They asked all of them for the names of trusted relatives and friends. The B-3 tracked down Italians who had never applied for US citizenship, while those who had and had been rejected were promised citizenship in exchange for information.

They had gathered quite a bit of data that the B-7, the unit responsible for analyzing the intelligence, was evaluating and classifying numerous strategic memoranda.

At this point, Haffenden concluded, there was only one move remaining: to convince the entire Sicilian Mafia organization to agree to serve the cause of liberation. Was there a leader among them charismatic enough to able to persuade his counterpart in Sicily to be on their side?

Licata had once again hit the nail on the head. That was the question he wanted the Lieutenant Commander to ask. Saro told Haffenden that the man he was looking for was the same one who had been able to stop the sabotage attacks at the Port of New York. Lucky Luciano was the only one who could convince their Sicilian cousins to side with the Americans.

Of course, all this would have a price. Though it was beyond his jurisdiction, Haffenden promised to bring the matter before the US attorney general, the only authority capable of deciding on a possible reduction of sentence. He told Saro and Polakoff that even District Attorney Hogan, as well as Governor Dewey, who had sent Luciano to prison some years ago, had already agreed to a retrial with a view toward a possible pardon.

Polakoff personally brought Luciano the news of the meeting with Haffenden, the request from naval intelligence, and the promise of a potential retrial to drastically reduce his sentence.

Lucky Luciano realized that this was his last card to play if he was to be released from prison any time soon. He still had twenty-four years to serve *if* he was a model prisoner—otherwise forty-four more years. So he agreed to go to Sicily secretly and meet with Don Calò, the Sicilian Mafia's *capo dei capi*, or "boss of bosses."

As a landing place, Luciano suggested the Gulf of Castellammare, where there were many coves still controlled by friends who would protect him.

Naval intelligence would arrange the trip and his stay in Sicily. But Haffenden demanded that he be accompanied by Saro, whom he had come to trust. Once Luciano gave the island's bosses his instructions, Saro would be their contact in dealings between the Americans and the Sicilians.

Chapter 51

On maps, Villalba is a tiny dot on a hill just under two thousand feet in elevation, in a rugged district of central Sicily that locals call the Vallone—"deep valley"—in the heart of the Madonie. Calogero Vizzini was born in this cluster of huts and stinking hovels, with no roads, no running water, and no sewers, where animals find shelter in the same dwellings as the peasants.

Don Calò, as everyone respectfully addressed him, was the son of destitute people; he had no lofty ancestry, no uncles who were monsignors or gabellotti, yet thanks to a keen criminal mind and a remarkable tactical intuition for seizing opportunities in constantly changing conditions, he managed to reach the apex of Mafia power in just a few years.

When he was still a young man of twenty, Don Calò was able to gain credibility and prestige by offering his services as an intermediary between the robbers who infested the island and the landowners. His first success came when he was chosen by the famous bandit Francesco Paolo Varsallona as his sole liaison with the noblemen in the area. Don Calò was like an employment agency of a criminal nature, providing landowners and gabellotti with private guards, or campieri, to protect their lands. Naturally, the clients of this particular "agency" underwrote a kind of insurance that safeguarded them from theft and extortion.

Calogero soon became known throughout the Vallone, as well as in the neighboring provinces, as a "connected man"—that is, a man you could depend on. The people he recommended were absolutely trustworthy. This activity enabled him to develop a vast network of people that included not only men with more or less clean criminal records but also noblemen, large landowners, politicians, and monsignors.

As time went by, this extensive system of collaborators and supporters formed the nucleus of a true, tight-knit family, or *cosca*. Calogero won the respect and esteem of the major landowners, managing to acquire for himself lands and estates that the legitimate owners could no longer maintain. Obviously, he was involved with the law on numerous occasions, but he always came out clean; only once was he disgraced by going to prison. No one ever managed to find him guilty of the thirty-nine murders, six attempted homicides, thirty-six holdups, thirty-seven burglaries, and sixty-three extortions that he had committed or ordered. This was the "man of honor," Lucky Luciano and Saro Ragusa were to meet with in Sicily.

Late one night in spring, Luciano was taken from his comfortable cell at Great Meadow and transported to a secret airport used by naval intelligence, near the Hudson River. Waiting for him there were Saro and Charles Haffenden. On the airstrip, a brand-new Douglas C-54 Skymaster that would take them to England was warming up its engines.

Haffenden informed Luciano that they would not be landing in the Gulf of Castellammare on the northern coast of Sicily because the submarine that was to transport them couldn't get there by that date. Instead, from the Mediterranean island of Malta they would board a fishing vessel that would drop them off on the southern coast near Gela, landing near a small promontory west of town. From there two villagers with a car would take them to the meeting with Don Calò. The boss had already been informed and had agreed to meet Luciano near Palermo.

Immediately afterward, they would make their way to the coast of Capo Grosso on the north shore, midway between Palermo and Termini Imerese. There a fishing boat would be waiting to ferry them to the submarine that would take them back to Malta, from which they would then head back to America.

"Can we count on you returning to the States, Mr. Luciano?" Haffenden asked as he accompanied him and Saro to the hatch of the four-engine aircraft.

Luciano squinted his eyes, as if to focus better on the commander: it was his typical expression that brooked no argument. "No one is virtuous enough to be spared from temptation, Commander, but we're Sicilians. Sicilians have nothing but their word, and we're capable of dying for it." He shook his hand and boarded the plane followed by Saro, who couldn't stop admiring his every gesture.

An infantry unit, headed to a battalion stationed in England, had already boarded the C-54. Saro and Lucky sat down side by side on the wooden bench that ran the length of the compartment.

"This is my first time on a plane, Mr. Luciano," Saro told him.

"Call me Charlie," the other replied affably, adjusting his position on the uncomfortable seat. "Better get used to it. They'll make you act as go-between, so you'll be traveling a lot."

The plane taxied on the runway and began readying for takeoff.

"Charlie, have you met Don Calò?" Saro asked him.

"I was only seven when my mother and I left Sicily to join my father in America. But I still remember my mother telling us about this kid who at just twenty-five had already become a respected man. She would tell us those things to make us see that 'America' could also be found in Sicily and that there was no need to leave our land. She argued about it with my father, who felt humiliated by her words. He was a machinist; he worked in a brassware factory in Brooklyn. But hard work doesn't make money," Luciano said in a knowing way.

"But how did Don Calò get to be the *padrino di tutti i padrini*—the godfather of all godfathers—in Sicily?" Saro persisted.

"Through friendships," Luciano replied enigmatically. Then he went on: "You have to bestow favors and always make yourself available to people so they will then feel a moral obligation of gratitude and loyalty toward you. If you analyze those who are successful in life—government officials, industrialists, landowners, entrepreneurs—all of them excel at this. All men are corruptible: either they're greedy for money, or they want to appear powerful.

"But let's grab some shut-eye now. They got me up at three this morning." He turned up the collar of his jacket, crossed his arms, stretched out his legs, and closed his eyes.

———

In the early afternoon, they touched down on a secondary runway north of Bovington Camp in southern England. The infantry unit piled off the plane, and only Luciano and Ragusa remained. The copilot walked back with some sandwiches and said that, once they'd refueled, they would immediately take off for Malta. They would arrive at their destination within three hours.

And so they did. Thanks to favorable winds, the plane landed at the airport in Malta about ten minutes early.

That same night, at the port of La Valletta, they embarked on the *Santa Maria*, a trawler with a Sicilian crew. Saro embraced the three fishermen who spoke in his dialect. It had been several years since he'd heard that mixture of countless influences that formed his regional dialect. Suddenly he thought of his family. He smiled when he imagined promise of that night. How naive they'd been!

Once they boarded the vessel, it promptly moved out to sea toward Gela. It was the middle of the night when they came in sight of land. The moon lit up the coast enough for them to make out the small promontory near which they would be dropped off. They saw the flare of a lamp, and then a second and third in quick succession. It was the all-clear signal.

———

Saro and Luciano got in the military dinghy and, paddling briskly, ran ashore some minutes later. After four years, Saro once again touched the soil of his native Sicily. But he had no time to be moved by it because two men were waiting for them on the beach, signaling for them to hurry up. One of the men gave them dry pants and shirts, while the other hid the skiff in a cleft in the rock. The first man said his name was Michele and the second, the younger one, was Nicolino. It was the only words they spoke.

As soon as Saro and Luciano changed clothes, they followed Michele and Nicolino to a black Fiat Millecento parked on the road nearby.

"We have a long way to go. More than a hundred miles, almost all on dirt roads, so we won't run into the Black Shirts. Still, we'll have to pass through Agrigento and then Caltanissetta." Michele sounded nervous. He knew that if they were stopped, they would end up in jail until the end of the war.

"Do you know who I am?" Luciano asked.

"No, voscenza, they didn't tell us, sir. They just asked us to be sure and treat you with kid gloves."

Luciano smiled and leaned back against the seat, giving Saro a meaningful look.

———

Now sixty-five years old, Don Calò had returned to Villalba after his term in prison, to lead the life he'd always lived. A sober, unassuming life, in a modest house, where he was looked after by a spinster sister, Marietta, in whose name he had registered a substantial share of the Belaci estate. The elderly woman took care of her unmarried brother, serving him with the frugal, industrious diligence of a priest's housekeeper. Calogero Vizzini's thriftiness was not due to avarice, but to an age-old respect for the value of things.

The meeting between Lucky Luciano and Don Calò, the greatest *padrini* of all time, was an event that all mafiosi would look back on with great emotion. It was like Christians witnessing the union of the Father, the Son, and the Holy Spirit, the latter represented by Saro Ragusa on this occasion.

When they finally arrived at Don Calò's house, Saro and Lucky Luciano were surprised and somewhat disappointed to see the kind of place he lived in and how he was dressed. Especially Luciano, who, as an American, viewed power as a force to move people and money through managerial flair and determination. Don Calò appeared before his unknown guests wearing striped pajamas, the top open in front to reveal a freshly laundered undershirt, and a pair of leather slippers on his feet. The elastic waistband of the pajama bottoms came to just above his stomach, completely covering his big belly. Don Calò invited them into the dining room, where they sat around the table on old wooden chairs with straw seats. The dutiful Marietta prepared coffee made from real Brazilian coffee beans, a rarity in Italy at that time.

"The landing of the Allied troops in Sicily is imminent," Luciano began. "The fascists' days are numbered, and the Americans are asking for our help to gain the support of the island's population."

Lucky Luciano told him his story, to clarify his role in the whole affair, recounting the visits the US Navy's intelligence chief had made to his jail cell. The fate of the war in Europe was in their hands. This could mean a number of things, Luciano explained. In return for the favor, at the end of the conflict, they would have a chance to place their men in prominent positions in future administrations. And they could work directly with the armed forces command to maintain order in the cities and towns. At long last, the Mafia and the Cosa Nostra would be officially recognized.

Don Calò listened in silence. His gestures were extremely slow and wary. From time to time he nodded, to show that he was following what Luciano was saying. And as Luciano gradually ran through the future scenarios that would come about in exchange for the "favor" granted to the invading troops, Don Calò got a sense of the important deals he could look forward to for many years to come.

He also realized that his power, dimmed by the five years he'd recently spent in prison, would return, making him more formidable than ever. All of his trafficking would have the tacit approval of the occupation troops. Don Calogero Vizzini would enter Sicily's history as his people's greatest benefactor.

Don Calò was not much for fine words and grand phrases, so when Luciano finished explaining the facts, his only response was to get up from his chair, walk over to his guest, take his hand, and make him stand up. Saro automatically rose too and saw the big Sicilian clutch the slim Lucky Luciano in a forceful embrace. Luciano, more astonished than ever, put his arms as far around the don as he could, returning the hug. Then Don Calò, still scowling, but aware of the importance of the moment, planted a kiss on his mouth—a kiss that Luciano couldn't dodge.

As they were leaving, the American boss took a yellow silk scarf out of his bag and handed it to Don Calò, explaining that in a few months, someone, probably a soldier, would show up with an identical scarf. That man would be his representative. Don Calò was to do what he asked, to ensure a successful landing.

Don Calò took the scarf and unfolded it. An *L* had been embroidered in the center, in black thread. Still looking grave, he said, "It stands for Luciano, I suppose."

"No. It stands for *Lucky*—that is, *Fortunato*"—the other replied with a smile.

Don Calò balled up the scarf in his fist and put it in his pajama pocket. "I will treasure it dearly" were his last words, and with that, they said good-bye.

Chapter 52

In the weeks that followed, the Sicilian populace was exposed to a subtle, insistent wave of propaganda. From the major cities to the most remote villages, everyone knew that the Americans were about to land to liberate them from fascist oppression. Everyone was ready to welcome the foreigners with open arms. The war would soon be over. Fascism was almost defeated, and the people were exhausted.

Mothers told their soldier sons not to fire so much as a single shot at the liberators, but to surrender and thereby save their lives. Mussolini himself had decided that it should be mainly Sicilian soldiers who would defend the island's soil. Among the ranks of the five divisions, two brigades, and one regiment stationed on the island, three-quarters of the troops were born in that region. And, as Don Calò himself had said, lending a hand to the infiltrators planted by US intelligence was an easy way to earn merit points for the postwar phase. With the landing imminent, desertions were numerous, in part because the soldiers were worried about the families they'd left behind in their villages.

Sicily had been hammered by bombings since the beginning of the war. Messina, more than any other city, was a target because of its strategic location. Ninety percent of food supplies and war equipment passed through the strait between the island and the mainland. But other cities weren't spared, either: Palermo, Augusta, Trapani, Siracusa, Ragusa, and especially Catania, which suffered the most devastating bombardment, with over three thousand bombing victims in a single day. The strategy of those attacks was aimed at crushing Italian morale.

Shipments of goods ceased almost entirely. Bread and pasta disappeared from the markets. Meat had become a distant memory for most people, soap could not be found, and nor could oil and sugar. There was no choice but to buy those foods on the black market, which increased prices astronomically.

In those gripping days, many of the four million Sicilians alleviated their hunger by eating carobs, which had previously been fed to donkeys, horses, and pigs. In such a climate, people's anger against the government was ready to explode. In May 1943 the front page of a Catania newspaper bore a photo of the Duce under the banner headline "The Fiend Responsible for the War." Copies sold out within hours.

Amid the social and political turmoil, the Mafia, now backed by the Allies, had gone back to exerting its control over the region and over basic food products. Palermo was supplied with 450,000 rations of wheat, matching the reputed number of its inhabitants. In reality, during the months of bombing, two-thirds of the citizens chose to evacuate to the countryside, where everyone had a brother, cousin—someone he or she knew. When the rations were distributed to those who had remained in the city, there were at least 300,000 left over, which were regularly sent off to be sold on the black market.

Don Calò also worked directly with the counterespionage forces. He told his affiliates that to support the invasion, they had to collaborate with their American friends by every available means, even if it meant sabotaging the enemy's weapons. Over the course of the spring, German armored tanks belonging to the Goering Panzer Division stationed in the province of Palermo experienced mysterious breakdowns: someone had diluted the oil in their tanks with water. Some of the vehicles suffered melted engines and had to be pulled out of the units. Ships weren't immune from sabotage, either, and many cargo vessels were forced to remain at anchor as a result of tampering.

Salemi, in those frenzied days of late spring, had its heroes. The Italian Aosta Division and the Nazis' Fifteenth Panzergrenadier Division, part of which had been assigned to defend Caltanissetta, had been camped in the countryside outside the town. Roughly a dozen assault guns, four half-tracks, six Panzer Tigers, and five trucks with a convoy of heavy artillery and related logistical supplies were about to set out from the plain of Salemi to reach a new post near Caltanissetta. Though it was confidential information, the convoy's departure soon became public knowledge, thanks to some young women who had been cavorting with soldiers from the German tank corps.

In recent years, a substantial group of antiregime dissidents had formed in Salemi. One of the most active factions was represented by Nicola Cosentino, the deceased Rosario Losurdo's former campiere; Turi Toscano, the salt miner; and Peride Terrasini, the charcoal burner. Joining them in the last few months was Pepè, the grandson of Nini Trovato, the mayor's factotum. His grandfather was unable to control the young man and feared for his life. He'd told Pepè more than once that he shouldn't be seen with those people. Nini Trovato was well aware of the means that Jano Vassallo used to "straighten out" those with a "dirty conscience," as he called it. But Pepè, though he had not yet turned eighteen, had a mind of his own. He too wanted to fight for a better life, since the fascists, drawn into the war by the Germans in 1940, were only paving the way for a future of slavery.

Word of mouth carrying Don Calò's instructions had reached the ears of a few honorable men in Salemi, and the four friends had quickly rolled up their sleeves and set to work, wanting to be recognized as worthy participants of anti-German resistance. On one occasion, the four had sabotaged a truck used to requisition sacks of grain from Losurdo's farm. Pepè, being small, had crawled under the vehicle and loosened the oil pan screw just enough to make the oil leak out a little at a time but not enough to look like sabotage. A few days later, the truck's engine seized, and the poor mechanic was chewed out by the corporal.

The convoy's departure could be an opportunity to score another act of sabotage. But what could they come up with? Turi Toscano had an idea. The following night, they drove off toward the coast in a cart loaded with picks, shovels, hammers, and nails. They knew that the convoy would be headed south to Castelvetrano and from there east along the coast to Agrigento, before continuing to its destination.

They exited at Santa Ninfa, went past the town, and at the large junction leading to Castelvetrano on the right and Partanna on the left, they switched the signs. But their work wasn't over. Turi had also devised a masterful finishing touch.

They drove on to Partanna, less than four miles from the intersection, and on the outskirts of the village took down the sign indicating its name and replaced it with one they'd prepared ahead of time, marked "Castelvetrano." Finally, to complete the hoax, they stuck a new signpost in the ground, with an arrow and the word *Agrigento*.

It was still night as they approached Salemi, satisfied to have completed a mission that would undoubtedly earn them the praise of the Allies and Don Calò himself.

Pericle Terrasini was up on the seat, driving the mule, while his three friends sat in the cart, laughing and joking, imitating the Germans' faces when they discovered the prank. It was Pericle who first spotted Jano Vassallo and his Black Shirts stationed on the road leading back to town.

"There's Jano!" he called out, instinctively pulling in the reins so that the mule came to a stop.

"Christ!" Nicola Cosentino swore. "What are you doing? Go on, keep going."

Péride slackened the reins, and the mule started walking again.

"Let me do the talking," Nicola whispered, climbing onto the seat next to Péride. They drove up to the group of combat leaguers. The whole gang was there, Nicola thought: Ginetto, Cosimo, Prospero, Quinto, and even Nunzio.

"Hey there!" Nicola raised his hand in greeting.

"Nice night for a drive," Jano said sarcastically, taking hold of the mule's bit; the animal stopped patiently.

"We had a party for my sister Assuntina," Nicola replied.

"And those are your party clothes?" Jano laughed, shaking his head.

"A simple gathering; she got engaged to Toni."

"Who, Toni the *babbalucco*? That idiot?" He looked around for his men's approval; up till then they'd remained pokerfaced, not saying a word. A few smirked.

"No, Toni the mule driver," Nicola answered seriously. He took the reins from Péride and cracked the whip so the mule would start walking again. "He loaned us his cart to get home."

But Jano stopped the animal that was about to set off again, holding the bit tightly. "Where do you think you're going, Nicola Cosentino?"

"I told you, home."

"Wanna bet you'll end up in jail tonight?" Jano threatened him.

"Why? What did I do? What are you accusing me of, driving a mule without a license?"

He managed to hold his own against the Black Shirt, but Jano was tired of playing cat and mouse. "I've been keeping an eye on the four of you for some time. And tonight I finally caught you with your hands in the cookie jar. Are you dealing in the black market? Or worse yet, are you playing along with the infiltrators? Don't you know there's the firing squad for insurgents and saboteurs?"

No one answered.

"Well? Nothing to say?" He handed the mule's bridle to Ginetto.

He walked around the cart and leaned his fists on the wagon bed, which had no rear panel. First he stared at Turi Toscano, who met his gaze for a while. Then he turned to the boy sitting on the cart bed, his head lowered.

"Pepè, what are you doing with these people?" Jano asked him. Instead of looking up, the boy's head sank even lower between his knees.

"Do you want to give your grandfather a stroke?" Jano persisted. But the boy didn't answer.

"Leave him alone. Take it out on us if you have to," Turi Toscano spoke up.

"I'm not talking to you, Turi," Jano said and turned back to the boy. "So, Pepè, are you going to tell me what you were doing tonight with your friends?"

After still more silence, Jano walked around the cart, came up behind the boy, and whispered in his ear: "You're young, but maybe somebody explained to you how the 'box' works. In any case, I'll tell you myself: it's an instrument that loosens the tongues of even the most hardened bastards."

The boy covered his ears and was about to burst into tears. Then he turned around and shouted at him, "We didn't do anything! Nothing! It was only a prank, just for laughs!"

"That's enough, Jano, stop hounding him," Nicola Cosentino spoke up. "I'll tell you what we did: we signed an insurance policy for when the Americans come. Your days are numbered, people like you. You lost, Jano, face it. You and your friends have no future anymore. Fascism is finished!"

"Who filled your head with such grand ideas?" Jano shot back, but his tone was no longer sarcastic.

"Everybody in Sicily knows that in a few weeks the Americans will come to liberate us. Those who collaborated with them will be rewarded. Those like you who continue to fight for the Duce and a king who betrayed us will get what they deserve," Nicola Cosentino said.

"Who's saying these things?" Jano asked seriously.

Nicola replied just as seriously, "You know who Don Calò is, don't you?"

Jano considered for a few seconds.

"Let's make a pact, then," he proposed. "I'll close my eyes and ears to what you did tonight. And you'll put in a good word for us when your American friends arrive." He walked away from the cart and with a nod ordered his cronies to step back. His gang of bullies looked at him in surprise, not understanding the reason for his change of heart. Ginetto thought it was a ploy to catch their quarry unawares once they reached their destination; Nicola and the others thought so too. It wasn't Jano's style to let his prey go once he sank his teeth into them.

The four friends were so sure that Jano and his men would attack them unexpectedly that they set out toward the town's piazza with terror in their hearts, not saying another word, constantly looking behind them.

In reality, Jano, like a skilled quick-change artist, had sensed that the direction of the wind was changing, and had made up his mind to take the leap and side with those who would be steering things during the period following the dictatorship's collapse. But to get an endorsement like that, he would have to exact it from an undisputed authority. He decided to go see Don Calò.

It was late afternoon when he got to Villalba, accompanied by Ginetto, who had driven the truck the entire way. Jano had someone point out Calogero Vizzini's house and told his friend to wait in the piazza. Thursday afternoons were set aside for people making petitions. Anyone—not just the inhabitants of Villalba, but from nearby villages as well—could approach Vizzini and plead a cause. Don Calò would solve the problem one way or another, depending on who he knew. Rarely did a petitioner leave without being satisfied. That could happen only if the person who sought remedy did so against the interests of someone who was a closer friend than the supplicant himself.

The door of the house was open. There was complete silence, and Jano tried to get the attention of someone inside. "May I come in?" he called loudly. An elderly man appeared from a corridor and shuffled toward him, motioning for him to lower his voice.

"Come in; that's why the door is open," he whispered.

The old man led Jano to a small, bare room, where a row of straw-bottomed chairs were lined up along the wall, all but one of them occupied. When Jano entered, everyone's eyes turned toward him. Jano was wearing his black shirt, and Black Shirts weren't viewed kindly in Sicily. Then they all went back to their ponderings. Jano whispered a greeting and took the last empty seat.

"Did you come a long way?" the farmer sitting next to him asked suddenly.

"Yes, from Salemi," Jano replied.

The old man nodded, as if sympathizing with him for the long trip he'd made. "People come here from as far as Palermo. Even people who are well off."

"Are you here for Don Calò?" Jano asked.

The old farmer wasn't used to smiling, but he almost did, given the young man's naive question. "Dear boy, and why are you here? For *zu* Calò, right?" The residents of Villalba affectionately referred to Calogero Vizzini with the title *zu*, "*zio*" or "uncle."

"It's my first time here," Jano explained.

"May the good Lord sustain him for eternity. Every village should have someone like him. He's the only one capable of setting things straight. Only he has all the qualities to be a real *omu*—a decent human being."

It was already evening by the time Jano's turn came. He entered the dining room of Calogero Vizzini's house. Don Calò was seated on one side of a table that must have served as a desk, dining table, and countertop, with heaps of papers scattered all over its surface. In front of him was an empty coffee cup. Jano sat down in a chair across from him. Their conversation took the form of a monologue, as Don Calò heard him out without asking any questions. Jano told him that he was tired of serving the Duce, who, when you came right down to it, hadn't really done much for Sicily. In fact, by waging war against the Mafia, he had weakened and depleted the organization. Jano regretted the choices he'd made, and he now wanted to make available to Don Calò the power he had accumulated over those years—along with the young men under his command, who followed him unquestioningly.

Don Calò made a note of his name and the town he came from and then dismissed Jano, telling him he had nothing to worry about. When the Allies came, he too would have his assignments to carry out and his just rewards. Now, though, he had better take off that "clown suit"—referring to Jano's shirt—and await his instructions. Jano kissed his hand. He hadn't thought it would be so easy to wash his dirty linen after years of abusing people.

Chapter 53

After their meeting with Don Calò, Saro Ragusa and Lucky Luciano were taken to the north coast, near Termini Imerese. From there a Sicilian fisherman's small boat ferried them to a submarine waiting offshore, which in turn brought them to Malta. Then a Douglas C-54 transported them back to America. Twenty-four hours later, Lucky Luciano was once again in his cell at Great Meadow, but with the firm hope of being able to leave it someday.

Saro, meanwhile, hurried to Ferdinando Licata's hotel to report on how the mission had gone. He didn't find him there, however, and no one knew his whereabouts.

The prince was busy completing the most critical phase of his plan— the most delicate and difficult to implement because it had to be endorsed by none other than the district attorney himself, Frank Hogan. Stating who he was and reminding them of the terrible attack he'd suffered at the feast of Saint Ciro, resulting in the death of his beloved grandniece, Licata was received by Hogan on the same morning Saro returned to the United States.

It was with some apprehension that Licata climbed the stairs to the New York County District Attorney's Office, not because he was afraid of facing the chief prosecutor but because he feared having the plan he was about to propose rejected. If that happened, his entire strategy would collapse.

Frank Hogan was waiting for him and immediately offered his condolence on the death of his niece. Licata thanked him, then sat down in the chair in front of the desk.

"Mr. Prosecutor, I am Italian, though of English origins," the prince began. "The attack I suffered made me reflect a great deal on the *malapianta*: the bad seed that we have imported here in America."

"Are you referring to the Mafia organizations?" The prosecutor was precise as always.

"Exactly so. I was thinking about what could be done to weed out this disgrace to all Italians, Mr. Prosecutor." He spoke in such strong terms to give the impression that he was practically more Italian than a seven-generation native. "After racking my brains, I came up with a strategy for us to get rid of them legally. Well, Mr. Prosecutor, it's so obvious it was staring me in the face!

"It's simple: all we have to do is 'return to sender.' That is, ship them back to where they came from."

"But we can't force a citizen out of the country; he'd have to have committed a crime."

"That's not what I meant," Licata explained patiently. "You must create a legal provision—a regulation, as you attorneys call them—by which if a foreigner is suspected of belonging to a Mob or a Mafia family, at least one of whose members has been tried and convicted of a crime against the common good, that person may automatically be expelled from the United States and sent back to his homeland, with the stipulation that he can no longer return to the States. The individual will be labeled as an undesirable. Just think how great the benefit could be to the entire society, Mr. Prosecutor."

"We would have to consider a specific judicial order."

In his heart Licata was elated, because Hogan had not rejected the idea a priori. "I've talked to people in my neighborhood about this, and everyone supports the idea of expelling the undesirables," Licata pressed.

"I know you are a guiding force for the people on the Lower East Side. They even call you Father," Hogan said.

"Actually, some call me *u patri*, like in the old country," Licata explained. "But I see that everyone here in the DA's office is well informed."

"We do our best." If he'd had tail feathers, the prosecutor would have fanned them out like a peacock.

The prince felt he had won him over and took the plunge. "If you'd like, I could show you how to separate the wheat from the chaff," he went on, in that simplistic jargon that made the powerful feel at ease.

"How is that?"

"I could provide you with a list of undesirables. That way, your work would be minimized." There, he'd said it. Now all he had to do was wait for Hogan's reaction, though for a moment the prosecutor seemed at a loss. Licata took advantage of it and continued: "Of course, you would have to determine whether the individual was a greater or lesser danger. I would simply point out the persons who were, let's say, a more likely risk: those belonging to Mafia families."

That wording seemed less compromising to the DA. In any case, Hogan thought, such a list would be invaluable to him and his men.

"Okay, Mr. Licata. The idea seems promising. I'll refer it to my staff, and then we'll see about turning it into a judicial regulation. Meanwhile, not to waste any time, let's do this: while I try to resolve the legal issues, go ahead and compile the list and get it to me. Naturally, everything must be done in the strictest secrecy," he concluded, rising from his chair and moving toward the prince.

"Naturally, Mr. Prosecutor," Licata stood up, and the two men shook hands heartily to seal their pact.

In one fell swoop, Frank Hogan would get rid of a good part of New York's dregs, while Ferdinando Licata would wipe out his troublesome competition without firing a single shot.

Licata's list included the names of about two hundred previous offenders drawn mostly from the lower ranks of the families. But there were also some crew bosses, and a few kingpins. Jack Mastrangelo had agreed to help him with the job, though he didn't fully understand the usefulness of such large-scale finger-pointing.

But Licata could see farther ahead than anyone else, and Mastrangelo had confidence in his foresight.

A few days later, when the prince handed Frank Hogan the list of undesirables, the prosecutor rubbed his hands together excitedly over the explosive document. He promised him that he would make appropriate use of it.

As often happens, however, there was an informer in the DA's office. Despite the fact that Frank Hogan had kept the document confidential, someone still managed to photograph it and bring a copy to Tom Bontade, along with the whole story of the undesirables.

"Fucking bastard!" Bontade exploded when the mole had finished telling what he had seen and overheard between Hogan and Prince Licata. "Anyone who makes a deal with the cops is a gutless coward, and certainly no Sicilian. That contemptible scumbag has to die," he told Aldo Martini.

Bontade scanned the list and saw that the names of all his men were on it. "You're on it too, Martini," he said to his bodyguard, but he saw that the names of soldiers from the other families were there as well. Inconsequential recruits, minor killers, but also crew bosses. One name alarmed Bontade: at the bottom of the list he found that of Saro Ragusa. He thought for a few seconds.

"This guy is really a piece of garbage! Just think, he even betrayed his right arm, Saro Ragusa. Apparently he wants to ditch him. It's typical of him. He uses people and then gets rid of them." By his logic, this was the only explanation that could have led the prince to add Saro's name to the list of undesirables. Bontade realized that he finally held the cards to beat Licata. He would bring Saro over to his side by telling him about the betrayal as well as what had actually happened at the Blue Lemon. He had a witness who had been present the night the prostitute and her client were beaten.

The prince, Bontade concluded, had made a fatal mistake.

———————

In recent months, Saro's life had taken a rather bitter turn. No longer having any real friends, he now communicated only with the men recruited by Licata. But all they could do was agree with everything he said. He missed the good old days with Dixie and Isabel. The girl's death had devastated him, and the thought of Mena was too distant.

But he reached the depths of despondency with the arrival of a letter delivered to him by a fellow townsman, Roberto Naselli, who had managed to stow away on a ship sailing from Lisbon, Portugal. The letter came from Stellina, Saro's younger sister, who lived in Marsala and had entrusted it to the man.

Holding it in his hands, Saro kissed it like a cherished treasure; then he opened it and read it anxiously:

> *My dear beloved brother, forgive me for writing to give you bad news. Just yesterday I heard from someone I know, who fled from Salemi, that the fascist forces arrested our parents and poor Ester because they are Jews. The tavern owner Mimmo Ferro and another dozen or so villagers were deported along with them. We don't know where. I'm afraid that they will come and take my family too and for that reason Dinu and I have decided to leave town. My dearest brother, I cannot tell you where, in case this letter should not reach your beloved hands. I embrace you with all my love, as always, Stellina.*

The force of those few desperate words sapped any remaining will he might have had to go on living. From that day on, as soon as he could, Saro drowned his thoughts in an opium den in Chinatown, where Madame Wu treated him like a son. But instead of mother's milk, she gave him a deadly blend to smoke that sent him into a world of mists and fog.

It was as he was leaving one of those "salutary" sessions that he was seized by Aldo Martini and another of Bontade's hounds. They pushed him into a Cadillac and, holding him firmly under their feet, brought him to Tom Bontade's bunker in Beechhurst.

When he stood in front of the boss, Bontade told him that he had nothing to fear and handed him a glass of whiskey. Saro sank onto the sofa and drank. His head was still woozy, and he hoped the alcohol's kick would jolt him back to reality. He focused on Bontade, who now stood in front of him holding a sheet of paper.

"Read this. It concerns you personally."

Saro grabbed the paper and glanced at it absently. It took some time to recover a sufficient degree of attention. All he saw was a list of names, and he declined to read them.

"What is it?"

"It's a list of undesirables: people who will sooner or later be sent back to their country of origin and who will no longer be able to set foot in America. Go ahead, read the names," Bontade urged.

"I don't feel like reading all those fucking names." Saro tossed away the sheets, which landed at Aldo Martini's feet.

Martini was quick to pick it up and hand it to him again. Meanwhile, Tom Bontade lost his patience and shouted, "It's got your name on it too! Read it!"

This time Saro did as he was told and quickly scanned the list of names until he came to his own: Saro Ragusa.

Bontade jumped in before he could ask.

"That's a copy. The original is in the Prosecutor's Office. I can't tell you how I got it because the document is confidential. Top secret," Bontade was already relishing the moment when he would make his disclosure. "Aren't you going to ask me who drew up the list?" he asked after a while.

Saro looked up. "Who is the bastard?"

"Your dear friend Ferdinando Licata," Bontade replied.

"That's bullshit."

"It's the absolute truth. I know it's difficult to swallow, but it's true. Those who know him realize that such duplicity is nothing new for him. He gets people to help him, and then after using them he throws them in the trash."

"That's bullshit, I'm telling you!" Saro yelled firmly.

"Then tell me: Does the Blue Lemon mean anything to you?" Bontade asked cruelly.

Saro felt lost. What did Bontade know about the Blue Lemon? He tried to appear casual. "It's a club in Chelsea. I went there a few times."

"How come you don't go there anymore?"

"I never said that."

Bontade knew everything, it seemed to Saro. Would he blackmail him now?

"I'll tell you why: because you supposedly beat up a beautiful girl named Marta there, along with a poor, innocent john. That's how come."

Now he had Saro's back against the wall.

"There's a 'but,' however," Bontade added cryptically.

"I said you 'supposedly' beat up, not 'beat up,' and you know why? Because in reality, you didn't kill anyone that night; you were too drunk to even lift your little finger."

What was Bontade trying to say? What did he actually know? Saro was silent.

Bontade's face was close enough to nearly touch noses. "It wasn't *you* who attacked those two. *They* let you believe that. I have a witness who saw it all. He was present at the scene. I'm telling you: it wasn't you who beat up that bitch and her client."

The revelation inched its way into his brain like a tapeworm. The idea became more and more unbearable. Saro resisted it with every ounce of strength in him, but the more he thought about it, the more likely it seemed.

"Think about it. Think back to that night: you were drunk. Do you have so much as a *shred* of recollection of having killed the man or the woman?" Bontade pressed him, seeing that Saro was about to give in. "You can't remember because you didn't do it. Your memory only goes back to when you passed out on the bed. Then a burly guy came in, his face disfigured by scars. My informant got a good look at him. You know him. He's buddy-buddy with your boss, Prince Licata. Jack Mastrangelo came in after you, clobbered the woman first, then the man, with his bare hands. Then he smeared blood on your hands. He skinned your knuckles by scraping them against the wall. Finally, in the dead of night, when no one was around, he hoisted you on his back and took you away from there, to a dark alley."

"That's all bullshit!" Saro kept protesting, but he was about to cave.

"That's exactly how it happened, and don't ask me why your boss and his henchman staged that lovely performance. The fact is, they implicated you and made you seem like a murderer. I don't know why, maybe to be able to blackmail you one day. Who knows?"

Saro was a bomb ready to explode. The effects of the opium and whiskey, coupled with Bontade's words, were making his temples pound with the rhythm of a jackhammer. Those words summoned up the most heinous memory of his life, an event that had shaped his recent years and plunged him into despair with no way out. He sprang from the couch, enraged.

Bontade twisted the knife. "I understand, it's terrible to feel betrayed by one's friends. Those who tell us they want to help us, who give us a chance to become who knows what. To them we give our all—even our life if need be. And then we find out that the first chance he got, that benefactor of ours became our destroyer. 'Saro this paper says it clearly,' Saro Ragusa.'" He waved the list of undesirables at the young man. "Ferdinando Licata—*u patri*, as you call him—compiled this list to get rid of all the little men he no longer needs. Licata has to die!" So saying, he rose from the couch and handed Saro a short-barrel .38.

Saro grabbed the pistol and asked, "Is that it?"

Bontade nodded.

———

The prince's niece had never gotten over little Ginevra's death. Every day, Betty went to the cemetery and spent hours in front of her daughter's resting place. She planted little flowers around the grave, shifted the rag dolls from one side of the stone marker to the other. Ever since the day of the attack, she hadn't wanted to see her uncle, whom she viewed as responsible for what had happened to the little girl. Her daughter's tiny body had cushioned the blast and saved her uncle's life, whereas *he* should have been the one to protect the child. The woman was unable to come to terms with what had happened.

Ferdinando Licata felt that it was time for him to reach out to his beloved niece again. He spoke with her husband, who'd been trying to drown his sorrow over the loss of his daughter by working nonstop. That morning, Nico took him to Brooklyn, to Green-Wood Cemetery, where Ginevra was buried. He spotted Betty on one of the steep little hills of the cemetery, busy wiping off the gravestone with a cloth. Licata remembered how moved he had been, that day at the Port of

New York, when he first saw her again after so many years. As on that day, he felt a lump in his throat. He couldn't begin to imagine the pain his niece had suffered over the loss of her child.

The prince was holding a bouquet of daisies. He crossed the lawn, heading toward Betty. Nico let him go ahead. The woman looked up from the grave and saw him standing in front of her, nervously clutching the flowers. She didn't say a word and went back to wiping the marble more fervently.

"Elisabetta . . ." Licata whispered.

The young woman couldn't hold out any longer. Turning to him, she grabbed his shoulders and clung to him desperately. Ferdinando's strong arms encircled her as he buried his face in her hair, choking back tears. Betty burst into uncontrollable sobs of release. They embraced like that for several long minutes as Nico stood watching them, moved as well.

Then Betty collected herself. She slipped out of her uncle's arms and wiped her tears with a small handkerchief. "*Zio*, Ginevra is looking down on us from heaven."

"Now she's happy. And she's scolding me because I called you Elisabetta and not Betty." Licata smiled sadly.

His niece smiled too. Then she noticed her husband and went over to hug him too.

Suddenly a voice behind them shouted, "What a performance! Crocodile tears from Prince Licata!" Saro, distraught and beside himself with rage, was gripping Tom Bontade's .38.

"Saro, are you drunk? Why did you follow me?" Licata cried.

"To tell everyone what a bastard you are! You have a black hole where your conscience should be. Look at him, people! This is *u patri*. A father without children, because he devours them!"

"Saro, that's enough! Calm down!" Licata tried to impose his authority.

"Now that I know what you're capable of, I despise you!" Then he turned to Betty and Nico, who were completely stunned by the verbal attack. "As long as you're useful to him, this gentleman places you on a pedestal. Then when he no longer needs you, he throws you away with the trash. That's what he does to everyone, and that's what he did to me too."

"Have you lost your mind? Whatever they may have told you, it's a lie!" Licata insisted.

"A lie? What about this?" He pulled the list of undesirables out of his jacket pocket and waved it in the air. "This list was written by you!"

Then he spoke to Betty and Nico again: "This is a list of people who will be expelled from America permanently because he so decided. And my name is on it too! That way, Prince Licata will be rid of his closest collaborators!" He pointed the gun at him, determined to shoot.

"No!" Betty's scream drew his attention. "Your destiny follows you relentlessly, Zio. You can't run from yourself! And the loved ones closest to you have to pay for your decisions! Enough is enough now! Stay away from me! Stay away from us!"

She grabbed Nico's arm and forced him to leave. Licata watched her storm off; then he turned angrily to Saro.

"Do you mind telling me what's got into you? Is it that shit you smoke, clouding your brain so you suddenly get these crazy impulses?"

"I know all about it. You lied to me—you and Jack Mastrangelo. The two of you manipulated me like a puppet! You treated me like the world's biggest idiot. I won't stand for it. Not even from you."

"I don't know what you're talking about."

"About the Blue Lemon! Go on, tell me about the Blue Lemon! Tell me how Mastrangelo beat up two people, and then you let me think it was me. Do you deny it?"

Someone must have seen Mastrangelo and leaked the truth to Saro, Licata thought. "Who told you that bullshit?" the prince asked uncertainly.

"Your pal Bonrade. He described the scene in complete detail. You lied to me. You've always lied to me, even when you lay dying in a hospital bed. You made me think I had been the one who murdered those two people. And you betrayed me. You betrayed me when you wrote up this list. A person like you only deserves to die." He pointed the pistol firmly at Licata.

"Wait, Saro. I didn't betray you. I swear to you. I never betrayed you."

"Too bad." Saro fingered the trigger.

For the first time in his life Ferdinando Licata felt he was done for. "I've always protected you! You're the person I care most about in this world! I swear!"

"Too late." He stiffened his wrist, as Mastrangelo had taught him, to be ready for the gun's recoil.

Licata understood the young man's desperation. "Saro, don't shoot! I swear I never betrayed you. I could never betray my own son!"

"You'll try anything, right?"

"It's the truth. You're my son, Saro. My son! I'm your real father." Licata's sorrowful tone left no room for doubt.

Saro lowered the pistol. "Don't screw around with me! Don't fuck with me!"

Licata went to him. "You've always known that the Ragusas aren't your natural parents, haven't you? That you were adopted by them, right?"

"They're my only parents."

"And they've been exemplary with you, but your real mother's name was Carole." Licata was moved as never before. "She was a beautiful English girl: adventurous, cheerful, free, and easy. We met in Sicily. She loved to travel. We fell in love at first sight. I spent the happiest days of my life with her. Unforgettable days. They are imprinted in my mind, and I will carry them with me to the grave."

Saro was stunned. That revelation only confused his thinking even more.

"You are the fruit of our love."

"I'm your son?"

"Yes," the prince replied quietly.

"Then why did you give me up for adoption?"

"It is the greatest regret of my life," Ferdinando Licata finally confessed, releasing a weight that he had carried for well over twenty years. "I'm to blame. I'm solely to blame . . .

"Forgive me, Saro, forgive me." He took the hand that still clutched the pistol and kissed it. Saro drew back his hand, frightened at seeing the prince in that state. He had never seen him so vulnerable and weak. "It was my fault. I was almost forty years old, and I was afraid to marry a woman, to have a child. The work I was doing would not allow me to have enduring bonds. I could be blackmailed. I gave you and Carole up in exchange for power."

"You abandoned me."

"Carole died two days after giving birth. They couldn't stop the hemorrhaging. I refused to see you for fear of becoming attached to you. I was insane. Only a madman acts like that, but at the time, things were tough. There was no room for family ties," he said, resuming his usual irrefutable tone. "I chose the most decent people in Salemi, and I gave you up to be adopted by them. Dr. Ragusa was a decent man and an educated one. He was an excellent father to you. I always kept track of you, thinking one day I would be able to tell you everything and be reunited with you. I never wanted for you to learn the truth in circumstances such as these. Unfortunately, fate often arranges things differently from what we have planned."

"Very touching. But why saddle me with a murder that I didn't commit?"

"You must believe me. Given your respectful ways, you would never have gotten far in this world of wolves. I had to bring out whatever evil there was in you. Believing that you had committed that murder would give you enough self-assurance in crime to be able to move confidently among killers and thieves."

"Yeah, that incident changed my life."

"That's what I wanted. And as for that list—well, it's a red herring. Haffenden, the commander of naval intelligence, and I decided to put your name on the list to allow you to come and go in Sicily without suspicion. In fact, you'll have to leave for the island with the first contingent of OSS secret agents who will prepare for the landing of the American troops."

"Sounds like a very complex scheme."

"Yes. It's a brilliant scheme. But I haven't told you everything yet. I have great plans for you. The landing will play in our favor. You will manage the subsequent normalization period. You and Don Calò will put friends of friends in strategic posts essential to our future dealings, and you will be their boss. I'll remain in New York and see to maintaining a direct line with you. You and I will control the Cosa Nostra's main areas of trade. Do you realize what that means?"

Saro was struck by Licata's words. Then he embraced him, as he had never done with anyone. And for the first time in his life, he murmured, "Papa."

Chapter 54

Jack Mastrangelo hadn't heard any word about his niece for several weeks now.

Bontade had told him not to worry. As long as he was alive, the girl had nothing to fear.

Mastrangelo's investigations had petered out. He didn't believe Bontade; on the contrary, he was afraid his niece may have already been killed, and the thought of it drove him mad.

But Aurora wasn't dead. Indeed, the enforced wait, the fear of those men who took turns around her, the violent acts of one who, unseen by the others, stroked her private parts, awakening unfamiliar sensations—all these things had dispelled the constant fog that clouded her brain.

With each passing day, images and people popped up in her mind, impressions that her psyche had hidden away in a corner so as not to upset her. She saw and recognized the face of her mother. She remembered her name, Elena. She remembered her screaming desperately. And she remembered those big hands around her neck, squeezing, squeezing, until the woman fell on top of her.

Her thoughts were distinct, and the scene, which she went over every day in her mind, invariably made her cry. But it was the kind of crying that made her feel better.

She remembered the faces of the ladies dressed in black, their heads wrapped in white cloth strips. She could remember some kind ones among them and some less so.

Aurora also remembered the little garden behind the house. One day it occurred to her that if she could remember, she could also speak like she had at one time. She tried to say "Hello, Aurora." But only an incoherent croak came from her mouth. She had to exercise her vocal cords. She was sure she would be able to talk. She looked around. She spent the hours of the day waiting for meals, admiring the objects that had been stored up in that room, unable to imagine what fate had in store for her.

———

By mutual accord, Licata and Mastrangelo decided it was time to take action.

Every year in late spring, Bonrade's Beechhurst estate had its final cord of firewood delivered. The pickup truck stopped on the side of the main building. Besides Aldo Martini, Bonrade had insisted on having three trusted bodyguards with him: Vincenzo Sanfilippo, Antonio Vella, and Peter Alaimo, illegal immigrants who had recently arrived from Italy and had been given to him by a cousin in Sicily.

Vincenzo and Peter thoroughly checked both the truck and the two men who had brought the load. Everything seemed okay, so they ordered the two men to unload the wood and stack it in a corner of the garden.

The bodyguards kept an eye on them until the pickup disappeared down the road.

A few days later, in the early morning, Antonio Vella went to get an armload of wood for the fireplace in the living room, where Bonrade had lately started having his breakfast. As he lit the wood, Antonio Vella had no idea that the last load had been sprayed with a deadly, highly toxic substance. Prolonged exposure to fumes resulting from the burning of the toxin would, in the long run, fatally poison anyone who inhaled the vapors.

Tom Bonrade came down early that morning and asked for the newspaper. He had insisted on maintaining his usual routines, even after the incendiary article in the Sun.

Bonrade ate his anise biscotti with his favorite apple jam. He sweetened his cup of milk with honey. He read the news of the day. As fate would have it, just that day there was a strong wind that kept the fireplace from drawing properly. A bit of smoke seeped into the room.

Vella, crouched beside the fireplace, trying to keep the smoke from drifting back, was the first to fall to the floor, foaming at the mouth. Then Peter Alaimo; he too afflicted by pulmonary spasms. He doubled over, gasping in pain, and spat out a strange bluish froth, then lay still.

Bonrade was alarmed. He called Aldo Martini. At that instant the phone rang, and in a flash he remembered what had been written in the fabricated article in the Sun: the corpse had been found answering the phone. Terror took hold of each and every cell in his body. He approached the telephone that kept ringing insistently. Then he grabbed the receiver.

"Hello, you bastard. How does it feel to have death breathing over you?" The voice was Prince Licata's. "There's someone here who wants to talk to you."

Bontade's lungs struggled to take in oxygen. He could barely breathe. The voices came to him confused. His brain was less and less oxygenated, and he had to sit on the floor, his legs no longer supported him.

Now Mastrangelo was on the phone: "You have a few minutes to surrender your soul to the devil. If you tell me where Aurora is, I'll let you have the antidote to the poison. There's a doctor outside your gate. If you talk, you can still save your hide. As soon as you tell me where she is, I'll give him the order to inject the drip. It's up to you, make up your mind."

Bontade was finding it increasingly difficult to breathe. His mouth was filled with thick saliva. "She's right here. Hurry. . . hurry. . . I'm dying." He struggled to get those few words out.

There was no doctor outside Bontade's house. The old mafioso collapsed on the floor with the phone still in his hands. He tried desperately to suck in a breath of air. But the inability to breathe was now irreversible. The spasms were horrific as he clung to the still remaining thread of life with every ounce of strength he had.

Mastrangelo cursed himself for having ruled out from the start the possibility that Aurora might be in the most obvious place, Bontade's "bunker." He started speeding toward Queens—to hell with the traffic lights. In his heart, he was terrified of getting there too late to save his niece. He didn't understand how the toxin could have acted so quickly and with such virulence. The chemist they'd recruited had promised it would be diluted enough to cause extreme illness and death only after several hours of exposure.

Mastrangelo arrived at the house. There was no one to stop him. He put on his gas mask and entered from the back. On the hallway floor, he saw Aldo Martini, whose eyes were glassy. He then ran to the living room and saw Bontade, still clutching the phone. The fire was burning and kept giving off poisonous toxins. He raced through every room of the house. Instinctively, he called the girl's name at the top of his lungs. He didn't find her in any of the rooms. Bontade couldn't have been lying when he was at death's door.

Suddenly he heard a voice: "Here! I'm down here." He had never heard Aurora speak; it couldn't be her.

The voice was coming from the basement. The door leading down to the cellar was unlocked. Mastrangelo ran down the steps and, in the center of the room, surrounded by stacks of objects, he saw Aurora.

"Here, over here."

She was speaking! So she could speak! Mastrangelo bent over her. She was lying on a kind of mattress set on the rough cement floor.

"Aurora, I'm your Uncle Jack—your mother's brother. Do you understand my words?"

"Yes, Uncle Jack." The girl was having trouble breathing. Painfully she opened her eyes and raised a hand to stroke her uncle's cheek.

"If only your mother were here." Mastrangelo kissed the hand she'd reached out to him. "Come on, let's get out of here." He pulled out a handkerchief and wiped away the saliva that flowed abundantly down her chin. He put his mask on her. But Aurora's breathing was now a rattle.

He mustn't lose another minute. He took her in his arms, she smiled at him, and then she closed her eyes, overcome by the spasms crushing her chest. Mastrangelo held her tightly and headed for the stairs. For a moment, he staggered and had to pause to catch his breath. Now he too felt intense pain in his chest and struggled to breathe. Summoning all his strength, he took the steps one by one. The door was at the top of the stairs, but it seemed like it was at the end of a tunnel. The dazzling light blinded him. He steadied himself against the wall and went on climbing. Just a little more effort, and he would make it. All of a sudden Aurora's body went limp in his arms, its weight doubling. He knew the girl was dead, but irrationally pushed away the thought. He mustn't give up. He'd never in his life been a quitter, and he wasn't about to start now when he had to save his niece's life.

At last, he reached the door. Now they had to get out of the house in a hurry. He rushed down the corridor, but his chest heaved, and a fitful cough made him expel a clot of blood that stained the garment of the young woman whose head now dangled lifelessly. Jack Mastrangelo fell to his knees, spent by the effort he'd made thus far. Tenderly, he laid Aurora's body on the floor. He unbuttoned his shirt and tried to breathe, but the jagged ache in his chest pierced him like a sword. He tried to contain the sharp blade with his hands, but the stabbing pain spread through his body. He fell back. He turned and looked at Aurora. Her mouth seemed to form a smile. He reached out to her, and even that simple act was an effort. He felt like crying or shouting in despair over such a rotten fate, but he couldn't do either. His hand reached the girl's hand and he placed it over hers, as if to keep the promise he'd made so long ago to his beloved sister. Then he opened his mouth gasping for one last breath of air, but it was no use.

The phony news story about Tom Bontade's death, so minutely described in the *Sun*, had made the rounds of the city at the time and had led to much teasing by the other bosses, not only in New York but also in Las Vegas and Chicago. The paper had issued an apology, and the reporter had been fired. But when the event reported back then became a real news item, an icy chill descended on all the Mafia families in the various districts. Such a thing had never happened. Everyone knew who was behind it, but they were careful not to let on. Ferdinando Licata had won everyone's respect—even those who hated him for his rapid rise.

When Roy Boccia, in his basement cell at naval intelligence, found out from one of the guards about what had happened, he was seized by panic. Terror became his daily bread. He finally decided to cooperate with the cops, realizing that as soon as he stuck his nose out of prison, Licata would have him killed.

He asked for a meeting with the district attorney. He wanted to make a confession. When the prosecutor called him in, he said he was ready to testify in court against Saro Ragusa. He admitted that he had seen him assault Vito Pizzuto in a warehouse at the port, chaining him up and torturing him to death.

In exchange for his testimony, however, he demanded that he be given a new identity and passport so he could build a fresh life in another part of the world, far from New York.

Based on the allegations of that eyewitness, public prosecutor William Brey issued an arrest warrant for Saro Ragusa. He was unaware, however, that Saro had meanwhile been enlisted by the OSS—Office of Strategic Services—for Operation Husky.

Chapter 55

In strictest secrecy, Saro Ragusa was picked up one day in midspring by two soldiers in civilian clothes and escorted to a military base near Washington.

There, along with a dozen other young men of Sicilian origin, he was given intensive training in how to use automatic pistols and submachine guns, how to assemble a bomb and recognize detonators and explosive powders, and how to use a radio for communications, as well as the basics of karate. Lastly, he made three parachute jumps, one by day and two others at night. The instructors informed the Sicilian-American operatives that they would parachute onto the Sicilian coast under cover of darkness.

The group was part of the Office of Strategic Services, the intelligence services division established during that period by a volcanic Irish attorney in Washington named William "Wild Bill" Donovan.

The OSS was divided into several sections. Secret Intelligence, dedicated to operations in occupied nations; Secret Operations, the liaison for operations to be carried out with resistance forces in countries occupied by the Germans; Morale Operations, the section for psychological warfare; the X-2, devoted to counterintelligence; and Research and Analysis, the investigation unit charged with providing political, social, and economic data about the countries in which they operated.

Within the Secret Intelligence branch, there was a subdivision called the Italian Section, created by a certain Earl Brennan. The key figures were Vincent Scamporino, charged with leading the section, attorney Victor Anfuso, and Max Corvo, barely twenty years old.

The section had been formed to organize a group made up essentially of native Sicilians, who were to initiate the task of infiltration aimed at supporting the upcoming Allied invasion. To obtain information about Italy, the team drew on a pool of six million Italian-Americans. They sought collaborators among Sicilians who had been forced to emigrate not only because the fascists had never cared about their region but also because the regime had treated them as criminals, sending soldiers and carabinieri to oppress the population.

When Prince Licata asked Haffenden about the possibility of recruiting Saro Ragusa for the Italian Section, the leaders were happy to enlist him in the unit.

Max Corvo's men covertly infiltrated every area of the island, looking for minefields, military facilities, command centers, airstrips, antifascists—in short, any information that might prove useful to the forces that were preparing for the invasion. In particular, they had to convince the Italian soldiers to lay down their arms, since fascism had been defeated, and each man had to think about his own future: one that would be shared not with the Germans but with the Americans and the British.

Saro, along with a dozen other Sicilians, was dropped into the Corleone area on a moonless night.

It was not the softest of landings. He ended up hitting a stone wall, the kind used to mark the boundaries of a field, and the parachute dragged him over a large prickly pear. The cactus's sharp spines pierced the rough cloth of his pants, causing him excruciating pain. According to the instructions Saro had been given, first he was to fold up the parachute and hide it under a bush. As he painfully set about recovering the fabric, he was surrounded by two farmers pointing their shotguns at him. They asked him who he was, and Saro replied in dialect that he had come to prepare for the arrival of the Americans. Reassured by those words, the two men helped him pack the parachute back together and then led him to their nearby cabin.

There he could see firsthand the extreme poverty to which his people had been subjected. Malnourished children, undoubtedly with lice and bedbugs feasting on them; women who'd aged before their time; clothes that were coming apart at the seams; homes that could only be called hovels; malaria; and resignation in the men's eyes, crushed by a government that had left them at the mercy of those in power. But he also observed in them a proud, indomitable dignity and an awareness of their own worth.

The man made the women and children leave and told Saro to lie down on the straw mattress; he would pick out the spines of the prickly pear for him. Saro took off his shirt and pants, and the old man set about his task with infinite patience.

Saro had been dropped into the heart of the island, where US general George Patton would pass with his armored columns. Naturally, he knew nothing about the tactical plans for the invasion. His orders were to contact the Mafia bosses and persuade them to cooperate with the American troops. Saro, however, also had another assignment, given to him by Ferdinando Licata: he was to take advantage of his situation by laying the groundwork for repositioning the bosses at the top levels of the new government, while also appealing to the Sicilian Independence Movement championed by attorney Andrea Finocchiaro-Aprile. Up until the advent of fascism, Aprile had served in three legislatures as deputy from the electoral district of Corleone, considered the headquarters of the Mafia Council.

Finocchiaro-Aprile dreamed of the island's independence from Italy and was willing to make alliances with anyone in order to realize that goal: first of all, with the party of the big landowners, well represented by Lucio Tasca, who, with the motto "Sicily and Liberty," saw separatism as the best way to safeguard privileges and fiefdoms. And then with the top Mafia bosses: Calogero Vizzini of Villalba, Giuseppe Genco Russo of Mussomeli, Greco of Croce Verde Giardini, Virgilio Nasi of Trapani, Vincenzo Rimi of Alcamo, and Vanni Sacco of Palermo. All were very much in favor of eliminating the dictatorship, which, besides sending many of them to prison, had taken control of their territory. The Mafia required democracy, not dictatorship, in order to flourish.

While Saro was busy creating a cover that would allow him to move freely in the area without arousing suspicion, Jano and his men, in their new guise as supporters of the family bosses, turned into saboteurs. Better yet, following the orders of Don Calò, whom Jano now familiarly called *zu* Calò, they began robbing supplies brought to the artillery redoubts in unescorted trucks.

For Sicilians, life became a living hell. Every day, squadrons of Allied fighter planes took off from Malta to support bombers that came from North Africa to drop their explosives on cities and military positions. The bombs were democratic; they did not discriminate. They shelled the famous Hotel San Domenico in Taormina, where German field marshal Albert Kesselring maintained his headquarters, and razed the town of Palazzolo Acreide, where the Italian army's Napoli Division was headquartered, almost completely neutralizing the unit. For nine days, the Sicilians lived in terror of the nightly bombings, which nearly always struck areas where there were clusters of troops or military commands.

The Italian Section's efforts had produced excellent results. Saro in particular had a stroke of luck. After the mission in Corleone, where he was able to obtain a promise of cooperation from the local families, he headed for Gela to await the landing and be reunited with the OSS group.

As a cover, Saro dusted off his old line of work as a barber. He went around from farmhouse to farmhouse offering to cut the farmers' hair or trim their beards and mustaches in return for some vegetables or a chicken egg.

In the countryside around Gela, he was welcomed by a gabellotto named Giovanni Scirè, who asked Saro to spruce him up. His son would be marrying a local girl in a few days. Scirè was a jovial, ruddy man who apparently hadn't suffered any hunger pangs as a result of the war, since he and his family seemed well fed and in good health overall. The son had even found time to fall in love.

As he was sharpening his razor on the leather strop, Saro asked him, "Is your son on matrimonial leave?"

"I don't know. Why are you asking?"

"Just curious. I wondered which battalion he was in. I have relatives scattered throughout most of the island." He got ready to shave the man's beard.

"The war is over now. Too bad, because the party's over for us as well," the gabellotto said with regret.

"Are you are a supporter of the Duce?" Saro goaded him.

"Are you kidding?" the man said angrily.

"Well then? I don't get it."

The man lowered his voice, as if not wanting to be overheard: "The Italian naval command is nearby."

"Not in Enna?"

"The general staff is in Enna. The naval command is here. Their rations are limited, so they ask us to supply them with all sorts of things, and we make them pay black market prices. They're used to eating well, those fine gentlemen." Saro's antenna immediately went up, but he launched into the kind of populist claims that everyone can always agree on. "While we go hungry."

"Have you ever seen a grand gentleman who was any different? They're all alike." Scirè was sprawled in the chair, hands folded over his belly, eyes half closed, taking pleasure in having his beard shaved.

"Where is the command?" Saro tossed out the question casually.

"In Baron Giovanni Moleti's villa. There are generals and officials coming and going. By now it's an open secret. All of Sicily knows the naval command is there."

"Have you ever been in there?"

For Giovanni Sciré, having come in contact with the gracious world of the upper ranks was a source of great pride. "Of course! I'm the one who brings them their chickens and hens. Inside the rooms, the walls are hung with large maps of Sicily. The tables are covered with piles of papers. There's also a large safe. I'd never seen one before."

"Where is the safe?"

"In the central room, where they all are. They put it near the portrait of Baron Giovanni Moleti's great-grandfather. He was one of Garibaldi's Mille—the One Thousand—you know," Sciré told him.

It wasn't difficult for Saro to locate the villa. It had been constructed in the eighteenth century, with spacious, lushly planted grounds which had not been maintained for some years. The façade was rose colored, and on one side there was a grand terrace overlooking a valley that sloped down toward the sea. To the left of the main building stood a small house, also rosy pink, with a red-tiled roof; in earlier times, it had served as the servants' quarters, but now it housed troops assigned to guard the naval command. That was all that could be seen from the road. Saro set his mind to opening the safe, but to do that, he would need some friendly help and support from Gela's Mafia. For several days, he studied the situation, noting that the command's routine worked somewhat like an office's: a soldier arrived around eight o'clock in the morning to open the command. Officers and generals got there at ten and departed around seven in the evening, leaving a couple of soldiers to stand guard outside. The Moleti family could then enjoy a little privacy, at least until eight the following morning.

The job did not present insurmountable difficulties. All he had to do was neutralize the two guards. As for the rest, the baron's family didn't worry him at all.

To swing into action, however, Saro needed at least three men ready for anything. He approached a major player, a certain Vincenzo Lanzafame, who had trained him for the upcoming landing. The man was actually happy to be of use and assigned Saro three of his best men.

The two soldiers in the outbuilding's small kitchen were preparing a dish of spaghetti *al pomodoro* when they were surprised by Saro's team. Bashed with clubs wrapped in damp cloth, they fell to the floor unconscious. The three mafiosi looked at Saro, as if to ask for his permission. Saro thought they were waiting for him to compliment them.

But one of the three, moving to the platter that sat there ready to eat, said, "Are we gonna let it get cold?"

In times like those, wasting food was a sin. They divided the spaghetti up, filling two more plates, and ate silently, gobbling it down in just a few forkfuls.

Their bellies filled, they left the small house and headed toward the villa.

As cautious and discreet as they had been not to make too much noise, the baron had noticed the unusual commotion behind the windows. He opened the door of the villa before the mafiosi could get out their lock picks. Saro and the others were alarmed, but Giovanni Moleti was quick to reassure them. He welcomed them as liberators and asked Saro, the only one of the crew he didn't know, if it was true that the landing was now imminent and that the bombings actually meant that it was just a matter of days.

Saro confirmed his hunch. The baron invited him in and showed him the naval command room.

The gabellotto's description was fully accurate. Saro saw the painting portraying Baron Moleti's ancestor. Beside the fireplace stood the safe. He asked if he could open it. The nobleman practically beat his breast, apologetic about not knowing the combination; he begged them to believe him.

To speed things up Saro decided to blast it open with a small charge of dynamite he'd brought with him.

The door flew off, and what he saw inside would have made any spy ecstatic: dossiers, maps, encrypted documents, envelopes bearing the eagle of the Third Reich. There was information about the positioning of Italian ships, and the Luftwaffe's deployment over the Mediterranean. There were even confidential orders for the Wehrmacht's divisions in Italy. Saro hurriedly slipped all the papers into a satchel, said good-bye to the baron, and left the villa with the three mafiosi. He separated from them shortly afterward, promising to remember them and Vincenzo Lanzafame.

Twenty-four hours later, the satchel was in the hands of OSS agents, who delivered it at once to Vice Admiral Kent Hewitt, commander of US naval forces in European waters.

———

The bombing of the island's main cities reduced many of them to rubble.

The appointed day for the Allied troops' landing was July 10, 1943.

Rather than gathering at a single assembly point, the assault fleet's ships had sailed from various ports—Port Said, Alexandria, Tripoli, Sousse, Sfax, Algiers, Oran, Bizerte—joining forces once at sea. Nothing like it had ever been seen in living memory. The imposing armada consisted of 2,590 transport vessels, 1,800 landing craft, and 280 warships.

The Fifteenth Army Group was under the command of British general Harold Alexander, and when they neared the coast, they would be divided into two other task forces: the US Seventh Army, commanded by Lieutenant General Patton, which would land on the beach at Gela; and the British Eighth Army, commanded by General Bernard Montgomery, which would come ashore south of Siracusa.

According to the strategy devised by the British and American generals, Montgomery's men were to head toward Messina, to close off the escape route and hem in the Italian-German forces, while Patton would keep the west side of the island in check.

Left to oppose these shock troops was a demoralized Axis army. Nearly all the Italian infantry, artillery, and gunnery units were made up of Sicilians who feared for their families and despised the regime that had treated them like stepchildren. In addition, their outfits and equipment were in desperate shape. They had no shoes, not to mention uniforms. Some soldiers wore a regulation jacket and civvies for pants, while others wore military pants and civilian shirts. And when it came to armaments, the situation was truly pathetic. Besides numerical inferiority, since the thirty-eight Italian and nine German battalions were facing sixty-nine Allied contingents, there was the inadequacy of their weapons, which were few and in poor condition.

Chapter 56

With the second wave, OSS members landed in Gela, arriving in force to support the agents already present on the island. Their main task was to interrogate prisoners and civilians to obtain information about routes through the countryside, minefields, and gun emplacements. Additionally, they were to continue looking for the individuals designated by Luciano to ask for their collaboration.

The two landings were quite successful. In particular, Patton's Seventh Army encountered almost no resistance in Gela, while Montgomery was able to enter Siracusa the same night of the landing.

By the end of the invasion's first day, more than a thousand Italians had already been taken prisoner, and at least that many had thrown down their rifles and fled to the countryside to hide. After a week, the number of prisoners had grown to twenty-two thousand, half of them Sicilian. The OSS men suggested sending them home, since the fields needed laborers for the upcoming harvest. That way, American logistics operations wouldn't be strained to the breaking point.

The idea made headway in the commanders' minds as well. The Allies would allow all soldiers who had surrendered to return to their villages.

Operation *Tutti a Casa*—"Everybody Home"—allowed over thirty-five thousand Sicilian troops to abandon the war, and by so doing, to save their lives, thereby accelerating the collapse of the Italian army in Sicily.

———

On the morning of July 14, four days after the start of the invasion, an American fighter plane flew over the skies of Villalba, attracting the attention of farmers and the village's few inhabitants. The pilot aroused their curiosity by making a couple of turns at low altitude over the church rectory, as if to display a yellow flag with a big black *L* in the center, fluttering cheerfully from the radio's forward antenna. At the third turn, the pilot tilted the plane 45 degrees and dropped a large satchel near the residence of Monsignor Giovanni Vizzini, the village priest and brother of the famous Don Calogero Vizzini. It contained a silk scarf identical to the one waving from the plane's antenna. The satchel was to Lance Corporal Angelo Riccioli of Palermo.

The following day, the same fighter plane flew over the area of Cozzo di Garbo, where Calogero Vizzini's home was located, and dropped a second satchel right in front of his house.

The bag was marked "*zu* Calò" and was picked up by one of Vizzini's household staff and delivered to its intended recipient.

That same evening, a local farmer known only as Mangiapane set off from Villalba at full speed, galloping toward Mussomeli. He carried a message penned in dialect by Calogero Vizzini.

The message was top secret, and Mangiapane had instructions to swallow it if he were stopped by anyone. It was addressed to *zu* Peppi, Giuseppe Genco Russo, the local boss in Mussomeli.

Couching his words in the Mafia's colorful idiom, Don Calò had written to tell him that on Tuesday the twentieth, a certain Turi—evidently the head of a family in the Polizzi Generosa area—would accompany the armored divisions (which he called "calves," to the "fair" in Cerda, while he himself would leave the same day with the bulk of the troops (cows), the tanks (wagons), and the commander in chief (bull). *Zu* Peppi was to make sure their friends prepared hotbeds of resistance and possible shelters for the troops.

At dawn the following day, Mangiapane returned with *zu* Peppi's response, assuring Don Calò that the herdsman Liddu had taken care of laying the groundwork for the resistance.

On July 20 Patton's tanks approached Salso Inferiore. A jeep carrying two soldiers and a civilian messenger broke away from the column and headed for Villalba at top speed, thirty miles ahead of the advance guard. Fluttering on the jeep's antenna was the yellow flag with a big black L in the center. Unfortunately, shortly before reaching the road to the village, the driver of took the wrong fork and headed for Lumera. There he ran into an Italian patrol, the rearguard of the Assietta Division. When they saw the American jeep, the Italian soldiers opened fire and hit the messenger, who fell out of the vehicle. Under fire from the Italians, the driver had no choice but to turn around and quickly return to where he had come from.

The messenger had been killed instantly. His body lay in the road for several hours. A passing villager stopped his cart and took the leather pouch that was still slung around the man's neck. Inside he found an envelope addressed to Calogero Vizzini. A few minutes later, the envelope was in *zu* Calò's hands.

On the afternoon of the same day, three American Sherman tanks arrived outside Villalba. The first of the three flew the yellow flag with the black *L*. The turret hatch opened, and a man with a Sicilian accent asked the curious onlookers to go call Don Calò, who appeared a few minutes later in shirtsleeves, his jacket folded over his arm, and a cigar in his mouth. He approached unhurriedly, not so much because of his considerable bulk but because that's how *"uomini di panza"*—men of substance—walk. The don was accompanied by his grandson Damiano Lumia, who had immigrated to America but had been stuck in Villalba when the war broke out.

Without saying a word, Calogero Vizzini took his yellow scarf out of his pants pocket and showed it to the tank's crewman. The man signaled for him to climb in, and Don Calò, together with his grandson, who was fluent in English as well as Sicilian, disappeared from Villalba for eleven days.

———————

Saro and the Italian Section team had proved invaluable in directing the tank columns. Their information turned out to be consistently accurate, clearly the result of his group's diligence in carrying out its intelligence activities.

William Donovan himself, the man responsible for forming the OSS, had gone to Sicily to see the work firsthand and, naturally, to accept the general staff's compliments. Donovan also had to attend to several delicate covert missions, such as the release of about a hundred mafiosi imprisoned by the fascist regime on the island of Favignana. It was one of the promises that had been made to Luciano in exchange for his help and that of the Sicilian Mafia.

Nonetheless, for the armies of Patton and Montgomery, the advance through the island was not easy. While many Italians chose to abandon their uniforms, many others put up a heroic fight on Sicilian soil. After the relatively easy conquest of Gela, Patton faced vigorous counterattacks from the Livorno Division and Germany's Goering Panzer Division, while Montgomery was stopped outside of Catania, which resisted to the last man.

———————

Sergeant Charles Dickey of the FBI arrived at Patton's headquarters in the midst of this inferno, having come directly from the New York DA's Office. He had been sent by prosecutor William Bray with a warrant for the arrest of Saro Ragusa, accused of killing Vito Pizzuto.

Saro, returning from a mission, was immediately handed over to the sergeant. When Donovan was personally notified of this grave interference, he in turn ordered Vincent Scamporino, head of the OSS section, to resolve the matter at once and to "kick the FBI intruder's ass back into the Mediterranean." As a civilian, Scamporino had pleaded a million cases and was skilled in dialectics. He met with the sergeant in one of the offices of the Seventh Army command center. Saro was behind bars in a cell at the carabinieri headquarters in Gela.

The OSS section head introduced himself and wasted no time in laying into the sergeant. "I'm Vincent Scamporino. There's a war going on out there, see, so I don't have much time. Let's try to understand each other quickly."

"And I'm telling you right now, my friend, that I'm not afraid of either your rank or your threats. I'm here to serve justice. There are no good days and bad days where justice is concerned; every day is the same. War or no war, Saro Ragusa is accused of having killed a man. There's an eye-witness who says so. So he has to come with me to New York to prove his innocence before a jury. Have I made myself clear?"

"Maybe you didn't get what I said." Scamporino was furious and couldn't contain himself, shaking his finger angrily at the other man. "A war means that people—or, rather, American soldiers—may live or die depending on whether I and my men, including Saro Ragusa, are able to provide them with the most reliable information possible." He raised his voice and could be heard even on the top floors of the building.

"Now, I want to know how the fuck you people fit into all this! What the hell do you bureaucrats, sitting there warming your chairs behind a desk, know about what's going on here on this fucking island! That man is saving the army money, valuable time, and, above all, human lives! The lives of American young men! He should be commended by the taxpayers, by American mothers, and by you, mister pain-in-the-ass FBI nobody!"

The sergeant's tough shell wasn't even scratched by Scamporino's outburst. He replied coolly, "It's simply a matter of fairness, Major. Justice treats everyone the same, and we cannot —"

Scamporino didn't let him finish his sentence: "You know where you can stick that justice of yours?"

"Okay, I get it. Let's try to meet halfway: I'll let Ragusa go now so he can continue his war efforts. But as soon as all this bedlam is over and his work is no longer needed, I'll arrest him and bring him to New York. Does that sound all right with you?"

Vincent Scamporino accepted the compromise. The sergeant started to hold out his hand, but the major walked out without so much as a glance.

Saro was set free at once and permitted to return to his intelligence activities, but he often found Sergeant Dickey lurking behind him. The man wouldn't let him out of his sight, not even to go to the toilet.

Meanwhile, Patton's army had branched into two sections in Agrigento. The first, commanded by Patton himself, continued around the coast to Palermo, which the swaggering American general captured on July 22. The other company headed inland, it too advancing toward Palermo. Once they were reunited, the two units would make their way toward the crossroads of Cerda, a village not far from Termini Imerese, where they would meet up with the Third Corps of Patton's army, which had encountered fierce resistance from the Goering and Livorno Divisions.

The operational plan described in simple terms in Don Calò's encrypted note had been successful. The two divisions had hemmed in the Italian-German forces, closing off any possibility of their retreating to Messina, where the strait presented an escape route to the mainland. At that point, Don Calò was brought back to Villalba, accompanied by two American officers. The don had explained to them that his jurisdiction ceased at the Cerda crossroads. The boundary marked the division between the authority of the *mafia dei feudi*—the landowners Mafia—which he controlled, and that of the *mafia dei mulini*—the millers mafia—run by the ruthless families of Caccamo. Still farther on was the *mafia dei giardini*, the gardens Mafia, which controlled the distribution of water.

The two officers didn't wholly understand the reasoning behind those divisions, but nonetheless they thanked Don Calò for his help and took their leave with perfect military salutes.

The day after Don Calò's return to Villalba, at the carabinieri station, he was appointed mayor of the town by Lieutenant Beehr, Mussomeli's civil affairs officer. The villagers were ecstatic and shouted, "Long live Don Calò! Long live the Mafia!"

The Americans allowed Don Calò, his men of honor, and the mafiosi under his jurisdiction to carry firearms "in order to safeguard against possible transgressions by the fascists, to carry out with authority the tasks assigned to them by Mayor Calogero Vizzini, and to serve as backup to the carabinieri if necessary."

Once the fascist mayors were removed, the Allies needed to appoint new local administrators. It was natural for them to turn their attention to those individuals who had always been hostile to the fascist regime, or to those who enjoyed authority and prestige, without checking whether that prestige derived from unlawful activities.

And so, many members of the Mafia, credited as antifascists, ended up filling important government positions.

Giuseppe Genco Russo was appointed superintendent of public assistance in Mussomeli. In Raffadali, in the province of Agrigento, Vincenzo Di Carlo, the underboss of the local family, was assigned to head up the grain requisitioning office. Max Mugnaini, a known drug dealer, was chosen to manage American pharmaceutical warehouses in Italy. In Vallelunga, Turiddu Malta was appointed mayor. For the office of mayor in Racalmuto, Don Calò designated a former associate, Baldassarre Tenebra. For the first time in their lives, the most powerful exponents of the Mafia organization were placed in political roles. In order to quickly secure control of the island, the Allies weren't overly fastidious, often falling for schemes hatched by local leaders, frequently instigated by Saro Ragusa himself.

In those heady days of late July, the Cosa Nostra thus took to operating openly again. Its men had infiltrated many of the offices in the new administration. They were able to do legally what up until then had been considered illegal, and this time it was their benefactors, the Americans, who paid for it.

In Corleone, the command center, a safe containing money earmarked for the XII Army Corps actually disappeared. In Vallelunga one night, some people broke down the doors of the pharmaceutical storehouse, looting everything that could be carried off, especially penicillin, the prodigious new miracle drug. In Montemaggiore Belsito, hundreds of overcoats set aside for the winter vanished. Not to mention the disappearances of gasoline tanks, telephone cables, flour, and wheat. For dealers in the black market, they were unforgettable days.

With the capture of Messina by Patton on August 17, the Sicilian campaign could be said to be over. The bare figures reported that in the thirty-eight days of the campaign, 4,875 Italians, 4,369 Germans, 2,899 American soldiers, and 2,721 troops from the British Commonwealth had lost their lives.

To mark the end of the conflict, a large celebration was arranged at the summer home of the marquis of Torrearsa, Enrico Ferro. All the area's notables were invited: the landed aristocracy, British and American officers from the nearby command center, and friends of friends.

Lieutenant Colonel Charles Poletti, US Army civil affairs officer on the island during the entire period of military rule in Sicily, was also present. In civilian life, Poletti had been an attorney, a profession he abandoned first to serve as a justice of the New York State Supreme Court, and later to pursue a political career.

Nearly all the representatives of Sicily's oldest families were invited to the event, along with the most powerful Mafia figures. Vincent Scamporino and Max Corvo took advantage of the occasion to proudly present nearly all the members of their Italian Section group, among them Saro Ragusa in his brand-new American uniform. Behind Saro, as usual, was his shadow, FBI Sergeant Charles Dickey, who was eager to be able to finally drag him back to a cell in New York.

Scamporino approached Dickey and asked him to give Saro some breathing room, at least for that night, and let him enjoy the victory to which he could say he'd contributed. The sergeant, unfazed, replied calmly that he would stand aside, but the following morning, he would put Saro on the first military plane bound for the United States.

The party was made livelier by torrents of wine and a great many joyous toasts. A band, composed of American soldiers, played Glenn Miller's latest hits. Ladies of the Sicilian bourgeoisie danced with American officers in their smart uniforms, while their husbands tried to cozy up to those in charge of trade operations, to put together lucrative business deals.

Then, as in any self-respecting brotherhood, someone furtively handed out notes to twenty-eight people: invitations to a secret meeting to be held the following day at the Colonnas' palazzo in Palermo.

Saro wanted to enjoy those last remaining hours before he had to return to America. Among the swarm of guests, he thought he spotted Jano Vassallo, wearing an elegant dark pinstriped suit, a white shirt, and a tie.

Saro pushed through the crowd and stood before him. "Jano, what a surprise. What happened to your black shirt?"

Jano returned his contempt. "The same thing that happened to your shabby rags." He turned and, taking the arm of the young woman who was with him, walked away. The girl looked back for a moment and then ducked her head. Saro was struck by a scathing pain in his chest.

Mena. It was Mena, more beautiful than ever, wearing a floral silk dress that showed off her slender legs. Her hand rested on Jano's arm as he displayed her like a trophy.

In a heartbeat, the fleeting glimpse of Mena awoke in him sensations that he hadn't felt for a long time. Her sweet name rose to his lips.

"Mena," he whispered, as if to convince himself he wasn't dreaming.

Then the tender feeling vanished, replaced by rancor. Saro had been living with hatred for some time now; it had become his overriding emotion. He was furious at the injustices of life and destiny.

Sometimes, however, when life seems inevitably headed toward an adverse destiny, providence itself comes rushing to our aid.

The following morning, in fact, Roy Boccia—detained in a cell at the Manhattan precinct by his own choice, to protect himself from any vendetta on the part of friends of the Cosa Nostra—was brought a cup of Italian espresso. Needless to say, it was his last cup of coffee.

When the fact was reported to prosecutor William Bray, he raised holy hell, shouting that he would put the entire police precinct in a cell. He had lost the chief witness for the prosecution. Consequently, all charges against Saro Ragusa were definitively dropped.

Chapter 57

When Vincent Scamporino arrived at his office in Palermo the next day, he found a cable from the New York DA's Office on his desk, informing him that the prosecution's witness Roy Boccia had been poisoned in his cell and was dead. Saro Ragusa could be considered free on all counts.

Scamporino was pleased to be the first to give Saro the good news, since the young man was an invaluable member of his group. Then he phoned Sergeant Dickey and told him to come to his office because he had a document from the New York district attorney to show him.

With that news, Saro's life took a wholly unexpected turn. Completely different scenarios opened up to him. He had seen himself as a man on the run, wanted by every police force in the world. A man without hope. Now, overnight, he was cleared, free to be able to choose. How many people are given such an opportunity? He owed it all to *u patri*, his father. But there was still a thorn in his side: Mena. Before making any other decision, that thorn had to be removed.

Once again, as they had done so many years earlier, twenty-eight of the island's most prominent individuals came to meet in the same red drawing room of Palazzo Cesarò, having been convened by Finocchiaro-Aprile. It was the first official meeting for Sicilian separatism. The assembly consisted of the agrarian aristocracy, which feared the revolutionary winds of the North. There were also some genuine autonomists, whose aim was to oppose the centralized policy of Rome. Finally, there was a group of Mafia bosses, well represented by Don Calò, and some American and British proponents of the liberation forces, among them Charles Poletti, the US Army civil affairs officer.

During the meeting, the main articles of Sicilian separatism were drawn up. The final document proclaimed more or less:

The Committee for Sicilian Independence fervently and enthusiastically salutes the armies of England and the United States of

America and their indomitable leaders, and expresses to them, from this first solemn moment, the people's profound and heartfelt gratitude for having helped rid them of the uncivilized, barbarous, and deplorable fascist domination. Our highest aspiration is that Sicily be promoted to a sovereign and independent state under a republican form of government. After putting Italian unity to the test for many decades, during which time the island has been distressed to see that it has never been considered in the same way and on the same level as other regions [. . .]

Our agenda now is: Sicily to the Sicilians [. . .]

The Committee is therefore counting on England and the United States of America to support the plan for the creation of a sovereign and independent state of Sicily founded on democratic principles [. . .]

Naturally, this new state included the Mafia organization as well.

Salemi had not been spared by the bombings, either. The main target of the liberators' squadrons was the small wooded area at the foot of the hill on which the town stood. The bombers were aiming to strike the Goering artillery divisions hidden among the trees. But many cabins located on the outer edge of town had also been destroyed by mistake.

Now that military operations were over, the young men from the Italian Section had been allowed to go see their relatives.

Though Saro had no family to return to, he wanted to see his old friends and his home. As he approached the houses, he was overwhelmed by old memories: some happy and some bitter. It seemed like a century had passed since he had been forced to leave Salemi. He ran into Carlo Vacca, Armando Caradonna, and some others he had known from his barbershop days. They greeted one another, though half-heartedly. The war had dampened the urge to smile.

He headed toward his house. The fighting had passed over, barely touching it. But the door was ripped off its hinges, the windows shattered. He stood motionless, staring at those beloved walls for what seemed like an eternity. A woman came by with a bucket of water on her head. He didn't know her; he'd never seen her before.

After she walked on, he entered the house where he had grown up, surrounded by the love of his parents, Peppino and Annachiara Ragusa: those two extraordinary people who had never attached any importance to the fact that he was adopted. The floor was littered with roof tiles, broken glass, bits of plaster. In the center of the room, overturned on the floor, he recognized the dining table. He spotted a notebook on the ground, picked it up, dusted off the black cover, and opened it. He recognized the wobbly handwriting of his father's former pupil Turi Toscano. "All men are born with equal dignity. Only decent work sets us free." Reading those words, he could no longer control himself and burst into sobs.

Sometime later, he returned to the jeep and headed for the Piazza del Castello and what had been Mimmo Ferro's tavern. He hoped to meet his old friends there. Two men were sitting silently in the doorway smoking a cigarette, passing it back and forth between them. Saro didn't know them, probably they were other evacuees. He went inside but there was no longer the usual cheerful commotion. People sat at the tables with empty glasses. Some played cards. Besides Armando Caradonna, he spotted a few more old acquaintances: Domenico the barber, Curzio Turrisi, and Ninì Trovato, the town crier, who strode toward him with open arms as soon as he recognized him.

"Saro! *Saruzzo beddu!*" He embraced him with sincere emotion. Then he looked him up and down and admired his uniform. "Have you become an American?" he asked ingenuously.

"I landed with the Allies."

A crowd of people clustered around Saro. Now everyone wanted to greet him; even those who didn't know him.

"You came with the 'saviors'?" Curzio Turrisi asked incredulously.

"Oh, sure, with the 'saviors,' as you call them, Curzio."

"Come here, have a drink with us. You're our guest." Ninì nudged him over to the bar.

"Sorry, but this round is on me." The new tavern keeper set the glasses on the counter and began filling them.

Ninì noticed the young man's sad look. "Mimmo was taken away by troops and the SS, together with your family. That day was a tragedy . . ."

Saro bowed his head.

"Dr. Ragusa didn't deserve what they did to him," Curzio put in.

"But we mustn't think about the worst. We must be optimistic," Domenico the barber said.

The tavern keeper stepped aside, and Saro, looking up, saw a magnificent landscape behind him, painted on the tavern's bare stone wall. It was a view of Salemi and the countryside surrounding the town. The colors, style, and the particular scene made him recall a very similar painting he had seen in New York at La Tonnara.

"That painting wasn't there before, Curzio, did your brother do it? Is Salvatore Turrisi back?" Saro asked.

"We haven't heard from Salvatore in years. What makes you ask if he's back?" Curzio asked.

"Because there's a painting just like it in New York, in a trattoria—in fact, I'd say it's exactly the same. The owner is Elisabetta, Prince Licata's niece. She told me your brother, Salvatore Turrisi, painted it."

"Did she say how he was?" Curzio asked anxiously.

"Actually, no. But apparently he was getting by okay—"

"That painting was done by Ciccio Vinciguerra," the tavern keeper interrupted, referring to the man who had been saved by the prince after being dragged from a truck by Jano's gang. "He offered to do it for free. I let him eat here the entire time it took him to paint it. He's a good man. He never speaks."

"*U pisci*," Saro said, referring to him by his nickname: the Fish. "I didn't know he too could paint so well."

As the old friends drank the new barkeeper's wine, remembering Mimmo's generosity, their thoughts went to all those who would never return. Saro said good-bye then, intending to return to the command center in Palermo.

Leaving the piazza, he noticed that the walls of the Castello had been spared by the bombings. He looked up and saw the sentry box at the top of the embankment. That tower too was intact. That watchtower was linked to one of the most beautiful memories of his life. He decided to climb to the top of the walls.

He entered the door of the house facing the Castello, went down to the cellar, and walked through the long tunnel that connected the building to the Castello's dungeons. This time he had a flashlight with him. He still had fond memories of Mena following him fearfully. He climbed up to the landing where the long spiral staircase began, leading to the sentry box on the walls. There he recalled with emotion the moment when he'd put his arm around the girl's waist, with the excuse of protecting her from tumbling down. Her luminous green eyes had made him fall for her instantly. That sensation of falling in love was indescribable and the night of the fireworks unforgettable.

From the top of the walls Saro's eyes swept over Salemi's green valleys. He saw the patchwork of cultivated fields, the destroyed and abandoned shacks, life gradually starting to return again. He decided to leave and turned and saw two green eyes boring through his.

Mena had noticed him drive up in the jeep from a window of her new home in Piazza del Castello. Seeing Saro again had awakened a flood of memories. She had to face him. She wanted Saro to know the truth; *her* side of things.

She watched him go into the tavern. When he came out not long afterward, she knew where he would go. Now, as they looked into each other's eyes, she would have liked the ground to swallow her up rather than have to face his rancor.

"Mena . . ." Saro murmured in a faint voice. Seeing her appear before him was a shock.

She was wearing a brightly patterned dress with a stylish skirt. A rarity in those days, but evidently Jano didn't let her want for anything.

"Hello, Saro," she said breathlessly, her chest heaving from the climb.

"I never thought I'd find you here."

"I haven't been back since that time. I need to talk to you," she said lowering her eyes.

"Mena, what happened? Why didn't you ever answer my letters? We made a promise to each other."

"I missed you. All hell broke loose when you left. From the time you went away, the Black Shirts ruled over the town like tyrants."

"Not one letter—you never answered me."

"I never got anything from you! Saro, I swear to you! In fact, I thought you had fallen in love with someone else."

"We promised to wait for each other. Don't you remember?" Saro said again.

"Yes, but things change. *We* change."

Saro thought of Isabel at that moment. "What could I have done?" Mena asked. "Don't crucify me—not you too!" The turn her life had taken had profoundly altered Mena's spirit.

"But how could you agree to such a compromise!"

"Saro . . ." She wanted to shout out her love, but she was bound to another man, and her honor kept her from betraying her legitimate spouse.

"How could you have married such a despicable individual!" Saro was incensed, but he would have liked to hold her firmly in his arms and offer his forgiveness.

"You can't understand. You were far away. You might never have come back, like many of our men. I hadn't heard from you."

"But I wrote to you." Suddenly it occurred to him: "Oh, I get it, Jano must have intercepted my letters. There was no reason to marry a sadistic bully, however."

"He's the father of my son."

"I don't want to hear that. You and I belong to each other! Nothing else should have mattered!" Saro shouted.

Mena began to cry.

"My life ended the night you left."

"How could you marry Jano?"

"He said he would take everything my family had: the land, the farm. I did it for my mother and my brothers."

"It's hard to feel sorry for someone like you!"

Mena couldn't take anymore. She wiped her eyes, turned and disappeared into the darkness of the stairs.

Sergeant Charles Dickey of the FBI had nothing more to do in Sicily. His mission had ended with the death of Roy Boccia, the prosecution's chief witness against Saro Ragusa.

He was ready to return to New York on the first available plane. Every day, there was at least one flight headed back to the United States. He had already said his good-byes to Donovan and Scamporino, and he couldn't wait to see his family again. Dickey was only twenty-five, but he had a wife and two children waiting for him.

As he was packing his duffel bag, someone knocked on his door. He went to open it, and there stood Jano Vassallo.

The man asked if he could come in; it was urgent that he speak with him. Dickey invited him into the small room of the Palermo hotel that the OSS had requisitioned, designating it as its headquarters.

The sergeant knew Jano because more than once he had seen him escorting Don Calogero Vizzini from one feudal domain to another. He opened a bottle of whiskey and poured some into two glasses. Jano took a drink and sat down on the only chair in the room, while the sergeant sat on the edge of the bed.

Jano came straight to the point: "I know you came here to arrest Saro Ragusa for a murder that he committed in America—and that you'll have to go home empty-handed."

"His main accuser was killed in prison. We can't proceed against him," the sergeant explained regretfully. "He's a free man now."

"I could furnish evidence of certain crimes that Saro Ragusa is committing behind the US Army's back," Jano said bluntly.

"Like what?"

"He's one of the main organizers of the black market. He hijacks trucks with drums of gasoline, spare parts, and provisions, which he then sells on the black market. He bribes the drivers and warehousemen. He also has his hands on medicine and drugs supplies."

"We're aware that we're being robbed. But when we catch them, they're always petty criminals. Up till now, we've never been able to snare the ones who run the wholesale trade."

"Saro Ragusa is one of them. I can arrange for you to catch him in the act. Afterward, it will be up to you people to make him confess the names of the leaders of the organization. I assure you that it will leave you all speechless," Jano promised.

"What do you want in return? All Italians who do you a favor always want something," the sergeant challenged.

Jano's self-respect was offended, but he couldn't act like an affronted, upright citizen just now. It was true: he did want something in return.

"A favor for a favor, Sergeant Dickey. I'll hand you Saro Ragusa on a silver platter so you can have the satisfaction of throwing him into a cell for the rest of his days. And in return, I ask that justice be done to a certain Prince Ferdinando Licata, who fled to America four years ago. In 1920 the prince was an accomplice in a double homicide."

"A double homicide committed twenty-three years ago in Italy?" the FBI sergeant repeated. "Don't you think it's a little too late to seek justice?"

"He had the Marquis Pietro Bellarato and another individual, impossible to identify, killed by Rosario Losurdo, a gabellotto in his employ."

"So you give me Saro Ragusa in the act of stealing our supplies, and I'm supposed to arrest this Prince Licata in America along with his—what's the word?—gabellotto, right? His gabellotto Rosario Losurdo for a double homicide committed twenty-three years ago."

"Losurdo is dead. All I want is Prince Licata."

"It's really true that you Sicilians never forget. And may I ask the reason for such hatred?"

"Prince Licata ordered the slaughter of my family. I was just a child when my family members were killed. I was spared because I hid under the bed, but I saw it all. Those images are seared in my brain. They butchered my aunt and my uncle and two of my siblings, but they never managed to find my father, the outlaw Vassallo. The weapons were found hidden on Rosario Losurdo's farm. No one ever paid for that massacre. But I will never forget it, until my dying day. That's why I'm asking for revenge or justice. I leave it to you to decide."

"I see. If this Prince Licata is now living in the United States, it's not a bad idea to get rid of him, seeing what he's capable of."

The two men shook hands, sealing their pact.

Before taking action to obtain the extradition of Prince Ferdinando Licata, Sergeant Charles Dickey conducted an investigation to ascertain whether the facts were true. He heard the testimony of the witnesses who were still alive. He began by questioning Curzio Turrisi, who had been the main source pointing the finger at the outlaw Gaetano Vassallo as the perpetrator of Marquis Bellarato's murder. In actuality, Curzio Turrisi admitted to him that he'd been forced to come up with that name in order to avoid being subjected to the "box." His torturers wanted him to denounce the bandit because Vassallo was the only proof of Prince Licata's involvement in the affair.

Carabinieri Marshal Mattia Montalto confirmed the general outline of Curzio Turrisi's story, although he personally didn't believe that Prince Licata would go so far as to order a man to be killed over a land dispute. He told the sergeant that everyone in town called him *u parri* because of the compassion he showed toward the poor and the peasant farmers. But opinions for Sergeant Dickey had no probative value.

Other witnesses confirmed the facts as well. At the end of his brief investigation, Dickey decided to see if he could somehow arrange to have the prince extradited as the man behind the 1920 murder of Marquis Pietro Bellarato and the subsequent Borgo Guarine massacre, carried out in an attempt to capture the outlaw Gaetano Vassallo.

While Sergeant Dickey was trying to gather evidence of Licata's guilt, Saro was organizing the "transfer" of goods from the army's warehouses to those of Don Calò.

In those tumultuous months, amid the chaos of a still uncertain war, the Americans, busy reinforcing the positions they'd won and making plans for a continued advance toward northern Italy, weren't very exacting about checking on where the rerouted food supplies ended up. They didn't care who the recipients were; for them, it was enough to satisfy the population's hunger. As for how that happened, that was none of their business. The officials themselves found it more convenient to share the incoming provisions with the Mafia organizations rather than oppose them.

Half of the supplies ended up at charitable institutions, while the other half found its way to black markets in various cities, not only in Sicily.

Saro had his eye on a shipment of motor oil stacked in drums near the Salemi field camp. He had arranged for two Canadian drivers to transport the goods to a farmhouse near Villalba, providing them with counterfeit ID papers. He had promised the Canadians a little money and, even better, the company of two prostitutes.

At dawn the next day, they were to load the truck and set out immediately for Villalba.

But Saro didn't know that one of two drivers, Robert Miles, had already been contacted by Jano Vassallo, who had promised him twice as much as what he would get from the Mafia to transport the contraband oil drums. The Canadian promptly reported to Jano that Saro Ragusa had hired him to convey the barrels to Villalba.

It was what Jano had been waiting for, for some weeks. He summoned Sergeant Dickey to his house, away from prying eyes, and told him about the shipment that was leaving at dawn the following day. It was the evidence they'd been looking for: Saro Ragusa would spend his next twenty years in a maximum security prison.

Chapter 58

The conversation between Jano and Sergeant Dickey was overheard by Mena, who was hidden behind a door. As soon as the two men left the house, the young woman decided to go to Saro. She spoke with Nennella, her maid, telling her to give the child his supper. She had an errand in town but would be back as soon as possible. If Jano came home, meanwhile, she was to tell him that she had gone to bring her mother some milk.

She hid her face under a long black shawl and set out for the boardinghouse where she knew Saro was staying.

The porter was surprised to see her there. She greeted him and had him tell her Saro's room number. On her way up the stairs, she ran into a soldier embracing a local girl. Both women ducked their heads to avoid being recognized. Mena was well aware that the visit could be fatal to her reputation. She knocked on the door and went in. Saro leaped off the bed when he saw her. She stood in the doorway for a moment, and then closed the door behind her and rushed into his arms. They held each other close, locked in each other's arms for several long minutes.

How often Saro had imagined this scene during his lonely nights in New York! His lips sought those of the young woman, but she avoided the kiss and slipped out of the embrace.

"Saro—forgive me. I don't want to give you any false expectations," she stammered, unable to find the right words. "I'm not here for us. Jano met with Sergeant Dickey a little while ago. They know all about tomorrow morning's oil transport. They're setting a trap for you."

Saro's mind was in turmoil. He couldn't understand the reason for Mena's decision to marry Jano. He stepped closer and grasped her wrists.

"Mena, I love you. I love you just as I did when I left. Why? Why?" He was gripping her arms so tightly it hurt.

That was when Mena caved in. She had never revealed her terrible secret to anyone. "I too never stopped loving you. But you must swear that what I tell you now will not change our lives."

"All right, I promise."

Mena collected her thoughts and chose the most appropriate words to keep Saro from flying off the handle. "One evening when I was sadder than usual over your having gone away, Jano came to see me at the farm without my family knowing. Well, I was devastated by your absence and by my father's death. I was vulnerable. I tried to push him away . . . but he took me by force.

"Then, to make amends for the dishonor, he agreed to marry me."

Saro, shattered by the revelation, clung to Mena desperately.

"We have to bury our feelings, because they have no future," Mena continued forlornly. "If you love me, as you say you do, you must at least not bring shame on me.

"Saro, my love, good-bye."

———

At dawn, Saro had the barrels loaded onto the two trucks. He gave one of the Canadian drivers, Robert Miles, the bill of lading and told him that he would be waiting for them at the farm in Villalba, where they would unload the drums.

The two trucks set out for the specified destination, but just before Palermo, at the junction to Cristina, the convoy was ordered to stop.

The roadblock had been set up by Sergeant Dickey, with Jano's assistance and that of a couple of US military police. A simple sawhorse placed across the road barred the first truck driven by Robert Miles.

The FBI sergeant approached and asked him for the transport papers.

"Where are you headed?"

"I'm supposed to deliver these drums to a farm in Villalba," the driver replied casually.

The sergeant glanced at the papers, but he knew he wouldn't find any irregularity. "We'll escort you. I want to see who's taking delivery of this oil shipment."

Behind him, Jano was gloating with pleasure. Saro was finally trapped.

The sergeant climbed into the back of the truck to check out the drums. He struck the metal with the butt of his pistol, but instead of a solid thud, there was a kind of hollow echo. He tapped the other barrels as well, and they all resonated with the same dismal sound. He called the driver then and ordered him to open one of them.

The man obeyed, and the sergeant could see that the drums were empty. The ones in the other truck were empty as well. The US military was taking twenty empty oil barrels on a joyride through Sicily! Dickey turned red with rage. He shouted at Jano that he couldn't get away with fucking around with him that way; that he'd make him pay for it. He wanted to get to the bottom of it. He told Jano to come with him to the location indicated on the shipment papers and then ordered the driver to carry on with his mission.

Dickey, Jano, and the military police headed for Villalba in the jeep, covering the seventy-five miles of mountain roads in record time. When they got there, they asked the way to the Caprile farm.

Jano was afraid of being recognized by Don Calò's men. He asked if he could hide, and much to the amazement of the sergeant and the two MPs, who couldn't understand the peculiar quirks of the Italians, he ducked under the seat.

The farm was deserted. The house had been abandoned for some time. Looters had cleaned it out, carrying off every object and piece of furniture that could be moved. Dickey and his men scoured the surrounding area as well, and in the neglected vineyard, one of the MPs found something that surprised the three of them: scattered in the fields were the sun-baked ashes of the carcasses of about a dozen trucks. The vehicles had apparently been unloaded, hidden among the rows of vines, then sprinkled with gasoline, set on fire, and left to their fate.

On the basis of this finding and the testimony of the two Canadian drivers, who declared that Saro Ragusa had been the one who loaded those empty drums and ordered them to transport them to the farm in Villalba, a new warrant was issued for Saro's arrest.

Naturally, the Americans' search, led by the vile character who was hiding in the jeep, did not go unnoticed by the ever-watchful eyes of Don Calò's men. The old Mafia boss was informed of what was happening at the Caprile farm.

"Find out who that bastard is," *zu* Calò ordered.

———

Later on Jano returned home. As soon as he saw Mena, he realized that she could have been the one who warned Saro about the trap. Without even asking for an explanation, he slapped her. Nennella ran to protect her, as she always did when the two argued and Jano raised his hands to his wife. "Stop! Don't you touch her!"

"Nennella, don't butt in!" Jano yelled angrily, his breath jagged. "She has to learn to keep her mouth shut." Jano then turned on Mena, who sought cover in the arms of her faithful housekeeper. "You were the one who warned your lover, weren't you?" he roared.

"She has no lover! You have a hole in your head, that's what!" Mena thought how incredible it was that how Nennella could stand up to him, undaunted by his violence.

Their little son appeared in the doorway of the room in tears, frightened by his father's shouting. Mena broke away from Nennella's embrace and rushed to reassure the child.

"Rosario, you mustn't cry. Come, my love." She picked him up. "You see? Everything is all right."

She carried him over to her husband. "There now, Daddy will let you ride piggyback . . . Take him, Jano."

Jano was forced to take the boy and swing him up to sit on his shoulders. The child's tears turned to smiles. Mena clapped her hands to hide the anguish in her heart.

———

Sergeant Dickey, with an arrest warrant for Saro Ragusa, went to pick him up at the Salemi field camp where an OSS detachment was stationed. But in response to the arrest order, Saro showed him a series of merit certificates and a special clearance from the United States Army Command officially endorsing him to the other Allied commands and bureaus of the Allied Military Government in Sicily. Dickey, despite insistent appeals to high-ranking military offices that he take Saro into custody, nonetheless had no concrete evidence that the man had been involved in anything illegal. The only charge against him was arranging for a shipment of empty drums to be delivered to a farm where twenty or so trucks had been set on fire. But that didn't prove anything.

Wartime requirements necessitated the services of that individual who on more than one occasion had demonstrated that he was invaluable to the war effort. In the end, Dickey was once again forced to give up.

———

Meanwhile, after a contentious debate, the New York district attorney's office had informally agreed to hand over Prince Ferdinando Licata, despite the fact that several judges had opposed Dickey's request. They felt it was inappropriate, at a time like this, with war operations still ongoing in central Italy, to rake up events from more than twenty years ago. America shouldn't get mixed up in those "family quarrels," as the judges put it. But in the end, they all agreed that it was better not to wrestle with the FBI, Sergeant Dickey would conduct his investigation, and afterward, they would decide what should be done.

The only direct testimony pointing to Ferdinando Licata as the hand behind the Bellarato homicide was the account that had been given by Prospero Abbate before prosecutor Tommaso Amato of Marsala back in 1939.

Jano had very cleverly sent the sergeant off on the track that he himself had laid out years ago. Fortunately, both Abbate and the prosecutor were still alive. Amato had retired to devote himself to his cherished botanical studies, while Abbate, like his Black Shirt comrades, had managed to go into hiding at the opportune moment to avoid serving in the Social Republic, the puppet state of Nazi Germany during the latter part of the war.

The former prosecutor admitted truthfully to Sergeant Dickey that Prospero Abbate's confession had seemed false at the time. Dickey thanked him for his candor and asked to see the confession transcript, which he studied carefully, word for word. Attorney Amato was right: it seemed like a little speech that had been memorized.

He decided to close the case. Even for a bulldog like him, the matter went too far back. He would find it hard to uncover any credible evidence after so much time had passed. Moreover, he told Jano, he hadn't kept his word, either. He was supposed to hand him Saro on a silver platter, but he had tricked them both.

Jano, nonetheless, had an ace up his sleeve: an eyewitness who had never wanted to appear but whom he would now convince to testify. Dickey gave him one last chance.

After Mena's explanation, Saro still couldn't understand how she could so easily have given in to that despicable man. He knew the strong sense of honor that was in the girl's blood. It could be traced back to her father's dignity and her mother's sense of modesty. The last time they'd seen each other, she had implored him not to bring shame on her—"you at least," she'd said to him despairingly. He couldn't help thinking of her. He found the most trivial excuses to end up wandering near her house.

One afternoon he saw her return home with two large bags of vegetables and the child toddling after her, clinging to her skirt. The boy stumbled over a pothole, fell, and began to cry.

"Saruzzo, will you watch where you're going?" she scolded him. She put one of the bags down on the ground and picked him up. "There now, don't cry. Look, here's Nennella." The nanny took him from her arms, and the boy calmed down immediately. "Rosariuzzo," she said, "Nennella made you a *cassata* that will make you lick your chops!" The woman beamed, and the boy smiled with her.

Meanwhile, Mena picked up the second bag and with a brief run caught up with Nennella and the child. Together they disappeared through the door of the house.

Saro entered the tavern and asked with feigned indifference, "What's the name of Mena's son?"

"Rosario Saruzzo," the few customers frequenting the inn at that hour chorused in reply.

His heart skipped a beat. A flash went off in his head. Mena hadn't lied! It was true: he was the only one she'd loved! She had loved him so much that she'd bamboozled Jano by naming her son not after his grand-father, as it might seem, but after her first love, him!

———————

To lend a semblance of legality to the testimonies and at the same time authenticate the documents by the presence of bona fide military judges, Dickey obtained the collaboration of two American magistrates. He had a couple of teacher's desks from the local elementary school brought into the large town hall chamber, where films were once screened, and had the judges sit there.

He demanded that the citizens of Salemi be present at the interroga-tion. If anyone recalled any piece of information about that long ago murder, he was to speak up and report it.

The witness, a surprise arranged by Jano, was Nunzio, the son of one of Rosario Losurdo's foremost campieri, Manfredi.

Nunzio had been twenty years old at the time of the events. He had never wanted to talk, so as not to get involved in that ugly affair. But now, given that they wanted to shed some light on Marquis Bellarato's murder, he'd decided to come forward. That was the version Jano told the audience. In actuality, Nunzio was doing Jano a personal favor, and no one could say no to Jano.

When he entered the chamber, a few voices from the back shouted "Fascist!" To make the testimony seem even more solemn, Dickey had the witness swear on the Bible, which everyone viewed as an eccentricity on the part of the investigator. Nunzio stood in the center of the hall, in front of the two officers, with his back to the audience, and began answering the sergeant's questions.

Briefly, he stated that on the day Marquis Pietro Bellarato was killed, he was in the vicinity of the palazzo. All of a sudden, he saw Rosario Losurdo run out the back door. He noticed him because the man appeared distraught, and his clothes and hands were smeared with blood. He acted like someone who had just committed a murder. He saw him take off in a hurry, and a few minutes later the fire broke out. He didn't remember anything else.

Prospero Abbate's testimony was also heard, as he repeated the account he'd given four years earlier to the prosecutor from Marsala. His deposition electrified the spectators, who murmured animatedly as he described the marquis's murder in abundant detail. He spoke of Losurdo trying to persuade the marquis to withdraw the option on the land, and then told of Losurdo grabbing the poker and striking Bellarato repeatedly on the head. Abbate was extremely meticulous, describing the blood that splattered the killer, who then wiped his face and hands on his clothes as best he could. Finally, he told of Losurdo's making his escape after setting fire to the draperies and furnishings. He, Abbate, was hiding behind a curtain, terrified. At the time, he was only eleven. He waited for Losurdo to run out, and then he got out of there too.

"But a second corpse was found, Dickey pointed out. "Did you see a second person in the palazzo?" the sergeant asked him.

Abbate shook his head. He had always believed that Nicola Geraci, the other corpse, had been carried into the burning palazzo later by Prince Licata—because Geraci was an enemy of the prince, who had himself been involved in the deal to purchase the former Baucina estate. The sergeant was satisfied with the witnesses' statements. The two military judges exchanged looks as if to say that the case was all too clear.

Also in attendance in the chamber were Monsignor Albamonte and the parish priest Don Mario; Nini Trovato and his wife, Tina; Curzio Turrisi with his wife, Vincenza, and his son, Biagio; plus Jano, Nunzio, and the entire combat league group that, just prior to the Allied landing, had managed to renounce fascism and blend in with the town's antifascists. The only one missing was Ginetto. Someone had shot him in the back right before the Americans arrived. Also present were Mena and Nennella, who hugged Rosario as if he were her own son. In the back of the hall sat Saro. All in all, the majority of Salemi's population was there—or what was left of it.

The sergeant turned to the public and declared gravely, "On the basis of these testimonies, I hereby charge Prince Ferdinando Licata, soon to be extradited from the United States, with the murders of Marquis Pietro Bellarato and Nicola Geraci, which took place in 1920. If there is anyone in the audience who wishes to add further information, he is asked to please step forward."

An unreal silence descended over the room. No one dared breathe for fear of shattering the tense mood that hung in the air. Then someone from the back rows raised his hand. Everyone turned around and saw Tosco, Marquis Bellarato's servant, get to his feet. The man walked to the center of the room and stopped in front of the two desks. The sergeant stood beside the military judges, waiting for him.

"You are?" Dickey asked.

He stated his name with great dignity: "My name is Tosco Bellarato." One of the two judges wrote the name on a sheet of paper.

"Are you a relative of the marquis?" the sergeant inquired.

"I'm his half brother. His father was my natural father." He glanced at the two judges, who were impassively taking notes.

Seeing Tosco walk toward the center of the room, one individual in the audience had a start: Nunzio.

"Did you live with your half brother?" Dickey continued.

"I was his servant and his laughingstock."

The Americans didn't understand what he was referring to, whereas the whole town did.

"Explain what you mean," Dickey persisted.

"He had his way with me. I was also his lover, just to be clear." The words fell on the foreigners' heads like a guillotine blade. Then he continued: "A pack of lies was told today. Someone said he saw Losurdo run from the palazzo, covered with blood. It's not true."

"Tosco, you should be ashamed! Go home!"

All eyes turned to Nunzio, who had bellowed those words, beside himself. But Tosco went on, undeterred: "I'm not the one who should be ashamed. Nature made me this way. Someone else should now be ashamed!" He pointed a finger at Nunzio. "He's a perjurer. He couldn't have seen Losurdo escape, because he was in bed with me on the day of the fire."

Those words had the impact of a bomb. Everyone in the room began shouting, arguing with one another, some hurling insults at Nunzio and some at Tosco. Nunzio tried to make it to the door, but following the

428   Vito Bruschini

sergeant's abrupt orders, the two military police got to him first and stopped him.

In a flash, the sergeant and Jano saw their theory fall apart. When calm was restored in the chamber, the sergeant asked Tosco if from his room it was possible to hear what was happening in the drawing room where the marquis had been when he was killed. Tosco stated that it wasn't possible to hear anything.

Then the sergeant turned to Nunzio: "Do you deny knowing this man, let's say, intimately?"

Nunzio ducked his head between his shoulders.

Jano couldn't believe what he was hearing. "A fairy," he murmured.

Meanwhile, another hand went up from the center of the audience. Once again all eyes turned toward the new witness.

A name echoed through the hall to everyone's astonishment: *U pisci.* Ciccio Vinciguerra, the quiet, bearded man who had showed up in Salemi about ten years ago from God knows where, made his way through the people who crowded on either side of him.

"The man who killed Marquis Bellarato was Salvatore Turrisi," said the man, whose rumbling voice few in the room could say they'd ever heard.

"That's a serious accusation you're making," Dickey told him. "Who is this Turrisi?"

This time it was Curzio Turrisi who stood up. "I am Salvatore's older brother. My name is Curzio Turrisi. Salvatore disappeared at the time of the murder, and no one has seen him again since then. We all thought he immigrated to America."

The sergeant turned back to Ciccio Vinciguerra. "Why are you so certain it was Salvatore Turrisi who killed the marquis and Nicola Geraci?"

"Because he told me so himself."

"And where is he?"

"I met him more than ten years ago in New York. Then I came back to Sicily, and I never heard anything more about him."

"What did he tell you?" Sergeant Dickey asked.

"Salvatore had it in for the marquis because he had accused Salvatore of raping and killing a young shepherd, forcing Salvatore to go into hiding and join Gaetano Vassallo's band. Instead, it was the marquis himself who raped and killed the shepherd boy in a fit of rage. But Salvatore wasn't cut out to be an outlaw; he was a good campiere, that's what he was. One day Rosario Losurdo went to see the bandit Vassallo. Prince Licata's gabellotto asked Vassallo to steal the marquis's cattle. He just wanted to blackmail him: if Bellarato gave up the option on the Baucina estate, he would return the herd. Otherwise he would slaughter every head of cattle. That was when Salvatore Turrisi conceived the plan to murder the marquis. It would be easy to let the blame fall on Losurdo—and that's just what happened.

"But there was an unforeseen event, Salvatore told me: a fire accidentally broke out in the palazzo. He was about to make his escape, and when he opened the door, the blaze spread like wildfire, sending all the wood furnishings, and especially the heavy drapes, up in flames. It came as a real surprise to him to discover Nicola Geraci hiding behind one of the curtains. Geraci was the representative of the Socialist Party's cooperative, the Farm. That disgusting worm must have been playing a double game, because he was a socialist, and the marquis was notoriously allergic to any politicians of a red stripe. Evidently money makes all ideologies see eye to eye. So the two had agreed to get their hands on the Baucina estate and then divide it between them.

"To make a long story short, Geraci was engulfed in flames, and Salvatore told me that he was unable to help him. He saw him die in unspeakable agony. At that very moment, Turrisi thought that this might be a unique opportunity for his future: if he were to be identified as the charred corpse, unrecognizable as a result of the fire, no one would be looking for him anymore. Best of all, he could break away from Vassallo and his band. His action was quicker than his thought. He tore the aluminum Saint Christopher's medal off his neck and threw it onto the cadaver. Nicola Geraci, therefore, died accidentally. I felt it was my duty to tell the truth because two people were about to be unjustly accused, and Tosco Bellarato gave me the courage to speak up!"

Once again a great uproar broke out in the hall. Ciccio Vinciguerra's disclosure had literally shaken everyone's thoughts. Curzio Turrisi, bent over in his chair, his head in his hands, was crying like a baby. His wife tried to console him, but it was no use.

Amid the commotion, Vinciguerra turned to Jano and claimed his attention in a gravelly voice: "Jano! I have the truth for you too. Remember Michele Fardella? I was there when he was captured and executed by the antifascists along with Lorenzo Costa. Before he died, he wanted to get a load off his conscience that had been weighing on him for years. He confessed to me that the Borgo Guarine massacre was committed by the Royal Guard under Costa's command. For all those years, Jano, you were taking orders from the man who killed your family!"

That revelation had a resounding impact on the townspeople. Jano was stunned.

Saro took advantage of the great confusion to approach Mena.

"Mena, I have to talk to you," he said, taking her hand.

"Not here, Saro—not now. You're crazy!" she replied, terrified, trying to break out of his grip.

"Here and now." Saro gave Nennella a meaningful look. The nanny, unruffled as always, had picked up the child, as if to protect him from the agitated voices around them. "I'll leave. I'll wait for you outside with Saruzzo," she said to Mena.

Saro led Mena by the hand to an office adjacent to the main chamber. He closed the door, shutting out the frantic shouting of Salemi's citizenry.

"I have to know the truth: Did you give my name to your child?" Saro asked softly.

Mena's magnificent green eyes filled with tears. For entire nights she'd dreamed of being able to embrace her true love, but she always chased away the thought so as not to dishonor her husband. But now there he was, asking her about Saruzzo. Mena finally gave way and burst into tears, letting it all out. Impulsively, she clung to Saro and kissed him on the mouth with all the pent-up passion from those four long years. She put aside her reserve; she had to tell him how much she'd loved him and still loved him.

When their mouths broke apart, Mena stared at him, lost in reverie. She had memorized every inch of his skin. She wanted to drink her fill of him, if only she could. "Saro . . . Saro . . . light of my eyes," she said finally, fighting back more tears.

Holding him close, she brought her mouth to his ear and whispered softly, "Saruzzo, thanks be to God, is the fruit of our love." Saro drew back and stared at her, shocked.

"It's true: Rosario is your son." The big secret was revealed. Mena had sworn to herself that she would never divulge it, but once she saw Saro, deciding on the truth was inevitable.

"Rosario is my son?" Saro exclaimed, still incredulous.

"Things didn't happen with Jano the way I told you the first time. Jano raped me; he took me by force. But he didn't know I was already pregnant. I demanded that he marry me to make amends, and when Rosario was born, I arranged with the midwife to make him believe that the infant was premature. How I cried over you, Saro, so far away! So many times I prayed the door would open, and you would appear.

"Then I became resigned to him; to his violent ways. But I hate the man who destroyed our love and my life."

Those last words left Saro grimly resolute. He had a score to settle now. The two kissed again, passionately. Meanwhile, the uproar in the chamber was subsiding, so they went back in.

In accordance with the two military judges, Dickey declared the case closed. He later sent a cable to New York requesting that they search for Salvatore Turrisi.

People began leaving town hall, chatting about what they had learned thanks to Vinciguerra. Everybody was congratulating him and thanking him for having restored the truth in their traumatized town.

When everyone had gone, Curzio Turrisi went up to Vinciguerra, his heart full of gratitude. The two men stared at each other for several long moments. Ciccio Vinciguerra's face was concealed by a bushy beard, and his long hair reached to his shoulders, but his eyes were bright as diamonds. Then Ciccio opened his mouth and showed Curzio a space where his incisor was missing. Smiles lit up both their faces; then they gripped each other in a passionate, trembling embrace, barely managing to choke back their tears. Curzio gave Ciccio a kiss on the cheek and whispered with a smile, "Finally, we meet again, you rotten son of a bitch—no offense to our mother, God rest her soul."

Chapter 59

Saro Ragusa's mission had been a big success. New York's former governor, albeit briefly, Charles Poletti, had supported every move he and his friends made, never once getting in the way of their activities.

In his own interests, Poletti made the most of the advantages of his office and set up an import-export business in New York with Jimmy Hoffa, a big shot in the Teamsters union, who had been rumored to have ties to organized crime.

Saro, with his military uniform giving him license to come and go, was able to coordinate the entire black market with considerable skill: not only the market for foodstuffs, clothing, fabrics, and shoes but also drugs and narcotics in particular. But the real business, besides that of morphine, was arms trafficking, financed with money from the other lines of trade.

In those months, Sicily was an arsenal: there were weapons abandoned by Italian soldiers, by retreating German troops, and by the Americans themselves, who relegated them to the scrap heap the first time they misfired.

Don Calogero Vizzini, Villalba's boss, had a veritable army of campieri in his employ, among them Jano Vassallo and some of his former combat league buddies.

One evening Don Calò sent for him. Jano was expecting a recognition or some special assignment. He had demonstrated to the old boss that he was capable of any iniquity.

But Don Calò broached an unlikely subject for a mafioso to bring up to a subordinate. "It's none of my business," he began after sending away everyone in the room, "but there are some nasty rumors going around about your wife and Saro Ragusa. I'm sorry to have to tell you, but I'm doing it for your own good. You know how much I care about you."

"That *cornuto!* The bastard—for years he's been stuck in my craw," Jano pointed to his gullet.

"Actually, you're the *cornuto*—the cuckold."

The severity of Don Calò's words caught him off guard. No one had ever spoken to him that way.

"Don Calò, you shouldn't be so harsh toward me—"

"If you can't be the boss in your own home, how can you demand obedience from your men?"

"That bitch . . ." Jano muttered through clenched teeth.

"You see? You take it out on her, whereas it's her lover you should silence."

"First I'll take care of him; then it will be her turn." Jano was beside himself with rage.

"I want to help you, Jano Vassallo. I've learned that today, at sunset, they will see each other at the Chiarenza mill."

"Has Saro Ragusa let you down?" Jano asked, aware of how close his longtime nemesis was to Calogero Vizzini.

"He put matters of the heart before business. He can't be trusted," *zu* Calò pronounced.

Jano was delighted to hear those words. With Saro out of the way, only he would remain by Don Calò's side. The old Mafia boss wanted to get rid of Ragusa, and the excuse of a crime of honor would pacify even those who had high regard for Saro and saw him as *zu* Calò's right arm.

———

Jano was familiar with the Chiarenza mill. It was halfway between Salemi and Trapani, close to Lake Rubino. He figured the two lovers wanted a protected place, away from prying eyes. Jano left his horse about a half mile away from the mill and walked the rest of the way, careful not to be seen by anyone. Finally, he came in sight of the mill. It was a stone structure, on the bank of a stream fed by a nearby pond. The wooden wheel stood stationary because of a bomb that had damaged the mechanism. Evening was falling, and he recognized Mena's buggy near the door. What Don Calò had told him was true.

Jano was carrying his shotgun. He walked to the door. It was unhinged and leaning to one side. He bent under it and went in, taking care not to make any noise. He wanted to surprise the two while they were making love. But not a sound could be heard in the place. He walked down a corridor and reached the door leading to the machinery room.

From there too, not a sound.

He opened the door and entered the room, stepping over fallen beams and splintered wood on the ground. He looked around. The gear works, drive belts, and big wooden cogwheels were still covered by a thin film of flour, as if the workers had simply left for the day and would be back the next. Jano advanced to the center of the room, where the horizontal cogged axle of the big wheel that dipped into the waters of the stream stood.

A voice behind him, cold as ice, took him aback.

"*Dui su' i putenti: cu avi assai e cu non avi nenti.*" "Only two have power: those who have a lot and those who have nothing."

He spun around and saw Prince Ferdinando Licata emerge from the shadows.

At his side was Saro Ragusa and, behind them, three of Saro's men. Except the prince, all were armed with rifles. One of the three men went up to Jano and took the shotgun out of his hand.

The prince stepped forward and stopped a short distance from his adversary. "Surprised, Jano?"

Jano Vassallo realized that he had been sold out by Don Calò. He knew he was done for.

"It's the day of reckoning; time to settle accounts," the prince spoke calmly as usual.

"I'm not afraid. Screw death, I don't give a damn about it," Jano spat contemptuously.

The prince shook his head and smiled. "You see, you won't be the one screwing; the other lunatics who will be living with you starting tomorrow will be screwing you."

"Get it over with, Prince Ferdinando Licata! Kill me! I'm not afraid," Jano repeated.

"It would be too easy for us and too good for you. Sorry, Jano, but I have other plans for your future. For example, I'll stuff you with drugs, but not too much, because I want you to be fully conscious when I feed you to the sex maniacs. That's right, because I've decided to have you locked up in one of our worst lunatic asylums with a diagnosis that will give you little chance of recovery. You'll live for years and years steeped in your own excrement and that of your numerous lovers. And don't think you'll be able to kill yourself, because I'll see to it that you lack both the strength and the will to move. You'll live like a larva. It's what animals like you deserve."

Hearing that chilling verdict, Jano dropped to his knees. He grabbed Ferdinando Licata's ankles, pleading with him: "*Patri*—have mercy on me!" He kissed his shoes, but Licata kicked him and broke his grip. He headed for the door, while Jano began banging his head on the bare ground, until two of the men forcibly pulled him up and gave him the first morphine injection.

––––––––

The night following these events at the Chiarenza mill, a meeting was called between the heads of the Sicilian Mafia and those of the American Cosa Nostra. The United States was represented by Ferdinando Licata, while the bosses of the twelve major families spoke for Sicily. Various spheres of influence were established. In Sicily, Don Calò would still control the Commission while Saro Ragusa received the recognition of the *padrini*, who "kissed his hands" as a mark of respect and gratitude for all that he had done to restore them to the top levels of power in Sicily. In the United States, Ferdinando Licata was named, along with Vito Genovese, as the Commission's main point of contact, replacing Lucky Luciano, who two years later, consistent with the prince's strategic plan, would be freed and deported back to Italy, he too under the official pretext of being an undesirable.

During the meeting, Don Calò asked what happened to Jano Vassallo.

"He lost," Saro replied. The old boss nodded, satisfied, and asked no more questions.

A few months later, once Jano's "mental illness" became established, the Vatican annulled his marriage to Mena Losurdo, on the grounds that his psychic flaw had been concealed from her at the time of their nuptials.

A year later, Mena and Saro realized their dream of love, and little Saruzzo was finally able to embrace his real father: Saro Ragusa, the new boss of Salemi.

––––––––

Such was life in Sicily in those days: a cup of bitter gall.

Acknowledgments

My thanks to all the "fathers."

The "father" of a novel is never solely the author. It all began six years ago, when Sergio Fumasoni, a dear friend who has lived and breathed publishing since he was in short pants, tried to convince me to write a story about the Mafia. At the time, Vincenzo Labella (writer and producer of *Jesus of Nazareth*, *Marco Polo*, and other miniseries), sent us an article from the Los Angeles *Herald Tribune* by Stash Luczkiw, in which the poet regretted that stories like *The Godfather* were no longer written. The article was inspiring, and I accepted the challenge. It was Fumasoni who gave me a starting point: among his papers, he had a 1945 dossier on the sinking of the *Normandie*. I wrote *The Father—Il Padrino dei Padrini* (*The Godfather of Godfathers*), which Fumasoni brought to Carmine Parmigiani, a film producer. Parmigiani was immediately excited about the story and in turn passed it on by email to a friend of his in Los Angeles, Fabio Mancini, a producer at Paramount. The producers of the "majors"—the major film studios—presented it among their selections for fall 2007. At the same time, Parmigiani also had the manuscript read by director Alessandro D'Alatri, who, more than anyone else, saw a strong likelihood that Prince Licata's story might stir movie audiences' emotions. D'Alatri instantly took action and proposed the novel to the publisher of Newton Compton Editori, Raffaello Avanzini. I will never forget the day we received his "okay," and he showed me the cover of the book. Finally, the last "father" of this book is actually a "mother": namely, Giusi Sorvillo, the novel's editor. It's always smooth sailing with Sorvillo; she can wield a pen like Benvenuto Cellini's chisel.

To all of them, I offer my sincere gratitude and warm recognition for bringing me to the result you hold in your hands.

But there are still two people who are in my thoughts at this moment. The first is Giuliana, my wife from time immemorial, who from time immemorial has supported my dreams. To her I apologize for all the sacrifices that she's had to make to get to this day. The second one's name is also Giuliana, and she is my daughter. For her I wish a life full of dreams—and that they may come true.

Rome, October 13, 2009

About the Translator

Anne Milano Appel, PhD, is an award-winning translator whose latest translations from the Italian include Paolo Giordano's *The Human Body*, Andrea Canobbio's *Three Light-Years*, Goliarda Sapienza's *The Art of Joy*, Claudio Magris's *Blindly*, and Giovanni Arpino's *Scent of a Woman*. Most recently her work was awarded the John Florio Prize for Italian Translation (2013) and the 33rd and 32nd Northern California Book Awards Translation Prize for Fiction (2014 and 2013).